Death on the Marais

Death on the Marais

ADRIAN MAGSON

First published in Great Britain in 2010 by
Allison & Busby Limited
13 Charlotte Mews
London W1T 4EJ
www.allisonandbusby.com

A CIP catalogue record for this book is available from
the British Library.

10 9 8 7 6 5 4 3 2 1

13-ISBN 978-0-7490-0834-5

Typeset in 13/16 pt Adobe Garamond Pro by
Allison & Busby Ltd.

Paper used in this publication is from sustainably managed sources.
All of the wood used is procured from legal sources and is fully traceable.
The producing mill uses schemes such as ISO 14001
to monitor environmental impact.

Printed and bound in the UK by
CPI Mackays, Chatham ME5 8TD

For Ann, as always

PROLOGUE

Picardie, France – 1963

She was going to die. She could feel it, her life ebbing away as surely as fine sand through fingers. The thought caused her more sadness than fear; less a sense of foreboding than a cause to wonder what lay ahead.

Maybe it was the drugs. She didn't know much about the effects of what a doctor at one of the parties had called hallucinosis, but she'd sensed this odd disconnection before. It wasn't usually this bad. And never in water.

The water. Seconds ago it had been over her chest and soaking into the heavy uniform jacket with the hated decorations. Now it was lapping at her chin, the waterlogged material dragging her down like lead weights. A splash, and she tasted it, cold and oddly chalky on the palate. She clamped her lips shut, fighting to breathe through her nose, eyes tight shut. But the bruised tissue around her septum hurt too much. In desperation, she inhaled…and choked. It could only have been a drop, but it felt like a bucketful, instantly blocking her airways and inducing panic.

God, how her chest hurt! She wondered if she had a broken rib. She could only recall one punch, but that was last night and seemed to be an age away. There must have been others.

She pushed back the pain, managing to thrust her head above the surface. She tried to shout, but her throat was constricted by fear. Besides, she was too far from any source of help and her cries would go unheeded, lost among the trees and in the shrill dawn calls of the marshland birds.

The water was intensely cold, especially around her feet. She kicked out, fearful at what she could not see, too terrified to look. She had never liked swimming; her imagination always too colourful to dismiss as benign the depths beneath her or whatever creatures might be lurking there. Yet oddly, seeing her hands floating before her, this water seemed as clear as day. And there was an unnatural brightness around her. It reminded her of when she was a child, pretending to swim as her mother filled the bath. Back then, when her mother was alive, swimming was always safe.

She reached out desperately for the bank, and felt a slimy texture beneath her hands. Her fingers sank into a chill, paste-like substance with no solidity, offering nothing onto which she could hold. She felt like a spider she'd once seen trapped in a soup bowl, tiny feet scrabbling for purchase until it had stopped, too exhausted to go on.

She began to slide further down, the water a rising blanket around her face and now tinged red by the blood from her broken nose. She kicked harder, bubbles bursting in a thin trail from where air had been trapped in her clothing. Another brief respite. She took a deep breath, felt the urge to cough. If only she could take off the jacket that was weighing her down, then she might have a chance. But the uniform buttons had been hard to do up in the first place; they would be even harder to undo.

A crackle of vegetation sounded from nearby, and she looked up, desperate for a helping hand, a friendly face. Maybe a villager out hunting early. Or maybe not. Scared out of the copse where she had been hiding since last night by the sound of a car arriving, she had tripped and plunged head first down a steep bank, the flash of cold water replacing one panic with another.

'Help…help me!'

A familiar shadow, framed by the thin dawn light, loomed over the water's edge. She felt pathetically grateful, reaching up to take the helping hand.

But grasped only empty space.

Then strong fingers clamped down on her scalp, and suddenly she had no buoyancy left. Her kicks were futile. Instead, she watched through the clear water as the bank, brilliant white, slid past her face, and below her the bottom of the pool, like a funnel leading into blackness, approached all too quickly.

CHAPTER ONE

Lucas Rocco? Insubordinate bastard. And insolent.
A good cop, though.
Capt. Michel Santer – Clichy-Nanterre district

To Inspector Lucas Rocco, the gathering in the churchyard looked too casual to be a riot, too small to be a funeral. Newly exiled from his home base in the Clichy-Nanterre district of western Paris under Interior Ministry orders, and assigned to the village of Poissons-les-Marais, in Picardie, north-west France, it was a welcome distraction. He turned off the car radio, killing in mid-sentence Johnny Hallyday, the current singing heart-throb *de choix*, and left his Citroën Traction outside the local café to find out what was commanding such a gathering in this flyspeck of a place.

'It's a bomb, I tell you.' A compact, nut-brown man in a greasy old bush hat was speaking round a spit-stained *Gitanes* with the assurance of one who knew about such things. The focus of everyone's attention was a large, cylindrical object lying in a shallow depression in the chalky soil next to the gravelled pathway. Tapping the rusted metal casing with the toe of his boot brought a sharp intake of

10

breath among the crowd, who all stepped back a pace.

'Probably from the Great War,' said a phlegmatic woman in a black headscarf and chequered apron. She stood hugging an armful of leeks to her ample bosom like a character from an old painting. 'It looks old enough.'

'No way,' Bush-hat disagreed. 'Those little kites wouldn't have been able to lift anything this big.'

'Doesn't look that much to me,' muttered an old man in traditional *bleus* – the uniform jacket and baggy trousers of the working man in rural Picardie. In spite of the warm weather, the trousers were tucked into a pair of enormous rubber boots, the tops reaching his knees.

Bush-hat lifted an eyebrow, assured of his audience's attention. 'You think? A bomb this big would take out an area about three hundred metres in radius, no problem.'

Since three hundred metres was roughly the length and width of the village, a remote spot too small and insignificant to even figure on the map of northern France, and they were standing right in the centre, it caused the crowd to move back another respectful, but entirely useless, three paces.

Rocco found himself standing next to a heavy-set man in a green vest and thick corduroys. The man turned and nodded affably.

'Did he say bomb?' Rocco wasn't yet used to the accent in this part of the country, although he'd understood most of what was said.

'That he did,' the man replied. He had a deep, almost melancholy voice. 'Don't worry: it's what passes for excitement in these parts. You the inspector?'

'I am.' Rocco was surprised: news had travelled faster than he'd expected. 'Lucas Rocco. How did you know?'

11

The man thrust out a calloused hand, which Rocco shook. 'Lamotte. Claude will do. I know lots of things. Also,' he nodded back towards the Traction, 'the big black cop machine is a bit of a giveaway.' He turned and called, 'Hey, everyone – it's our resident *flic*.' He smiled shyly at Rocco. 'No disrespect; better out than in, as they say.'

'None taken.' Rocco waited as the crowd turned to stare at him. Their reactions were mixed. He reckoned suspicion – a natural response to policemen everywhere, even among policemen – won out by a long nose, with surprise and fleeting interest not far behind. He let it wash over him. At just over two metres in height and built like a useful prop forward, he'd long given up on the idea of blending in anywhere among normal society. Crims, prizefighters and soldiers, OK; others, forget it. 'I've been called worse.'

'Not yet, you haven't.' Claude gave Rocco another inspection, eyes dwelling on the heavy shoes, the broad shoulders and the angular, powerful face topped by a scrub of black hair. 'Stick around, though, and you might.'

'They don't like the police?'

'They don't like anyone. Comes of living in a rural shithole, ignored by everyone, including our esteemed *général*.' He spoke with quiet cynicism, but if he was worried about causing offence, he didn't show it.

Rocco shrugged. Charles de Gaulle, soldier and current president of the Fifth Republic, lauded and loathed in fairly equal measures, was a man he rarely thought about. 'I think he's got other things on his mind at the moment.'

'The Algerian thing?' Claude nodded sombrely. 'That's all done and dusted, bar the shouting. Up to them, now.' As if sensing Rocco's lack of interest in the political desires of the

12

once French-held North African territory, now just a year on from independence, he nodded at a tall, skeletal character standing to one side. 'Monsieur Thierry over there,' he said, returning to the matter in hand, 'looks after the churchyard. It's his way of getting a free pass into Heaven. He found the bomb while returfing. Looks a big bugger.'

Rocco had seen bigger in Indochina, but scrubbed that mental picture. Best not go there; barely ten years ago, it was still too recent to forget and offered only dark shadows waiting to greet him.

Besides, it didn't look much like any bomb he'd ever seen.

'Who's the expert?' Bush-hat was now bending and sniffing noisily at the object like a terrier inspecting a rat hole, dribbling cigarette ash all over it. Small and brown as a nut, the man looked as hard as the soil he was standing on, as much a product of the land as the crops in the fields.

'Didier Marthe. He's a scrap man. Anything worth selling, he'll break it down and flog it. He spends all day hitting things with a big hammer.' He tapped the side of his head. 'I think the vibration affected him over the years.'

Didier, Rocco noticed, was missing the thumb and first two fingers of his left hand, and his face looked shiny on one side.

'Looks like he suffered for his art.'

Claude laughed. 'He hit a grenade a little too enthusiastically one day. It was a dud, but still had enough life in it to stop him playing the accordion.'

'Now there's a blessing.' Lucas paused, did a double take. 'He hit a live *grenade*?' It made him wonder if there was, after all, some truth to the slanderous rumours about country folk circulated among his former colleagues, who rarely, if ever, ventured outside the city limits. 'Tell me you're kidding.'

'Unbelievable, but true. World War Two, British, I think it was. He doesn't usually bother with them – they're too small and not worth the effort. He prefers artillery shells, the bigger the better. And bombs like this one.'

'You make it sound like a full-time job.'

'It is. The last big one he found was next to the school eighteen months ago. He'd just finished clearing the ground around it and went to get some lifting gear when it blew up. Knocked him flat on his arse and blew the roof off the schoolhouse. Luckily, the kids were on holiday.'

'For him, too.'

'Not the way he saw it. All that metal, fragmented to hell; he got totally tanked and cried for three whole days.'

Rocco grunted. No wonder the scrap man was so interested in this find. Large, oblong and rounded, it had a hefty hexagon nut at the end protruding from the ground. The casing was covered in a thick scale of rust, no doubt through being buried in the chalky soil of the Poissons-les-Marais churchyard with only the ancient village dead for company. Quite how such a monster had lain overlooked for so long was a mystery, although he knew these things worked their way to the surface from time to time, like pebbles in the garden.

'Lucas Rocco,' murmured Claude, stretching out the words and pronouncing Lucas the American way, with the 's'. 'You're not from these parts, are you?'

'I'm relieved you can tell.' Rocco wondered how long the dissection would go on for. Probably days, given the fact that so little else seemed to happen here.

'Easy. You don't look shifty enough.'

'What have people here got to be shifty about?'

'Everything. Nothing. Living and dying, mostly.'

'I'll bear it in mind.'

'You'll be looking for somewhere to doss down, I suppose?'

Rocco decided he might get to like this man – if he didn't have to arrest him for something first.

'I might. Are you the local psychic, or a letting agent?'

'If I was either, I'd die of boredom. You've seen the café?'

'I have. Not my thing.' His recommended billet above the *bar-tabac*, where he'd just stopped to check out the facilities, was too public, and the smell of stale beer and cigarette smoke too invasive, for his tastes; he'd lodged in too many similar fleapits over the years to look on them with affection. It was at best a stopgap until he found something better; somewhere he could call his own space while he considered what the hell he was supposed to be doing out here.

'Go see Mme Denis, down Rue Danvillers.' Claude tilted his head towards a lane running off at an angle from the village square. 'Last but one on the left. She has the keys to an empty house down there. Plenty of room to park the cop machine, too.' He grinned knowingly. 'In your line of work, you'll feel right at home.'

'Why?'

'A man was murdered there years ago.'

CHAPTER TWO

Rocco? Arrogant and disrespectful.
Lieut. André Thomas – head of administration and
accounts, Clichy-Nanterre district

'Say again?' Rocco stared him down, his voice a growl, and
the grin faded quickly.

'Only kidding. It's a nice place. Peaceful.'

Then the crowd moved and the man named Didier
Marthe was in front of them. No doubt aware that he'd
lost his audience's attention in favour of the new arrival, he
stared belligerently up into Rocco's face, craning his head
with difficulty.

'What are you doing here, *flic*?' he demanded, cigarette
bobbing angrily. 'We've done nothing wrong. It's a bomb,
that's all. Not a drama; not an arrestable offence…unless
you go around locking up explosive devices these days?'
He turned and sniggered at the crowd, seeking support
against the outsider, the cop. 'They turn up all the time,
these things, like turds on a sheep farm. The whole area
was one big munitions dump back in forty-four, and
what wasn't stored here was dropped like bird shit by

the British as they scuttled back to England.'

'Easy, Didier,' murmured Claude. 'He's a newcomer. Show some respect, huh?'

'Respect?' Didier spat on the ground, easing the gobbet around the cigarette. 'He'll have to earn it like everyone else!'

Rocco stood his ground, although he was trying not to gag. It wasn't the little man's aggressive demeanour, nor even the potentially deadly object sitting just a few feet away which bothered him: rather, Didier's breath, which was toxic enough to kill a chicken at ten paces. A mixture of *vin de pays*, cheap tobacco and several other unnameable substances, it wafted out in a vicious cloud whenever he spoke, enveloping anyone within range in its evil embrace.

'We'd best call the *gendarmes*,' Monsieur Thierry called out anxiously. 'Before it goes off and flattens the village.' He looked in a state of shock, staring in awe at the spot where his shovel had hit the casing with some force. A silvery scar was clearly visible where the rust had been chipped away.

'What?' Didier spun round in horror, and Rocco could guess why. The fire brigade was the first force called on in emergencies, but the local brigade probably wasn't equipped to deal with explosives. The *gendarmes*, while less popular – and likely viewed by cynics as expendable – would keep whatever they dealt with as evidence. 'Why let those thieving maggots get their hands on it?' Didier turned back to Rocco, including him in his contempt and huffing out a fresh wave of halitosis.

Rocco fought to hold on to his breakfast. The idea that this man might take a hammer to the thing simply to prevent the police from confiscating it was frightening. But short of surrounding it with armed guards or decking him, he couldn't think of any way of preventing it.

'What do you say, Inspector?' The question came from Thierry, looking to officialdom for support – probably a rarity in these parts, Rocco guessed. Anyone representing the government or its agencies would clearly be viewed with hostility and caution.

He shrugged, wondering what made them think he was an expert on bomb disposal. Then it hit him: if anything went wrong, blame the *flic*. It was probably an English bomb, made in Coventry or some such hellhole, and since the English were probably no more popular in these parts than the police, what could be more fitting? Barely twenty years since the end of the last global conflict centred on France, the debris of two wars was just as fresh in people's minds as it was in the ground beneath their feet.

He was about to suggest evacuating the immediate area and calling in the *gendarmes*, as Monsieur Thierry had suggested, when a man pushed through the crowd. He was dressed in filthy overalls and carried a canvas tool bag.

'Philippe Delsaire,' Claude informed Rocco helpfully. 'He's what passes as a plumber in these parts. Also farms a small plot outside the village. Gambler, too.' He rubbed his fingertips together. 'Not a bad plumber or farmer, but lousy at cards.' He grinned knowingly.

Everyone watched as Delsaire stared hard at the object. Then he stepped forward with a large wrench, and without warning, gave the hexagon nut a resounding thwack.

In spite of his doubts about the object being a bomb, Rocco felt his testicles shrink and witnessed fleeting images of his past life go by at speed. A collective groan testified to others sharing this same life-death experience. Even the mad bomb-basher, Didier, looked fleetingly alarmed, while Thierry crossed himself and muttered something obscene.

The newcomer struck the object again. But instead of the expected flash and monumental explosion that should have sent Poissons-les-Marais into orbit like a space rocket, the nut simply fell off, and out onto the grass glugged a stream of rust-coloured water.

Delsaire smiled and tossed the wrench into his tool bag.

'Water container,' he said simply. 'A prototype. Only seen a couple of them in my time. The design never caught on.' He pointed to where the water was bubbling out. 'With only one hole you can't get a steady flow, see? Probably fell off a lorry and got buried.'

As Delsaire walked away, whistling, Didier glared around, daring anyone to say a word. Then he calmly scuttled forward and claimed the container as his property.

The crowd left him to it, some looking almost disappointed that a discarded water tank wasn't about to reduce them and their village to microscopic dust particles.

Rocco was about to return to his car when Claude stopped him.

'So what's a city detective doing out here?' he asked. 'We're just a pimple on a cow's arse. It's not like there's any real crime – nobody's got anything worth stealing. And certainly nothing to trouble an *inspecteur*.'

'I've no idea,' said Rocco truthfully. 'They haven't told me.' Captain Santer, his boss, had merely presented him with his new orders, an accommodation warrant and directions, and told him to go and investigate cowpats until further notice. All part of a new nationwide initiative, he had explained vaguely, a small grinding of a very large wheel in the Fifth Republic's efforts to modernise its police force. So far, Rocco judged, going by what he'd seen, as initiatives went, it was a case of wait and see.

'There must be a reason, though.' Claude was gently insistent, like a friendly dog with a bone, teasing out the goodness.

'Why?'

'There's a reason for everything.'

'Ah. You're a philosopher as well as a psychic.'

'No. Just that I know how the official mind works.'

'Lucky you. When you've got a minute, perhaps you can fill me in.' He nodded. 'Thanks for the tip about the house.'

CHAPTER THREE

Rouen, Haute-Normandie

Ishmael Poudric rubbed his eyes and glanced along the hallway towards the front of his house. Someone was at the door. Lowering the large pendulum eyeglass which old age and too many hours spent poring over photographs had rendered necessary, he checked the clock on the wall of his study. Nine o'clock. Who could be calling at this hour? Time was no longer a medium he allowed to control his life the way it once had, but at his age it was a commodity too valuable to waste. A glance at the window confirmed that darkness had fallen without him noticing.

The knock was repeated. It sounded urgent. Maybe his son, Etienne...a problem with the business. No. He would have called first.

He stood up with a grimace, bones protesting, and eased away from a desk cluttered with the results of years of his work: the negatives, slippery and undisciplined, like small children; the cardboard mounts for slides; the photo prints in black and white, some aged and fading, others bright and new.

He opened the front door and was surprised to find a woman smiling at him. She was dressed smartly and conventionally enough, even if, to Poudric, she looked a little plainer than any woman should do. Pallid, almost, as if illness or circumstance had drained all the colour from her skin. She appeared to be in her middle years, although he had long ceased to be any kind of judge when it came to the ages of women.

'Can I help you?' he queried politely. After a lifetime of service behind a camera and a shop counter, it was a difficult habit to break.

The woman held out a cutting from a magazine. He recognised it immediately. It was from a history journal about the building of an archive for a university library, by one Ishmael Poudric, photographer, once of Poitiers in Aquitaine, now retired to Saint-Martin just outside Rouen.

'I read about you,' the woman said. 'You're building a photo library about the Resistance movement.'

'That's correct, madam – but it's very late…'

'I know – and I apologise for the discourtesy,' the woman said hurriedly. 'My name is Agnès. Agnès Carre. I'm a student of Modern History, and was wondering if you could help me?' She delved into a pocket and produced a slim envelope. 'I will pay you for your time.'

'To do what?' Poudric was surprised. There were not many offers of money these days, now he had given up his photography business – well, other than favours for a few friends now and then. And this project he was working on was out of love, not financial gain. With younger photographers out there, armed with the latest technology and new ideas, his skills as a snapper were fast becoming outmoded.

'I'm looking for some photos for a thesis I'm writing.' Agnès smiled tiredly and brushed back a stray hair. 'Can I come in and explain?'

Ten minutes later, his curiosity satisfied and the envelope containing the money lying invitingly on his desk, Poudric was delving through a long photo file box, flicking aside index cards and humming, a habit he had never quite managed to lose. His visitor was sitting quietly, nursing a cup of tea he had prepared for her.

'Ah.' He stopped and lifted out a print and its negative, both encased in a thin protective sleeve. 'I think this is the one.' He turned from his desk and showed her the print.

She took it carefully, holding it between her fingers, the way he had, and tilted it to the light. The snap showed a group of people, all dressed in rough, working-style clothing. Six men and one woman. They were huddled around a fire in the open, expressions sombre, most of them facing the camera. The men were armed with rifles, some with bandoliers of ammunition across their chests. The woman sat at one end of the group, a pistol in one hand and a knife in the other. The man next to her had a hand on her knee. With its dark tones and grim connotations, the scene pulsed with atmosphere.

'I took that,' Poudric explained, remembering the occasion with unusual clarity, 'one evening near Poitiers. I had worked hard to gain the confidence of this group and persuaded them to sit for posterity.' He gave a faint smile. 'This particular group was communist in its affiliations, but they were brave people, all fighting for what they thought was right. To be frank, it was risky having this done – for them far more than me – but when one is faced with history in the making, you take whatever opportunity comes along. And there were damn few weddings or celebrations requiring my expertise at the time.' He chuckled dryly at the memory.

Agnès nodded, not taking her eyes off the photo, as if mesmerised. 'Do you have others of this group?'

'There are some, but I would need time to find them. The collection is not in order yet.'

'In that case, this one will do.'

'I will have to copy it – it's the only one I have. I'll need an address to send it to.'

'I would rather take it now.'

'Now? But it's late… I can send it first thing tom—'

'That won't be possible.' Agnès seemed suddenly agitated. She leant over and picked up the envelope. 'I'm travelling tomorrow and need it immediately.' She opened the envelope and counted out some notes. 'I'm sure you still have your equipment?'

Poudric hesitated for a moment. Then need overcame tiredness. He had a powerful sense that this woman, whatever her claims, was no student of History, and had an ulterior motive for acquiring this photo. The energy coming from her was almost palpable. But who was he to judge? He folded the notes into his shirt pocket and stood up. 'You will have to give me time to set it up and for the print to dry. Would you care for more tea while you wait?'

The woman sat back, her face calm again. 'No. Thank you. I've been waiting long enough. A few more minutes won't matter.'

CHAPTER FOUR

Rocco? An uncultured ruffian. He needs locking up.
J de Montrichy – deputy mayor's office,
Clichy-Nanterre district

Rocco knocked on the rear door of the cottage Claude had directed him to the previous day. It was on the outskirts of the village, along a narrow lane leading out into an open expanse of rolling pastureland. A sign pointed to the next village, Danvillers, five kilometres away, along a surface which looked little used and was dotted with cowpats drying in the early morning sun.

The house was small and sturdy, surrounded by flower and vegetable beds with barely a spare centimetre of unused space. The earth had been tilled to a fine grain, the borders straight as a city block and without a weed in sight. A large chicken run stood at the end of a long garden, but the inhabitants appeared to have free roam of the place, with one old hen nestled contentedly by the back door in a small dust bowl of her own making.

The air smelt gamey, buzzing with a swirl of fat, lazy flies. Rocco had passed two farms on his way down here, both with large manure heaps inside enclosed yards and crawling with chickens, so he was hardly surprised by the insect life. It wasn't unpleasant, though, and certainly better than the noxious air in the café where he'd forced down the half-baguette and bowl of hot chocolate which passed for breakfast, topped off with toxic tobacco fumes from the patrons at the bar.

The cottage door opened to reveal an elderly woman with white hair and thick glasses. She was of medium height and compact, dressed in a blue apron over a grey dress, with a triangle headscarf pinned carefully in place.

'You're the *inspecteur*?' she said, and motioned him inside.

'That's me.' He was no longer surprised at the way information was circulating in this place. There was no telephone wire to the cottage, so he put it down to some secret sort of underground network known only to the locals. Or maybe they had a team of fleet-footed kids doing the rounds, letting everyone in on the latest news as it happened.

The cottage kitchen was clean, simply furnished and like walking into a museum. But it was homely and neat, a small oasis of tranquillity hung with the smells of cooking and soap. Fading photos of a large man in cavalry uniform sitting astride a huge white charger were dotted around the room, and Rocco recognised the atmosphere of widowhood.

Mme Denis went to a sideboard and pulled open a drawer, extracting a small bundle of keys. She dropped them on the heavy table, then went to a stove and picked up a coffee percolator.

'I brewed this fresh for you,' she said. 'Big man like you

needs a stimulant to keep going. My husband was a big man.'

Rocco didn't really want more coffee. But he sensed a ritual about to unfold and that he was a central part of it. A refusal might offend.

She produced two heavy, brown cups and filled them with coffee, then took an aluminium jug of milk and a cardboard box of sugar cubes, and slid them across the table, motioning him to sit. She had strong hands, Rocco noted. It explained the orderly garden.

'The house next door,' she said, sitting down with a sigh, 'is available. It's clean and dry, although you'll have to put up with the *fouines* in the attic.' Lucas must have looked blank, because she said, 'Fruit rats. They're everywhere in these parts. You don't get them where you come from?'

He shook his head. Paris had plenty of rats, both two- and four-legged. But not the fruit variety.

'They're harmless,' Mme Denis assured him. 'They make a bit of noise in the attic at night, scrabbling around up there, but as long as you don't leave food out, you should be fine.'

He drank his coffee, which was as strong as boat varnish, but good. He added sugar cubes and milk. Then he began the negotiation for the rent. If he stayed at the local *bar-tabac*, where the regional HQ in Amiens could get hold of him easily by telephone, they would pay his board. Opting to get his own place meant he would have to pick up the bill himself.

He decided that if all he had to worry about was a few fruit rats, he could put up with the expense. A telephone, though, was a must. He mentioned it to Madame Denis.

She pursed her lips. 'There aren't many in the village, although they put up the wires. The mayor, of course – he's got one. And the *garde champêtre*.' She smiled. 'Be warned, though: you'll get a lot of visitors if you have one of those put in.'

'But I'm a policeman – a *flic*.'

'Doesn't matter. When people want to call friends and family, you'd be amazed how forgiving they can be. What about your laundry?'

'No problem. I used to be in the army. I'll manage.' It wasn't something he had given much thought to.

She cast a critical eye over his clothes, which consisted of a long, dark coat, dark cotton shirt and charcoal trousers – the latter Swedish imports and expensive – and his shoes, which were from London. Good-quality clothing was one of Rocco's few luxuries. 'Those fine fabrics won't last long out here, not if you pound them to death in a sink. There's a laundry service calls by twice a week. Leave it in a bag with Francine at the co-op and they'll pick it up and return it in two days, sometimes three. You'll need to plan what you wear.'

When he had finished his coffee, she led him out of the house and along the lane to the house next door. Rocco was pleasantly surprised: it was a large, villa-style property set back off the road behind a railed, overgrown garden. Outhouses and a garage stood off to one side, and the rear plot disappeared into the distance, sprouting a vast wilderness of unknown species.

'Are you a gardener?' she asked him, handing him the keys.

'No idea,' he said frankly, staring at the expanse of

rampant territory waiting to be tamed. 'I had some tulips in a window box once.'

She looked unimpressed. 'Flowers. What happened?'

'They died.'

She made a *phuitt* sound. 'In that case, you'll need the services of Arnaud.'

'Is he a landscape gardener?'

She smiled indulgently at the term. 'You're a city boy, aren't you? Arnaud pretty much lives at the café. He'll do whatever needs doing. Just make sure he completes the work before you pay him, otherwise he'll be drunk as a skunk for a month.'

She watched as he unlocked the door. It opened onto a large kitchen-cum-general room, with a small electric cooker and a separate wood fire and range with a water tank attached. There was a plain sink and drainer. The air smelt musty and dry from a lack of circulation. Another room lay at the back, leading, Mme Denis informed him, to the bedroom.

'No running water?' he said.

'No. Along the main road, where they laid the pipes, but not down here. The toilet's outside by the outhouse.' She gave him a sideways glance. 'There's a pump, though. I presume you're more familiar with pumps than flowers?'

'Of course. Most good bars have them.'

She snorted. 'Glad you have a sense of humour, Inspector. When it drops below freezing and you have to melt the ice first, you'll need it. Come.' She led him out to the side of the house, where a pump stood in the lee of a large wooden outbuilding. It had an elaborate, cast-iron handle and spout, with a metal cap on the top. A tall plastic jug stood beneath

29

the spout. She lifted the hat. 'You prime it with water, then jiggle the handle until it starts to pull.'

'And when it freezes?'

'Stack straw around the base and set fire to it. Works every time. Won't boil the water, though.' She lifted the corner of her mouth and chuckled at her own wit.

Rocco smiled and followed her to the front door. He remembered what Claude had said. 'Has anyone died here recently?'

'Not that I recall. Why – do you intend holding séances?'

He watched her as she pottered away, shaking her head. Then he stepped inside and inspected his new home. He found a scattering of dust-layered furniture, all plain and sturdy, but useable. Solid. Rodent droppings were scattered across the floor, and a bat was hanging in one corner, small and sinister. Something furry and dead lay beneath the kitchen table. The back rooms were large and airy, and apart from an ill-fitting French window in the back living room, it was pleasant and comfortable.

He went back outside and primed the pump with a slosh of rainwater from the jug; jiggled the handle which groaned like a donkey, then felt the pump stall before water began gushing out. It looked crystal clear. He tasted it. Not exactly *Pouilly-Fumé*, but it would do.

Still better than the café, anyway.

After a brief tidy-up, which lifted more dust than it laid, Rocco walked back to the café to collect his car. The bar was empty, so he took advantage of the quiet to check in with his former office in Clichy-Nanterre.

'What do you want?' Captain Michel Santer, a tough,

overweight man from the Jura, sounded harassed as usual. 'I thought you'd be on a horse by now, chasing sheep rustlers.'

'They don't do sheep,' Rocco told him. 'Cows, though, lots of them. And village idiots with a death wish. Any news for me?' *A transfer back*, he thought, *would be nice.*

'No. I'm too busy trying to cover for you. Since you buggered off, we've had two bodies turn up, as well as twelve reported burglaries, two bank raids and one minor riot caused by students demanding better facilities. It's like there's been a mini-crime wave in celebration of your departure. Oh, and the mayor's wife lost her chihuahua in the Rue de Bord.'

'If it went missing down there, tell her to try the Korean restaurant at the end. What about my replacement?'

'Hah! He didn't turn up, did he? Seems the turnip got on the wrong train and ended up in Toulouse. I've told them they can keep him. Anyone who can't navigate their way round this city is as much use to me as tits on a pigeon.'

Rocco laughed. 'Not a good start, then.' Like all 'initiatives' this one had begun with a shuffle of bodies all around the board, from the Med to the Channel ports, with movements in manpower creating gaps everywhere, not all of which could be filled quickly enough. A bureaucratic charade, in other words, a result of the Fifth Republic trying to prove it had more balls than the recently lamented Fourth had ever done by introducing new policing methods.

'What about the new emperor?' He was referring to the impending arrival of the new divisional *commissaire*. The officer classes were also part of the elaborate game of musical chairs.

'Not yet here.' Santer laughed. 'It wasn't personal, you know, moving you. I doubt someone saw your name pop up on a report and thought: *I know – let's have some fun and move that awkward bastard, Rocco, out to the sticks. It might mean disturbing the entire French police establishment, but what the hell – it'll be worth it just to piss him off.*'

'You know that has the disturbing ring of truth.'

'I already told you, it was a nationwide plan; our new boss was hauled out of Bordeaux and dumped on us just like you've been dumped on those lucky country folk in Picardie and so on along the line. When the top men at his level get moved, it sets off a ripple effect throughout the ranks. You and every other bugger who was moved got caught up in it like flies on dog shit.'

'That's all it was?'

'That's all. It's about sharing services across the whole police network. We loan inspectors to the regions, they let us have some of their big farm boys when we need a bit of fresh muscle for the CRS, we all cooperate on forensic and cross-border issues, blah, blah, blah. It's called "integration".'

'Sounds too good to be true.'

'Amen to that. It's the latest thing, probably copied from America, so don't go and cock it all up by being awkward. You should think yourself lucky and enjoy the holiday. Oh, and don't forget, you're responsible to the local station, nobody else. No magistrates, no mayors – you go straight to the local *commissaire*.'

Rocco felt his spirits plummet. Reporting to the uniforms? That's all he needed, being told what to do by brass buttons. Still, it might be an interesting departure from the norm. Initiatives came and went, whatever their names and aims. As for the high-level *commissaire* being hauled out of a distant regional office and slipped into an outer Paris district, that was a clear indication of impending elevation to a more senior post. All the grey beards at the top of the command structure were doing was making sure the incomer was sufficiently groomed and had the straw picked out of his ears before being allowed to mix with the nobs in the Ministry of the Interior. In the meanwhile, everyone else shuffled across the board like chess pieces, just to show they were cooperating.

He told Santer about his move to a house on the outskirts of the village, and that he would collect messages from the café until he got a phone fitted.

'What's wrong with the café?' Santer demanded. 'Christ, I'd *love* to be billeted in a café for a few weeks: drinks on tap, bar billiards to play every evening and out from under my wife's reach? You don't know when you're lucky, you big ape!'

'Yes, and everyone listening to every word I say,' countered Rocco. 'They already know more about me than I do. I want to keep some distance.'

'Fair enough. Be a misery guts. Oh, a bit of advice: touch base with the local *garde champêtre* as soon as you can. It's a minor courtesy but worth doing. He'll be your best source of information, in case you need it.'

'What exactly does a *garde champêtre* do? I've never met one.'

'He's a rural cop. Bit like the rangers in the USA, only without the bears – and he probably rides a bicycle. But keep him happy and he'll look after you. And just remember that

33

he's all that keeps the peasants from marching on this city with pitchforks and tar barrels and wheeling out Madame Guillotine.'

'Jesus, there's a thought.'

Rocco cut the call and got through to the PTT service centre. He explained to three people in turn that he needed a telephone fitted urgently, and each time he was told to wait before being passed on. 'It's for official police business,' he explained to the bored-sounding clerk who finally agreed to take some notes. He gave the man his new address.

'There's a cop in Poissons-les-Marais?' The clerk sounded sceptical. 'Mother of God. I was born near there. What have they done – decided to join the twentieth century?'

'They're working on it. How quickly can you do it?'

'*Pfffff*... You've no chance. You'll have to join the queue like everyone else.'

Rocco bit down on a surge of impatience. Dealing with petty bureaucrats like this was the one thing guaranteed to spoil his day. 'Let me speak to your supervisor,' he snarled. 'This is urgent!'

'I *am* the supervisor,' replied the man tersely. 'And you'll still have to join the queue like everyone else. If I let every person who claimed to be a cop jump the queue, we'd have rioting in the streets.'

'Wha—? I *am* a cop, you imbecile!'

There was a click as the connection was cut.

Rocco slammed the phone down, nearly dislodging it from the wall. He swore at length, roundly calling into question the man's family history, sexual proclivities and the likelihood of his ever fathering anything but deformed goats.

When he turned round, he found several customers – farm workers by the look of them – gathered in the bar behind him, listening in silent awe to his tirade.

'Government business,' he growled. 'We talk in code.' He strode from the bar, wondering just how much they'd heard and wondering how easy it would be to get them to take up pitchforks and tar barrels and march on the PTT offices.

CHAPTER FIVE

Rocco? Pushy...dogmatic...intuitive. He gets results.
Capt. Michel Santer – Clichy-Nanterre district

Rocco climbed in his Citroën and headed along the main street to the eastern end of the village, where the landlord of the bar had told him the *garde champêtre* had a cottage. He had no guarantee of a warm reception, since the man might resent a city detective landing on his doorstep without warning, viewing him as a threat or an informer, possibly both. But as Michel Santer had suggested, it would be the simplest way of getting to grips with his new territory, and he wasn't about to ignore good advice.

He reached the village boundary and found a rambling but tidy daub-and-wattle bungalow on a large plot of land. Most of the garden was laid to vegetables, the exception being a bed of dark-red roses in the front. At the side of the property stood a lean-to garage and a large chicken house, with vine creepers snaking everywhere, unchecked and gnarled with age.

He got out of the car and knocked on the front door.

The noise echoed around the garden and filtered off into the fields, while back in the village, the church bell sounded thin and suitably soulful. He'd seen no sign of a priest yet, and hoped that would remain the case.

The door opened and Claude Lamotte smiled out at him.

'I'm looking for the—' Rocco began, before noticing Claude's uniform trousers and shirt, complete with shoulder badges. 'You're the *garde champêtre*? You didn't say.'

'You didn't ask.'

Rocco felt a ruffle of irritation, sensing he'd lost a point or two. Instead of coming here and opening up relations on a genial, if slightly superior note, given his rank as an inspector, he realised this rural policeman had gently played him.

Claude peered past Rocco's shoulder at the big black Citroën. 'Yours or the department's?'

'Mine.'

'Good choice. Discreet, underplayed – blends in well with the scenery.' He grinned.

'It's a car,' Rocco countered tersely. He had to concede, though, that the man was probably right. Back in Clichy, it wouldn't have raised an eyebrow; out here, it was as subtle as a hearse at a wedding. Still, he wasn't going to give in without a fight. 'It does the job it was built for.'

'Fair enough. Come in.' Claude led the way into a smart but sparsely furnished living room, with a small kitchen off to one side. 'You want coffee?' A percolator was bubbling steadily on a small stove, filling the air with a heady aroma.

Rocco looked around the room, absorbing the

atmosphere. There was a large dresser, a sideboard, a dining table and two leather armchairs. Few ornaments and no softness. A man's room, he thought. No woman's influence here, although there had been, once, evidenced by a piece of crochet-work in a frame on the wall. A large plastic-covered map of the area was tacked to another wall, and below it, on the sideboard, a pile of books and folders which Lucas recognised as the official detritus of a serving police officer.

'Why not?' His stomach rumbled, a leftover, he was sure, from Mme Denis's brand of paint stripper. But since he was intent on getting to grips with the locals, including this man, who was to all intents a colleague, he could stand another cup.

Claude filled two cups and pushed sugar across the table. 'Help yourself.' He sat down and picked up his coffee. 'So what can I do for you, Lucas?'

Rocco sat across from him and tasted his coffee. It was very good. 'For a start, thank you for the information about Mme Denis. I'm now the tenant of the end house in Rue Danvillers. It doesn't seem to have a name or number.'

Claude smiled. 'It doesn't need one. It's already being called the cop house.'

'No kidding.' He noticed a black telephone sitting on a small side table. 'I need a phone, though. There are too many big ears flapping at the café. Any ideas?'

Claude reached across and scooped up the handset and dialled a number from memory.

'Dédé? It's Claude. I need a phone fitted yesterday. Police, yes. Hang on.' He covered the mouthpiece and looked at Lucas. 'My cousin, Dédé. Can you run to a decent bottle of Armagnac?'

'If they sell it at the co-op.'

'They do.' He gestured at the telephone and said softly, 'Sorry – it's the way things work here, but we don't make the rules, right?'

Rocco suppressed a smile. Out in the middle of nowhere and he got a phone fitted with one call. In Clichy, it would have taken weeks, and threats of physical harm – and even then the job would have been botched.

'Thank you,' he said and sipped his coffee. 'When can he do it?'

Claude went back to the phone. 'No problem, Dédé. When can—? Really? That's superb, my friend. See you soon.'

He put down the phone and smiled triumphantly. 'Tomorrow. He's in the area. If you leave your door unlocked, he'll do it on his way through. Leave a chalk mark on the floor where you want it fitted.'

'I owe you one.'

'Yes, you do,' Claude agreed. He leant back in his chair. 'So, to what do we owe the pleasure of this posting?' He was clearly referring to Rocco's presence in the area and saw the favour as having earned information in return.

'Musical chairs,' Rocco explained. 'There's been a shake-up of various departments and regions, and I've been sent out here as part of an exchange initiative. Someone else is sitting in my chair, another is sitting in *his* chair and so on. It's nationwide.'

'Sounds like bureaucracy. In my experience, such initiatives are an important man's way of becoming even more important. But why you and why right here? Why not Amiens?'

'Me? Well, if you listen to the politicians, I've come to bring order to the countryside: smite the robbers, murderers, thieves and philistines.'

'Philistines. We don't have many of those around here: the local priest sees to that.'

'Then he and I have something in common.'

Claude sniffed. 'You make it sound like a holy war.'

'It is. And God help anyone who gets in my way.' He smiled. 'In the meantime, I thought I'd come and say hello.'

'That's nice.'

'And get a briefing. Do you get *any* crime here at all?'

Claude puffed out his cheeks. 'Well, we do, but what we call crime and what you call crime is not the same. You city people get cars stolen, our crims steal the odd chicken. You get riots and gang fights, we get the occasional punch-up over a game of bar billiards or somebody's brand of politics. No offence, but none of that needs detective skills.' He stood up and went over to the map on the wall. 'Poissons sits in a shallow valley, and shares space with a river, a canal, and the *marais*, all to the south of here.' He stabbed a finger on each in turn, ending on a large expanse coloured pale green. 'The *marais* runs for about three kilometres along the valley, and about half a kilometre deep. Here in the village, it's mostly a couple of lakes surrounded by trees, but further out to the west, there are four more lakes, all much more open.'

'Are they linked?'

Claude tilted his head. 'Not like they used to be. There's a narrow stretch joining them up, but only the locals know about it. When I patrol out there, I use a Canadian.' Rocco must have looked blank, because he added, 'It's a canoe;

slides through weeds and other rubbish like a knife across butter. And it's quiet. If anyone's there who shouldn't be, they don't hear me coming. The best way along the valley by water is along the canal, which is further out.'

'Still used?' Rocco couldn't recall seeing one, but he knew many of the country's canals were still in use.

'Sure. Some freight traffic, but it's dying. Losing out to the big trucks. It's near the station; you go over a bridge but it's masked by trees so you wouldn't know it was there.'

'What about the village?' As far as Rocco knew, his 'patch' was as deep and wide as his superiors chose to make it, and probably encompassed an area several hundred kilometres square; but his immediate interest was Poissons. He could hardly live here and not show an interest.

'Not big. About a hundred houses, mostly stretched along the main street. A shop, church and school...and the café you know about. Most people here work on the land, the railway or at factories in Amiens. There are a dozen small farms, a couple are bigger ones, and lots of open country. We're still in the horse era, here; there are a couple of tractors but that's it. The farmers don't have the money for mechanisation on a big scale.' He sat down again and finished his coffee, his briefing done. 'So, where are you from? Before Paris, I mean.'

'Here and there. All over. The army, then the police; I moved around a lot.'

'Indochina?' The last big conflict the French army had been engaged in.

'Yes.' Rocco's response was deliberately brief. He wasn't ready to talk about it with strangers. It was best kept locked in a private box, waiting for the memories to dim and fade.

He was still busy working out how to hurry that process along.

'Married?'

'Was, once. It didn't work out.' Something else he wasn't ready to discuss. Emilie hadn't been able to stand the stresses and strains of first, being an army wife waiting at home for his return from distant lands and conflicts, and second, the same sort of job, only closer at hand and just as unpredictable. In the end, she had left. 'You?'

'Was also. She died.' Claude flicked a glance at a photo of two adults and two small girls in a frame on the wall. They were all smiling, but the photo looked several years old. 'And the kids…well, they waited 'til they were old enough and buggered off to the city.'

'You see them?'

'Not much. We talk now and then – when I can track them down. But it's another language these days.' He shrugged. 'They're good girls – just different.'

They sat and looked through each other for a few seconds, accompanied by the ticking of a clock.

When the telephone jangled, it startled them both.

Claude scowled. 'It hardly ever does that,' he announced. 'Except for my sister in Nantes. She likes to remind me of her latest dress size and the birthday of every child in the family. She thinks I'm made of money.'

He picked up the hand-piece and listened, and Lucas watched as he turned slowly pale.

'OK. At once,' he said softly. 'I'll be there. Yes, of course directly.' He put the phone down and adjusted its position on the table, then looked at Lucas with a grave expression.

'Your sister?' said Rocco.

42

'I wish. What I said about not having much crime here? I spoke too soon. That was Monsieur Paulais, the stationmaster. There's a British military cemetery about a kilometre outside the village, close to the station. It's alongside a wood.' He gave a small shiver and stood up, pointing at the map on the wall. 'It's a nice spot. Very… peaceful as you would expect, for that kind of place. The gardener – an Englishman named John Cooke – arrived for work today and found a body in the cemetery.'

Rocco resisted the temptation to ask where else would you find them. 'A visitor had a heart attack?' He knew that many old soldiers and their families made pilgrimages to the battlefields of the two world wars. Understandably, some of the older ones from the conflict in 1918 were not in the best of health. The journey out here often found weaknesses otherwise left undiscovered.

'No.' Claude reached for his jacket on the back of the chair. 'Not this one.' He rubbed a hand across his face. 'We may have need of your investigative skills sooner than I thought.'

Rocco's senses prickled. He finished his coffee and stood up. 'Why?'

'The deceased is a woman and she's wearing a Gestapo officer's uniform.'

CHAPTER SIX

Rocco? Unorthodox. If they don't walk,
he brings them in under his arm.
Lieut. Pierre Comorre – Custody & Records Office
– Clichy-Nanterre district

The British War Graves cemetery of Poissons-les-Marais lay off the side of a dusty, rutted track which went on to bury itself in a stretch of thick woodland on the side of a hill. The cemetery consisted of a walled oblong roughly fifty metres by one hundred and fifty, dotted with military regularity by evergreens marking the boundary like silent sentinels. A long, low, brick-built construction in the style of a cloister stood at the near end, and a tall memorial cross pointing to the sky dominated the serried ranks of white marker stones which filled the cemetery grounds, surrounded by trimmed lawn and flower beds. A smaller brick structure stood in one corner, partially concealed by a privet hedge.

Rocco parked behind a grey Citroën 2CV van and climbed out of the car. The afternoon heat hung heavy over the wheat fields on either side of the track and a family of crows in the woods gave voice to the new arrivals, while a skylark sent out its call high in the air. Rocco tried to spot the small bird but gave up. He turned and flicked a practised eye over his surroundings. Vehicle access was bumpy but OK, so the mortuary wagon would be able to get up close. They were two hundred metres from the road, but since passing traffic was limited, there would be no problems with crowd control. Unlike the city, he reflected, where even a rumour of an unexplained death was sufficient to bring out the ghouls and freaks, eager to play their part in the drama.

Turning back towards the way they had come, he could just make out the church steeple in Poissons, rising above a range of trees surrounding a series of small lakes between the cemetery and the village. A line of poplars showed the location of the canal just north of the railway line, but there was no sign of boat traffic.

Following Claude's directions, he had driven through the village and along a winding lane past an area called the *marais* – the marshlands – and down past the village railway station. This was little more than a small brick building on a raised platform. A simple striped barrier to stop traffic stood alongside the road, with a counterweight on one end to help the stationmaster lift and lower it.

To Rocco, more accustomed to city scenes, it was like another country. Narrow roads with no vehicles; clusters of houses but few people; cultivated land, clearly productive and well maintained, but no sign of workers.

Then he became aware of the smell.

'*God on a bicycle!*' Claude coughed as he joined Rocco by the front of the car. 'What the hell is that?'

'Death.' To Rocco the aroma was all too familiar.

Heavy and sickly, it hung in the air like a curtain, thick enough to taste. 'Come on.' He led the way into the cemetery and saw a man sitting at the far end of the cloister with his back against the wall. He looked unnaturally pale and was staring across the cemetery with a tight expression etched on his face. Probably trying not to breathe in, thought Rocco. It never works, no matter how hard you try.

'John Cooke – the Englishman,' whispered Claude, one hand clamped across his nose. 'His French is so-so.' He wagged his other hand in a see-saw fashion. 'Actually, for an Englishman, not bad.'

Rocco strode along the walkway, his footsteps echoing around him, and watched as Cooke stood up to greet them. Up close, he was the quintessential Englishman: tall and thin, with blue-grey eyes and a neat moustache, fair hair. He wore dark-blue overall trousers and a check shirt, and had the wiry, sun-bronzed arms and face of an outdoor worker. Right now, however, the tan on his cheeks was struggling to stay in place.

'Mister Cooke,' Rocco said in English, and introduced himself. 'Inspector Rocco. I understand you found a body.'

'That's right. Over there.' Cooke looked surprised and relieved at hearing his own language. 'Glad I don't have to explain this in French. I could do it, of course, but… Anyway, come this way and I'll show you.' He set off out of the cloister and across the carefully tailored lawn, leaving the two policemen to follow. He walked like a soldier, Rocco noted, easy strides, back straight.

'You speak English,' muttered Claude, tapping Rocco's arm. 'You didn't say.'

Rocco gave a ghost of a smile, remembering his surprise at finding Claude was the *garde champêtre*. 'You didn't ask.'

Cooke stopped alongside the giant stone cross set in the centre of the lawn. It had a stepped platform beneath an oblong base, and the main stone of the cross was inlaid with a bronze sword, the tip of which was running with verdigris.

Like green blood, Rocco thought sombrely.

Cooke gestured to the far side of the platform, and moved back to allow them to pass. 'I hope you've got strong stomachs,' he said. 'It's not pretty.'

Rocco stepped around the cross.

The woman was lying on the stone platform, arms flung wide, one leg bent beneath her. She had a dark, mottled tinge to her facial skin, which was bloated and pincushioned out of shape. Her pupils were milky-white, half-closed, and she could have been anywhere between twenty and sixty – it was impossible to be certain. Her hair was mousy, lank and crusted against her head in tangled snakes, and one cheek was pulled back in a cruel facsimile of a smile. But that was the only detail Rocco could determine immediately without a closer examination.

She was dressed, as Claude had said, in the stark black uniform jacket and skirt of a Gestapo officer, complete with a swastika armband, leather belt, shirt and tie. The collars of the jacket bore a twin lightning-bolt insignia and three pips, and the black forage cap lying by the woman's side was decorated with white piping.

'You found it like this when you came in?' Rocco asked Cooke.

'Yes. I had to call in at Peronne first thing this morning; I only got here twenty minutes ago.'

'Can anyone confirm that?'

Cooke lifted an eyebrow. 'What – you think *I* might have left her here? Bit obvious, isn't it?' When Rocco said nothing, he added dispiritedly, 'No, I didn't see anyone to speak to.'

'And there was no one here when you arrived?'

'No. The place is hardly Piccadilly Circus.' He paused, apologetic. 'That's in London.'

'I know where it is.'

'Right. Of course. If we get any visitors, it's usually not until after midday. Otherwise it's just me and the chaps.'

'Chaps?'

Cooke gestured vaguely towards the lines of white stones. 'Them. Trouble is, they don't talk much.' He gave a thin smile.

English humour, thought Rocco.

'When were you here last?'

Cooke thought about it. 'Three days ago. I have to cover several other cemeteries; this one is the easiest to maintain, so I don't come every day.'

Rocco bent to peer more closely at the woman's face. No significant marks, although it was hard to tell with the lumpy state of the skin. But he noted what might have been a small bruise on the side of the woman's neck. She wore a single silver-and-enamel earring in the shape of a yellow-and-white flower – it looked like a marguerite – in her left ear, but nothing in the right. The yellow centre showed sharp and bright in contrast to the body and the dark clothing.

He ran his fingertips across the skirt and jacket. The

material was heavily creased and the fabric damp – in fact, worse, it was soaked through. Several white marks showed on the fabric and were repeated around the welts of the shoes, and tendrils of weed were dotted here and there on the clothing and wrapped around her legs like dark-green centipedes. Her black stockings were ripped and laddered, exposing the flesh underneath which bulged through the mesh like uncooked pork.

'Did it rain here last night?' he asked.

'No. Hasn't for days.'

'What did you do after you found the body?'

'I didn't touch anything, if that's what you mean. It was obvious she was dead, so I drove to the station and got Monsieur Paulais to call Claude. I think he also called the police in Amiens.'

Great, thought Rocco. It won't be long before the circus gets here. He'd have liked more time to study the scene in peace, but that was no longer in his hands. He turned to Claude. 'How long before they arrive?'

'About an hour…thirty minutes if they've got nothing else on. Depends whether Monsieur Cooke mentioned the uniform.'

'I told them.' Cooke took up the conversation in French, his accent evident but not bad. 'It seemed pretty important… I thought it might galvanise them into action a bit sooner.'

It would do that all right, thought Rocco. Finding a corpse dressed like Himmler's sister is not the kind of thing you ignore, not in France. He lifted the forage hat, which was dry to the touch, and opened it. There was no name tag.

Claude looked glum. 'If Paulais called the police, he'll

have called the press, too.' He rubbed his thumb and fingers together. 'Money. In these parts, this will be a big story.'

'You think we get bodies in Gestapo uniform turning up every day in Paris?' Rocco shook his head. 'Where's the closest stretch of water?'

'To here?' Claude jutted his chin back towards the village. 'The canal, just the other side of the railway. After that, the lakes and the *marais*. Why?'

'The clothing's wet through. She was in water until very recently.' He touched the skin of the dead woman's leg. It was covered in a slimy film.

He turned his thoughts to what would be needed here, if it wasn't already on the way. The full works, undoubtedly – forensics, scene of crime, mortuary service…and Lord knows who else would want to get in on this act, with that uniform. Poissons-les-Marais wouldn't know what had hit it.

Claude read his mind. 'This is going to get messy, isn't it?'

'Very. I hope you had a good night's sleep, because this could be a long stretch of duty. You ready for it?'

'Me?' Claude looked surprised. 'I'm a lowly *garde champêtre* – the regular cops won't want me around.'

'It won't be up to them, though, will it?'

'Really? What do— Ah.' The light dawned. 'Of course – this is *your* patch now.'

'Too right. They sent me down here; I might as well do my job. So stick around.'

CHAPTER SEVEN

*Rocco? Big and scary. A bit nuts. Women seem
to like him, though, lucky bastard.*
Capt. Michel Santer – Clichy-Nanterre district

'Monsieur Paulais says we can use the station waiting room
if we need to.'

Claude had driven off earlier in Rocco's car to speak to
the stationmaster. He had returned immediately with the
news. 'As I thought: he called the papers as well as the
regional radio news channels. He's already dressed in his
best uniform, hoping to get interviewed.'

'He's welcome to it,' said Rocco. 'Can you put up a
barrier across the lane? The last thing we need is the press
trampling all over the scene.'

'We could leave your car parked sideways across. They'd
have to drive onto the fields to get past.'

'That won't stop them, will it?'

'Not until Duchamel, the farmer who owns these fields,
sees them flattening his crops; then he'll come and shoot
their tyres out. Anything for a bit of sport. I can arrange it,
if you like.' He looked positively eager at the idea.

'Stop it. You'll be selling tickets next.'

'Hey, not a bad thought. By the way, you should get yourself something more practical than the Traction. Nice car, but not good for driving over these tracks. Too low for one thing: you'll wreck the suspension within a week.'

Rocco hadn't thought much about the kind of terrain he'd be covering until he arrived. City streets were either good or bad, and you took them at your own risk. But at least you went with the knowledge that they were usually passable. As he'd already seen here, anything less than a metalled road was little better than a cart track.

'What do you drive?' He hadn't seen a car at Claude's house, although there had been a building big enough to house one.

'2CV Fourgonnette. Amazing vehicle.' Claude looked enthusiastic. 'I once saw a farmer overturn one in a field. Then he and his son flipped it back over and away he went.' He dropped his lower lip. 'A bit rippled here and there, I grant you, but as good as new.'

'Thanks. I'll keep this for now.'

'Your funeral.'

'Uh-huh.' Rocco looked up towards the wood behind the cemetery. 'Where does the track lead?'

'Nowhere much. Only the farmers go up there, to their fields.'

'And the wood? Or is it just a wood?'

'Christ, no. You don't want to go in there. It's an old ammo dump, full of shells, bombs and grenades. You step on the wrong thing and *baff!* – you lose a leg. Or worse.' He gestured towards his groin with a grim chopping motion.

'Wasn't it cleared?'

'No. The commune kept asking, but there was never the money or the men – the experts. One suggestion was to lob in a couple of mortar shells and stand well back.' He grinned. 'That would have been worth seeing.'

'It didn't fly?'

'No. It was vetoed on grounds of insanity. And despoiling the countryside.' He spat on the ground. 'Like they worry about that kind of thing.'

Rocco paced back and forth, returning to study the ground between the cemetery gate and the monument where the body lay. He'd already taken a stroll around the inside of the cemetery while Claude was away, and had seen nothing helpful: no clues revealing how the dead woman had got here, no telltale tracks, no arrows pointing to the guilty party. He stared at the hump of the body, now covered by a tarpaulin Cooke had got from the tool shed, the brick structure in the far corner of the plot. The forensics boys weren't going to be happy, but it was better than allowing the legions of flies waiting to get in on the act to begin feeding, especially with this heat.

He wondered who the woman was. Had been. And why she was dumped here. She certainly hadn't died in this place. The clothing, with the exception of the hat, had been in water; and he'd seen similar bloating to the skin on bodies pulled out of the Seine, which indicated that she had been immersed for a while. Then there was the uniform. Was it someone's idea of making a point? If so, it was a grisly one. He deliberately hadn't tried the pockets of her jacket yet, which might yet yield a clue; that would be best done with the forensics team in place, in case they found anything that might deteriorate rapidly and be lost as evidence.

'Lucas!'

He turned. Claude was looking towards the main road where three vehicles – a black saloon and two chunky police vans, all with their roof lights flashing – were speeding towards the turn-off.

He walked to the entrance gate to meet them.

The man in charge was a cheerful-looking individual with a red face and a well-developed middle. He hopped from the car, followed by men from the other vehicles, and watched as Rocco approached.

'Who are you?' he queried. 'This is the scene of an unexplained death.'

'Good description,' Rocco congratulated him. He took out his transfer orders and calling card. The officer read the details carefully, eyebrows lifting.

'OK, that changes things, I grant you.' He ducked his head. 'Captain Eric Canet, Amiens *Préfecture*. We heard someone new was coming. My men are at your disposal, Inspector.'

'I appreciate that.' Rocco shook the captain's hand, relieved that Canet wasn't about to jump on his soapbox over who had primary position. By rights, Rocco should have presented himself at the Amiens office prior to coming here, but he had seen no reason to do so until absolutely necessary. 'My colleague is *Garde Champêtre* Lamotte, based in Poissons, and the other man is the cemetery gardener, John Cooke. He's English.' He gestured towards the monument. 'The body is at the base of the cross, covered with a tarpaulin against the flies. There are no obvious signs showing how it got there, or even the cause of death…but I'll leave that to you and your men to determine.'

'Of course.' Canet acknowledged the courtesy and flicked a signal to his men. They began to mark out a pathway from the gate to the monument, examining the ground as they went. 'To be honest,' he added softly, 'rather you than me on this one. Is it true about the Gestapo uniform?'

'Yes.'

'God help us. That's all we need, stirring up old memories. That's always bad news.' He paused and nodded towards the stone cross. 'If you'll excuse me?'

'Help yourself.'

Canet set off in the wake of his men and disappeared behind the memorial. He reappeared two minutes later and walked back to join Rocco. He looked pale around the eyes, his sights fixed on the ground.

'Holy Mother,' he muttered. 'I've seen some stuff in my time, but that...'

Rocco nodded. They all would have seen far worse before, but the shock value in what lay beside the monument was the degree of contrasts: the bloated, stodgy skin of the dead woman against the black of the hated uniform.

Canet walked to the gate and spat onto the track, then wiped his lips. 'Sorry,' he murmured, and checked his watch, glancing towards the road.

'You expecting somebody?'

Canet nodded. 'You won't have been made aware of it, but we've just inherited a new divisional *commissaire*, starting today. It's part of this big reshuffle. He's from Marseille.' It was clear from Canet's wry expression that he looked on the senior officer's move to Picardie as an odd, not to say controversial one.

'Know anything about him?'

'No. I was on leave until today and came out here as soon as I got in. His holiness was doing an arse-kicking tour of the *sous-préfectures* this morning so I don't even know his name, only that he's ex-military from way back. But I do know he'll have something to prove…which is why he's on his way here to take charge of the investigation.'

'Oh, joy.' Rocco was dismayed. *Commissaires* didn't usually involve themselves in such matters, limiting themselves instead to making announcements to the press and their superiors in the Interior Ministry about successful outcomes and an increase in performance statistics. He could foresee an argument looming; one he would probably lose.

Canet sniffed in agreement. 'Well…I'm not surprised. This thing looks like being a touchy subject – the Gestapo kit and all. It could make good headlines for him if it breaks quickly, bad if it doesn't, in which case you'll get responsibility.'

Rocco smiled. 'Cynic.'

Canet shrugged fatalistically. 'With good reason: I've seen it all before.'

Just then, the sound of car engines intruded on the quiet and both men turned. Two gleaming black saloons were approaching along the main road, moving at a sedate clip.

'Shoulders back, stomachs in,' said Canet, hitching up his trousers and stepping through the gate. 'You ready for this?'

'Not yet.' Rocco had better things to do than tug his forelock for a bunch of self-important desk jockeys. He decided to take a tour of the outside perimeter of the cemetery instead. It might also offer a chance of getting upwind of the awful smell for a while. If standing on ceremony was important to the brass, they would wait. If not, they'd have to follow him and get their shoes dirty.

CHAPTER EIGHT

Rocco? A nobody...a rebel...reckless.
Lacks any respect for authority.
Col François Massin – former brigade CO,
Indochina campaign

Rocco turned left out of the gate, then left again, following the wall across the width of the cemetery. The ground here was rough but easy to read, where neither weeds, grass nor farmers' crops had taken root, leaving a half-metre perimeter of hard ground to follow like a path. There were no signs of disturbance, no footprints to help him except a few paw prints, and lots of rabbit droppings; a dead thrush, half-eaten by maggots and, a yard into the field, the carcass of a larger bird – a wood pigeon dead on the wing, no doubt the random target of a farmer's rifle.

He was pretty sure the narrow strip of ground here was much the same as the day the men who had built the wall had packed up and left. He walked on.

He reached the next corner near the tool shed, where it looked as if access might be easy, and studied it carefully. Nothing. No marks on the wall to show anyone had climbed it, no traces of fabric caught on the rough brickwork. The ground below it was unmarked. Then, as he turned up the long stretch of wall abutting the wood at the top, he saw movement in the trees.

Rocco stopped and crouched as if examining the ground, all the while checking the tree line. Something or someone was up there, but he couldn't see any detail. A flick of a branch, a change in the pattern of shadows, then it was gone.

He continued walking, head moving from side to side, and eventually reached the end of the wall where it butted up against the wood. The atmosphere here was still, densely packed with overgrowth, with not even the rustling of leaves on the branches to break the silence. He breathed deeply, sniffing the air, enjoying the raw smell.

He turned and followed the top wall across the width of the cemetery, the wood on his right shoulder. But he was no longer interested in the ground: he was already certain that whoever had dumped the body in the cemetery had gained access through the gate, not over the wall. Instead, he concentrated on listening to the silent mass of greenery to his right. It was thinner here, he noted, where selective trees had been felled or had fallen to nature. It allowed the air and light to penetrate, and there was a breeze, too, like a whispered conversation, the leaves and branches setting up a chaffing, clicking sound as if discussing man's intrusion on this quiet place.

It reminded him of a jungle he'd once come to know, also a place of whispered noises and shadows. His head began to ache and he shivered, mentally pushing away the flickering images trying to intrude. No time for that; never time for that. He breathed deeply until his mind was quiet and his inner vision began to clear, the pounding in his head gradually subsiding. His hands, though, were clammy. He wiped them on his coat and forced himself to concentrate.

One thing he'd learnt in Indochina was that among trees and vegetation, human smells stand out far more than they ever could in a city street. And if you had the nose and the patience, not to say the nerve, you could tell if a stranger was close by simply using your senses.

Especially one who smoked *Gitanes* and had the body odour of a dead badger.

He wondered what Didier Marthe had been doing among the trees, watching the cemetery. Was it coincidence? Was he scouring the wood for shells to break up and just happened to be here? Or did the scrap man have some other reason for skulking around?

By the time Rocco got back to the cemetery gate, the two black cars were parked fifty metres down the track, the doors hanging open. Three men in smart uniform were walking towards him, one tall man in particular leading the way. The others – drivers and gofers – stayed smoking and chatting among themselves, no doubt glad to be rid of the brass for a few minutes.

The tall man, bearing the badges of a divisional *commissaire*, spoke to Canet, who turned and pointed a thumb towards Rocco.

The senior officer stood where he was, clearly waiting for Rocco to join them. Rocco held his ground. He was being stubborn and would probably regret it, but he was beyond jumping through hoops for uniforms with nothing better to do than step on other people's feet. Instead, he turned away, running his eye over the cemetery boundaries, trying to read what had happened here. If the men – and he was only guessing it had to have been more than one – had brought the dead woman through the gate, any traces they had left, such as footprints, would be indistinguishable against the grass, especially now Cooke and everyone else had tramped back and forth.

The one thing he didn't know for certain was how the woman had died. Only that water had been involved in some way, either before, during or after death.

A crunch of footsteps sounded on the track behind him. He turned to find the three newcomers metres away, with the tall officer in the lead. He looked less than happy, his body language stiff and foreboding.

In the split second that he saw the man's face, Rocco felt as if he'd been punched in the stomach. The features, although older and more lined, were instantly, shockingly familiar. The expression was just as aloof, the bearing as pompous as he remembered and he was transported back to 1954. In that brief moment of realisation, of remembering, he saw that the officer remembered him, too.

Rocco steeled himself and wondered what malevolent twist of fate had sent this man here, to the same patch of soil as himself. Because when he had last set eyes on Colonel François Massin, the officer had been cowering in a foxhole in Indochina, screaming like a frightened girl.

CHAPTER NINE

Rocco? He shouldn't be allowed out!
I'm totally innocent, I tell you…he had no right…!
Roni Ahkmoud – convicted serial killer and rapist
– Clichy-Nanterre district

'What are *you* doing here?' There was no warmth in Massin's greeting, no sign of even feigned familiarity, merely a frosty expression of disdain.

And of hesitation. *As well you bloody might*, thought Rocco, *you cowardly, high-born bastard*. Partly due to this man and his colleagues in the high command, a lot of good men had died in those far-off jungles and rice fields, victims of bloody battles and lethal mantraps. Others had been taken prisoner, only to emerge months later from captivity, broken and sick, ghostly versions of their former selves in body and spirit.

'My job,' he replied. 'Investigating a murder.'

He wondered whether Massin remembered that Rocco had seen him in the foxhole, had witnessed his naked fear on display. Or had he managed to blank the entire incident from his mind?

He was surprised that his former CO had managed to

migrate across to the Sûreté Nationale. What strings had he pulled to do that? No doubt friends of friends pulling strings in the invisible network of former colleagues encountered and nurtured in the elite French military academy of St Cyr. After being evacuated out from the battlefield in a state of pure funk, Massin must have seemed ripe for a career no more stressful than counting beans, far away from the sight of his former comrades – at least, the few who had survived – and indeed anyone else who might know what had happened. Yet here he was, resplendent in the uniform of a senior police officer, a pillar of the establishment.

'Your job? Who says it was murder?' The senior officer's nose quivered as if he had just caught the first smell from the body. He looked away, momentarily distracted.

'You got that?' said Rocco abruptly. 'That stink in the air? It's called putrefaction. Decomposing tissue. It happens when a body has been in a warm place, or under ground or in water. The bugs and larvae begin attacking the tissue, laying eggs and eating their way inside. You might like to take a closer look…since you're heading up the investigation.'

If Massin recognised the challenge, he ignored it. But a flicker of revulsion crossed his face. Or guilt, thought Rocco. Maybe even lack of guts, given his track record. Give him five minutes near this place and he'd be away back down the road to his office like bald tyres on a skidpan.

'I'm perfectly familiar with the aftermath of death,' Massin replied stiffly. 'What I want to know is, who ordered you here, to this region?'

Rocco shrugged eloquently, a gesture calculated to annoy the man. 'Me? I'm merely following orders. Part of the latest barmy "initiative" cooked up by someone with too much time on his hands, who thought investigators should be out in the country slopping through cow shit instead of in the cities, solving major crimes.'

'Take yourself away. Now. You are dismissed.' Massin was almost quivering with rage, his body stiff as a brush. Behind him, his two companions had stopped a few feet back, watching and listening.

'Excuse me?' Rocco gave the man his most insolent stare. He wasn't sure whether a *commissaire* had the power to throw him off an investigation; it had never arisen before. Maybe this might be the moment he found out.

'I said you are dismissed. I do not want you on this investigation!' The words snapped out, surprising the other two men and causing the drivers and assistants to fall silent. Captain Canet and Claude watched from a distance.

'Sir?' One of the other officers, braver than the other, stepped forward. He looked at Rocco as if he had made an obscene suggestion, then introduced himself with a brief nod. '*Commissaire* Perronnet.' Then in a soft aside to Massin, 'Is something wrong, sir?'

'Yes. This man is not needed here. I want him elsewhere – anywhere. But not here!'

Perronnet looked momentarily nonplussed. He touched Massin on the arm and murmured, 'A word, sir?'

They turned away and talked in undertones, leaving Rocco staring into the distance. But he caught fragments of conversation, most of it coming from the junior officer.

'…lead investigator…has a very good record…sent here from Paris…nobody else available…could be *political*…the uniform…neo-Nazi movement.'

When they turned back, it was as if a switch had been

thrown. Massin's face was more composed, and he was looking at Rocco with eyes that no longer held open dislike. He's struggling, though, Rocco thought sourly. Like a cobra studying a particularly juicy-looking rodent.

'Very well.' Massin appeared to reconsider his decision. It took a few moments, during which the junior officer said nothing, but stared at Rocco with an intensity which conveyed a simple message: *Don't say a word or you're on traffic.*

'It seems,' murmured Massin finally, forcing out the words, 'that you are necessary to this investigation after all.' He lifted his chin, haughty and begrudging. 'You have primary responsibility and I want regular reports on your progress, copied only to me. Nobody else. You understand?'

'Perfectly,' said Rocco. In other words, so you can stitch this up any way you like, you dumb shit, he thought dourly. Kill it off if it looks like causing inconvenient embarrassment, dumb it down if it can be passed off as a minor crime. Claim the credit if it goes hot.

Massin turned and strode across the lawn to the monument, accompanied by the second officer, leaving Perronnet studying Rocco with an open air of interest.

'He doesn't like you much, does he? Do you always affect people that way?'

'It's my friendly nature,' said Rocco dryly. 'Never mind, I'll try to weather the disappointment.'

A raised eyebrow. 'Insolent, I see. Is there history between you?'

Rocco thought about it for two seconds. He didn't have to spell out his past to this man; if Perronnet were really that interested, he could delve into the personnel files. If he did, he'd no doubt be unable to resist taking a peek at Massin's file, too, and something told him that would not be available for scrutiny. 'Not that I'm aware of.'

Perronnet looked sceptical. 'Didn't sound like it to me.'

'If you don't believe me, you could always ask him.'

Perronnet looked surprised by the challenge. He seemed about to reprimand Rocco, but merely said, 'Maybe I will.' He looked across the cemetery as the two men returned, both looking pale, Massin with his jaw clenched tight. 'But let's get this cleared up first, shall we?' he continued softly. 'And maybe tomorrow, you might do the courtesy of presenting yourself to the station and making your acquaintance with your colleagues. Just a suggestion to the wise.' With that, he turned and fell in with the others, accompanying them out of the gate and back down the track.

'You should try pissing on electric cables,' said Claude. 'It's a lot less dangerous.' He joined Rocco to watch the cars reverse down the track. 'I've never heard anyone talk to a *commissaire* like that before and survive.'

'You heard?' He'd thought Claude and the others were out of earshot.

Claude smiled. 'I might be getting on a bit, but my hearing's still good. You know the top man – Massin, is it?'

'It's a long story.' He turned and watched Canet and his men at work around the monument. He might as well leave them to it; for now, he had other things on his mind. 'Tell me without looking in that direction, why would Didier Marthe be in the woods behind the cemetery?'

'Didier?' Claude visibly strained himself not to look

CHAPTER TEN

Rocco? Contrary…dogged…astute.
Capt. Michel Santer – Clichy-Nanterre district

Didier Marthe's home was a large, ramshackle house at the end of a twisting, narrow lane near the centre of the village. Following Claude's directions, Rocco steered over a series of potholes and deep ruts into a wide, sunken yard containing an ancient manure heap, dark and evil-smelling. Twenty metres away, across from the house, a fast-flowing stream cut between the yard and a belt of poplar trees and disappeared towards what Rocco judged to be the road leading towards the station, where he and Claude had just driven. He recalled a slight hump in the road near the village outskirts, just before the first scattered houses, and guessed it might be where the stream ran beneath the road.

He stopped the Citroën and climbed out, and was struck immediately by the silence hanging over the property. Everywhere else he had been, from the village centre to the cemetery, birdsong was evident and plentiful; here there was none, only the clack-clack of a loose shingle on the side of an outbuilding.

'Does he have a vehicle?' There were none in sight, although plenty of recent tracks were evident in the dried mud of the yard. They criss-crossed each other, showing where the wheels followed the same route around the yard in a circle, entering and leaving.

Claude nodded. 'A Renault van for carrying his scrap. He's probably got it with him.'

'Where does he keep it?' Rocco counted two barns and three smaller outbuildings scattered around the place. Most were as shaky as the house, but the barns looked plenty big enough to house cars, vans or tractors. He walked over to the nearest barn and kicked back one of the twin doors.

The grey nose of a battered Renault stood inside.

He touched the bonnet. 'Hasn't been used recently.'

Claude stared at the van as if it might disappear in a puff of smoke. 'Damn. I was sure he'd be out in it.' He looked at Rocco. 'Maybe it wasn't him you saw in the woods.'

'It was him.' Rocco walked up to the front door and pounded on it with his fist. The sound reverberated through the house. No answer. He tried again, the wood quivering and, just in case Didier Marthe had gone deaf, finished with a kick.

'You don't hold back, do you?' said Claude. 'Is this how they do things in Paris?'

'No point pissing about – not in a murder enquiry.' He knocked again, but the sound reverberated through the building.

The front door was bracketed by two massive artillery shells. Although the casings were pitted and dull, the noses were shiny at the tip, as if a hand had been laid on them in benediction each time someone passed. To one side stood a heavy wooden bench fitted with an enormous metalworker's vice and covered with a variety of hammers, pliers and hacksaws, and odd scraps of lead, brass and other rusted metal. The tools and cast-asides of Didier's unusual trade.

'Let's just say he was in the woods looking for shells. Wouldn't he have taken his van to haul them back in? No point making two trips.'

'Of course, normally. But...' Claude looked unsure, and for the first time it occurred to Rocco that the two men might be friends. Yet here he was assuming otherwise and relying on this man to help him.

'Are you with me on this?' he asked casually. 'Because now's the time if you want to bow out and go tend your roses. Is Marthe a friend of yours?' It was rough, bordering on offensive, but he needed to know where they stood. Having Claude Lamotte working half-heartedly would only undermine his task.

Claude looked offended. 'Me and him – *friends*? That stunted little bigot? Christ, no. What made you think that?' The denial had a natural ring of authenticity and Rocco breathed more easily.

'Sorry. Just making sure. What's his story, then? Is he married?'

Claude puffed out his cheeks and inspected a small cannon shell lying on the table. 'Not married, no. What sane woman would have him, with this lot? He arrived here about five years back, from somewhere further south. He's openly communist and proud of it, but he's no political brain. The only factor preventing him being a Trotskyite is he probably can't spell it. He hates fascists, priests, Americans, the British, industrialists and Parisians…but not necessarily in that order. If he's got any real friends, I've never met one, although he got pally for a while with a neighbour along the street. All in all, he keeps to himself, even when he's in the café.'

'No kidding.' Rocco remembered the man's bad breath. He studied the two artillery shells. 'I bet he doesn't get too many repeat visitors.'

'Probably not.' Claude put the cannon shell down with utmost care and looked at Rocco across the bench. 'You think he's involved in that woman's death?'

Rocco shook his head. 'I'm a detective, not a medium. I just wanted to see where he lived, that's all. A man's home can tell you all manner of things, if you know how to look. Most of all, though, I'd still like to know what he was doing in the wood behind the cemetery.'

'Coincidence?'

Rocco turned and walked towards the stream and stared out at the trees. 'Coincidence is a lame defence. You'd be amazed how often it crops up, though. What's over there?'

'The *marais*. The lakes. Take a straight line from here and it's a short walk. We passed them on the way back, although they're not easily visible from the road.'

'Handy.' Rocco walked along the stream to where a huge weathered tree trunk had been laid to form a rough footbridge across the stream. The top surface had been chopped flat, the axe marks clearly visible, and wide cracks ran the length of the trunk. He bent down and inspected the dirt at the end of the trunk.

Claude said, 'I wouldn't step on there if I were you.'

Something in his tone caught Rocco's attention.

'Why?'

Claude looked faintly embarrassed. 'I don't know if it's true, but four years ago, not long after he arrived, some boys coming back from fishing in the *marais* saw Didier putting something in those cracks. They used this as an unofficial short cut home.'

'And?'

'He told them the bridge was booby-trapped. Anyone stepping on it would be blown to bits. They swore he wasn't joking.'

'What did you do?'

'Me?' Claude shrugged. 'I looked into it, of course, him being a stranger still. But I couldn't find anything. I thought he was having them on...you know, playing the mad, bad bastard just to keep them off his property.'

'And was he?'

'Not sure. About a month later, there was a hell of a bang in the middle of the night. When we got down here, we expected to find Didier in bits around the yard. Instead we found a young wild boar spread all over the bridge, blood and guts everywhere.'

'What did Didier say?'

'He claimed it must have picked up a grenade he'd been working on. I couldn't prove otherwise, so had to let it drop. Since then, nobody's been near the place.'

Clever, thought Rocco. An effective way of Didier ensuring his privacy – unless he was as mad as a snake.

As they walked back to the car, Claude waved a hand around at the yard. 'So what does this tell you?' he asked, as if clues were jumping off the ground to be counted. 'Anything?'

'Not much. Not yet.' Rocco slid behind the wheel, eyes on the house. No movement, no sounds. Too quiet, though. 'One thing I do know: he's in there, watching us.'

'What? But how? We came directly here.' Claude looked ready to get out and go and beat on the door, but Rocco put out a restraining hand.

'Bicycle. There are tracks leading off and on to the footbridge, and a half-smoked *Gitanes* – fairly fresh, if that's not a contradiction. He came straight across from the road to the station, cutting out the loop. He must have just beat us.' He started the engine. 'Never mind. Now I know a bit more about him than I did ten minutes ago.'

'Such as?'

'He has a back way into the *marais*, and whatever he was doing in the woods, he wasn't out looking for shells.'

CHAPTER ELEVEN

Sgt Rocco? Solid...professional. Pity he hates officers.
But hey, who doesn't?
Capt. Antoine Caspard – Gang Task Force
– Paris Central

As tired as he was after his busy introduction to Poissons, Rocco's first night in his new lodgings was disturbed by a series of skittering and rolling noises in the attic above his head, and with tangled thoughts of Colonel François Massin, now divisional *commissaire* of police. The other tenants Mme Denis had warned him about were plainly unperturbed by the new arrival, and seemed to be playing football from one side of the attic to the other. It was only when he eventually leapt out of bed and charged up a narrow flight of steps into the loft space that he discovered the floor littered with dry walnuts. Of the fruit rats, there was no sign.

He went back to bed, where Massin intruded against an unwelcome backdrop of shattered trees, ruptured earth and the cries of the wounded and dying. He turned on his face, trying to blot out the memory of that final battle, but the images remained crisp and vivid, leaving him bathed in perspiration, the sheets tangled around his body like snakes.

* * *

Massin. The commanding officer had come up to the forward positions against orders, trailing two nervous adjutants, hands on their guns and alert for the first Viet Minh to hurl himself over the earthworks. Rocco, from his position near one of the guns, had watched the officer strutting about the lines in his immaculate uniform, by turn snapping at battle-weary troops like a teacher controlling recalcitrant children, then reassuring them about reinforcements and a change of tactics that they all knew would never come. Already all but surrounded by enemy forces, they were too exhausted to be astonished at the stupid self-importance of the man, most turning their backs as he approached, to avoid the embarrassment of eye contact.

Seeing what he perceived as a gap in the defences, Massin had ordered more men forward, ignoring the more experienced NCOs who had seen it for what it was – a killing zone. Low down, with only one way in and one way out, it was overlooked by enemy positions, whose snipers had already notched up too many unwary sentries.

An hour later, after a blizzard of fire, just three men came struggling back. The others had fallen victim to a heavy machine gun on a distant hill, no doubt smuggled into position under cover of a previous barrage.

Shortly afterwards, they heard the opening barrage coming in as the Viet Minh began their final assault. The ground shook as the shells rained down on the inadequate dugouts housing the worn-out mix of French, Vietnamese and legionnaire defenders. Plumes of earth, bodies and material seemed to float in the air, each explosion creating another gap, another hole in the line. More men lost.

Turning to help a mortar team which had lost a man to a

sniper, Rocco saw Colonel Massin stumble out of a dugout, face white and uniform dishevelled, staring around as if he could not understand the events that were unfolding. His mouth was working, but in the noise and confusion, his words went unheard. Another barrage came in, and Massin fell into a foxhole, where he lay screaming and kicking his legs, hands over his ears, his cries finally shrill enough to find a gap in the furore and reach the ears of the men on the defences. One of the nearest had turned his head and looked at him with mild detachment, then spat on the ground in disgust before turning to resume firing.

Then the order came to get Massin out. Too big a trophy to risk him being captured, said the instruction; bring him out by whatever means possible.

Rocco and two others were assigned to the task, along with Massin's two adjutants. Under covering fire from the men on the front, they had moved on foot through the last known gap left towards the rear. As the small group moved out, the incoming barrage grew more intense, pounding the positions in a deadly, relentless drum roll. By the time they had covered a desperate, muscle-burning thousand metres, the barrage was beginning to fade. Another five hundred metres and it fell silent altogether, save for an occasional haunting gunshot.

Rocco slept, his dreams vivid. Eventually, at eight, he pitched himself from his bed feeling like death, his head reeling. He put on some coffee, then walked around the large garden, head up and tasting the morning air. It was fresh and cool, completely free of his usual intake of petrol and other inner-city fumes, and he breathed deeply for the first time in years.

A honking at the front of the house drew him to the front gate, where a grey Renault 2CV Fourgonnette stood in the middle of the lane. Mme Denis and two other women were standing by the rear doors. The driver, a lugubrious man in his sixties, waved a thumb towards the back. 'Help yourself, Inspector – settle up at the end of the week.'

Rocco went through the greeting rituals with Mme Denis and her companions and helped himself to a baguette. He studied the car, remembering Claude's recommendation of its finer points. Somehow he couldn't see himself even squeezing inside, let alone driving one. He ambled back to the kitchen, where the aroma of coffee was replacing that of dust and mouse droppings, and settled down at the table. Breaking off one end of the baguette, he chewed the still-warm bread with relish, chasing it down with a mouthful of coffee. Stretched his legs out and sighed.

For the first time, Dien Bien Phu and everywhere since – even Clichy – seemed a long way away.

By ten, nursing a mild headache, he was heading back towards the cemetery. On the way he stopped outside the co-op and went inside. He was greeted by a raft of pleasant smells. A pretty, dark-haired woman was serving, and nodded in reply to his general good morning. The three other customers all turned and murmured back, eyeing him at length without a flicker of embarrassment before going back to their shopping.

Rocco forced a smile and waited; it was worse than being before a promotion panel. When the queue had gone, he selected some cheese, cooked meats and pickles. If he was going to live in the country, he might as well get used to country living, preferably without too much effort.

The woman rang up his purchases and put them in a bag.

'Having a moving-in party, Inspector?' she said with a smile. He was surprised, expecting more reserve towards an outsider. In Paris, he would have been served with little or no exchange, treated like the stranger he was.

'This is the first course,' he replied, and handed her the money, instantly feeling out of place, an amateur. The truth was, he had come to prefer the larger city shops, where contact was minimal and the choice was endless and not open to comment. Here, the scrutiny felt almost intimate. 'Perhaps you could recommend a main course?' He wasn't sure where that had come from, and began to look for a way out.

'Chicken's good,' she replied, 'and easy to cook.' She took off a cotton serving glove and held out her hand. Her fingers were soft and cool, but with a firm grip. 'Francine Thorin. Welcome to Poissons, Inspector. We don't bite, you know, unless you're an inspector of taxes. Then we just won't serve you.'

'Rocco,' he said briefly, feeling the conversation getting beyond his control. He gestured towards the door and said, 'Thanks. Sorry… I have to be going.' He turned and walked out, face burning, and felt her smile boring into his back all the way out of the door.

Back at the cemetery, he inspected the ground around the monument. There was no sign of John Cooke, and all traces of the body and the crime scene markers had been cleared away.

He wasn't expecting to discover anything new, but he

sometimes found that going back to the scene once all the evidence had been cleared away opened up new lines of thought and insight. But not this time. If there was something there, he wasn't seeing it.

He walked up through the cemetery to where it abutted the wood, and hopped over the wall. Stepping cautiously into the trees, he negotiated a straggly wire fence half-buried in the undergrowth, recalling what Claude had said about the deadly contents of this place. He felt a shiver run up his legs at what might be lying in wait beneath his feet, and stood for a moment, absorbing the atmosphere, tuning in to the scenery around him. The breeze was lighter than yesterday, but there was still the rustling in the leaves, like whispering gossips, their words sibilant and foreign.

No images today, though; no clamminess.

He breathed easily and studied the ground. He was standing roughly where he had seen Didier Marthe yesterday. Over to his right, a patch of nettles lay crushed and bent. Further on, a section of ground cover had been disturbed, in clear contrast to the area immediately around it. Marthe had walked across here, trying to stay on open ground, where his traces would be less likely to show. No doubt the poacher he had once been…or maybe was still.

Rocco followed the trail, stepping carefully in Marthe's footsteps, not deviating from the route by a centimetre. Although much heavier than the scrap man, he figured he was reducing his odds of setting off anything if he trod the same path.

At the edge of the wood, he found a large patch of what he thought looked like bluebell leaves, bent and broken, long past their prime. Nearby, on some disturbed soil, was a faint zigzag pattern too regular to be made by nature, and a thin line of flattened plants leading away towards the track.

Bicycle tyres.

He followed the marks out onto the track and walked down past the cemetery. There, the signs ran out.

By midday he was in Amiens, working his way through various levels of administration at the station, showing his credentials and transfer papers and trying to commit to memory the names of those he met. Most of the officers and civilian staff were cordial, with a few wary greetings, mostly among the other detectives manning their desks. He guessed that they had heard about him from Canet, who was out on a job, and were suspicious about his presence, a spy come to haunt them and report on their work. The air around them was a thick fug of cigarette smoke, reminding him of the office in Paris, except that the atmosphere here was quieter, less frenetic, less an air of tension and more of passive duty.

He saw Perronnet in the first-floor corridor. The senior officer nodded cordially but made no comment, merely indicating a door further along. Rocco took the hint and went to the door. Knocked and entered.

Massin was seated behind a large desk perusing the contents of a buff folder. The office was sparsely furnished: no certificates on the walls, no cups or medals, no testimonials or glitter from a successful career. Rocco gave him the benefit of the doubt: maybe he hadn't had time to put them up yet. Still busy getting his feet under the desk and arse-kicking, as Canet had called it.

'Can I help you?' Massin stopped reading and stared at

him. 'You have any developments in your investigation?'

Developments, thought Rocco irritably. We've barely begun, he wanted to say, but settled for a vague, 'Nothing yet. I'm checking in, that's all. Keeping the paper shufflers happy. And I want to see what the pathologist says about the body.'

'Pathologist?' Light glinted on Massin's glasses. 'This office doesn't have that luxury. Not yet, anyway. I plan to change that.' He nodded sideways. 'The department, as such, is next door. I haven't seen it myself yet.' He closed the folder, his finger marking the page, and sat back. 'You should do well to remember something, Inspector. There are ways of operating out here that do not translate well from the city.'

'What's that supposed to mean?' Rocco had never liked the official use of cryptic talk when a direct order would work much better.

'It means you cannot go round cracking heads or throwing people into meat wagons out here.' Massin tapped the folder in his hand, and Rocco realised it was his personnel file, passed on from Clichy. 'Your record seems to indicate you have form when it comes to using harsh methods.'

Rocco sighed. He'd had just two complaints about excessive use of force in his career, both unsubstantiated. One against a child molester with a good lawyer, the other a pimp fond of using a razor on his girls' faces. Neither charge had made it to court, but the rumour had clearly remained on his record like toxic mud. Massin must be aware of that.

'I'll try to mend my ways,' he said flatly.

'See you do.' Massin winced slightly. 'As I understand

the situation, the "initiative" which put you out here places you in a unique position, Inspector Rocco. You have what amounts to a free hand in conducting investigations, no longer tied to the normal chains of command. That has not gone down well in certain parts of the justice system or the police. I hope you realise that.'

'I didn't ask for it.'

'Maybe so. But you've got it. Just make sure you don't get too freewheeling in your methods. Keep me informed of your findings.' Massin went back to his papers, a deliberately curt dismissal.

Rocco turned and left, annoyed by the man's arrogance but relieved to be out of his way. He had the feeling it was as close as he was going to get to being given the nod to carry on.

He walked across to a grey, single-storey block next door, where whatever passed for the pathology and forensics team did their work. He took the opportunity to take a few deep breaths: the combination of cleaners, chemicals and death in the busy Paris mortuaries was a smell he had never entirely got used to, and he doubted it would be any different here.

A sign hanging on the door advised callers that it was closed for lunch. No difference there, then. Rocco toed the door open and flipped the sign over. Lunch could bloody wait.

He was in a small corridor with doors leading off. All were closed, except for the first one spilling light and the rustling of paper, followed by a thumping noise. Rocco stopped in the doorway and waited.

The room was a small, cluttered office, holding a single desk, some filing cabinets and several wallcharts. A man in a white coat was working at the desk, desultorily marshalling a few scraps of paper and imprinting them with a rubber stamp. The air was surprisingly fresh, with only the faintest smell of chemicals to indicate what went on in the building.

'We're closed, can't you read?' the man said without looking up. He had a wisp of mousy hair, thin wire spectacles and looked far too pale, as if he spent too much time here among the corpses and chemicals. A plate of sandwiches sat at his elbow.

'You've just opened again,' said Rocco, and flipped his calling card onto the desk. 'Are you the pathology person?'

The man read the card without touching it, then looked up at his visitor. He didn't appear surprised, although he looked faintly startled by Rocco's height. Rocco got the feeling someone in the detective office had buzzed ahead of his arrival.

'I'm a doctor, actually. Bernard Rizzotti.' The man stood up and lifted his chin, but without offering his hand. 'We don't run to a pathologist; I'm on attachment only. However, I can tell you that I completed a preliminary examination of your... um...deceased. Interesting case, from the point of view of the uniform, but pleasantly straightforward, I'm relieved to say.'

'Glad you approve,' said Rocco dryly. 'Cause of death?'

'Drowning.'

'That's it?' Rocco had been certain there would be something else. A drowning seemed too mundane, especially with the body left in the military cemetery.

'Yes. Why do you ask?' Rizzotti's forehead developed a ripple of dismay. 'You have other facts I should know about?'

The way he put the question suggested it was unlikely.

Rocco explained about the bruise on the neck. 'I know the body had been immersed in water, but I didn't expect drowning to be the primary cause.'

'Why not?'

'Let's call it instinct.'

The doctor's lip curled. 'Really? Ah, you mean that vague, inexplicable sense you people refer to as "gut feel", which takes precedence over the precision of modern science? The intuitive ability to make leaps of the imagination which the most advanced laboratories cannot match? Maybe it works every once in a while where you come from in Paris, and in those ridiculous films from America. But not in this building. Not with me.' He sat down and folded his hands in his lap, then flapped them open and smiled condescendingly as if to ask, *So what now, clever Dick?*

Rocco moved to the side of the desk and leant over the doctor until his face was close enough to make Rizzotti flinch. 'I'm sorry "people" like me don't share your entirely scientific view of the world,' he said softly. 'But that's the way we are. Now, I'd like to see the body, *Doctor.*' He was holding himself in with difficulty. What he really wanted to do was to dangle this little prick by his throat and shake him until his teeth fell out. He'd seen too many deaths before, many from a variety of causes that were not immediately obvious, and the last thing he needed was some self-satisfied, corner-cutting medic playing a game of trump-you with blind science.

Rizzotti went pale and blinked, trying to squirm away sideways in his chair. 'That's not possible.'

'Why not?' Rocco thought about calling Perronnet, but

decided against it. It would be momentarily satisfying to see this white-coated jerk taken down a peg or two, but ultimately it would serve no purpose. And being in a senior officer's debt didn't appeal, either. He picked up the plate of sandwiches and balanced it in his hand as if he were about to hurl it across the room. 'Are you going to show it to me or do I have to tear the place apart?'

'You can't – it won't do you any good.' Rizzotti swallowed hard and stared at the sandwiches, his Adam's apple bobbing like a fishing float on a line.

'*Tell me!*' Rocco muttered, and made as if to tip the plate into the waste bin by the desk.

It was enough. Rizzotti finally gave in.

'The body has gone.'

CHAPTER TWELVE

Rocco? Impatient…eager…jumps in with both feet sometimes, but no fool.
Sous-Brigadier Gilles Nevalles – Ecole Nationale de Police – Clermont-Ferrand

Rocco put the plate down. 'Gone where? We haven't finished the investigation…'

Rizzotti stuck out a hand and reclaimed his sandwiches before Rocco could pick them up again. 'I'm aware of that, Inspector. But you'll have to take it up with your superiors. The body was claimed by a representative of the family first thing this morning. They had a release signed by a magistrate in Paris and countersigned by Central Administration.' He opened his hands again. 'That's all I can tell you.'

'You're kidding. How could anyone get a release signed so quickly?' Rocco felt as if the ground had been swept from beneath his feet. Nobody but *nobody* moved this fast to take a body out of the system before a full investigation had been made. Not unless the examining pathologist – in this case a pretend pathologist – was either negligent or easily leant on. He decided to do a bit of leaning himself, pressing over Rizzotti until the medic back-pedalled in his chair like a kid on a toy bike.

'I can't help you, Inspector,' he gabbled. 'It came in, I made a preliminary inspection, it went out again. I deal in facts, and the fact is simply that the woman drowned.' He reached out for the papers on his desk as if grasping a lifebelt and held up a single sheet. It showed an outline diagram of the human body, with notations at various points, presumably marks or cuts that Rocco hadn't been able to see. 'This was my initial inspection copy. As you can see, I found several marks – mostly small cuts or abrasions – but nothing specific or suspicious. Some mud around the face, which is usual in these cases, where the body may have become inverted in the water. There was a bruise on her neck, here' – a cross had been placed on one side of the neck consistent with where Rocco had seen the mark – 'but it was not serious enough to have killed her. At least,' he smiled thinly and without humour, 'not unless the person who administered it gave her the kiss of death.'

'What?'

'A love bite, Inspector. Not a bruise in the way you mean.' He sat back, his features softening slightly. 'I'm sorry you have had this taken away from you. I sympathise, really I do. What I can tell you is that the woman had a large amount of fresh water in her lungs and a considerable amount of alcohol in her stomach – possibly Martini, whisky – a mixture, anyway. There were also traces of drugs, but I have not yet had the results back.' He lifted his shoulders. 'In my opinion, she got drunk, fell into some water and was unable to extricate herself. It happens all the time.'

'What kind of drugs?'

'Well, I'm pretty certain we're not talking about headache pills.' He stood up and shot his cuffs self-importantly. 'I think you need to find out where she was just prior to her death, Inspector. That will answer a lot more of your questions than any scientific evidence.'

'Really? I thought science could provide all the answers.' Rocco turned and walked out, then turned back. Something he'd forgotten: the clothing. 'What about her uniform?'

'Ah, yes. That we have retained. What about it?'

'Did you check the label?'

The surgeon blinked. 'I don't follow.'

'The tailor's label. Every piece of clothing has one, even the cheapest backstreet T-shirt. It's a trick we unscientific plods use to tell us where the clothes came from.'

'I see. Of course – excuse me.' Rizzotti sidestepped Rocco and left his office in a rush. He was gone several minutes. When he came back, he seemed rattled. 'I'm sorry, Inspector, but you were correct. There is one label, in an inside pocket. But not that of a tailor. It is Louis Pheron et Fils. Costumiers.' He held out a piece of paper with the details written on. 'I confess we...I...had not thought to check that. It was sewn inside a jacket pocket. We checked the clothes first thing for identification papers and personal items, of course, but found nothing.'

Rocco nodded and let Rizzotti stew. It might do him good. Pheron et Fils. He'd never heard of the name, but it told him something else about the dead woman: she had not been a member of a revivalist Gestapo club, come back to hoist a contemptuous finger at French sensitivities. Nor had hers been a genuine German body buried and preserved for the past 20 years and uncovered as part of some sick neo-Nazi plot. She had simply been a woman in fancy dress, probably attending a party where she had picked up the love bite.

Tasteless, perhaps, even sick, given that particular uniform. But not a crime and not the first he had come across.

'Was there anything else about the clothes that you did manage to notice?'

Rizzotti bristled, on the defensive, but Rocco was beyond caring. The man had been careless. 'Such as?'

The hat, for one, he wanted to say. It was dry. How come, if she fell into water? But he decided to keep that to himself. 'Anything in the pockets? Any marks on the clothing? Come on, you know what we "people" look for.'

Rizzotti's eyes dulled as he trawled his memory. 'There were no obvious tears or rips, if that's what you mean. The fabric was worn around the hems and wrists, but that's quite common. The pockets were empty.' He shrugged. 'There were some chalk marks here and there, but again, nothing especially helpful. The area in this region is full of chalk – she could have picked it up sitting on the ground or falling down a riverbank.'

Nothing helpful, then. Now all Rocco had to do was find out where she had been and how come she had been spirited away from this place so quickly and easily. If he did that, he might discover her identity.

'How long has she been dead? Do you know that much?'

'Not for certain. There are signs, but I am not skilled enough to tell for sure; it is not my area of expertise. They are making swift advances in scientific circles…in America and Germany – the British police, too. But without access to funds and better facilities…' He stopped as if aware of sounding too critical.

'So guess. You're a doctor. One day, a week, a month?'

Rizzotti lifted his shoulders. 'A guess? Three days, not more. There are…' He hesitated.

'Go on.'

'I think the body was taken straight out of the water after death before being kept…somewhere.'

At last. This was getting somewhere. 'What makes you think that?'

'The level of deterioration is more advanced than that of someone drowned and left for any length of time in the water. I worked with an aid agency in the Congo once, after a flood. Many of the bodies retrieved were wrapped in sheeting and stored awaiting identification. This had similar signs.'

Rocco lifted an eyebrow. 'See? You do have expertise – you just didn't know it.' If Rizzotti was right, the body had been kept somewhere before being dumped in the cemetery. And to be still wet, it must have been wrapped in plastic or heavy canvas. It might explain the smell and the slimy film on the skin.

He wondered how far he could push the doctor. He had already shown himself to be malleable by allowing the release of the body, and by Rocco himself. He had nothing to lose by pressing him further.

'I need names,' he said.

'Names? What names?'

'Don't piss me off,' warned Rocco. 'The names on the release papers; the name of the dead woman.'

'I don't know. How would I know who she was? I told you, there were no identification—'

'Maybe not. But *someone* must have known. How else would they have got the release papers prepared? Or is someone going around claiming unknown bodies for fun?'

Rizzotti's mouth opened and closed in confusion. He looked dazed, like a guppy in a tank, thought Rocco. But he thought he knew why: it was probably the one question the doctor had been dreading.

He said nothing, waiting for the doctor's conscience to tell him what to do. It was one of those moments when intimidating silence was far more effective than open threats.

'The papers have already been sent to the main office,' Rizzotti muttered finally, his voice dull, 'awaiting transfer onto microfiche. We don't have the facilities to duplicate them here. I'll...have to see if I can get them back.' He shrugged and looked beyond Rocco as if wishing himself far away from this suddenly cramped office.

Rocco sighed. Short of frogmarching the man across the yard and into the main building, it was the best he could hope for. 'All right. I'll wait to hear from you.' He scribbled Claude's phone number on his card. 'Call that number and leave a message. I'll call back.' By the time that happened, he hoped to have his own phone installed and ready to use.

'I can't promise...' Rizzotti began, then saw the look on Rocco's face and appeared to think better of it. 'Right. I'll call you.'

'If you don't,' Rocco growled. 'I'll come back. And you'll have more than your sandwiches to worry about, I promise.'

Rocco returned to the main office and asked to see their collection of telephone directories. A beefy man in a tight shirt silently waved a ham sandwich towards a cupboard against one wall. After a few false starts, he found Pheron et Fils listed at an office in Malakoff in the south of Paris. He took a quiet corner desk away from the other staff and dialled the number. No reply.

He called Michel Santer.

'Christ, you're still alive, then?' his former boss greeted him. 'I've been fielding calls about you ever since yesterday. What are you trying to do, Rocco – get an early ticket out?'

'What kind of calls?'

'High-level ones – the kind I can't ignore. A divisional *commissaire* named Massin was the first up. He sounded thoroughly pissed. Then a Captain Canet was on, talking about you and a female body in a Nazi uniform. I thought maybe you'd got into some weird stuff out there among the buttercups, but he put me straight. He was OK, actually, just sounding you out. And this morning, as I was about to enjoy my first coffee, another senior shirt named Perronnet bent my ear. Sounds to me like you've gone in with both feet first, same as usual, and upset the big boys. What's going on?'

'I'll tell you some other time.'

'Oh. Right. You've got company.'

'Yes. What did the two seniors want?'

'Background stuff, mostly. Where you'd come from, what you'd done – the usual crap-shovelling when someone wants to stick it to you and needs a personal, non-official edge. I told them you were a royal pain in the neck and couldn't find your arse in the dark with a sniffer dog, and I was bloody glad to have got rid of you. Did I do right, Lucas?'

Rocco smiled. Santer never called him Lucas unless he was taking the rise. He also knew his former boss wouldn't have said anything detrimental, but neither would he have over-buttered the bread. 'Thanks. I appreciate it. Now I need a favour.'

'Of course you do. And I'd like a longer penis, but I doubt that'll happen, either. Go on.'

Rocco explained briefly about the body in the cemetery, and the tag in the uniform. 'The manufacturer's name is Pheron et Fils, costumiers – probably on the theatrical side. Can you check them out for me?'

He heard the scratching of pencil on paper. 'OK, will do. I'll send your replacement. He finally turned up this morning like a spare wheel on a horse and cart. He's already got lost twice, so this should be just up his street. Anything else?'

'Yes. Can you make sure he stays zipped about it? No written notes.'

There was a long pause. 'Any particular reason for that?'

'I'm not sure. The body's already been released.'

'Jesus, that was quick. How come?'

'Somebody had the right paperwork.'

'Where from?'

Rocco smiled. Santer was right up there with him. For a body to be released so quickly and with no questions, only the best papers would have sufficed. And those could only come from one source. 'Paris. I don't know the details, but I hope to get them.'

'Good luck on that one. Who was the dead Nazi – de Gaulle's favourite niece?'

'As soon as I find out I'll let you know.'

'Do that.' Santer hesitated. When he spoke again, it was in a low voice. 'Watch your back, big man. When the big fish start taking notice of minnows, it's time to look for a handy rock to hide under. I don't know what you're getting into, but it could get messy.'

The phone clicked and Santer was gone.

CHAPTER THIRTEEN

Rocco? He's a cop. Always will be.
When he's not, he's sweet.
Emilie Rocco – ex-wife

By the time he got back to Poissons, it was too late to do anything useful, so he drove to the house and parked the car. The day's heat blanketed the front garden, oppressive and still, and he stood for a moment, enjoying the tranquillity. It was something he'd rarely found in Paris, where he had always been too close to others and their lives, too concerned with the next case on his list or the ones he had been forced by the pressure of work or political imperatives to consign to the backlog files.

He reached the front door and found a cardboard box on the step. A note was tucked inside the flap.

A man should eat. I hope you cook better than you grow tulips. The man installed your telephone already. You must be a Very Important Policeman.

Mme Denis was looking after his welfare. He glanced towards the hedge separating the two properties and made a mental note to slip some money for the food through her

94

letterbox. He took the box inside. It contained the basics of survival which even he could live on: milk, butter, cheese, eggs, a knot of fresh-cut herbs which he guessed might be basil and coriander, a box of sugar cubes and a bottle of wine.

The phone was standard black, perched on top of a telephone directory. An official subscription form was tucked under the handset. The instrument looked worn with use, with a coil of wire long enough to reach anywhere in the house, and a number was written on a yellowed piece of card affixed to a slim tray in the base. Dédé had evidently used a spare model to jump the queue. Not that Rocco cared; at least he was connected. He picked up the handset and heard the welcoming burr down the line. Wondered for a moment who to call to test it out, then decided it could wait.

He made an omelette, which he could cook with his eyes shut, thanks to his ex-wife's teaching, and listened for sounds of the fruit rats overhead. Silence. Maybe they'd gone out for the evening. Or they'd seen his gun and decided to find another home before he started blasting holes in the ceiling.

It reminded him that be hadn't cleaned the weapon for a few days, so he hoisted it out of his coat pocket and laid it on the table for later. He had a cleaning kit in the car and would find it therapeutic to go through the familiar exercise. The gun was a MAB .38 with a seven-round magazine. He had used it just twice in the police, and one like it a few times in the army. There were moves afoot to equip the police with another more up-to-date model, but Rocco had got used to the feel of the MAB and couldn't imagine using something else just because it was to be the new standard model.

As soon as the omelette was ready, he scooped it onto a plate and poured a glass of wine, and sat down to eat his first meal in his new home.

He came awake with a rush at four in the morning. There was a scurrying sound overhead, but he knew it wasn't the fruit rats which had disturbed him. Neither was it a physical intruder. Something more insidious had reached a hand into his sleep and dragged him to the surface; some dark thought at the back of his mind, nudging him awake.

His throat was dry and raspy. He'd been lying on his back. He scrambled up and reached for a glass of water, draining it in one gulp, then sat back in the dark and waited for whatever had been swirling around in his head to settle and become clear, as he knew it soon would. It had been one of the reasons Emilie had finally left; one of many, at least. She had accused him of living the job to the exclusion of all other facets of their life, evidenced by him often shooting bolt upright in the middle of the night in a eureka moment, dreams morphing back into reality. Like now. Sometimes the moments led somewhere tangible, sometimes not. But the damage had been great enough to rob him of her patience, then finally, her love.

He shook his head and forced his mind back to the job in hand. The dead woman had to be someone: someone's daughter, sister, maybe wife or mother. But whose? And someone important, if the paperwork to release the body was any indication. He would have to see whether Rizzotti showed some balls and came up with the names he needed. The bigger question was, where had she been prior to and immediately following her death? The wet clothing could be from any number of sources close by: the canal, the river or the lakes. But if Rizzotti was correct and his own instincts were right, the state of the body showed the drowning couldn't have been in the last twenty-four hours. Alcohol and fresh water…and maybe drugs. A lethal combination. Yet not necessarily suspicious. It could have been a genuine accident: too much to drink, a few pills maybe, followed by a stroll too close to water.

Folly wasn't necessarily murder.

Except that someone had discovered the body, but instead of alerting the authorities, had kept it for a while before placing it where it would eventually be discovered. Somebody with an acute lack of sensitivity.

The presence of alcohol raised a few questions. If a party guest goes missing – even one in a tasteless uniform – there would be questions asked. The police would be informed, the area searched, the family and friends expressing fear and loss, the usual incomprehension when someone – especially a woman – disappears. The area would be buzzing with rumour, gossip and innuendo.

Yet none of that had happened.

Either nobody cared…or they didn't know. Or did they not want to know?

He lay back down, then sat up again when a rooster crowed nearby, the harsh, gurgling sound drifting on the air with the clarity and reach of a bugle. He checked his watch. Almost five-thirty; time had passed swiftly. He shrugged on some old, lightweight cotton trousers and a T-shirt, and a pair of battered gym shoes: his training gear. His chances of getting back to sleep were less than slim, so he opted instead for a workout run. It was his first in three weeks, but it would help shake out the cobwebs.

He went out into the lane and turned away from the village. No sense in scaring the neighbours; he didn't expect too many of them had a training regime other than the hard, physical labour which made up their days. He worked his way up to a gentle trot, breathing deeply and swinging his arms as he made his way out into the open countryside. The birds were just beginning their chorus, and he nodded a salute to them as he passed by, an intruder in their midst, wincing at the pain in his knees and already wondering if this wasn't a few steps too far.

At seven, warmed by his run and a simple breakfast of toasted bread and coffee, Rocco reached the *marais*, taking a track off the road leading to the station and the cemetery. Laid with a thin surface of aged and cracked tarmac, it meandered through a belt of tall poplars, skirting three small lakes and a vast, untamed stretch of reed beds, regularly dotted with notices saying FISHING – PRIVATE. The morning sun filtered through the branches of the trees and reflected in patterns off the water, giving the area a shimmering, unreal quality. Rocco felt the Citroën wheels dip each time he strayed off the tarmac, and his gut tilted at the idea that the ground here might swallow him and the car without warning at any moment.

He nosed the car into a large clearing with tyre tracks in the surface showing where other vehicles had turned to go back to the road. The end of the line for anything on four wheels.

He stopped with the nose pointing back along the track

and killed the engine. Opened the door to let the air in. It smelt loamy, with a background scent of rotting vegetation and standing water. He got out and looked around.

A large wooden lodge dominated the clearing, standing proud of the trees behind it yet merging into the foliage as if camouflaged. It was plainly old, with peeling walls and weather-worn shutters over the windows, and a layer of soft moss on the shingle roof. A broad veranda ran the length of the front, with a wooden rail in the style of houses in the American Deep South. No rocking chairs, though, Rocco noted. No welcome mat, either.

He stepped onto the veranda and felt the rough planks flex beneath his weight. His footsteps made a hollow noise over the crawl space beneath, but the place had been built to last with seasoned hardwood – a wise move situated here in the marshes. He tried the front door, which had a shutter over the central panel, but it, too, was locked tight. He walked along the veranda to the end, and looked round the corner of the building. There was no garden to speak of and no fence – merely a patch of rough grass and weeds stretching back several paces to a reed bed. Beyond the reeds lay a large expanse of water, surrounded on all sides by trees, reeds and tangled underbrush. The nearest sign of life was a family of ducks about thirty metres away on the water, and the occasional plop of a fish jumping.

At the other end of the veranda he found the same scenery, with the addition of an overturned aluminium rowing boat lying just out of the reeds, a large barbecue bay and a metal rack which he guessed was for fishing rods. He hopped over the veranda rail and walked across the grass for a closer look at the boat. Worn and dented in places, the soft metal was scarred along the sides. There was no sign of an engine mounting, but he guessed that on a lake this size, oars were the best form of propulsion.

He turned to study the rear of the lodge. It boasted two large windows and a narrow door, all tightly shuttered. Whoever owned this place believed in security, and he wondered if the locals had a reputation for helping themselves when the owners were away.

It would be an ideal place for parties, he decided. Unusual, even slightly sinister, especially at night, but maybe that's what gave it a special cachet among its visitors. What better place to let loose and have a fling without anyone overlooking you?

He returned to the front of the building, making a mental note to find out whose name the place was registered in. City folk, no doubt.

He stopped.

Claude Lamotte was standing by the front steps. His feet were planted solidly, his weight balanced, and he had a shotgun slung across one arm.

Rocco felt his throat go dry.

The twin barrels were pointing right at his midsection.

CHAPTER FOURTEEN

Rocco? I barely remember the man.
Not one of our best, in my opinion.
François Massin – former brigade CO Indochina
campaign – now divisional *commissaire*, Picardie

'Taking a chance, bringing that thing in here,' said Claude genially, nodding back at the car. 'Ground's very soft off the road. Swallow a man whole in the wrong places.'

The shotgun barrels hadn't wavered and Rocco felt the muscles in his gut contract. The idea of it going off even accidentally at this range didn't bear thinking about. He tried to ignore it.

Very carefully, he slid a hand into his coat pocket and felt the reassuring heaviness of the MAB.

'So I gathered,' he said. He moved across the front of the house as if to study a poster wrapped around one of the heavy wooden uprights. The move was to take him out of the line of fire, but when he stopped and looked back, Claude had turned with him. 'Could you point that thing somewhere else?'

'Oh, sorry.' Claude moved his hand and the gun broke. He extracted two red cartridges. 'I was out hunting rabbits.

You get used to walking around locked and ready to go in this place.' A harsh sound broke the silence, and Claude glanced up into the trees behind the lodge. He inserted one of the cartridges, flicked the barrels up again. They locked into place with an efficient click, and he sighted at a crow sitting in the uppermost branches. Then he lowered it without firing.

By the time the barrel swung down again, Rocco had his gun pointed towards Claude through the fabric of his coat.

He still wasn't sure about Lamotte. He was local, after all, and knew everyone and probably everything: which way was up, which was down; the good, the bad and the plain indifferent. He was genial, too, and appeared to have accepted Rocco's arrival with genuine ease. Many would have been grudging at the very least, downright resentful at most. It didn't mean he was up to anything, but Rocco had spent too many years learning not to take anyone at face value or to drop his guard too quickly.

As he stood there, wondering whether Claude was going to break the shotgun again, he detected the smell of the oil he'd used last night to clean the MAB, the aroma set off by the warmth of his hand. It had been relaxing, he remembered, and he'd taken his time, dismantling the weapon piece by piece, the movements practised and smooth.

The metallic aroma, coupled with the sunlight through the trees, the thick, green carpet of reeds and the enforced silence after the clicking of the shotgun, reminded him of a long time ago. The close atmosphere of the jungle rushed in on him like a train, filling his head with images of the thick canopy, the narrow trails with their booby traps and their brightly coloured flowers, the darting flight of small birds and the sudden heave of soil and greenery as someone stepped on a mine or snagged a tripwire.

'You all right?' Claude broke the gun and stepped towards him. 'You look like shit, if you don't mind me saying.'

Rocco shook his head. 'I'm fine. Had a bad night, that's all.'

'You should try walking instead of running in the morning.' He grinned at Rocco's look of surprise.

'Someone saw me?' He could have sworn there had been nobody about. So much for a cop's eyesight.

'Someone will always see you. It's the way things are around here. You in training for anything special?'

'No. I got used to it in the army, then at the police academy. It helps me think. That's the theory, anyway. I should do it more often.' He gestured towards the poster on the upright. It was advertising a tag wrestling match two weeks ago. 'I thought this stuff had gone out of fashion.' He watched Claude out of the corner of his eye, his hand still on his gun.

'In Paris, maybe. Out here, though, they still have a taste for dramatic combat and the occasional spot of blood. Modern-day gladiators minus the lions.' The poster showed a ludicrously muscular man in a flowing cape, wrestling costume and a full head mask, eyes glinting through holes cut in the black fabric. He appeared to be snarling at the camera, but might easily have been yawning. 'Him especially. *Shadow Angel...man of mystery*.' He read out the banner line in a dramatic hiss and smiled, eyes crinkling around the edges. 'That's what they're already calling you in the village: Shadow Angel.'

'Why?'

103

'You dress like an undertaker, you're built like a brick shithouse and nobody knows who the hell you are…only that you look as if you're about to give them a kicking.' He shrugged. 'Not their fault – they've seen too many bad *flic* flicks.'

'In that case, I'll try not to disappoint them.' Rocco nodded at the house. 'Who's the owner?'

'No idea. The mayor might know: he collects the local taxes. I heard it's a businessman from Paris, uses it for fishing and hunting parties at weekends. Brings his friends down to show what fun we ignorant peasants have in the *marais*.' He pulled a wry face. 'Beats me why they come here, though. Hardly St Tropez, is it?'

'There aren't any photographers here scouting for Bardot skinny-dipping, that's why. Much more private.'

'I suppose. It's closer to Paris than the Med, too. And people around here mind their own business. Most of the time.'

Weekend parties, thought Rocco. A brief rush of excitement for the idle rich with too much time on their hands and not enough ways to fill it. Hell, why not? They paid their taxes, they were entitled. The same thing happened in reverse in Paris: people drifted in for a weekend of fun and frolics away from the faces they knew back home. Nobody got hurt, nobody knew. Well, mostly. Unless you bumped into your next-door neighbour doing the same thing.

Claude was watching him closely. 'You think the dead woman was here?'

'Most likely. She wasn't local, was she?'

'No. She wasn't. How do we find out who she was?'

'No idea. Not yet. But we will, sooner or later.' He related what Rizzotti had told him, then stepped away from the lodge and gestured at the *marais*. 'Can anyone fish here?'

'Sure. If they have a permit.'

'And do they?'

'Mostly, yes. Apart from a few kids.'

'Are there other places like this?'

'Sure. Come on, I'll show you. Watch where you walk, though, in those shoes. Tread where I tread.'

Claude set off past the lake, heading further into the trees. Rocco found the going difficult, his soles slipping on the reeds and grassy undergrowth. It was possible to imagine someone hurrying through here and stumbling. It would be so easy to skid off the track and into the nearest stretch of water.

Why did he imagine someone hurrying? The thought bothered him, but instinct told him he was right. Whatever had occurred hadn't been right here, but maybe not far off. All he had to do was find the place. Then the rest would become clear.

His coattails snagged on a cluster of thorns and he stopped to work them loose. He felt the soft ground shift underfoot as he twisted his body, the heavy air settling around him, with only the squelch of Claude's footsteps to break the silence. He was reminded of the other oppressive landscape. Back then, though, he'd been dressed appropriately, because the landscape and those who lived in it had learnt to fight back with lethal force.

He shook off the thoughts and watched Claude, dressed in semi-hunting gear, in his element and easing through the vegetation with barely a whisper. He needed to get some appropriate clothing of his own, if he was to stay here any length of time.

Shadow Angel. Christ, if Santer ever found out, he'd wet himself.

Skirting more reeds around a second, smaller lake, and watching for Claude's indications about soft ground and patches of dark mud, Rocco spotted another lodge. This was smaller than the first, but built in the same style. It was also locked and shuttered and weather-worn, standing on a smaller patch of ground, but plainly designed for the same function.

'Does the same person own this?'

'I don't think so – I believe it's a dentist from Lille, but I've never seen him.'

Claude wandered off and inspected the front door, then disappeared round to the rear. Seconds later he was back, gesturing to Rocco to follow.

Rocco went after him and rounded the corner of the building. The back door stood open, and a clear trail of damp footprints showed just inside the door.

CHAPTER FIFTEEN

Rocco? Relentless...doesn't give up.
Sgt R Desbordes – Contreband Task Force
– Provence-Alpes-Côte d'Azur

'Not mine,' Claude said. 'Recent, though.' He lifted one boot to show Rocco the sole. It was heavily moulded with a zigzag design, whereas the footprints on the floor were smooth with no discernible pattern.

Rocco moved past him and listened. If someone was inside, they were keeping very quiet. A random intruder from the village, come to see what they could lift? Or the owner, spooked by hearing their voices? If so, how had they got here? There were no signs of transport other than Rocco's Citroën, nowhere else to park nearby.

He pulled out his gun and motioned for Claude to stay where he was.

Searching the place didn't take long. The downstairs was one big room, with a tiny enclosed lobby at the front door. The main room had a kitchen area at one end, with a basic sink and drainer, a two-hob Calor gas cooker and a bar for serving or preparing food. The room was clean and tidy, although well beyond the first flush of newness, and the air held a faint tang of bleach. Rocco checked a pedal bin near the sink; it was empty. An open stairway ran up the rear wall and disappeared into a large hatchway in the ceiling. It was difficult to see much detail because of the shutters, but Rocco got the general layout.

He exchanged a look with Claude, then walked up the stairs, making no effort to hide his progress, but treading warily. By now, anyone here would know of their presence. If a startled owner was about to erupt out of a cupboard brandishing a lump of firewood, he wanted them to know he was coming.

Like the downstairs, the upper level was one large area, with two single beds and two bunks. Two wardrobes and a mirror completed the furnishings. There was a bit more light here from a round porthole window at one end, just enough to see that there were no hiding places and everywhere looked clean.

'Someone's been here in the last half-hour,' said Claude, as Rocco walked back downstairs. The footprints near the back door were still glistening, and it was clear that whoever had been here had progressed no further before turning and going back out.

Rocco bent and checked the lock, a simple tumbler mechanism. There was no sign of the door having been forced, and the tongue was shiny and well oiled.

'Whoever it was had a key.' He pulled the door shut behind them and said, 'Could be a cleaner.'

Claude shrugged. 'Not a local. I'd know otherwise. And why leave the place unlocked?'

'Maybe we scared them off. Anywhere else we should look?'

'Right here? Only one other place, smaller than this, at the back of the *marais* – but I just came by there on my way in. It's a ruin...unused and wide open.' He smiled. 'A weekend visitor got drunk and hung himself from the ceiling a few years ago; the local kids believe it's been haunted ever since and give it a wide berth.' He gestured back at the lodge. 'I was about to check this one when I heard your car. Some sounds carry through these trees.'

Rocco led the way back towards his car. It all seemed perfectly normal. A small village, miles off the beaten track; a couple of lodges used for weekend parties of hunters and fishers. No rush, no fuss, no noise. What could be more innocent? It seemed odd that the owner or owners didn't use someone from the village to clean for them, but it was hardly illegal.

He noticed a small wooden jetty that he'd missed on his way to the second house. It jutted out onto the larger lake, sandwiched and almost hidden from view by the reeds. He veered off and stepped onto the planks, testing his weight first. He had no wish to go for an unscheduled swim, and no desire to drive back to the house in waterlogged clothing. But water had always held a strange fascination for him.

'Watch yourself,' called Claude. 'You step off there, you'll go straight down.'

Rocco peered down into a murky brown sludge dotted with lily pads. The atmosphere here was heavy with the smell of rotting vegetation, and out on the water the air was thick with the swirl of flies and midges. Moorhens and coots, startled by his appearance, scuttled away protesting into cover, while a kingfisher flicked past and disappeared into the trees.

'A few years ago,' said Claude, joining him with care, the jetty quivering under their combined weight, 'a kid on holiday jumped off one of the jetties here. Not this one, though. Nice day, warm weather, must have been the most natural thing in the world to go for a swim.'

Rocco waited for the punch line.

'His body came up three weeks later. It's like soft toffee down there, waiting to grab you.' Claude shivered and walked back. 'Still gives me the creeps when I think about it – and I have to come out here regularly.'

'Not nice.'

'No. You ever used that in anger?' Claude was looking down at Rocco's gun. He'd forgotten he was still holding it.

'A couple of times.' He checked the safety and sighted on a log thirty metres away in the middle of the lake. He hadn't been to the police range for a few weeks, although regulations required all officers to put in regular practice and submit score cards. Somehow he never found the time. He assumed the position and breathed in. 'Firing.'

The first shot smacked out and lifted a splash of water two metres beyond the log. It caused pandemonium in the trees, as a score of birds lifted in panic and streaked away into the sky, protesting loudly. The echoes of the gunshot followed them through the *marais*, followed by another two as Rocco pulled the trigger in quick succession. Another splash with the second shot, then the log exploded as the third one took the damp wood in the centre.

He waved away a veil of gun smoke and looked at Claude. The *garde champêtre* was staring at him, mouth open.

'Sorry,' Rocco said. 'Looks like I need the practice.'

'You reckon?' Claude shook his head and stepped off the jetty. 'Didn't look that way to me.'

They returned to the Citroën and Claude bummed a lift back to the village. Just before they reached the end of the track, he tapped Rocco's arm and pointed off to one side. 'Stop here a moment. There's something I want to show you.'

Rocco stopped the car and they climbed out. He followed Claude for fifty metres into the trees, where they emerged into a small clearing, the middle of which was taken up by a circular stretch of water approximately ten metres across.

'It's called the Blue Pool.' Claude pointed into the water. 'Take a look.'

Rocco stepped up to the edge of the water and felt the hairs on his neck stand up.

The water was crystal clear all the way to the bottom, and about the same depth as the deep end in a public swimming pool. It was also the same colour blue, and the sides were uniformly curved, like a giant soup bowl.

'I don't get it,' said Rocco. He'd never seen anything like it. And after the impenetrable murk of the lake just a short distance away, it was a distinctly odd contrast.

'Creepy, isn't it?' said Claude. He bent down and dug his fingers into the side of the pool just below the waterline. When he brought his hand back up, his fingers were covered in soft chalk, like cream cheese. 'It's something to do with the chalk and the chemicals in the soil. It never gets dirty except after a storm, when mud gets washed in, and always stays the same depth. And nobody ever goes swimming in here.'

'Not even kids?'

'Especially not kids.' He pointed to the bottom. 'See that small dark area right in the middle?' He stood up and cast around until he found a short branch, heavy with mud. He dropped it into the water and hunkered down to watch. Within seconds, the branch, too heavy to float, began to slide down the curved side of the pool until it reached the centre.

Then it was gone.

Rocco couldn't help it; he stepped back from the water's edge with a start. 'What the hell happened?'

Claude shrugged. 'I think it's a freshwater spring, like a fumarole. Anything near the neck of the inlet gets sucked down by some kind of back pressure.' He stood up and pulled a face. 'Actually, I don't have a clue how it works, but that's what a water authority inspector told me a while back.' He bent and scooped up a handful of water and tasted it. 'Try it. It's as good as Evian.'

Rocco shook his head. 'I'll take your word for it.' He tried not to think about what else might have got dragged down there over the years and left its traces behind. No wonder nobody swam in there: the very idea would give even strong men the jitters.

As they walked back to the car, he looked back at the first lodge, silent and anonymous, shuttered against prying eyes.

'I'd like to take a look inside,' he said quietly. 'What are the chances?'

Claude stopped and pursed his lips. 'I'll see if anyone knows who owns it.' He dipped a hand in his pocket and took out a slip of paper. 'Damn – I forgot. I had a phone call this morning. Wouldn't give me his name, said you wanted this urgently but he wants to be left out of it. He sounded a bit shifty.'

Rizzotti. Rocco studied the names Claude had transcribed onto the back of an old fishing permit. The first was the senior magistrate who had signed the release papers for the dead woman. The second was the name of the dead woman herself, followed by an address. He felt his gut tighten. It was near the Bois de Boulogne, an area he knew well. Big houses, expensive cars, entryphones on the gates and armed guards for those who found that kind of accessory a necessary part of life. Not the kind of place you went calling unless you had a solid reason for being there.

'She's not just anyone,' said Claude. It wasn't a question – he'd written down the name and evidently recognised it.

Rocco nodded. He didn't really care about the magistrate who had signed the release; he would keep for later. But if Nathalie Bayer-Berbier was who he thought she was, then she certainly wasn't just anyone.

'I need to go to Paris,' he said. He climbed in the car and motioned to Claude to get in. It was time to trust this man. 'But not in this.'

'You could go by train from Amiens. Hey – you've got a radio! I didn't notice before.' Claude began spinning the dials like a kid in a toy shop. 'Is this police issue?'

'No. I had to buy it. The Bayer-Berbier place is close to my old stamping grounds; there's too much of a chance someone will recognise my car.'

'Ah.' Claude nodded in approval as the soft tones of Françoise Hardy filled the car, interspersed with a hiss of static. 'Beautiful girl, lovely voice. I take it you're not going to ask anyone's permission, is that it?'

'Yes. I wouldn't want to disturb them.' It might be awkward if one of his former colleagues spotted him and word got out. Quite apart from treading on toes – maybe even those of his old department – he'd probably find his way blocked by politics, the shutters brought down tight. A favour called in, like the early release papers signed so efficiently by a senior magistrate, and the entire story would disappear under the rug. At least going in fast now, he might get some information before that could happen. He considered calling Massin, then dismissed the idea. It would be seen as calling in a favour from a big gun, and that was the last thing he wanted to do.

He drove back to Claude's house while Claude continued playing with the radio, sweeping the airwaves in search of some music, muttering at the stations playing rock by British and American imports. He was relieved when they arrived back at the house. Parked outside was a grey 2CV Fourgonnette, like the baker's car and a million others on the roads of France.

'Yours?' said Rocco.

'Of course. The best transport for my job – when I'm not using my bike, anyway. Of course, it would be even better with one of these radios.'

'Is that how you got to the *marais* – by bike?'

'Don't worry – I'll pick it up some other time.' He jutted his chin at the 2CV. 'How about it? Take us no time at all to Paris.'

'In that? I'd break something…or suffocate.' Rocco tried to imagine himself squeezing into the driving seat, and couldn't. It was built for midgets, not men of his build – and it had as much speed as a donkey.

'Why not?' Claude shrugged. He got out and jerked a thumb at a rack on the roof. 'There are thousands of them in Paris. Put a ladder on top and nobody will look twice.' He grinned. 'Especially if I drive. She's a bit temperamental, you see.'

It had its merits, Rocco had to admit. But there was a major drawback. 'Have you ever driven in Paris? It's not like the roads here.'

Claude's eyebrows lifted. 'I had a life, too, you know, before coming here. I was a cab driver for a while…in Paris and other places.' He looked triumphant at Rocco's surprised reaction. 'I had my share of big-name clients. In fact,' he tapped Rocco on the chest, 'I wouldn't be surprised if I knew the street where that poor woman lived better than you do.'

CHAPTER SIXTEEN

Rocco? A safe pair of hands. Hard but safe. Is he coming back?
Sous-Brigadier Etienne Stauff – Anti-drugs Initiative –
Nice district

The street was silent apart from the chirruping of house martins, with that deserted ambiance found only in exclusive neighbourhoods in the middle of a working afternoon. The kerbs either side were peppered with a democratic selection of dog turds and expensive cars, the former awaiting the unwary, the bumpers of the latter kissing gently in true Parisian fashion.

'You sure this is a wise move?' said Claude, not for the first time. 'Berbier's a powerful man. You could end up with your balls in a vice at the drop of a phone call.'

'What do you suggest?'

'Go through channels. Amiens. Massin. I know you don't like him, but he could clear the way for you – maybe get the locals in Paris to approach Berbier instead. That would take the heat off you.'

'It would also take days while they're all bending over touching their toes. Whoever killed Nathalie Berbier is getting further away. The more time we lose, the harder it will be to nail them.'

Claude was right, though: he was taking a risk coming here. Not checking in with the local *préfecture* first was a no-no, a breach of rules and etiquette. Even approaching the Bayer-Berbier family direct could have all manner of repercussions. But he figured he had the element of surprise on his side and that would be to his advantage, where going through channels would not. If he left it to the locals, they wouldn't even get this far: the Bayer-Berbier name alone would be sufficient to put the block on any questions, the matter consigned for ever upstairs amid a welter of obstructive paperwork.

He climbed out and walked along the street. He wasn't expecting any obstacles, but his dark coat and air of confidence would help him pass muster from anyone watching the area. If that failed, he might have to use more direct means. He scanned the house numbers set in blue plaques on the gateposts as he went, eyeing the interior of the courtyards where gleaming limousines stood waiting to whisk their owners on the next journey into the capital. The traffic noise from a nearby intersection was a muted buzz over the rooftops, a comforting reminder of activity after the rural quiet of Poissons-les-Marais.

He glanced back at the end of the street. He'd told Claude to stay on the move. Any longer than ten minutes in the same spot and a local patrol would be along to give the driver the once-over. With no rational explanation for being in the area, it would be inconvenient for both of them if they were pulled in.

He found the number and a bell push alongside an

entryphone. There were no identifying marks but he would soon find out if he'd got the right place.

'Yes?' an elderly woman's voice squawked from the speaker grill.

'Monsieur Berbier, please.' A phone call twenty minutes ago had elicited the fact that Philippe Bayer-Berbier, industrialist, war hero, diplomat and friend of politicians throughout the land, was at home. The small lie about who the call was from had been easy, made simpler by cutting it short mid-sentence. Phone lines were occasionally unreliable in Paris, even in these exclusive quarters, and nobody gave an interrupted call much thought.

'Who wants him?'

The sharp response wasn't quite what Rocco had expected, but he guessed it might have something to do with the death of a daughter of the house. Some normally mild-mannered people dropped completely out of character when faced with the death of a loved one.

'Police.'

The entryphone beeped once and there was a click as the gate locks disengaged.

He stepped into a courtyard paved with cobbles. In the centre stood a dried-up fountain with a bronze cherub pointing a chubby finger towards the sky. A thin veil of green mould covered everything as if the sun rarely shone here, and the overall effect was sombre and melancholy. The only relief was a gleaming Citroën DS sitting low at rest on the far side of the fountain. A stocky young man in a dark suit was rubbing the rear window with a duster, his other hand hovering by the front of his jacket. He watched Rocco cross the yard but made no move to intercept him.

Rocco spotted a recess leading into the building. Nothing so common as a front door, he thought, and wondered what had led to this architectural oddity. As he walked towards it, an elderly woman emerged. She was grey and stick-thin and looked as if a light breeze would pick her up and send her spinning away over the rooftops like a discarded paper tissue. Her skin was sickly white and mottled with age spots, her hair done in an elaborate perm which he was ready to bet was done once a week in an expensive salon off Boulevard Haussmann.

'What do you want with my son?' she demanded, gaze fixed on him like a bird of prey spotting a particularly juicy target. There was nothing frail or sickly about her eyes, he noted. Like twin coals in the dark.

'I'm afraid,' he said politely, 'that I can only discuss that with him.'

'What is your authority?' Her cheeks flushed red at his response, her annoyance clearly lurking just beneath the surface.

'That, too, is something I need only reveal to Monsieur Berbier.' He deliberately left off the Bayer part of the name to annoy her further. He had little time for the *grandes dames* of the city, who thought themselves above the law and able to parry questions from simple plodders like him by sheer force of personality or, when that failed, a bit of judicious name-dropping.

She blew out her cheeks in frustration, then shrugged and beckoned him to follow. Rocco trailed her slowly up a flight of tiled stairs, her hand grasping an elaborate handrail and her asthmatic breathing loud and wheezing in the confined space. She was wearing a pair of faded and threadbare slippers, with baggy stockings bunched around spindly ankles. He caught a distinct tang of expensive perfume. Not that he was any expert; he used to buy perfume for Emilie, back in the days when it was still an acceptable negotiating tactic for the hours spent at work instead of home, but the numerous scents seemed to him to be simply a variation on a theme.

When she arrived on the first landing, the old woman turned and put her face close to his.

'My son is under a great deal of stress at the moment,' she muttered savagely, her breath as sour as old milk. 'Matters of state, of course. Important matters. I don't want him upset further.'

'Well, I'll try, of course.' He wondered if 'matters of state' was the new expression among the elite to cover a sudden death in the family. If so, they probably had an expression for the deceased being found wearing a Gestapo uniform and pumped full of drugs and alcohol, too.

'See to it, otherwise I will speak to my friend, the *député*, and have you removed. He can do it, too. Like that!' She clicked her fingers with a sharp snap.

Rocco was debating whether to use a hip throw on the old woman or simply kick her down the stairs, when they were interrupted by a deep voice echoing down the stairwell.

'Maman!'

He looked up and saw a man standing on the bend of the stairs, peering down at them. The face was familiar: it was Bayer-Berbier. He was tall and elegant in a pear-shaped way, dressed in an immaculate grey suit and a white shirt. Rocco guessed him to be in his sixties. He had the short, stiff *brosse* style of hair affected by Frenchmen of an ex-military background, and the steel-grey eyes behind frameless glasses were cold and unemotional.

The old woman made a huffing noise and beat a retreat through a doorway, muttering something uncomplimentary as she went and hawking deep in her throat.

'My apologies,' said the man, coming down to meet Rocco. He held out his hand. 'My mother believes it is her duty to intercept all callers – my mail, too. She is concerned about my safety. Last week she placed some documents from my office into the fire because she thought the paper might be contaminated with germs.'

'I hope they weren't valuable.'

'They weren't, fortunately. But it took me three hours and a lot of telephone calls to make sure of that. How may I assist you?' His gaze was intense and Rocco had the feeling the comments about the man's mother were merely a smokescreen to break the ice and lower barriers. It was executed smoothly, man to man, equals for the moment in spite of their undoubtedly different stations in life.

'I have to talk to you about your daughter, Nathalie,' he said carefully, reminding himself that this man was so high up the food chain, he was probably accustomed to dealing with officials via his lawyer. Not that he could have faced the kind of discussion Rocco was going to have with him too often.

'Do you have some identification?' Berbier held out a hand.

No questioning of the subject matter, thought Rocco. No frown, no doubt in the voice, the way most normal people would react when a policeman came calling. Iced water in his veins. He wondered at the 'war hero' tag which had followed Berbier around. A glorious but secret period operating with the SOE, he recalled reading somewhere; keen to fight the Germans, Berbier – a captain at the time – had found his way to London and joined the Special Operations Executive, parachuting back into France to help the underground fight. The detail remained clouded but the myth grew stronger as his prominence increased.

He produced his card and handed it over.

Berbier studied it, rubbing a thumb across the printed surface. It was a gesture Rocco had seen before: a tactile check among those who cared about such things, feeling for embossed letters. A faint lift of the Berbier eyebrows might have been a show of approval.

'It is refreshing to see,' he said, 'that there are still those who take their work seriously. Were you with the military?'

Rocco nodded. 'Once. A long time ago.'

It was all Berbier seemed to need: Rocco was a policeman, therefore not a civilian, a man with credentials, therefore not a peasant. He slid the card into a top pocket. 'So. How could my daughter be of interest to you? A parking infraction, maybe? A traffic offence? She is sometimes a little careless about these things. You know how it is with the young, I'm sure.'

Rocco felt his breath go still. Was this man playing him or was he in denial? His daughter had been found dead, he'd claimed the body, yet here he was acting as if she were in an adjacent room, alive and well.

'None of that,' he replied, his mind racing ahead. 'When did you last see her?'

Berbier shrugged, pushing out a thin lower lip. 'I can't

recall precisely. Last week? Yes, last week. She has her own apartment in the fifteenth *arrondissement* – off Avenue de Félix Fau—' He stopped as if he had said too much, then recovered. 'We do not live in each other's pockets, Inspector Rocco. She is young, pursuing her own career...her own life.'

'Of course. May I ask what she does?'

'She works in fashion.' Berbier's eyes glittered, and Rocco felt the balance tip in the air like a tangible force, as if a decision had been reached. 'Tell me, on whose authority are you here, Inspector?'

'My own.' Rocco stared back steadily. He'd faced men like this before. They were powerful, confident and usually arrogant. They could, in the usual order of things, break a man like him with a simple phone call. 'I'm investigating the death of a woman in a village called Poissons-les-Marais, in Picardie. Her body was discovered in a military cemetery and was taken to the station in Amiens, where it was released on the orders of a senior magistrate.'

'And how does that affect me?'

'The body was released to this address.'

The sound of firm footsteps echoed from the bottom of the stairs. The chauffeur, Rocco was willing to bet, coming in response to some unseen signal. Berbier said nothing, his face blank. Then he took Rocco's card from his pocket and studied it again. 'This does not give your *préfecture*. If you are asking questions about some place in – Picardie, was it? – you do not have any jurisdiction in Paris.'

'I have jurisdiction wherever a crime has been committed,' Rocco replied softly, 'and wherever my investigations may lead.' He was treading on thin ice and knew it; like stepping without care in the *marais*. But thin ice had never stopped him in the past.

Berbier indicated the stairway. 'You have made a mistake. Please leave.'

'A mistake? Are you saying your daughter was *not* reported dead and her body shipped back here?'

'She couldn't have been. I spoke to my daughter only last night.'

'But you said earlier that you'd last seen her a week ago.'

If he'd been caught out in a lie, it didn't faze Berbier one bit. He nodded. 'I was being precise, Inspector. I last *saw* her a week ago. But I *spoke* to her last night.' He waved a thin hand. 'It was only a minute or two…just a brief hello and goodnight.'

He's lying. Rocco was stunned by the ease of Berbier's words. 'Are you sure?'

'Don't be impertinent.' Berbier looked as if he could spit fire. 'I will be reporting this matter immediately to the highest authority. How dare you come here with this ridiculous story? You will be lucky if you escape with your job and your freedom.' With that, he turned and walked back up the stairs, ramrod straight.

If that's his idea of grief, thought Rocco, left with no option but to make his way back down to ground level, thank God I'm not part of this family.

The chauffeur had stepped back outside and was waiting for him. The duster was gone and the man was standing squarely in his way, hands loosely clasped in front of him. He looked solid and tanned. Resolute. A man not to trifle with. Probably ex-para and full of spit, thought Rocco. Thinks himself unbeatable.

'Don't be a fool,' he said softly, advancing on the chauffeur without hesitation. 'You'll end up breathing through a tube.'

The chauffeur wavered...then stepped aside at the last second.

As Rocco stepped through the gate onto the street, he came face-to-face with two men. They were dressed in smart suits and had just stepped out of a black Citroën DS. Neither looked as tough as the chauffeur, but one was holding up an Interior Ministry badge, which trumped toughness any day.

'Inspector Rocco?' the man said.

'Yes,' Rocco replied. 'What do you want?' He knew what they were here for; Berbier must have called them the moment he'd shown up.

The man ignored the question and held out his hand palm upward. Rocco took out his wallet and showed him his badge. 'You realise,' said the man stiffly, giving it a careful examination, 'that you are outside your jurisdiction?'

'That's what Berbier thought, too,' said Rocco. 'I'm investigating a possible murder in Picardie. The victim lived here. That gives me jurisdiction.'

'That's not reason enough. There are channels, as you well know. Procedures. If we had every policeman running all over the country on a whim, there would be chaos.'

'And,' put in the second man with a show of teeth, 'we can't have that.'

Rocco took a deep breath. They were taking the piss, daring him to tell them where to go. The frightening thing was, he could see that they were absolutely serious. Official machines.

'You should read your latest bulletins,' he suggested. 'I've been given a roaming brief as part of a nationwide policing plan. Are you saying the Interior Ministry doesn't like the idea?' He kept his voice level: losing his temper with these men would be like fighting fog. Best try and use their own regulations and decisions against them.

'Enough.' The man handed back Rocco's wallet with a sour look. 'You say "possible" murder. Does that mean you're not sure? Do you have any proof which you can bring before a magistrate?'

Rocco sighed. The fight against bureaucracy was all about detail.

'You want to see my case notes?'

'Answer the question.'

'I have no proof. Yet.'

'Really? Yet you thought you could waste time by driving all the way here from – where is it you're from?'

'Poissons-les-Marais. It's a nice place, full of people who pay your wages. I doubt you'd know it.'

'You're right. I don't. Wherever it is, you'd best get back there. You're wasting your time here. Police time.' The man looked superior. 'I suggest you find something important to occupy your life, Rocco. Trying to catch the eye of people above your pay grade is not for the likes of you.'

The man was being deliberately insulting. Rocco contemplated wiping that supercilious expression off his face, but a grain of sense held him back. It was probably what they were hoping for: drive Rocco into a confrontation and it would give them an ideal excuse to rope him in and take him off the street. These two had not happened along here by accident; they were following orders. There could only be one reason for that: to derail his investigation.

A movement out of the corner of his eye broke his concentration. Another car had turned into the street and ghosted to a stop twenty metres away. Three stocky men in dark-blue kit and jump boots climbed out and stood watching. He recognised the uniforms. They were members of the CRS – *Compagnies Républicaines de Sécurité* – the unit charged with crowd control and head banging. One of them was spinning a short wooden baton into the air and catching it without looking, the smack of wood against flesh a clear warning.

Rocco turned back to the man in the suit. 'You're quite an offensive little prick, aren't you?' he said amiably. 'You must love telling your kids what you do when you get home at night. Must give you a real sense of pride, following orders from people like Berbier. Thank Christ you're not a real cop: you'd make me ashamed to share the same badge.'

He stepped round the two men and walked down the street. The three CRS men stood their ground, then one of them looked past Rocco and his eyes flickered in disappointment.

Rocco felt just as disappointed when they stepped aside.

CHAPTER SEVENTEEN

Berbier was standing at the window of his study trying to stifle a rising sense of panic when the door opened. It was the two men he had summoned from the Interior Ministry to deal with Rocco.

'Well?' He did not bother turning, intent on staring at the rooftops across the way, where pigeons were conducting their daily courting rituals. Flying rats, many people called them, but he found them amusing. Watching their pointless antics helped take his mind off the clouds he felt gathering overhead. Clouds he'd thought were long past being able to bother him.

'We warned him off, sir,' said the first man. 'But I don't know for how long.'

Berbier spun round. 'What? He's a plodding country bumpkin, for heaven's sake! This is intolerable. My daughter is dead, my family is grieving...and this *nobody*...' His hand made an angry, chopping motion in the air, the action replacing words.

'Problem is, he's not just a country cop,' said the second man. 'He's an experienced investigator with a tough record. He was transferred out of Paris not more than a week ago.'

'Really?' Berbier pounced on the information. 'Discipline problems?' That was the usual reason cops were sent into the back of beyond, where they could quietly wither and die. Maybe it was an opening he could use to his benefit. But the other man dumped cold water on the idea.

'He was moved as part of a national crime-fighting initiative to put seasoned investigators into rural divisions. They get a free hand to conduct their own affairs. It's a trial run.' He hesitated, then said, 'Rocco's got a reputation for being a hard-nose. We tried to get him to kick off but he wouldn't play.'

'Kick off?'

'Cut up rough. Even cops get themselves locked up for that.'

'It would have taken him out of circulation for a while,' explained the first man smoothly, with a warning look at his colleague. 'Unfortunately, it didn't work.'

Berbier looked from one to the other, his nose pinched and his cheeks pale. He sighed impatiently, trying to remain calm. 'In that case, I will need your assistance further. My daughter had a flat in the Fifteenth, near Félix Faure. Rocco now knows about it.'

'We know the place. What do you want us to do?'

'Get round there and remove any papers. Anything, you understand? Take my driver and get others if you need them.'

The two men nodded and left.

Berbier watched the men cross the yard, scooping up his driver on the way. He felt a worm of anxiety building in his chest. He already sensed from facing Rocco that the inspector was not a man he could steamroller out of the way. The two from the Ministry he could rely on for their silence and cooperation, as he could his chauffeur. But Rocco was an outside force who would not toe the line. No matter what bureaucratic or procedural obstacles might be placed in his way, he would eventually get round to Nathalie's flat. It was merely a matter of time and procedure. Whatever was there, whatever she might have felt resentful or malevolent enough to leave lying around that might implicate him in a scandal, had to disappear.

CHAPTER EIGHTEEN

Rocco? A gentleman. A cop, too, unfortunately,
but he always treated us like ladies.
Mme Viviane Bernard – escort services provider – Étoile

'I need to go back to Paris.'

'What – now?' Claude opened the door in his pyjama bottoms and an old vest, eyes heavy and ringed with sleep. 'It's five-thirty in the morning!'

'Blame the cockerel.' Rocco thrust a flask at Claude and stepped past him. 'Coffee. You drink, I'll drive.'

'OK. But why so early?'

'You know Paris. It's the best time to go. Chop-chop.'

Claude stumbled away to get dressed, leaving Rocco to wait and consider what he was doing. He wasn't looking for further confrontation with the Interior Ministry goons, but something had been nagging him all the way back from Paris and into the night: Berbier had mentioned his daughter's flat. He'd been cursing himself ever since for not going to see it. True, it might reveal nothing useful. But in his experience, the homes of murder victims always showed something, even if merely a side of their character that had been hidden from others.

'Is this a good idea?' said Claude, returning and tucking his shirt into his trousers. 'Those CRS morons don't play games, you know.'

'They won't stop us. They were there for show. You ready?'

Ninety minutes later, having almost tamed the wobbly gear shift on Claude's 2CV, Rocco drove through the outer suburbs of the city, keeping one eye out for a café with a line of taxis nearby. When he saw one, he pulled up outside and explained to Claude what he needed.

Claude disappeared inside, and returned five minutes later, smelling of wine. He shrugged at Rocco's look.

'Hey, I had to buy a drink – it's only polite. Anyway, I got what we need. I didn't think a Berbier would be in the directory, but Nathalie Berbier is – or was.'

Rocco nodded. 'According to her father, she's in the fashion business. People like that don't hide; they're like moths to a flame – they want everyone to know who and where they are.'

'Well, we know where she used to be. The cabbies in there told me the exact building.'

Claude took the wheel and pointed the nose of the car towards the south-western corner of the city. 'Fashion? Huh. They're as tight as a hedgehog's arse, I know that. Lousy tippers. I remember the street from my taxi days: full of students, hippies and rich kids pretending they were working class.'

Twenty minutes later they crossed the Seine over the Pont de Grenelle, and Claude eventually steered into a narrow street and pulled up outside an apartment block over a row of shops. The area was quiet, with just a handful of people

– mostly young – going about their business. Denim jeans were in evidence, as were lurid sunglasses and colourful hats and bags; exotic butterflies on display even at the break of day. It looked to Rocco like a place trying hard to be something it wasn't.

'Hasn't changed much,' said Claude, 'apart from the colours.' He nodded at the apartment block. 'Up there on the third floor. Number twelve. If you can get past the concierge. There's usually one – but you'd know that, anyway.'

Rocco nodded and checked his watch. Nearly eight. Just the right time for a raid. Motioning Claude to follow, he crossed the pavement and pressed the bottom button outside the building. The door buzzed and clicked open, and he found himself in a neat foyer facing an elderly woman with a ginger rinse and a face like a chow. A door with a curtain across the glass panes stood open behind her, the sound of Piaf drifting faintly from inside.

'Christ. What has the wind blown in?' The woman stared at Rocco, her face unfolding in recognition. She was small and neatly dressed in a blue skirt and cream jumper, and could have been anyone's maiden aunt.

Only Rocco knew better. He chuckled in disbelief. He doubted that Viviane Bernard was her real name, but it was the only one he'd ever known her by.

'You look well,' he said, and held out his hand.

She took it in both of hers and squeezed firmly, smiling coyly the way he remembered. But then, coy had once been Viviane's stock-in-trade, back when she ran a string of 'escort' girls operating out of a large apartment near the Arc de Triomphe. He knew because he'd had the dubious pleasure of pumping her for information whenever one of her girls took a beating from a drunken client.

'Lucas Rocco?' she breathed. 'It's been a while.' She glanced at Claude, who was eyeing them both in surprise.

'Sorry,' Rocco muttered, and made introductions. They shook hands. 'I thought you'd retired to the country.'

'I did. It was boring and far too quiet. I couldn't sleep so I came back here.'

'And became a concierge? You?' He allowed her to lead him inside her flat, which was surprisingly big and comfortably furnished. Or maybe not so surprisingly, he decided. Viviane had been a very successful madame for a lot of years, and it was rumoured that she had salted away a decent amount of money in the process. The bit she wasn't allegedly paying as protection money to senior policemen in the area, anyway.

'Not the concierge,' Viviane replied. 'I own the building and I didn't want to have someone else running it.' She shrugged. 'It seemed the best arrangement.'

Rocco revised his opinion of her financial acumen. She had evidently made more than he'd guessed.

'A drink or coffee?' said Viviane.

'Coffee would be nice,' agreed Rocco.

She smiled knowingly. 'I know how you like yours, but what about you?' She looked at Claude. 'You look like a man with hair on his chest, too.'

Rocco was surprised to see Claude blushing, before he replied, 'As it comes.'

'Give me a second or two.' Viviane shuffled away through a glass door and they heard cups rattling.

Rocco briefly filled Claude in on Viviane's history. He knew she wouldn't mind; she'd always been honest about her trade, with no concessions or apologies to anyone. Claude looked surprised but said nothing, merely lowering his bottom lip and eyeing Rocco with renewed interest.

'So, what can I help you with?' Viviane entered bearing a tray with three cups, cream and sugar. She served the two men before sitting down, then glanced at Claude. 'This man is a gentleman,' she said disarmingly, 'for a Paris cop, anyway. Always treated us like ladies and never expected or took a freebie. Not once.' She sipped her coffee, then seemed to realise what impression she might have conveyed and added, 'Actually, he wasn't a client, either. Strictly professional.' She beamed at Rocco then said softly, 'I heard about Emilie. A great pity; you two seemed set for the long one.'

Rocco shrugged. 'It happens.'

Viviane nodded and changed the subject. 'So, are you on a case? I heard you had left the city.'

'I am and I have,' confirmed Rocco, adding, 'in fact, I have an interest in one of your tenants.'

Viviane put her cup down. 'Who?'

'Nathalie Bayer-Berbier.'

The name dropped into the room and left a lengthy silence. A car hooted outside and a woman's laughter echoed along the street, followed by a truck engine and a scooter puttering past like an angry wasp. Normal noises off, lives being lived.

Rocco waited patiently for Viviane to say something.

'She's up on three. Number twelve. What has she done?'

'We know the number,' Rocco told her. 'I'd like to see inside her flat.'

Viviane eyed him carefully, then Claude. 'She hasn't been

135

CHAPTER NINETEEN

Rocco cursed under his breath. They were too late. 'Any idea who they were?'

'Her father's employees, I suppose. Polite but firm – you know the type. Not the kind to argue with. And they had a cop with them.'

Rocco and Claude exchanged a look. More official help. 'What did they want?'

'They took some stuff away. Not furniture – but boxes and bags. It looked like correspondence and things like that. I couldn't stop them because Berbier pays the rent.' She shrugged. 'Half my tenants have their rent paid by parents...or others.' She stood up and went to a flat wall cabinet behind the door. Opened it to reveal several hooks hung with keys and numbered cardboard tags. Taking one of the keys, she handed it to Rocco. 'Is the girl all right?'

'No. I'm afraid not.' Rocco took the key. 'How about friends, boyfriends, people she worked with?'

Viviane gave a huge shrug. 'You think I can keep track of that kind of thing? She's a young woman – she has more friends than I have ever known, probably more admirers than she can ever hope to enjoy. But she used to share meals with Sophie in number ten, across the hallway. I think they shared boyfriends, too, on occasion, but that's the old woman in me talking.' She gave a quick smile. 'Lucky her, if you ask me.'

Rocco stood up. 'It might be best if nobody knew we were here.'

'Nobody?'

'Not the local cops, not Bayer-Berbier or his polite but firm employees, and certainly nobody who knew Nathalie.' He shrugged. 'We're working off our patch.' He waggled his hand from side to side. 'It's a jurisdiction thing.'

'Ah. Understood.' Viviane would know all about jurisdictions, had probably played with them from time to time, too, to avoid too much interest from the law.

They left her alone and walked up three flights of tiled stairs. If there were any other tenants in the building, they were being very quiet. Flat 12 was at the end of a short corridor. A woman's bicycle stood outside, with another door – No. 10 – directly across the hall. Rocco knocked on No. 10 first. Best to try and see the friend, if she was in. He watched the peephole in the middle for signs of movement, of the light changing. But there was nothing.

He turned to the door of No. 12 and inserted the key. Pushed the door open.

The air inside smelt of soap and polish, with a hint of perfume. The atmosphere was warm and pleasant, a place to call home. He led Claude inside, noting coats on a rack inside the door, a small table piled with newspapers and some circulars. No mail, though. A pair of walking shoes stood neatly against the skirting board, and alongside them, a furled umbrella, bright and fragile-looking, as if a faint breeze would turn it inside out.

'What are we looking for?' said Claude softly.

'Anything,' said Rocco, 'that tells us where she was last week. A note, a letter, train ticket – anything.' He didn't expect to find much, after what Viviane had just told them. But all it needed was something the other men might have dismissed as inconsequential.

It took them ten minutes to search the three rooms and discover that the men had dismissed nothing. Most of that time was spent going through pockets, handbags and drawers, because there were no other obvious hiding places, nor, Rocco concluded, any reason for having one.

The flat was neat, plain, if expensively furnished, and spoke more of money wisely spent than a young woman splashing daddy's wealth around. It was comfortable and light, with white walls, and to Rocco looked like something copied from American tastes, currently sweeping Europe in the wake of the Beach Boys and other left-coast music.

It took a further two minutes to establish that there was not a scrap of paperwork in the flat. No letters, receipts, bills, postcards; no jottings or scribbled memos, no REMEMBER board; no notebooks, pads or work notes, no portfolios.

'They cleaned it out,' said Claude, huffing at the lack of evidence. 'Not even a single photo. Why?'

'Because it was quicker than going through it here,' said Rocco. Easier to just bundle it up in boxes or bags and look through it at their leisure. The last time he'd seen this level of cleansing was when he'd taken part in a raid on the house of a Turkish drug dealer. The man had got a tip-off just prior to the raid and had used his gang to clear the house of every scrap of paper, right down to his wife's magazines and shopping lists, in case someone had made a careless note which could implicate him.

He walked through the flat, absorbing the atmosphere and wondering whether Nathalie had had anything worth hiding or whether her father was merely being ultra cautious in the wake of her death. Maybe she was simply a young woman, as Berbier and Viviane had variously described her, working in the fashion business and having a good time. If so, she wouldn't have needed to hide anything.

Unless somebody else knew different.

He stepped into the living room. Looked at a telephone on a small side table near the front window. It was facing the window, as if someone had sat in the window seat to use it. There was a button on the base of the phone, the kind that releases the note tray in the base, like his own. He pressed it. The tray shot out, revealing a small notepad. On it was scribbled a name and a number in a neat hand.

Tomas Brouté – frid even – 21 J? 482787

He tore off the top sheet and showed it to Claude. 'Somebody's name and a phone number at the very least.'

Claude looked sceptical. 'You think? A bit too easy, isn't it? It could be a date on a Friday evening or a reminder for a lottery ticket number.'

'You think she would have played the lottery?'

'Good point.'

'And if it's a date, why write down the full name?'

140

'A poor memory…or lots of boyfriends.'

Rocco picked up the phone, listened for a tone, then dialled the number. 'Only one way to find out.' He waited.

No connection.

'Not a Paris number, then,' Claude concluded. 'Without an exchange, that's a lot of places left to cover. He picked up a directory from the floor and flicked through it. 'No Brouté in Paris, Tomas or otherwise.'

'I'll get a search done through the PTT.'

Claude looked doubtful. 'Good luck with that. According to Dédé they couldn't find their arses in a thunderstorm.' He shrugged. 'Still, who knows? With the power of the police behind it, they might perform a miracle.'

From out in the street, a furious honking of a car horn drifted up, followed by shouting. More horns were followed by more shouting.

Rocco stepped over to the window and looked down.

Two cars had stopped outside. Both black, both gleaming. In front of the first car, a man in a delivery uniform was standing by his truck, gesticulating at his trolley piled high with boxes. In response, the car driver got out of his vehicle and walked towards him, flexing his shoulders.

It was the chauffeur from the Bayer-Berbier house.

'Out,' said Rocco. 'We've got company.'

'Can't you pull rank?'

'It's not that kind of company. Besides, whoever they are, I'd rather they didn't know we were here.'

They hurried downstairs, footsteps echoing off the walls. As they rounded the last bend, someone began pounding on the front door, and they saw Viviane coming out of her flat.

She turned towards them and handed Rocco a key.

'Out the back,' she whispered. 'It's the same men who came last night. Post the key back to me when you can.' She clutched his arm. 'Did you find anything?'

He thought it better to lie, if only for her sake. She was a tough character, but she might find herself facing heavy opposition and he didn't want her compromised if they leant on her.

'Sadly, no. No answer from number 10, either. But thanks. Ring me if you think of anything that might help.' He pressed his card into her hand, his new number scribbled on it. Ducked his head and kissed her on the cheek. 'Give us two minutes.'

They were just clear of Paris when Claude slapped a hand on the steering wheel and swore. 'How did they know we were there? Are you sure she—?'

'I'm sure,' Rocco interrupted him. It was natural that Claude might suspect Viviane of having made a sneak phone call, but he was certain that she hadn't. 'They must have been watching the place. I should have noticed.'

'Maybe. OK, if you say so.' Claude thought it over, then shrugged. Moments later, he looked sharply at Rocco. 'What was that phone number again?'

Rocco took out the piece of paper from the telephone pad. 'Forty-eight, twenty-seven, eighty-seven.'

'Thought so.' Claude looked confused. 'But how—? *My* number starts with forty-eight. I bet yours does, too.'

Rocco pictured the number in the house in Poissons. *He was right.* 'Forty-eight, twenty-seven, ninety-three.' He turned and looked at Claude. 'Who else in the village has a phone?'

'His highness the mayor. Francine at the co-op. The café. Maybe a couple of others.' Claude shrugged, making the wheel wobble. 'I don't know. Not many. But there's nobody called Brouté; I'd know, otherwise.'

'Then he or she must be using another name.' Rocco scowled darkly and wondered what other secrets the village of Poissons was hiding.

CHAPTER TWENTY

'What the hell did you think you were doing?'

Massin sounded frosty, his voice snapping down the line like a whip. The phone had been ringing when Rocco got back home. It was nearly eleven and he had a feeling it might have been ringing for a while.

He gathered up the phone wire and walked through to the kitchen. While Massin continued ranting, he put on some water for coffee. If this went the way he was expecting, he might not get the opportunity later.

'You break with protocol,' Massin grated, 'you cross boundaries without as much as a thought to other regions and you interrogate an important man like Bayer-Berbier – all without clearing it with this office first! Who gave you the authority? Did I say you could proceed outside this division? Did I?'

'I couldn't get hold of you in time,' Rocco lied easily, and sat down to wait for the accusation that he and Claude had entered Nathalie Berbier's flat without authority and against instructions. Massin had clearly been in receipt of a shit storm from the Interior Ministry, and was now passing it on down the line in time-honoured fashion.

'Really? What was so urgent that you could break all the rules like this?'

'Because the body was removed from the pathology room by order of a Paris magistrate before I had completed my investigation. It struck me as suspicious.'

'You could still have gone through official channels.'

'The local station wouldn't have known anything about it. I needed to brace Berbier direct, not through a functionary with one hand on his arse and his eye on his career.'

A brief pause, then, 'What did he say?'

Rocco noted the change in tone. It represented a slight shift in Massin's response. Was the man going soft?

He relayed the brief conversation he'd had with Berbier. 'It amounted to nothing. He didn't confirm his daughter's death – in fact he claimed he'd spoken to her the previous evening, which was bullshit. He's either in denial or hiding something.'

'Thank you for that expert analysis,' said Massin dryly. 'But has it not occurred to you that he might be grieving? Or that being interrogated by a member of the police was too much, too soon? He's not a country farmer, you know.'

'Yeah, that occurred to me,' Rocco said. He got up to pour water into the percolator. 'The fact is, if he was a local farmer I wouldn't be having this problem. Berbier pulled strings and got his daughter's body lifted out of a police establishment before my investigation even began. Farmers don't get that privilege.'

A short silence, then, to Rocco's surprise Massin said, 'I agree. Even so, we operate with the consensus of the people. Don't forget that. Some of them have powers we cannot dream of.'

'Really? Damn. And there was I thinking we had a job to do and to hell with what the people thought.' He still couldn't work out what Massin was up to. After opening with angry bluster, the man was now sounding almost reasonable.

A door slammed not far from the other end of the phone, and Rocco heard Massin murmur a brief greeting, before the senior officer said, 'You have your instructions, Inspector Rocco. See that you follow them.'

Rocco immediately knew what was up. Massin had someone close by, listening to his end of the call.

'Are you telling me to back off?' he asked carefully.

'No. I merely suggest that from here on, you proceed with all appropriate attention to procedure. Do you understand me?'

The words were stiff with authority, yet Rocco detected a tone in Massin's voice which allowed flexibility of interpretation. There was something else: *Massin hadn't mentioned Félix Faure.*

'What if my investigation should take me back to the city?'

'Is that likely?'

Rocco thought about it. Massin wasn't expressly forbidding him from going back to Paris, in spite of the clash with Berbier and the Ministry men. As convoluted as he knew the official mind could be, it sounded like a blind eye was being turned.

'It's looking possible.'

'Explain.'

'Berbier must have learnt about his daughter's death within hours of her body turning up at Poissons military cemetery; otherwise, how could he have known to claim it? He might be an important figure, but it still takes time to get a senior magistrate to sign release papers for a possible murder victim.'

'I see. Were there documents on the body?'

'Not according to Rizzotti. She was simply a dead woman of indeterminate age. Someone must have told Berbier; someone who knew she was in the area. I intend to find out who that person is.'

'Very well. I accept your explanation and expect to hear no further complaints.'

The phone clicked off and Rocco stood there, trying to figure out what was going on. The call had filled him with unease, but not for having been caught out trampling across regional boundaries or bracing an important figure in Parisian society about the death of his daughter. Either Massin had somehow put aside who Rocco was, along with their history, or he was setting him up for a fall. And that could only be to get rid of him. Except that it would be a messy way of stitching up a subordinate. He must know that Rocco wouldn't simply curl up and go without making a fuss. So what was he up to?

He poured his coffee and took it through to get changed into fresh clothing. Whatever was going on, he still had a job to do. And worrying about the machinations of senior officers wasn't going to help with his investigation. All the same, he was going to have to watch his back a lot more carefully than he had done so far.

The one thing he was now certain of more than anything was that Nathalie Bayer-Berbier's death had not been an accident. There was too much of an undercurrent for that. And although he had no reason for suspecting her father's involvement, other than being a grieving parent with the ability to pull strings, he knew he hadn't even begun to unravel that knot in the proceedings.

He remembered that he hadn't yet tried the number from Nathalie Berbier's flat. There was no time like the present. He picked up the phone and dialled.

No reply.

He let it ring a dozen times, then replaced the receiver. Somewhere in the village of Poissons-les-Marais – or close to it – a phone with a direct connection to the dead woman had just been ringing.

All he had to do was find it.

He was just pulling on a clean shirt when the phone rang. It was Claude.

'Lucas? I'm at Didier's place. You'd better get down here.'

'What's up?'

'He's blown himself up.'

'I'll be right there.' Rocco snatched his coat off the chair where he'd dropped it last night and ran out to the car. Minutes later, he pulled up fifty metres short of the yard where Didier lived and parked his car facing back the way he had come. If the bang that had hurt Didier looked like spreading, he might need to get away fast.

Claude must have heard the Citroën. He met Rocco

at the corner of the house. He looked flustered and was shaking his head.

'What happened?' Rocco queried. He didn't want to think about what Didier might have been tinkering with, or how close he might have been standing to the two enormous shells either side of his front door.

'Not sure,' replied Claude. 'When I got here he was muttering about something being covered with mud. Maybe it was a grenade.'

'He's alive, then?'

'Yes. He's a tough bastard, but we'd better get him to hospital quick. Delsaire was here first and bandaged his arm, but he's losing a lot of blood. I figured you'd be a faster driver than anyone else.'

A few villagers stood in a cluster near the front door, and moved aside as Rocco approached. Beyond them, the house appeared to be without windows, grubby curtains flapping through the holes where the glass had been, the worn shutters hanging drunkenly from the brickwork and adding to the building's sorry look of neglect.

He pushed between the onlookers and looked down at a body lying on the ground. Didier was dressed in dirty blue overalls several sizes too big, making him look even smaller and wirier than ever. To Rocco's amazement, he was calmly smoking a yellowed *Gitanes* and smiling at the crowd as if he was sunbathing. His right hand had gone, along with a good portion of his forearm, and the rest was wrapped in a bloody rag. An empty brandy bottle lay nearby, which accounted for his apparent air of calm.

Near the front door was a small heap of wet sandbags.

The fabric was shredded and scorched on one side, with sand spilling onto soil coloured a vivid red. It was clear that Didier had used them as an emergency blast wall. Unfortunately, he hadn't let go of the grenade quickly enough.

Not surprisingly, there was no sign of the hand.

CHAPTER TWENTY-ONE

Rocco checked the bandage on the remains of Didier's arm. It was rough and ready but doing the job. Didier was still bleeding heavily, but with gentle pressure he knew it could be contained. All they had to do now was get the scrap man to a hospital before he died of shock.

'Bring your 2CV,' he told Claude. 'We can lay him in the back.' He looked at Delsaire, the plumber. 'Get something for him to lie on. Some old sacks from the barn.'

Delsaire nodded and hurried away, while Claude manoeuvred his 2CV into position. Once the sacks were in place, several men gathered round and lifted Didier into the rear of the car. It was far from ideal, but the patient was in no condition to voice an opinion.

Rocco drove as fast as he dared, with Claude keeping gentle pressure on the bandage. Nearly unconscious by now through shock and the effects of the brandy, Didier was rolling around in the back. Rocco figured it was a trade-off between some mild discomfort for Didier now, against the chance that he could die if they didn't get him treated as quickly as possible.

It took twenty minutes to get to the hospital in Amiens, with Rocco urging the underpowered car along every bit of the way and barging through whatever traffic they encountered. Fortunately, nobody tried to argue, no doubt seeing the 2CV with its lights on and clearly being driven by a reckless madman as something to be avoided.

As Rocco hurtled round the final bend in the hospital grounds and slid to a stop before the emergency entrance, Claude grasped his elbow.

'Best not say it was a grenade blew his arm off,' he advised. 'I'll tell them it was a tractor.'

'A tractor?' Rocco stared at him. 'Are you serious? What do you reckon they'll think you run tractors on in Poissons – dynamite?'

'It's just that...hell, the *paperwork*. We'll be tied up for hours.' Claude looked embarrassed at the proposed lie. 'Just a thought.'

He was right. Rocco weighed up the rights and wrongs. If the hospital called the police, as they were bound to do in cases involving explosives, there would be a full investigation, with the might of the authorities descending on them here and in Poissons. If that happened, he could say goodbye to his investigation.

He was saved from saying anything by the appearance of two hospital attendants rushing towards them with a wheeled stretcher. Claude heaved himself out of the car, before hurrying to the back to oversee the lifting of Didier from his resting place.

By the time Rocco parked the car and made his way inside, Claude was calmly drinking coffee and chatting away to a nurse on reception. There was no sign of Didier, although a number of other patients were waiting to be seen, sitting in a line of chairs against one wall. He assumed Didier's injury was probably novel enough to have gained priority.

'What did the doctors say?' he asked Claude.

'It's not good,' Claude murmured, frowning into his cup.

'I'm sorry.' Rocco was surprised they had been able to comment on the outcome so quickly. Didier wouldn't have the use of his arm again, but he'd seen men with far worse injuries pull through. Shock, maybe, always a difficult matter to foresee, had probably taken its toll, along with the ride here and a gutful of brandy hammering through his system.

'Oh, I don't mean that,' said Claude quickly. 'The duty doctor has seen, you know, grenade injuries before. He served in Indochina. He's already called the cops. I tried to get Didier to keep his mouth shut, but the imbecile was away with the birds and wouldn't listen.'

Rocco swore silently. He'd been half-ready to back up Claude's madcap story about a tractor, but with an experienced doctor able to tell explosive trauma from a tractor losing its big end, there was no way the story would float. If they knew anything about the locals, they would be aware that some occasionally did stupid things like attempting to dismantle the deadly remnants of two world wars.

He felt a measure of sympathy for Claude. As the local representative of the law, he might pick up some criticism for allowing such things to go on. But without patrolling every yard and garden in Poissons, he was powerless to stop it.

Approaching footsteps prevented further discussion. A tall man in a white coat appeared from a corridor. He was holding a small plastic bag in one hand and looked far from happy. He glanced at the receptionist, who pointed at Rocco and Claude.

'You are friends of the grenade injury?'

'Not friends,' Claude said defensively. 'Same village, though.'

'I see.' He eyed Claude's uniform shirt, then glanced at Rocco with the hint of a sneer. 'Doing your civic duty, I suppose. How noble. Are there many madmen like him where you come from?'

Rocco gave him a heavy look. He could do without this kind of annoyance. 'Cut the attitude, Doc,' he growled. 'We brought him in, that's all you need to know.'

The doctor looked wary and stepped back a pace. 'My apologies. Only, is the man insane or what?'

'He picked up a grenade,' Claude huffed. 'It happens.'

'Quite often, according to what he told me. He dismantles explosive devices for a living – usually much bigger ordnance than grenades. He said this one went off before he could unscrew the fuse.'

Claude leant forward. 'The stuff is unstable. He probably hit it too hard.'

'Undoubtedly. But doesn't he know he's supposed to report finding things like that?'

'How's he doing?' Rocco cut in. 'Will he live?'

'Yes. But he won't be playing cards for a while. And if he

gets anywhere near another bomb with a hammer, I'd leave the immediate vicinity, if I were you, because he's not going to be doing it with any precision.' He started to walk away, then paused and glanced at Claude. 'You'll have to wait, incidentally – your colleagues are on their way here. They'll want a statement. But I guess you'd know that, wouldn't you?'

'We're well aware of the procedure,' said Rocco. 'What've you got there?'

The doctor didn't even look at what he was holding. 'It's for the police.' He gave Claude another look. 'The proper ones. No need for you to concern yourself.'

Rocco sighed and held up his badge. 'I am the police, so enough with the crap. What is it?'

'Oh. You should have said.' The doctor held up the bag. 'This item was embedded in his forearm; probably blown there by the force of the explosion. Do you know what it is?' It was clear by his expression that *he* did.

Rocco studied the object inside the bag. It was the thickness of a pencil and made of pale metal, like aluminium. It had a ragged end, as if it had been broken from a longer piece, and was blackened by scorch marks.

He nodded. 'I know. What was Marthe's explanation?'

'He didn't have one. He lost consciousness before I could ask him. If he's using this technique for taking ordnance apart, Inspector, he needs locking up, for everyone else's protection if not his own.'

The doctor walked away, calling for the next patient.

Moments later, they heard a car squeal to a stop outside and a police *sous-brigadier* marched into the foyer, young, fresh-faced, self-important and austerely immaculate, his *képi* under one arm. He was followed by another uniform who stationed himself by the door. The first man glanced briefly at Claude before disappearing down the corridor after the doctor, clearly familiar with the layout. When he emerged a few minutes later, his face was pale and unfriendly. He strode up to them, eyes inspecting Claude with an expression of distaste.

'You're Lamotte.' he said accusingly. 'We've seen this kind of lunacy before. What's it this time – another idiot with a death wish looking for scrap?'

'A grenade,' Claude explained, stiffening under the man's eye. 'He picked up a grenade. I explained to the doctor.'

'So he said.' He turned to Rocco. 'You're the new inspector, aren't you? Odd you should be involving yourself with these people.'

'People?' Rocco felt his temper rising. 'What I do and who I get involved with is none of your business. We're in the middle of a murder investigation and we brought in a man who'd had an accident.'

'That's as may be.' The young man lifted his chin and Rocco guessed he didn't need to shave often. By his badge of rank, he'd probably put in about a dozen years, but that still put him at not much more than thirty, possibly less. 'But I have to report the facts of any explosions and related injuries. Further action may need to be considered.'

Rocco reached out and clamped a hand around the pompous officer's neck in a pseudo-avuncular manner, but with just enough grip to stop him talking. 'Great. That's good. Glad to hear you're so keen on the rule book. But listen to me, sonny. We don't have time to get caught up in any of your official rubbish. If you think otherwise, why don't you have a word with *Commissaire* Perronnet or Divisional *Commissaire* Massin. They'll set you straight. Now, if you'll excuse us.' He patted the man on the shoulder and walked away before he could argue, leaving Claude to throw up a vague salute and follow.

'What was that about?' said Claude, as they got back in his car. 'And what was in the bag?'

Rocco sat there, mind racing. What the doctor had found was something that no scrap man, no matter how unconventional, idiotic or desperate he might be, should have had access to. It was inconceivable that Didier Marthe was using it to break down grenades or shells. The idea was ludicrous, although he hadn't said as much to the doctor.

'What did Didier say when you first got to him?'

'I couldn't be sure. He was rambling on about something being covered with mud. Why?'

'Because whatever took his hand off wasn't just a dodgy grenade. It was part of a detonator. The kind used with plastic explosives.'

CHAPTER TWENTY-TWO

Claude stared at him. 'He was using *plastique*? That's madness.'

'Didier wasn't. But somebody was. It wasn't mud he saw on the grenade, either; it was explosive moulded and coloured to look like it. The question is, why would someone with access to that kind of equipment want to kill Didier Marthe?'

He told Claude to return to Poissons, and more specifically, Didier Marthe's house. Although unnerving to experience the other man's driving – and him a former taxi driver – it allowed him time to mull over what they had just learnt.

Plastic explosive, otherwise known as C3 or C4, was the current tool of choice for demolition work, bomb disposal…and guerrilla warfare. It was easy to hide, mould and place, and could be disguised to blend into almost any background. It had the added benefit that, with the right timers or detonators, it could be set off remotely.

Rocco had never used the stuff, but he'd seen it in action, employed by engineers to destroy traps in the jungle and bridges used by the Viet Minh. It was very effective in the right hands but, as he knew all too well, the right hands weren't the only ones capable of getting hold of it.

What he couldn't get his head round was the idea that someone had laid a booby trap for Didier Marthe. Whoever it was must have been watching him, and was aware of his movements and the methods he used in his insanely dangerous line of work. The only question was, what had Marthe done to warrant such an attack? From the little he had seen of him so far, he was quick-tempered and unpleasant, and could undoubtedly do with a bath or two, but that was insufficient reason to try blowing him to bits.

By the time Claude pulled into the yard of Didier's house, Rocco had worked his way through various possible scenarios, but without reaching one specific conclusion.

He got out of the car and walked over to the bloodstained sandbags. The area of the blast was easy to identify, with the focal point between the two arms of the 'V' formed by the bags. At the sharp end of the 'V' was a gap, big enough for a hand and arm to fit through. Although he had no way of verifying it until Didier himself came back, he guessed that the scrap man had somehow realised what he was holding and had thrust his hand between the sandbags to shield himself from the blast. Unfortunately, he hadn't been quick enough.

But where had he got the grenade from? Picking it up in the fields or woods would have been too random: there was no way the person who'd planned this could have known what he would do. That meant it had to have been left here for him to find – or handed to him by the intended killer.

He turned and surveyed the area for clues, but quickly dismissed it as a waste of time. The ground was a mishmash of footprints where everyone had gathered around Didier, and any trace left by whoever had been here before the explosion had long been obliterated.

He walked around the yard, trying to think it through. Didier's work was well known around the village. It presupposed that anyone watching him for any length of time would soon come to know his routine. And if Claude was correct about the kind of ordnance lying around in the countryside, he had an almost inexhaustible supply from which to choose. That meant he would spend relatively little time out searching, but a lot more here in his yard.

'The door's open.' Claude nodded at the house. The front door was sagging on its hinges.

It was too inviting to ignore. Rocco pushed the door back and stepped inside, ducking his head beneath the low frame.

The smell was the first thing to hit him. Sour with sweat, unwashed clothes and burnt cooking oil, the choking atmosphere was enough to make his stomach revolt. The light was poor, with heavy net curtains over the windows, now free of glass. The furniture was ancient, darkened by smoke and grease, with any visible surfaces covered in dust and mouse droppings, the remainder laden with dirty crockery, filled ashtrays and cooking utensils. Old newspapers and magazines spilt over from chairs onto the floor, most of them trodden flat and shredded beyond recognition.

There was no obvious sign of a telephone, he noted.

Three doors opened off the room. One led into a sleeping

160

area of sorts, made up with a single, unmade metal-framed bed with no sheets and shabby blankets, a wardrobe and matching sideboard on a bare wooden floor. A single bulb hung from the ceiling, a nipple of brown grease hanging from the thin glass. A second door led to a narrow stairway, but it was soon evident by the layer of dust on the treads that it hadn't been used in years.

The third door was locked, with a stone step just visible at the bottom. A cellar, Rocco guessed. He studied the lock. It was ancient but solid, and he decided to leave it. If there was anything down there worth seeing, he could come back another time.

'You see this?' Claude was standing by a small side table. Nailed to the wall above it was a bulletin board, the kind used by every police station, school and council office in the country. Among the various bills and notes pinned to it were several photographs, faded and discoloured by age and the toxic atmosphere of the room. Most looked like family groups, taken in the Thirties, judging by the style of clothing. But the one Claude was pointing at looked different. It wasn't old, not in contrast to the others, which were faded and grimy, although the subject matter clearly was. It had been pinned on top of the others, where its size and freshness made it stand out.

'Interesting,' Rocco murmured.

The photo showed a group of six men and one woman, huddled around a campfire. Their faces were gaunt, the expressions sombre and inward-looking. One man was turned away, his face blurred, but the others were staring into the camera. They all held rifles, and one or two had bandoliers of ammunition slung across their chests. The woman was holding a pistol in one hand and a dagger in the other.

'Resistance fighters,' said Claude. '*Maquisards*. I've seen pictures like this before, but not often. It was taking a hell of a risk having your face recorded like that. The Germans would have paid good money for this kind of evidence.'

Claude ran a fingertip across the faces, stopping on a thin individual sitting next to the woman. The man looked about forty years of age, although he might have been younger, and appeared to be leaning against the woman, with one hand resting on her knee. He wore a heavy jacket and a beret and, like the others, looked as if he had not eaten or washed in days.

Claude tapped the man's face. 'Look who we've got here.'

Rocco looked. Felt a jolt of recognition.

It was Didier Marthe.

'Did you know he was in the Resistance?' said Rocco. He slid the photo into his pocket: it would be another line of enquiry to consider, although he didn't hold out much hope of turning up anything useful. As Claude had said, the records of Resistance members were sketchy, and those in the know were inclined to be very secretive on the subject. In any case, it might not have any bearing on why someone had tried to kill the man.

'I never heard him say anything.' Claude shook his head in wonderment. 'You occasionally hear of someone being involved – usually after their death. But it's not something people talk about.' He shrugged. 'Those who do are usually the ones who like to *suggest* they were part of it, but weren't, if you know what I mean.'

Rocco nodded. It was the same with the Indochina campaign: those who had been there talked about it the least. He'd come across the braggarts himself. Sad, most of them, to be pitied for their pretence and their false lives. 'It might explain where Didier got his knowledge of explosives.'

'True. But so what? It's just an old photo.'

Claude was right; it was just an old photo. And unless he could come up with a plausible reason for Didier having plastic explosives and detonators in his home, he was making a puzzle where one did not exist.

As they walked outside, he automatically checked for signs of a telephone wire running into the house. He couldn't see one…but neither could he imagine Didier Marthe having many friends to chat with, either on the phone or face-to-face.

Later that afternoon, he took a walk round the garden, trying to empty his mind of conflicting thoughts about the dead woman and the nearly dead Didier. Two events in such close proximity in Paris would have been unremarkable: murders and assaults with no obvious bearing on each other occurred in adjacent streets every day. It was the way of things in heavily populated areas. But out here in the middle of nowhere? It didn't seem feasible.

He stopped beneath an old cherry tree and took out the photo of Didier Marthe and his fellow Resistance members. He turned it over. There was nothing to identify the group: no names, location or date scribbled helpfully for him to pursue. But there was a small blue stamp, an ink mark in one corner, in the shape of a triangle. He peered more closely and was able to decipher three letters, one on each side of the triangle. APP. The developer's name?

He went back indoors and rang Amiens, asked to be put through to Massin. The *commissaire* came on and went immediately on the offensive.

'Rocco, why are you involved with some idiot who wants to blow himself to bits? Your time is too valuable to waste on low-level misdemeanours.' Clearly, the officer at the hospital had wasted no time spreading the word about Didier's injury and Rocco's presence at the hospital.

'It might not be what it seems,' explained Rocco, cutting him off short. He wanted Massin's help, not to be tied up with pointless arguments about jurisdictions or the parameters of his work.

'What do you mean?'

'It's true the wounded man was messing about with a grenade, but I think it had been booby-trapped with *plastique*.' He took a deep breath and launched into his next statement before he could change his mind. 'There might be a *Maquis* connection.'

There was a long silence on the line, and Rocco could picture Massin sitting back and judging how ill-advised it could be to go trawling into the murky history of the wartime Resistance movement. Others had been drawn into it before when revenge killings occurred or old scores were settled. It was usually messy and unpleasant, with many of the people now in positions of power. Suddenly having their past deeds exposed to the harsh light of a modern-day murder investigation was something most of them wanted to avoid, and digging too deeply into them could threaten the future prospects of an unwary investigator.

'How do you arrive at that conclusion?'

Rocco explained about the photograph and its logo. 'It looks as if Marthe might have been in one of the Resistance groups. The only link is the photo shop which processed the print, but I don't have the resources or the leverage here to find it. I was hoping you could arrange a search.'

'You want me to put my name behind it, you mean? You've got a nerve, Rocco.' Massin sounded annoyed, but there was no way he could refuse the request without having a solid reason.

Rocco pressed ahead before Massin could find one. 'If someone is trying to kill this man, it could be something to do with his wartime activities. I'd rather stop it before he tries again and ends up killing a bunch of innocent villagers. Plastic explosive is hardly selective in its victims.'

The potential headlines were evidently clear enough for Massin to imagine. Equally clear to him would be the dangers of digging into events which few people wanted to uncover. 'All right,' he said reluctantly. 'Leave it with me. What about the other thing?' He meant Paris and the Berbiers.

'I'm making enquiries. There's somebody local who might know what happened. I just have to winkle them out of the woodwork.' It was as near a lie as Rocco had ever uttered. He didn't know if anybody in Poissons was involved, but the suggestion might be enough to keep Massin off his back.

He rang Claude. The *garde champêtre* sounded groggy. Rocco guessed he'd been taking a nap.

'How many suspicious deaths have there been in this area recently?' he asked.

'Suspicious? You mean murders? That's easy: none. Why?'

'And assaults? By that I mean anything beyond a bad-tempered punch-up?'

'Same answer. It hasn't happened. Sorry to disappoint you, Lucas, but life out here isn't like Paris. People argue, sure – even have lifelong feuds. But that's all it is. The last sudden death we had was last year, but that was a hunting accident. A visitor got careless in the woods and ran into a charge of buckshot. It happens, unfortunately; and for the fascists in the anti-gun lobby, far too often.'

Rocco was aware of the hunting and shooting argument: that many legal guns found their way into the hands of criminal elements, quite apart from the deaths caused in communities by accident or intent. 'You don't approve?'

'No. I mean, there are idiots out there with guns, we know that. But if the bureaucrats got their way, they'd shut it down altogether. Christ, it's un-French!'

Rocco laughed. 'Did anyone pursue the matter?'

'No. There was a witness standing right next to the man who was killed. He didn't see the shooter, but he said there was a big group of outsiders in the woods on a hunting weekend and it could have been any one of them. Whoever pulled the trigger probably didn't even know what he'd done. The Amiens office declared it an accidental death due to not knowing the local terrain.'

Rocco sighed. It looked as if Poissons-les-Marais possessed an almost surreal lack of crime, and the only occurrence which had come close was an accident. But that made recent events even more out of the ordinary. 'OK. Just working a line of thought, that's all.' He was about to put down the phone when a random thought occurred to him. 'Who was the witness to that shooting?'

Claude gave a dry chuckle. 'Funny you should ask. It was Didier Marthe.'

Rocco was jerked awake two hours later by the phone. He shook his head and checked the time. Six o'clock. He was beginning to regret having the damned thing installed.

'Rocco?' A vaguely familiar voice came over the line. 'Is that you?'

'Speaking.' He swung his feet onto the floor. 'Who is this?'

'Bernard Rizzotti – Amiens *préfecture*. You came to see me about the dead woman.'

'So I did. What have you got?'

'The results came in.' Rizzotti sounded subdued. 'It's maybe not what you were hoping for, though.'

'Go on.' Rocco experienced a sinking feeling. This wasn't going to be good.

'She was clean. Alcohol, yes – a fair amount, in fact. But no drugs.'

Rocco swore quietly. So, a simple accident: a young woman who'd had too much to drink went walking near water and fell in. It happened.

But Rizzotti hadn't finished speaking. 'There's something else. The deceased was pregnant.'

'You're sure?' Rocco flicked through the possibilities, wondering how that might tie in with Nathalie Berbier's death. Depression at finding herself pregnant leading to excess drinking and a fatal stumble in the dark? An angry lover – perhaps married – furious at hearing the news and pushing her into a river to silence her? Or the lonely realisation that she had made a dreadful mistake…and seeing only one way out?

'I'm certain. Without the body I can't tell how far gone she may have been, but I can tell you it wasn't physically obvious when I made my initial examination.'

'I understand. So why tell me now?'

'Well, because it changes things...her being pregnant.'

'I see.' It sounded like Rizzotti had a soft side. Rocco sensed that he wanted to say more, but was hesitant. 'If there's anything else, it goes no further.'

A long pause, then Rizzotti said quietly, 'This is not to be broadcast, you understand. I will deny all knowledge if you use my name in connection with this.'

'Go on.'

'When I first examined the stomach contents, there was some alcohol. But it was difficult to judge how much because it was mixed with a large quantity of clean water, as were the lungs.'

Proof of drowning at least. Then Rocco stopped. '*Clean* water? Not lake water?'

'Clean-ish, I'd say. Either from a fast-running stream where there's little or no pollution or silt...or near a source of natural water...say a spring.'

Fresh water. As good as Evian. He recalled Claude's words. The Blue Pool.

Rizzotti was still speaking. 'But to have fallen into water and been unable to get out would indicate a severe level of intoxication or the presence of a powerful narcotic, such as cannabis or heroin...maybe even one of the new synthetic drugs being manufactured in America. That would severely reduce a person's ability to function normally – especially a young woman.'

'So what's the problem?'

'The lab figures do not bear that out. They simply state the presence of a powerful sedative and the conclusion that the deceased consumed too many tablets in error, perhaps while intoxicated, and fell to her death in a stretch of water.'

Rocco felt the air hum around him. 'But you don't agree.'

'Most assuredly not.' Rizzotti sounded almost angry yet resolute. 'Her system showed signs of an excessive dose of barbiturates, that is undeniable. But to have reached the level stated would have required the digestion of a great many pills indeed. Yet I did not find any such residue in her stomach.'

'Which means?' Rocco sat up.

'The reported figures are mistaken…or ill-founded.'

'You mean they've been altered.'

'I can't say that for sure.' Rizzotti was careful to avoid levelling any direct accusation towards the forensic laboratory.

Rocco didn't push it. He might need the doctor's help later. Alienating him by backing him into a corner wouldn't ensure that, not now he'd come out this far.

'What's your conclusion, Doctor?'

'There is only one. If it wasn't in her stomach – ingested normally, in other words – there is only one explanation for such a high dose of barbiturates: she must have been injected with it before she died.'

A few seconds went by as if Rizzotti was aiming at the maximum effect. 'This was no drunken accident, Inspector Rocco. I think that poor woman was murdered.'

CHAPTER TWENTY-THREE

'Tell me about this.' Rocco dropped the photo of the Resistance group on Didier's hospital bed the following morning. The scrap man had been placed in a single room with a view over some gardens, a facility Rocco thought was better treatment than he deserved.

'Never seen it before,' Didier Marthe muttered sourly. The response was too quick to be anything but instinctive, but he was staring at the print as if it might bite him. 'Where did you get it?'

'Pinned to the noticeboard in your kitchen. What's that about – reliving old times?' Rocco turned to stare out of the window. Experience had taught him that while facial expressions could be feigned, there was often more to be sensed from the way a person spoke, and the timbre of their voice.

'You've been in my house? *Bastard!*'

Didier lashed out angrily, sending the photo spinning across the room.

'Calm down,' Rocco warned him, bending to retrieve the snapshot, 'before I sit on you. I'm pursuing a possible murder investigation, so yes, I went into your house. Anyway, the door was open after your little explosive episode.' He slapped the photo back down on the bed where Didier couldn't ignore it. 'You can try suing me for trespass if you like, but I wouldn't fancy your chances much.'

'Murder?' Didier instantly dropped the aggrieved expression and looked shifty instead. His eyes went back to the photo and lingered there in fascination. 'I don't know anything about any murder.'

'Attempted, in your case. Somebody tried to kill you, didn't they?' Rocco dragged up a chair and sat down heavily. He needed at least a litre of coffee, but it would have to wait. 'With the grenade.'

'I don't know what you're talking about. It was an old Mills, that's all. British. It blew up. Unstable crap.'

'Balls. It blew up because someone spiked it with *plastique* and a detonator.' Rocco leant forward, pinning Didier with his gaze.

'You're insane.' Didier looked away, rubbing subconsciously at the stump of his arm.

'They left it lying around for you to pick up. But you recognised the detonator or the explosive for what it was and tried to get rid of it. You weren't quick enough.'

'That's a fancy imagination you've got there, Inspector. How would I know about *plastique*? I only deal with ammunition I find in the ground.'

Rocco looked pointedly at the photo on the bed. 'You were in the Resistance. That photo proves it.'

'So?'

'You'd know all about explosives, how they worked. Tell me I'm wrong.' Didier said nothing, so Rocco pressed on. 'I'm guessing someone doesn't like you and they've decided to get even with you over something. Am I right?'

'No.' Another response that was too quick. 'Go screw yourself.'

'Wrong answer. There was a shooting accident last year in the woods. Guess who was standing next to the victim? You. A botched attempt on your life, was it? That didn't work either. You must have more lives than a cat. Care to share with me who might be after you, Didier? Hopefully, before any innocents get caught up in this little vendetta.'

'What's going on here?' It was the doctor Rocco had spoken to on the day he and Claude had brought Didier in for treatment. He was standing just inside the door, his expression chilly. 'This is not permissible! Why are you interrogating this man?'

Rocco sighed. He'd get no further now. Didier would duck behind medical protection. And if he pushed the doctor, Rocco would likely end up being hauled out of here by a couple of Massin's men.

'Apologies, Doctor,' he said politely. 'Only I like to try and find out as early as possible why someone will try to kill a man using plastic explosives. It's the protective side of our job, you know?' He looked at Didier and tossed a card on the bed, then snatched up the photo. 'If you have a relapse and remember a name, give me a call.'

'OK...OK. *Jesus!* The *plastique* is mine, all right? I was trying an experiment.'

Rocco and the doctor stared at Didier in surprise.

'What kind of experiment?' Rocco wanted to tell the

doctor to get lost, but he didn't dare lose the moment now it had come.

Didier shrugged and licked his lips, eyes flicking left and right. His good hand was shaking as if he was running a fever. 'What I do needs speed and lots of material, right? The quicker I can separate off the metal components, the more money I make. I was trying to use a small charge of explosive to split the grenade's casing and expose the guts.' He shrugged again. 'It didn't work.'

'Bollocks!' As convincing as Didier sounded, he knew the man was scrabbling for anything that could get Rocco off his back. The idea of anyone using plastic explosives to open up a grenade was ludicrous.

The doctor stepped forward, the focus of his attention now on Didier. 'But how do you come to have plastic explosives anyway? *Why* would you have such a thing?' Plainly the idea of possessing anything larger than a firecracker seemed astonishing to him.

'Tree stumps,' Didier blurted. 'I have lots of them on my property and burning them out takes too long.' Another shrug. 'Blowing them out is quicker.'

'Mother of God,' whispered the doctor. 'You people are truly insane.' He turned and walked out, shaking his head in disbelief.

'You'll be charged with possession of prohibited materials,' Rocco warned Didier. 'That carries a prison term. Unless...' He waited, sure that the wounded man would look for a deal if he could get one. A born survivor, he'd be quick to look for a way out of the dilemma. It had undoubtedly stood him in good stead in the Resistance, where quick thinking was a survival skill, and he would have lost none of that ability over the years.

'Unless what?' Didier looked sullen and defeated, but his eyes were sharp with cunning.

'Unless you stop being an obstructive pain in the arse and help me.' Rocco nodded at the photo. He had to get Didier focused on it: a trade of information in exchange for the illegal explosives charges being dropped. 'Who are the others in that group?'

'Christ, you expect me to remember that? It was twenty years ago in another life; they're probably all dead by now!'

'You aren't.'

'Might as well be, with this.' He waved the stump of his arm, then slid down in his bed with a heavy sigh and turned to face the wall. 'I need some rest. Close the door on the way out.'

Rocco realised that he had lost the initiative – for now, at least. Didier was tough all right. But for how long? 'Fair enough. Just one more question: who owns the big lodge in the *marais*?'

'How the hell should I know?'

'Because you damn near live in the *marais*, that's why.'

'So?'

'And it's just across the stream from your place. You trying to tell me you've never seen or spoken to anyone down there?'

'Of course I have. But they don't tell me their business – why should they? They're just lousy Parisians with too much money and no respect for the common man.' His shoulder moved under the covers. 'Show them the guillotine, I say. That'll thin out their filthy capitalist ranks.'

Rocco gave up. This kind of pseudo-political nonsense could go round in circles. But he was convinced Didier knew far more than he was letting on.

'I will find out what's going on,' he said, walking to the door, 'one way or another. But you'd better hope none of your neighbours get hurt in the meantime. Otherwise, it'll be *you* seeing the guillotine, not a bunch of posh partygoers from Paris.'

He made his way back out to the car, reflecting on what had just happened. As a first interview with a significant person in a case presented with a piece of evidence, it had been no different to most of the others he had conducted. Witnesses and suspects alike were often adept at expressing denial, then anger in equal measure. Mostly, it was just a matter of wearing them down.

As he climbed in the car, his thoughts returned to the photograph. The one impression uppermost in his mind was that Didier Marthe had never set eyes on it in his life before.

From the hospital, Rocco drove to the office where he found a detective making a pot of coffee. He introduced himself and they shook hands.

'René Desmoulins,' the man said. 'I heard about you.' He was in his forties, genial, with a thin moustache and a weightlifter's chest and legs. 'You want coffee?'

'Is it strong?' Rocco peered at the mixture; it looked like treacle.

'It'll float a brick if you want it to. Help yourself.'

Cups full, Desmoulins led the way to an empty office and closed the door. 'I'm supposed to be working on a petrol scam on the outskirts of the town,' he explained, sitting down. 'It's a crap job which nobody else wanted, and I drew the short straw. If you've got something more interesting, for God's sake let me in on it. I'm dying of boredom.'

Rocco smiled. At last, a potential accomplice.

'Who do I clear it with?'

Desmoulins grabbed a phone and pushed it across the desk in front of Rocco. 'You know Eric Canet?' Rocco nodded. 'Dial two hundred and forty-one; to you he'll say yes.'

Rocco dialled the number and Canet answered. He quickly outlined what he needed and saw Desmoulins making notes on a pad. 'It's not much,' he said, 'but I need someone to trawl through the records. This could go all the way back to the war.'

'Tell Desmoulins to get on with it,' said Canet with a smile in his voice. 'He'll much prefer that to the smell of petrol.' He cut the connection.

Rocco relayed Canet's agreement. 'You'll also have Massin's blessing if you need it.'

'Yeah?' Desmoulins looked impressed. 'That'll do me – I need all the blessings I can get. What have you got so far?'

Rocco showed him the photo of Didier and his fellow *Maquisards*. 'Not much, I'm afraid. This man's a local in Poissons, although he doesn't originate from there. He just blew himself up with a grenade – don't ask, it's complicated.'

Desmoulins laughed. 'Christ, we heard about him. Take one idiot with a hammer and a death wish – and boom. Why the interest?'

'Because I don't think the boom was an accident.

Somebody's trying to kill him. He calls himself Didier Marthe, but that might not be his real name. Run it past anyone you can think of: police, military, medical… I can't narrow the photo down to a specific location, but it would have to be somewhere with Resistance groups operating during the war.'

'Tall order. It could be anywhere.'

'Not really. There were large parts of the country without any organised resistance. I've a feeling he'd have been part of a known group, most likely communist in leanings.'

'How do you know that?'

'He's got a line in angry left-wing rhetoric that's too practised to be put on. If you can find any historians or archivists working in the field of Resistance groups and their affiliations, they might be able to help you. Massin is chasing up the source of the photo, so that might narrow it down, too. Liaise with him via Canet if you need to.' He handed the detective his card. 'Call me when you get something.'

'Will do.' Desmoulins made more notes, then stood up. 'Sounds a lot more fun than chasing down petrol crooks. Anything else I can do?'

Rocco suddenly remembered the telephone number he and Claude had found in Nathalie Berbier's flat. He read it out and Desmoulins scribbled it down. 'Get the PTT to run it through their records. I need an address for the subscriber. It could be a Tomas Brouté but I'll take whatever they've got. And I need it fast.'

CHAPTER TWENTY-FOUR

Rocco left Desmoulins and drove back towards Poissons, stopping at an agricultural supplies depot on the way for some rubber boots. He had no intention of making them a regular part of his wardrobe, but neither did he imagine that his ventures so far into the great muddy outdoors would be his last.

Continuing his journey, he wondered if his burgeoning network of worker bees, which now included Massin, a turn of events which still struck him as deeply bizarre, would accomplish anything. Maybe he was chasing shadows over Didier Marthe, but he couldn't sit back and do nothing; he had too deep-seated a feeling that there was something there worth following up. All he had to do was tease it out into the sunlight.

He turned his thoughts to Nathalie Berbier. It seemed unreal that her death could be so blatantly denied by her father, with what amounted to the collusion of the Interior

Ministry. It was almost an insult to the poor woman's name, no matter what her lifestyle. Whether she had died by her own hand, by accident or at the hand of another, the least he could do for her was get to the truth.

He stopped off at the *marais* on his way into the village, and parked in the turning circle near the first lodge. He climbed out and did a tour of the building, testing the doors and shutters for weakness. But it was locked tight, with none of the play usually found in wooden structures. Whoever had built this place had paid particular attention to security. Perhaps it was natural, being so isolated and open to random burglars when nobody was about. Or maybe, he reflected cynically, the owners had something worth hiding.

He debated going to take another look at the Blue Pool, but decided to come back later. Whatever was there could wait. Instead, he drove to the house, surprising himself by experiencing a feeling of homecoming. Over the years his lodgings had been merely another temporary home in a long list of places to lay his head. Some had been better than others, most were unmemorable. Yet this place was different. Or was it he who was changing?

As he climbed out of the car, he saw Mme Denis standing by the fence between the two properties. She was prodding at the ground with a stick, unaware of his presence. He waved to her but she seemed too intent on her garden. He shrugged. Maybe she'd discovered Colorado beetle in her potatoes.

His pleasure at coming home was soured slightly by finding a journalist's business card tucked into the metal grill over the glass panel of the front door. It bore the logo of a regional newspaper. He tossed it aside, not surprised that they'd managed to find him. In a village this small, it would have taken just a few minutes to discover that a cop was living in their midst. And the presence of a former Paris investigator would have been a clarion call for a story.

Inside, he bagged up his laundry ready to take to the co-op, then made coffee. While it brewed, he rang Claude and asked him for the mayor's phone number.

'Is this about the ownership of the lodges?' Claude queried.

'That's right. What's his worship like?'

'He's a pompous arse, but good on paperwork. Used to be a teacher in Amiens before retiring out here. His name's Poitrel.'

The mayor answered on the second ring and Claude's summary was spot on. Poitrel's tone and words would have been more suited to a university lecture hall than a tiny village, but Rocco had come across his sort before. He remained businesslike and explained what he wanted.

'I wish I could help, Inspector,' the mayor replied loftily. 'But that property is leased through a commercial agency in Lille. If they wish to give you the information, that's up to them. If you hold on one second, I can give you their name.' A clunk as the phone was put down, and he was back within seconds. He read out the details.

'Thank you,' said Rocco. The mayor probably knew more than he was saying, but was happy to pass the buck.

'No problem, I assure you. I've tried to ascertain the ownership before – for our administrative records, you understand – but to no avail. However, the owners pay – via the agency – all the taxes and fishing licences, and even paid for laying the track into the *marais* for the benefit of other visitors and locals. So I could hardly criticise them too strongly for wanting to retain their privacy.' His tone suggested he would like nothing better if he could get away with it, preferably with a crack team of riot police to break down the doors of the lodge.

A bureaucrat through and through, thought Rocco. But at least he now had another name to follow up, an additional link in the chain. He thanked the mayor again and rang the letting agency.

'I'm sorry, but that's impossible,' said the manager. 'We receive our instructions via a private holding company and have no means of checking ownership. In any case, we have no reason to do so. If, however, you're suggesting there's a criminal connection—'

'I'm not,' said Rocco, frustrated by yet more officious smoke being blown in his face. 'Not yet, anyway. If I need to, I'll be in touch.'

He dropped the phone on its rest. Evidently Berbier wasn't the only person with something to hide. It was possible the owner of the lodge was shielding himself for tax reasons – something of a field sport in France – or to avoid the property falling into the clutches of a disenchanted marital partner. Either way, it wasn't helping his investigation.

He grabbed his coat and decided to go for a walk. He hadn't yet had an opportunity to explore the village, but now seemed a good time to do so. It might blow some fresh air through his brain as well as acquainting him with his new surroundings. On the way, he'd drop off his laundry at the co-op. Before leaving, he took out the photo of Didier and the Resistance group and placed it on the table, slipping one corner under the directory. He hadn't yet figured out its place in the scheme of things, or even if it was simply a distraction. But as the only copy, it wasn't something he wanted to misplace or get damaged. Looking at it later with a fresh eye might unlock an idea or two.

The lane into the village was deserted, as was the square. A flash of black swirled in the doorway to the church. A priest, short and well fed, scowling at Rocco as if he represented a challenge to his authority. Then he was gone, the heavy door slamming behind him with ominous finality.

No sign of Thierry, the gardener, Rocco noted, but perhaps the shock of finding what he thought was a bomb had been too much for him. He saw the odd curtain twitching as he walked along the main street, but ignored them. He was still an outsider and a cop, a double jeopardy in this environment. It was no surprise if people were reluctant to speak to him. But he did spot the plumber, Delsaire, coming out of the co-op and climbing into a battered Renault. He waved him to a stop.

'Inspector,' said Delsaire, 'found out who owns that old water tank yet?' He chuckled wryly at his own humour.

'Working on it, but nothing yet,' Rocco replied, falling in with the joke. 'I might have to call in help from HQ.' Then, before Delsaire could trump him with another one, he added, 'Do you know who owns the big lodge down on the *marais*?'

Delsaire shook his head. 'Sorry, no. I did some emergency work there once, but that was arranged via some property company. Lille, I think it was. Why?'

'What sort of work?'

'A blockage in the bath. The floor got flooded when

a guest turned the tap on and went for a walk. Probably pissed if you ask me. The place had that kind of feel to it, know what I mean?'

'Not really.' At Delsaire's quizzical look, he added, 'In Paris, I'd know what you meant. But not out here.'

'Ah, I see. Well, you know…secluded location, comfortable furniture, lots of alcohol about the place. Expensive stuff, too: whisky, vodka, rum, old Armagnac…all way above my budget. Looks a bit of a dump on the outside, but much nicer inside. Whoever owns the place spent money on it. None of it local, though. I never got a look in, apart from that one job. Everything done there comes in from outside.' He pulled a face. 'Maybe they think we country turnips can't tell a copper pipe from a cow's arse.'

'True. One other thing: do you know of anyone locally named Brouté?'

'Brouté?' Delsaire frowned. 'Unusual name. Certainly not one I've come across. Sorry.' He paused and gave Rocco a sideways look. 'As to anyone knowing about the lodges, you should try Didier Marthe. He spends enough time wandering around down there.'

Rocco thanked him for his time and watched him drive away. Delsaire had been too relaxed to be telling anything but the truth, and there could hardly be a man who knew more about the village and its inhabitants than the local plumber. That left out most other people around here. Except maybe Didier, who wasn't being any help at all.

He walked across to the co-op and went inside. Francine was assembling a large blue plastic crate of groceries, packing them carefully and ticking off each item against a list. She smiled in greeting and stopped what she was doing.

'Hello again, Inspector. Settling in all right?' She stepped through a gap in the glass-topped counter and shook his hand. 'And eating well, I hope?'

'Getting there with both,' he replied. 'It's Lucas.'

She lifted her eyebrows. 'Is that Lucas Rocco or Rocco Lucas?' Her smile was impish and Rocco felt himself flush. He had a feeling she knew perfectly well the order of his name, and was teasing.

'Lucas is my first name,' he confirmed gruffly, and looked around to cover his confusion. What the hell was a pretty woman like her doing in a place like this anyway? 'Um... I gather I should leave my laundry here.'

She nodded and took the bag from him; picked up a ticket and pen from the counter, quickly scribbled down his name and pinned the ticket to the bag. 'There. In the system. They collect tomorrow and bring it back in two or three days, depending on the workload. Capes and masks are extra, though.' She giggled and blushed self-consciously. 'Sorry – couldn't resist it. We're a long way from civilisation here. Simple minds and all that. You must find it unsophisticated... after Paris.'

'Well, it has its attractions.' He coughed, aware that it had sounded like the lamest of chat-up lines. 'Sorry...that didn't quite come out...' He stopped. She was grinning at him, her eyes dancing, and he wondered if she was like this with everyone who came calling.

'Would you like some tea?' she asked. 'I was just going to stop for lunch.'

'Oh. Right.' He nodded, unable to think of a reason to say no. 'Tea would be nice. Thanks.'

She nodded towards the rear of the shop. 'Come through.

Don't worry, I won't kidnap you and subject you to some fiendishly barbaric sacrificial ceremony in the backyard.'

'I'm sure you won't,' he replied, and thought maybe he wouldn't object too much if she did.

She invited him to take a chair in the kitchen at the back and made tea, then sat down across from him with a packet of biscuits.

'I should be a better hostess,' she said, 'and offer you sandwiches, but my mother always said that was going too far on a first meeting.' She held out the packet and Rocco took one.

'Your mother was a wise woman. What if I come back this time tomorrow?'

She lifted an eyebrow. 'We'll have to see, won't we?'

He smiled at this and sipped his tea. It was Earl Grey, which had always seemed too fragrant for his tastes. Refreshing, though, after all the coffee he'd been drinking. He wondered what to talk about. 'You run this place by yourself?'

'Yes. Business is too slow to allow me to take on any help. With the young people moving towards the cities, the population's not exactly thriving.' She shrugged. 'It wasn't my chosen line of employment, but my husband died in a factory accident eighteen months ago and I had to do something. I heard about this place closing, so I decided to give it a go. I get by.'

'I'm sorry. About your husband, I mean.'

'Thank you. It was a shock, but I'm learning to cope.' She looked at him directly. 'How about you? Can we expect to see a Rocco family moving in down the road? I can offer good rates for regular customers.'

'No. No family.'

185

'Oh, I'm sorry, I didn't...' This time it was her turn to look embarrassed.

The silence lengthened until he grasped another topic of conversation. 'I see you deliver groceries, too.' He was referring to the crate she had been preparing in the shop, and wondered whether Mme Denis would be put out if he got his deliveries directly from the source. He suspected she'd take out a hex on him.

'A few,' Francine replied, then saw what he meant. 'Oh, that's a one-off. There's a party at one of the lodges this weekend. I got a phone call saying they couldn't get the usual delivery in time, so could I help?' She rolled her eyes. 'Could I? I've been wondering how to get on their list of suppliers: I need all the customers I can get, especially the bigger spenders.'

Rocco's ears pricked up. 'Which lodge is that?'

'The main one. It's got a name but I don't recall what it is. They said to deliver the supplies and leave them at the back. A cheque is on the way.' She shrugged. 'It's a gamble, but I could always burn the place down if they don't pay.' Her expression said she was joking, but her tone sounded oddly serious.

He smiled. 'If it comes to that, let me know and I'll show you how.'

'That's very gallant of you.' Her eyes twinkled. 'Are policemen allowed to do that?'

'It's a little-known service we can perform for special members of the community. Don't tell anyone or they'll all want it done.'

'Special already, am I? I can see I'm going to have to upgrade to sandwiches after all.'

Rocco felt the heat building around his collar as the jousting progressed, and wondered where it was coming from. He was never usually this open in a woman's company until he'd got to know her better. He hid behind another question. 'Do you have the name of the person who rang you?'

Francine frowned slightly. 'Actually, I don't. Why would you be interested? It's just a delivery.'

He realised he'd jumped in with both feet and tried to pull back. 'I was just interested. I need to speak to the owners about security. But nobody seems to know who they are.' He ducked his head and drank more tea, wondering why he felt so inept in front of her. Maybe it was lack of practice.

'Is this really why you came here?' Francine put down her cup, her smile fading. 'It is, isn't it? That's why you stopped Monsieur Delsaire outside, too.'

'No, of course not—'

'So this is how big-city police work – getting people to inform on their neighbours?' Twin red marks had appeared on Francine's cheeks, and her eyes had gone dark, as if a small storm was brewing in their depths.

Rocco wondered how to rescue the situation but realised that he'd already pressed her too far. With a man, he'd have been able to batter his way past it, but with a woman – this woman…

'I'm sorry,' he said, and stood up. 'Thank you for the tea and chat.' He gestured towards the shop. 'I'll see myself out.'

He stood up and left the room, feeling her eyes on him all the way. Outside, the muted voices of children playing seemed to mock him all the way back down the lane.

CHAPTER TWENTY-FIVE

Back at the house, Rocco called Michel Santer to see if his former boss had any news of Pheron et Fils.

'I've been trying to reach you,' Santer muttered sourly. 'Where the hell have you been? Dallying with some buxom farm girl, I bet.'

Rocco felt his cheeks heat up at the memory of a few minutes ago. 'No such luck. What have you got?' He could do with something to distract him from his clumsiness.

'Your replacement finally came back with some information on that costume hire place. Christ, but he's a plodder. As much wit as my big toe and half the personality. Anyway, he says they hire out costumes to theatre and film companies, and just occasionally, to a few private clients for parties and balls, that sort of thing. For private, read posh. All pretty much above board, by the look of it.'

'Who hired the uniform?'

'That's where he came unstuck, although to be honest,

he couldn't really do much about it. They refused to tell him who hired the Gestapo uniform, said he'd have to get an order from a magistrate to make the records available. Told him to get lost.'

'On what grounds?' Rocco felt his blood pressure rise. He should have gone to see Pheron himself and wrung the details out of them.

'They said their products were hired by people who would not approve of their names being released. He didn't have the authority to push it, so I told him to leave it and get back here.'

'Tell him thank you, anyway. Would it bother you if I spoke to them?' In spite of the warning from the Ministry man, Rocco felt impatient to get on with it rather than put in an official request for a magistrate's order and wait days for it to be granted.

There was a grim tone to Santer's voice. 'I wish I could say help yourself, my son, but I can't. I just had a call from on high. Orders are to leave well alone. It seems Pheron et Fils weren't just blowing hot air; they've got friends in high places and aren't slow to call on them when they need to.'

Rocco swore silently, then thanked Santer for his help. Next he rang Massin. He was reluctant to involve the senior officer again, but he needed to call on a higher level of authority. Without it, he was stumped. He told Massin what Santer had found about the costumiers.

'And you want me to intercede and unblock it?' Massin sounded less than thrilled, and Rocco wondered if the *commissaire* was losing his taste for this investigation the closer it got to Paris and the seat of power. He wouldn't be the first officer to baulk at stepping on the toes of the

189

high and the mighty for fear of losing future promotion prospects.

'It's the only solid lead we have.' Rocco decided to remind him of the facts. 'Nathalie Berbier was wearing a costume hired from Pheron et Fils for a party I believe was held at a secluded lodge in Poissons. So far we haven't come even close to finding out who organised it, who owns the lodge or who – apart from Berbier herself – was even present. It's like wrestling smoke – and Bayer-Berbier didn't make things any easier by claiming the body.' Nor, he wanted to add, did the magistrate who signed the papers, nor the unknown senior official who just put the block on Pheron et Fils being approached again. He also wanted to relay to Massin what Rizzotti had said to him about the barbiturate levels being ill-founded, but decided to hold off on that for a while. If it became unavoidable, he'd let it out and Rizzotti would have to take his chances.

'I'll see what I can do,' Massin said finally, adding carefully, 'but you should be aware of how this might be viewed in official circles.'

'How do you mean?'

'You are not, shall I say, unknown for clashing with authority.'

'That's diff—'

'And, as investigating officer on this case, already dismayed at being transferred to an unknown rural patch from your post in Paris, you were further annoyed by the dead body being claimed before you could complete your findings. You skirted round formal channels and clashed with Berbier, suspecting – not unreasonably, perhaps – that there was something being concealed about this young woman's unfortunate demise.' Massin paused. 'Am I wrong?'

'It's not like that.'

'But you can see how it might look to other eyes.'

Rocco sighed. Massin was right. It would look like a pissed-off inspector throwing his dummy from the pram at being dumped out in the sticks and imagining all manner of conspiracies. End of career, probably, helped along by Berbier and his buddies from the Interior Ministry.

'Does this mean you're dropping it?'

'Inspector Rocco.' Massin sounded suddenly cool. 'I would appreciate it if you did not insult my integrity.' The connection went dead.

Rocco ate a solitary lunch of a cheese sandwich, wishing he was sharing it with Francine, and mulled over what Massin had said. He still wasn't sure what game the senior officer was playing, and was half-expecting to find himself being pulled in by a squad from the Ministry and consigned to obscurity and a job counting *képis.* Whatever was going on in the background, he still had a job to do and could not allow himself to be derailed from his investigation.

He finished his lunch and called Claude. He needed the man's local knowledge.

'Tree stumps,' he said shortly. 'How do they get rid of them round here?'

'They dig them out, mostly,' Claude replied. 'The impatient ones dump petrol on them and let them burn out, but most just use muscle and do it the hard way, digging down through the roots or dragging them out with horses or a tractor. Why? You thinking of going into the land clearance business?'

'Not me. How about the really impatient ones. What do they do?'

Claude hesitated. 'You mean explosives, don't you?'

'Jesus.' Rocco felt his spirits flag. Maybe Didier hadn't been lying after all.

'There's the odd one uses dynamite,' Claude confirmed with reluctance. 'Put a stick under the root bowl and retire to a safe distance. Bam – problem solved.'

'Where would they get it?'

'There are one or two quarries in the region. Could be from them – I doubt their records are as reliable as they should be. Apart from that, I wouldn't know. Who are you asking about?'

Rocco explained about his conversation with Didier. 'If he did have plastic at his place, it does away with my theory that someone was trying to kill him.'

Claude made a soft noise over the line. 'He's lying. Think about it: that miserable cretin can lay his hand on more explosive material than the national armoury. Why would he need to risk buying dynamite from a dodgy source? Furthermore, he's never blown any stumps out because he doesn't need to clear the land. Only farmers do that.'

'You sure?'

'Positive. Any explosion on his land would be heard around the village – just like the one that blew off his hand. Ask anyone, they'll tell you.'

Rocco had been suckered. Didier had taken advantage of him being new to the village to spin him a story, probably on the basis that, to a city cop, it sounded perfectly reasonable and not worth checking further.

'What did he say about the photo?' asked Claude.

'That's the odd thing. I don't think he'd ever seen it before.'

'Really? It was on the board in his house.'

'I know. If he's telling the truth, then someone else put it there – possibly the same person who tried to kill him. Unsettle him first by reminding him of the past...then bam.'

'Christ, this is getting complicated. What next?'

'We check and recheck our facts. Can you meet me down at the Blue Pool in twenty minutes? There's something I want to look at.'

He went out to the car and saw Mme Denis on the other side of the hedge, hoeing her garden. She waved at him.

'You seem very busy, Inspector,' she said genially. 'This place hasn't seen such drama in years.'

'Sorry about that,' he replied. 'I'll try to get it under control as quickly as possible.'

She shrugged fatalistically. 'Good luck with that. I've lived here long enough to know everyone and everything, and do you know what, Inspector? There are always surprises. Always.'

He nodded at this touch of philosophy and got in the car, then drove down to the *marais*. The village was quiet. He eyed the co-op as he passed through the square, but the windows reflected blankly back at him.

Parking on the turning circle near the big lodge, he put on his new boots. There was no sign of Claude yet, but that was fine: he wanted time by himself to think things through. As he made his way through the undergrowth to the Blue Pool, he felt clumsy in the unaccustomed footwear, but at least it kept out the water soaking the ground underfoot.

He circled the pool several paces back from the edge, studying the various directions of approach from the *marais*. It quickly became obvious that there were few options available, either because of impenetrable bushes or stretches of soft ground oozing with dangerous-looking mud. Even a heavy plank of wood, no doubt having once been used to negotiate a stretch of soft ground, was being absorbed gradually under its own weight.

He moved closer to the pool, narrowing down the most likely direction, then went round to the opposite side and knelt down, running his eye over the long grass on the far side to see if there were any telltale signs from this perspective. He could just about make out a dark, zigzag pattern showing through the undergrowth where someone had walked or run, but it was too close to where he and Claude had stood on their first visit to be certain.

A car engine disturbed the silence. He recognised the urgent whine of a 2CV, followed by the tinny slamming of a door. Moments later came the tramp of footsteps and Claude appeared.

Rocco bent back to his task. Then he felt a jolt. A clump of earth had been torn away from the edge of the pool on the far side, like a bite from a pie crust. It was too distinctive to be mistaken, but had he been on the other side, where Claude was now standing, it would have been hidden by the overhanging grass. He stood up and walked round until he reached the spot, beckoning Claude to come closer. He needed another set of eyes to witness this. The grass here was flattened, and when he bent over to examine the edge of the pool, he felt the familiar thrill of the hunter finding a clue.

'See what you read from this.' He stood aside to allow Claude to examine the spot, and ran his eyes over the surrounding area of undergrowth. He could almost picture the scene like a shot from a movie.

Nathalie Berbier must have run through the grass from the direction of the lodges, her path just about visible from the bent and broken stems. Too heavy and coarse to adjust themselves easily, they had browned and gone dry, leaving a faint but discernible trail. Unaware of the danger in her path, she had run straight towards the pool. Propelled by whatever forces were driving her, she had been unable to stop herself in time, and had plunged over the edge. The water soaking into her uniform and whatever drink or substances had been in her system would have done the rest.

'Did she fall or was she pushed?' murmured Claude, reading the situation.

'I think she fell. If she was pushed, there would be signs of a struggle.'

He bent down alongside Claude and peered over the edge. As he had seen before, the sides were clear white with a blue tinge, curving gently like the inside of a giant cereal bowl, the surface smooth and unbroken all the way down to the dark funnel in the centre. He reached below the surface and dug his fingertips into the side, feeling a shiver worm its way down his back as they sank without resistance into the soft texture. There was no chance of anyone pulling themselves out with this stuff, especially a woman weighed down by wet clothing. He pulled out his hand and rubbed his fingers together.

Chalk. Soft and slimy. He wiped his hands on the grass and remembered the white substance on the dead woman's shoes and what he'd taken as scuff marks on her uniform.

'How did you arrive at this?' Claude sounded faintly sceptical, but Rocco could tell he agreed with the scenario. 'You had one quick look days ago.'

'Random signs, that's all.' He explained about the fresh water in Nathalie Berbier's lungs and stomach and the chalk marks on her shoes. 'This is the only place where fresh water gathers. Anywhere else and her lungs and clothing would have been full of silt.'

'Like the lakes.'

'Exactly.'

'I see. But how did the killer get her out without leaving more signs? She'd have been very heavy.'

Rocco led him to the other side of the pool to where he'd seen the discarded plank of wood. He had no proof of what he was thinking, but it seemed a logical explanation. 'I once saw a river cop use a ladder to get a drunk out of the Seine. No way he could have lifted him, so he used leverage instead. The killer would have slid this under the body, then dragged her along the plank until he could lift her clear.' He peered along the roughened wood and plucked a thread of dark cloth from the grain along one edge. 'There. Minimal traces left behind and just possible for a strong man to do.'

'Or two.'

Rocco shook his head. He'd discounted that possibility, although with no rational explanation other than simple gut feel. 'Two men would have left more traces: heavier treads, more difficult to conceal. This was one man being very careful.'

'So why take her to the cemetery? He could have dumped

her in one of the lakes or buried her in the marsh. She'd have been gone for good.'

'Because burying a body would have taken time. He might have been seen. And bodies have a nasty habit of reappearing. Dumping it elsewhere also took the connection away from the *marais*.'

'And the lodges.'

'And the lodges.' He turned and looked in the direction of the big lodge, hidden by the trees.

'Doesn't seem right, does it?' breathed Claude, as they walked back to their cars. 'Not in this place.'

'It never does,' Rocco said calmly. It was always the seemingly innocuous which carried the greatest threat. He'd learnt that very quickly in Indochina, a country of beauty and innocence masking horrible dangers. Only this time it wasn't some exotic and harmless-looking jungle clearing hiding unseen traps: sharpened stakes tipped with excreta to infect anyone who stepped on them. This was the equivalent to home territory, greenery just like that familiar from his boyhood. There were no poisonous dangers lurking here other than the occasional rabbit snare, no mines waiting for a careless footfall, no trained killers waiting in the greenery with AK47s set on rapid fire.

Just a clear, blue pond where nobody dared swim.

CHAPTER TWENTY-SIX

Rocco walked back into the house after saying goodbye to Claude and was greeted by the phone ringing. He sat down to take the call, then noticed the Resistance photo lying on the floor.

'Lucas? Hello…are you there?' It was Viviane.

'Yes. Sorry – I was just checking something.' He bent and picked up the photo, and looked around the room, the hairs on his neck rising. Everything looked normal, untouched, as he had left it…yet he was certain he'd wedged the snap under the phone directory.

'You wanted to speak to Sophie Richert,' Viviane continued, 'in number 10…across the hall from that young Berbier woman.'

'I did?' Rocco had to stop and think, separating in his mind the murder of Nathalie Berbier from the attempted murder of Didier Marthe. He'd found in the past that working cases in tandem like this caused moments of confusion, but never quite the way it was just now. Perhaps because these two had occurred in the same small corner of France, rather than in unconnected streets in the capital, often as distinct as foreign countries in appearance, atmosphere and population. 'I do, you're right.'

'Well, you'd better hurry. She's on her way to America for several months. She wasn't keen on being involved, but Nathalie was a friend and I said she could trust you. She'll be at the airport this evening at six. Can you meet her there?'

He looked at his watch. The airport meant Orly, on the other side of Paris. It would be a bastard of a drive but he could make it – just – as long as there were no delays. There was no guarantee that the young woman would have anything useful to add to his meagre stock of information on the background of Nathalie Berbier, but he couldn't pass up the opportunity to talk to her – especially as she seemed to be instigating it herself. In any case, once she was in the States, she might just as well be in another world and beyond his reach.

'Tell her I'll meet her in the bar near check-in,' he told Viviane. He remembered the small bar, usually crowded and smoke filled, the final watering hole for nervous flyers and, in his experience, criminals fleeing overseas one step ahead of the law. It wasn't the ideal place to conduct a murder interview, but it was the only familiar spot he could think of at short notice. 'Thanks. I owe you.'

He dropped the phone back on the stand and changed his muddied clothes for clean slacks and a dark shirt. As he grabbed his coat ready to head out to the car, his attention was drawn to the French window looking out over the rear garden.

A corner of the net curtain was jammed in the frame.

* * *

199

Orly Airport was a busy rush of travellers, meeters and greeters when Rocco dumped his car in a convenient slot and hurried into the main terminal building. It was just on six o'clock.

He entered the bar across from check-in. The atmosphere was as he recalled, heavy with smoke and chatter, the floor around the tables littered with luggage. A young woman was sitting by herself in one corner, glancing at her watch. She wore a short, red dress printed in an interlocking triangular pattern, and knee-high white boots which Rocco thought might be plastic. He assumed she was what young fashion workers thought of as stylish and cutting-edge. As he got close, he saw she was studiously ignoring the attentions of two men at the next table who were trying inelegantly to chat her up. Neither had luggage or looked remotely like travellers and he pegged them as professional airport lizards, trawling for an easy mark.

'Miss Richert?' He smiled at her and saw her react with a mixture of wariness and relief. 'Lucas Rocco.' He didn't want to use his title unless absolutely necessary.

One of the two men leant over and said loudly, 'Hey – granddad. Try your own age range, why don't you?'

Rocco turned and looked down at the men, then nodded his head towards the exit. If he was right about who and what they were, they would read the signs and move on. It took a moment or two, but they finally got the message, stood up and walked away without looking back.

'That was neat,' Sophie murmured. He wasn't sure if it was meant as a compliment until she added, 'The times I've wished I was with a guy who could do that.'

'It doesn't always work,' he said with a smile. 'Sometimes

200

I have to start throwing furniture. Can I get you a drink?'

'If you want. Whisky.' She had the lazy confidence of someone older, although he guessed she was no more than twenty-five. Maybe that was what going to America did for you: gave you years beyond your years. He couldn't recall what he'd been like at twenty-five, only that he'd probably been full of vim and holding a gun, which lends confidence of a different kind.

He caught the eye of a waiter and ordered two whiskies, then sat down across from her with a view of the concourse where the two men had gone. He didn't usually drink while working, but since he was – technically, at least in terms of time – off duty, he decided to relax the rule.

'Thank you for agreeing to speak to me, Miss Richert. How much time do you have?'

She checked her watch, an expensive gold timepiece, and shrugged with near condescension. 'Less than thirty minutes. How can I help?'

He paused while the waiter served their drinks, then said, 'You know what happened to Nathalie?' He decided to cut straight to the chase: there was neither time nor reason to be circumspect.

She nodded and sipped her whisky. 'She drowned in some river. I still can't believe it. She was such…fun. It's horrible.' She shivered and tossed her head. 'I'm glad I'm going away. Is that unkind, wanting to put it all behind me?'

'No. It's normal. How well did you know her?'

'Pretty well, actually. We were friends, I suppose.'

'So you moved in the same circles.'

'You mean did I know her other friends?' Sophie was quick to catch on and her reply was cautious. 'We had a lot of the same friends and acquaintances here in town, but we didn't live in each other's pockets.' She toyed with the glass and Rocco guessed she really didn't like whisky, that ordering it had been for show…or because of nerves.

He beckoned the waiter over and asked him to bring a glass of white wine. The man nodded and wheeled away, returning moments later with the order. He shifted the other whisky to Rocco's side of the table.

Sophie eyed Rocco for a moment, then shrugged and took a sip of the wine. 'That's better. Thanks. What were we talking about?'

'I need to know who Nathalie mixed with,' he replied curtly, aware of time ticking away. 'Not her "town" pals; not her beauty stylist or favourite pastry chef, or who cut her toenails. But who might have taken her away to a weekend party in the country with a bunch of strangers so she could end up dead. Like that.'

She frowned at his abrupt tone. 'Is this her father's thing?' she queried defiantly. 'Trying to make out it was something it wasn't?'

'I don't follow.'

'Well, it was a silly accident, wasn't it? Nathalie got pissed and fell into some water. Or is the great Bayer-Berbier saying it's something else? Are you under his orders? He's got a lot of influence with the cops, everybody knows that.' She took a slug of wine and glared at him, then looked away in contempt.

Rocco felt like slapping her. Could young people really be so arrogant in the face of death? He hadn't seen any news reports, so had no way of knowing what Sophie might have read or heard about Nathalie's demise. Whatever it was, Berbier *père* had probably put out a carefully sanitised version of events, avoiding any mention of drugs or violence. As if in their world, being merely *drunk* and dead was so much better than any other kind.

'Actually,' he said softly, projecting the words so that there was no possible misunderstanding, no way she could continue to treat the matter so coolly, 'Nathalie was murdered.'

He waited for the realisation to sink in; for the 'M' word to be analysed and understood in whatever narrow, selective thesaurus her world permitted. When it finally hit home, it was signalled by a large tear rolling down her cheek.

'That was unkind,' she whispered. And suddenly the defiant, arrogant light was gone, leaving behind a young woman facing up to the harsh reality of loss.

He nodded. 'You're right, it was. I'm sorry. But I need you to know what happened because I'm trying to find out who was responsible for your friend's death. And I only have...' he looked dramatically at his watch '...twenty minutes of your valuable time left.' It was rough but he was suddenly tired of having to tiptoe through the tank traps of convention and etiquette.

'How would I know who could do that?' she protested, her voice suddenly shrill as if finally tapping into a source of anger. 'God, I didn't know she'd been...you know. She loved life, for Christ's sake. She was fun to be with, and how anyone could hurt her I don't know! I don't know any of that shit!'

Rocco allowed her to vent. He was aware of heads turning their way, and saw the bar manager approaching like a large missile, twisting impressive shoulders and hips skilfully between the tables and chairs. Rocco waited until he was almost upon them, then whipped out his badge and waved him away without a word. The man turned and went back to the bar.

Rocco leant across the table, giving her one last chance to help. 'Listen, I want you to start talking about who your friend knew, who else I can talk to. Because I really want to find out who killed her. For instance, who or what is Tomas Brouté?'

It meant something, he could see that. It was evident in her face, in the way her eyes flickered at his mention of the name.

Yet she shrugged and glanced at her watch as if it meant nothing. 'Look, I'm sorry, but I can't help you. I've never heard of him.' She leant forward to pick up her bag, unwilling to look at him.

'OK.'

She seemed surprised. 'I can go?'

He shook his head. 'No. In fact,' he stood up and planted himself squarely in her way, bending and putting his face within inches of hers, 'if you don't help me *right now*, I'll stop you getting on the plane. I'll also inform the American immigration authorities that you are an undesirable, and that you're helping with my enquiries into the brutal murder of a young girl. Do you have any idea how long it will be before you *might* be allowed into the States after that? Try years – ten if you're lucky, more likely fifteen. The Yanks have strangely harsh views about importing potential foreign criminals, believe it or not.'

Sophie's mouth fell open with a gasp. 'You can't do that! My father works for the Finance Ministry—'

'No shit. You try pissing higher than me again and I'll get a couple of uniformed cops in here to haul you out in cuffs. It won't be pretty and I doubt Daddy will be impressed with you dragging his name through the news.'

She sank down slowly back onto her seat, her stunned expression betraying the realisation that Rocco wasn't playing.

'What do you want to know? I don't know what I can tell you.'

Rocco sat and pushed the wine glass towards her. She took a sip, her face ashen.

'Tomas Brouté,' he repeated. 'You recognised the name.'

'No.' She shuddered. 'Yes. At least, I've never met him. He's just a name Nathalie mentioned a couple of times... someone on the phone.'

'What was the connection between them?'

'Brouté arranges things for people. He's a middleman.'

Rocco felt his gut tighten. 'Things? What kind of things?'

'Events. Parties. Weekends.' Sophie looked sick. 'He was a creep. She hated him.'

'She said that?'

'She didn't need to. I saw her face whenever she was talking to him.'

'What sort of parties?'

'Drinking, talk – music, mostly, stuff like that.'

'And when it wasn't mostly stuff like that?'

She shook her head. 'Can't you guess? You're a cop.' She ducked her head and looked as if she were about to throw up.

'Did you go to them – the non-talk ones?'

'No! Never, I promise. It all sounded so…sordid. Nathalie was promised money if she went along and helped things go with a swing. She thought it sounded fun. I thought it would be full of rich old men looking for young girls to screw.'

'What made you think that?'

'Because I knew another girl who went to one and she said it was exactly like that.' She waved a hand. 'And please don't ask me who *that* was – she died of pneumonia in a clinic in Grasse two weeks ago.'

Rocco let it drop: if he had to pursue that one, it would be easy enough to do so later.

'You said Nathalie was promised money. Why would she need it – her father's rich?'

'Her father's a pig. So are his friends.'

In the background an announcement called for flights to New York. Sophie didn't react.

'Did you know Nathalie was pregnant?'

Her big eyes settled on him. She nodded. 'She started puking in the mornings; it was pretty obvious. When I asked her she didn't deny it. She was terrified it would become public.'

'Did she tell you who the father was?'

Another tear rolled down her cheek, and she brushed at it angrily. 'She said she didn't know. She didn't have a regular boyfriend – not like that.'

So, more than one possibility. Rocco wasn't surprised. 'No boyfriend you knew of, you mean?'

'No. We were close enough by then. If she got pregnant, it wasn't a boy.' The way she said 'boy' implied innocence, civility – a whole world away from any other kind. She finished her drink and pushed the glass away. 'She talked about getting rid of it, but she wouldn't have dared tell her father and didn't have any of her own money.'

An abortion. That would take a lot of money, doing it properly. Before and after the event. But was she desperate enough to go to these parties to earn cash for a stay in a clinic? Maybe so. Suddenly he began to see a possible motive for a young woman's murder. If she had approached the child's father – at least, the possible father – for help, the man might have seen a scandal coming and reacted with fatal consequences. It made sense and wouldn't be the first time it had happened.

'How many of these parties did she attend?'

'Four or five, I think. The first about three months ago, then every few weeks after that. Not many. She hated them in the end...but I don't think she had much choice.' Sophie stared into the distance, twisting her fingers together. Rocco finally let her go and watched her drag her way across the concourse, all ego and arrogance deflated like a burst tyre. He almost felt sorry for her.

It was going to be a long flight to New York.

CHAPTER TWENTY-SEVEN

'Lucas?' It was the voice of Detective René Desmoulins echoing down the line and dragging Rocco from a troubled sleep. He threw back the covers and stood up, joints protesting after the long drive to Orly and back the previous evening. He checked the time. Eight-thirty. God, he'd slept late again. It was becoming a habit.

'What have you got?'

'Not much yet – and nothing from official records on a Tomas Brouté. It's not an uncommon name, but not from this neck of the woods. Further south there are a few, and down on the Atlantic coast, but none called Tomas that I could find.'

'OK, no matter.' He rubbed at his scalp, feeling deflated. One pace forward and two back. Still, at least he had progressed slightly with the Berbier killing. Small mercies.

'Before you go,' Desmoulins said quickly, perhaps sensing his disappointment. 'I ran a check on that phone number you gave me. It's actually registered to a Jean-Paul Boutin at 3, Rue d'Albert in Poissons.'

The information brought Rocco fully awake. Where the hell was Rue d'Albert? He still hadn't managed to get a clear view of the layout of Poissons-les-Marais, as simple as it was. It had one through road, a square and maybe two or three lanes, one of them Rue Danvillers where he lived. He'd have to check with Claude later. 'Good work. See what you can find on that name, will you?'

'I already did that through the local registry. It's not much help, though.'

'Try me.'

'J-P Boutin died two years ago and the house has no current occupant listed.'

'You sure about that?' Rocco strode through to the kitchen area, dragging the telephone wire after him. 'The records aren't out of date?' He knew that local files were notoriously unreliable in parts of the country, relying on overworked administrative clerks toiling with ancient paper-and-card systems to keep them updated. With tight budgets and untrained personnel, it was an uphill struggle which had caused many a police investigation to flounder, starved of current detail about people and their movements.

'I double-checked. The only way to make sure is to go find the place and take a look. You want me to do it?'

'No need. It's just down the road from me. Anything from Massin on the photo shop?'

'Nothing yet. I'll chase him up.'

Rocco disconnected and dialled Claude's number. 'Boutin, Jean-Paul,' he said without preamble. '3, Rue d'Albert. You know him?'

'Jean-Po? Sure. He's dead,' said Claude. 'He lived along the main street – that's Rue d'Albert. You working beyond the grave now?'

'You could be more right than you know. Meet me there in fifteen minutes.'

'Make it twenty and I'll bring coffee.'

Rocco put down the receiver and got dressed, grateful for Desmoulins and his desire to work, and Claude for his perception. The combination of helpers might make this job a whole lot easier.

He walked down to the village centre and along the main street. He saw Francine outside the co-op, arranging a display of fruit. She looked slim and lithe, dressed in a skirt and blouse. He waved when she looked up but received a cool look in return. He dropped his hand and walked on.

At least she hadn't thrown rotten fruit at him.

There were few other people about and no traffic. A paper bag blew across in front of him, catching on a telegraph pole and fluttering in the breeze. It felt like a scene from a western movie, where the white hat walks towards certain death and dubious glory against the black hats at the other end of town.

Cue a cowboy's lament.

Claude was standing by his car outside a ragged plaster-faced cottage with shuttered windows. Posters had been plastered all over the available surfaces, displaying everything from soft drinks to the latest appearance of the overmuscled Shadow Angel and his fellow wrestlers.

Claude handed Rocco a mug of coffee and gestured at the cottage. 'This is it. Not much to look at, I'm afraid.

Boutin left it to a daughter nobody's been able to find yet. What's the story?'

Rocco sipped his coffee, then told him what Desmoulins had found. Claude looked dumbfounded at the idea of the man who had lived here being connected in any way with Nathalie Berbier.

'Jean-Po? You're kidding me. I knew the man. He was a bit reserved, didn't talk much, but he was just an ordinary man. No side, no attitude. Worked on the railways as an inspector and kept himself to himself.'

'Yet he had a telephone. Not many people do, here.'

'That's a surprise, I'll grant you. Could have been part of the job, though.'

Rocco tried the front door. The wood was weather-worn but solid, as if fastened firmly on the inside, with no play in it. Bolts, he guessed, top and bottom.

He stepped back and checked either way along the street. The cottage stood on the corner of the main street and the lane leading to Didier Marthe's house. To his left the street curved over a slight rise towards Claude's end of the village, while to his right a farm building and a few houses led back towards the co-op and the café, which was out of sight around a bend in the road. A telephone pole stood a few metres away, with a wire stretching across to the eaves of the Boutin cottage.

'How did Boutin die?'

'He tripped and fell on his way back from the café one night. They reckoned he'd had a heavy night at the bar. He was unsteady but otherwise OK. Someone thought they heard a car go by at about the same time but we never found any trace of one. He'd hit his head on a kerbstone, so it was written down as an accident while under the influence.' Claude pulled a face. 'Poor sod. A lonely life cut short.'

Rocco finished his coffee and handed the mug back. 'I don't suppose you have a crowbar in your car?'

'Actually, I do. What for?'

'I want to get inside. Find the phone.'

Claude looked doubtful. 'Shouldn't we check with the mayor first?'

'Only if you want a lecture on town hall semantics. Is there a back way in?'

Claude went to his car and produced a large crowbar, then led Rocco down the adjacent lane to the back of the cottage. A wooden door gave way with a good push to a small back garden, overgrown with weeds and bordered at the end by a wattle-and-daub barn or storehouse.

'That's Didier's barn,' said Claude.

Rocco put his shoulder against the back door of the cottage. Like the front, it was solid and unyielding. He tried the shutters. They felt a little lighter with a fraction of give. He held out his hand for the crowbar, but Claude shook his head with a grin.

'Hey, let me have some fun, why don't you?' He went to the nearest shutter and inserted the thin edge of the bar and threw his weight backwards. The wood cracked and gave way with a squeal, and the shutter popped open.

Rocco used his elbow to break the window and carefully slid his hand inside, feeling for the catch. Seconds later, he was in the darkened house and unbolting the back door to admit Claude.

If there had been any tidying up after Jean-Paul Boutin's untimely death, it had been minimal. Probably a local worthy doing an act of charity, Rocco surmised, and expecting a family member to come along soon afterwards to finish the job. Except that nobody had come, leaving a home, sparsely furnished but with evidence of a daily existence, suspended in time, a museum piece. Newspapers spilt over from a chair in one corner, while pots and pans, battered and blackened with age and heat, were piled beside the kitchen sink amid a jumble of plates and cups. A pile of men's clothing lay on another chair, stiff and crinkled, covered in a green mildew, and a pair of brown boots by the rear door were cracked and curled, the soles heavy with dried mud. Everything was layered in dust.

He nodded towards an open door showing a flight of wooden stairs. 'You check upstairs, I'll do the front.'

Claude grunted and went to take a look.

Rocco stepped through into the front room and switched on the light, surprised to find it still connected. More dust, more clothing, some empty wine bottles in a wastebasket. One armchair, a table and some bits and pieces.

But no telephone.

A clomping sound echoed through the house as Claude made a tour of the upstairs. It was, reflected Rocco, the saddest of sounds; the kind that houses shouldn't experience, but inevitably do.

He began at the front of the room and checked the walls at floor level, looking for signs of a telephone wire coming into the property. If the installation had followed the usual methods, it would come down inside one of the walls and exit somewhere convenient for the handset and cradle. All he found was a hole in the plaster where a wire might have been.

He checked the kitchen but found nothing there. He scowled. This didn't make sense.

He called to Claude. 'Is there a phone line up there?'

'No. Nothing.' Claude appeared at the top of the stairs. 'Have you tried the cellar? The door's right next to this one.'

Rocco turned off the light in the front room, then looked behind the stair door. Sure enough, there was another one. He opened it, found a light switch and descended a set of concrete steps, nose filling with the musky smell of mildew, damp and rodents. A bare light hung from the ceiling and revealed an empty, brick-lined room, unplastered and cold. Whatever might have been stored here once had been cleared out.

He found the wire in the top rear corner. It had been channelled down the wall from upstairs, and was barely visible in the poor light. He followed it with his fingers, but instead of it leading downwards, it took a sudden turn and went towards a small vent on the cottage wall on a level with the back garden.

Suddenly, Rocco knew where it was heading. 'Clever bastard!' He ran back upstairs to where Claude was waiting and switched off the light. 'Someone's been very astute. Come with me.' He led the way outside and turned left, then knelt down by the back corner of the building beside the air vent.

The wire was just visible coming through the vent, before dropping down and disappearing underground.

He looked towards the end of the garden, where it butted up against the barn. 'We'll have to do some digging,' he said, indicating the wire's probable direction, 'to see where this goes.'

Claude looked mystified for a second, then he realised what Rocco was saying. 'You think Didier took over Jean-Po's phone? I didn't see one in his house.'

'You weren't meant to. I think he broke in here when Boutin died and nobody came to claim the place, and re-routed the wire to his house. Nice free service and nobody the wiser.'

'But that doesn't mean he's connected to this Tomas Brouté... I mean, this is *Didier* you're talking about!'

'So?'

'But the man's a moron...he plays with bombs, for God's sake!'

'Which means,' Rocco pointed out, 'he's probably unhinged but not entirely stupid. He'd have the nous to rewire a phone from one house to another, no problem. That's why he planted it underground.'

Claude whistled. 'Out of sight, out of mind. Jesus, that is clever.'

Rocco picked up the crowbar and dug the sharpened end into the hardened soil around the base of the house, creating a small trench near the wire. Seconds later, he was able to pull the wire upwards, and was rewarded by seeing it moving away from the house towards the barn. Within minutes, they had reached the barn's wall, where they dug down and found where the wire had been fed through a hole in the plaster.

CHAPTER TWENTY-EIGHT

Minutes later, they were deep inside Didier's barn, clearing away a mountain of old farm tools, rotting hessian sacks, rusting bicycles, a seed drill and several worn car tyres. When they reached ground level and brushed away a thick layer of soil, it revealed the wire coming through the wall and disappearing under the floor. Using the crowbar, Rocco dug down just enough to confirm the direction the wire was going in.

'Straight towards the house,' he said. 'Come on.'

The building was a sorry mess, with the windows empty of glass and the shattered front door barely staying upright. Rocco kicked it open and began a search of the building, opening cupboards, moving mounds of clothing, old papers and broken household furniture. The air was foetid and nauseous, every item layered with a coating of grease and dust, with no apparent order to anything. Didier Marthe evidently lived his life in chaos, picking up things as and when he found or needed them, then casting them aside where he stood. In spite of that, it took very little time to search the downstairs. The upstairs was even easier, consisting of two bedrooms, both empty and filthy with age and neglect.

There was no sign of a telephone.

Rocco returned downstairs. Claude was inspecting a narrow cupboard close by the back door. It was fitted with a bolt and latch, but had been left open with a strong padlock hooked through the eye. Inside were the only clean items in the house. One was a conventional side-by-side twin-barrelled shotgun, the metal and butt scratched and pitted; the other was shorter, with up-and-over barrels, and had been well oiled and maintained, with a decorative stock and inlaid butt.

Rocco took out both weapons and checked them. Unloaded but clean. The smaller gun was light, balanced and comfortable to the grip. He wondered how a man like Didier Marthe, scratching a living from dismantling ancient ordnance, could afford a superior piece like this.

He replaced the weapons and locked the cupboard and moved over to the one entrance he hadn't been able to investigate. The cellar door was solid, with a large lock, and he noticed something he hadn't seen before: that the door frame had been reinforced, probably where the wood had rotted and given way over the years. Given the state of the rest of the house, he couldn't see why Didier had bothered.

'No key?' said Claude.

'No.' He was guessing that Didier was a one-trick pony: if he'd found a way of concealing the wire in the Boutin house, he'd use the same trick in reverse here. Which meant it would emerge somewhere underground – in the cellar.

'We going to break it down?' Claude was swinging the crowbar expectantly, eyeing the door with a faint smile. 'Wouldn't take that much, not the way I feel.'

But Rocco shook his head. He had a bad feeling about this house. Something wasn't right. Everything he'd seen so far had been too easy, too open and obvious. Yet all the indications about Didier's character said the complete opposite. Which meant they were only seeing what they were meant to see.

He pressed against the door. Immoveable. No give whatsoever. Even in new houses, doors gave a little. In old hovels like this, they flexed like paper. 'No. This is too easy. If Didier goes to the trouble of locking this cellar door, what is it that he doesn't want anyone to see?'

'The telephone?'

'Probably. But what else? He plays with bombs, you said that yourself. What's down there that would warrant a secure door like this?'

Claude's eyebrows shot up. 'You think he might have booby-trapped it?' He stepped back a pace, licking his lips. 'He's certainly crazy enough, I'll give you that. Anyone who'd do it to a bridge to stop kids trespassing is hardly sane, right?'

'Maybe.' Rocco broke off as a car drew up in the yard outside. Doors slammed, followed by footsteps approaching. As a shadow appeared in the doorway, he reached into his coat and put his hand on his gun.

It was a uniformed officer with a colleague a few feet behind him. Both looked wary and had their hands on their weapons. The lead man, tall and thin with a heavy, drooping moustache, waved his colleague to move to the side to cover him and gave Rocco a questioning look. 'Stand still, please. Who are you?'

Rocco told him, and the man relaxed, nodding at Claude. 'That's a stroke of luck. *Commissaire* Massin says to get you to call in if we see you.'

'You came all the way here for that?' He wondered what could be so urgent, and whether Berbier had found another way of firing a shot across his bows, this time for good.

'Hardly, no. It seems the owner of this place – Didier Marthe? – did a runner from the hospital. He's wanted on charges of using unauthorised explosives...and now theft and criminal assault with an offensive weapon.'

'What did he do?'

'He smacked a male cleaner with a metal tray. Took out a row of teeth and damn near caused him to choke to death. Then he stole his clothes, wallet and car keys and locked him in a cupboard before going on the run. It took an hour for the cleaner to be missed, so Marthe could be almost anywhere. Detective Desmoulins said we should try here in the village first in case he heads back this way. Other units are checking the roads. What's the story?'

'We're not sure yet. But you can probably add phone fraud to the charges, with more to follow.'

The man lifted his eyebrows. 'Sounds like a real one-man crime wave.' He looked around the room with distaste. 'Christ, what a dump.' He signalled for his colleague to return to the car. 'We'll head back, see if we can spot him on the way.'

Rocco nodded and watched them go. He didn't give much for their chances: wherever Didier Marthe had disappeared to, he would be making sure that the car he'd stolen stayed well hidden.

As they left, he saw an old, mud-encrusted shoe on the floor. He nudged it so that it was touching the cellar door, then followed Claude out into the yard.

They made their way back to the main street, Claude looking perturbed. 'I don't get it. I don't know Didier that well, but all this seems so...' He stopped, lost for words.

'Unbelievable?' Rocco suggested. 'Out of character?' He shook his head. 'People are never quite what they seem. It's always the quiet ones, the loners, who come up with the big surprises.' He stopped and looked back towards the house, a ramshackle place tucked away down a side street in the middle of nowhere. Like so many other houses on the outside, yet with a big difference on the inside. Something told him that so far, they had not even come close to knowing all there was to know about Didier Marthe.

Back home, he found another card from another journalist, this time a radio station. The vultures clearly hadn't tired of trying to find a story. He tossed it aside and rang Massin to fill him in on what he and Claude had discovered about the telephone switch. 'I can't fathom out yet where it all fits, but the number assigned to Boutin was written down in Nathalie Berbier's flat alongside the name Tomas Brouté.' The moment he said it, he remembered too late that he had not told Massin about his visit to the Félix Faure address.

There was a lengthy silence, then Massin said softly, 'How could you know that?'

He thought about lying, but decided against it. Lies begat lies and soon he'd be knee-deep in them with no way of explaining himself. And so far, for whatever reason suited him, Massin seemed to be giving him a fair degree of latitude and help. He didn't know why, but neither did he want to push that too far. He explained about their search of Nathalie's flat and the sudden arrival of the men in cars.

'Did they see you?'

'No. And we didn't leave any traces, either.'

'You trust this concierge woman?'

'More than most. She's an old friend.'

'Very well. But if Berbier hears that you gained entry to his daughter's flat, do not expect me to bail you out.' He paused, then added, 'As for the logo on the photo you found, it stands for *Agence Photos Poitiers* – APP. The shop closed during the war because of lack of chemicals for developing, but the owner opened up again afterwards before handing over to his son. He still has an interest, although he now lives near Rouen. His name is Ishmael Poudric. I told him you'd be dropping by and cleared it with the local police, so you shouldn't run into any jurisdictional problems.' He read out the address with directions, which Rocco scribbled on the reverse of the photo. He checked his watch. Nearly noon.

'I'll get right on it. Thanks.'

The phone went dead.

CHAPTER TWENTY-NINE

Ishmael Poudric lived, according to the directions given by Massin, in a village called Saint-Martin, not far out of Rouen. His home was one among a small development of bungalows with precision-ordered gardens and scatterings of ornamental stone chips in place of grass. It was clearly a retirement community for those with means who preferred a degree of comfort without the harsh labour of upkeep to spoil their idyll, and Rocco wondered at the once ingrained custom among Frenchmen of having a house with a garden and a place to grow vegetables. Maybe that was dying, too, along with its ageing adherents.

He knocked at the door and waited. Moments later a short, bearded man appeared and smiled in welcome.

'You must be the police investigator,' he said politely, and motioned Rocco to come in.

Rocco ducked his head and stepped inside, where Poudric led him through to a disordered study with piles of folders, files and boxes on every surface. Books lined the walls, mostly on the history and craft of photography. Ishmael Poudric may have retired, but he'd clearly not lost any interest in his trade.

'Is my being a cop that obvious?'

'It is when you're the only visitor I'm likely to get all week,' Poudric said dryly. 'Not that I'm complaining; after years of jumping to the requirements of others, I've got round to liking my own company.'

Rocco had explained on the telephone his reasons for calling, and he was relieved to see that Poudric had a brown cardboard folder placed squarely in the centre of his desk, with a slip of paper attached and Rocco's name scribbled across it.

He produced the photo of the Resistance group. 'As part of an ongoing investigation,' he said, 'I came across this photo. I wonder if you can shed some light on its origins?'

Poudric glanced at the photo and nodded. 'I remember it.'

'After all this time?'

'What – you think because I'm old that I'm senile? That an old man doesn't have command of his faculties anymore?' The response was quick but Rocco noted an amused glint in the old man's eyes, as if he were harbouring a secret joke. Then Poudric smiled. 'It's OK, son, I'm just teasing you. You look like a man with a sense of humour. Now, before we get down to business, would you like a drink?'

Rocco hesitated. Twice in quick succession could be interpreted in some quarters as a habit.

Poudric was persuasive. 'Join me, please. It's not often I get a visitor, and I was given a bottle of fine whisky a

223

few weeks ago which I haven't yet opened. It'll go stale otherwise.' His eyes twinkled and he lifted his eyebrows expectantly, like a child waiting for a treat.

'In that case, it would be impolite not to.'

Poudric chuckled with delight and shuffled out of the room, returning moments later with a bottle of Glenfiddich and two glasses. He poured two generous shots and raised his glass. 'To your good health, young man. And death to all our enemies.' He took a drink and sighed with pleasure. 'My God, that's good.'

'Hear, hear,' echoed Rocco, and sipped the fine malt. It was as smooth as silk, and he enjoyed the warmth as it went down, regretting that he was here on business.

Poudric smoothed his beard. 'So, how can I help? You want to know about this photo.'

'Yes. Where it was taken, who the people are…anything you can tell me.'

'Is it important?'

'I'm investigating an attempted murder.'

'Ah. In that case, let's not waste time.' Poudric took another sip of whisky, then put down the glass and rubbed his hands together. 'The shot was one of several I took in a clearing near Poitiers in June 1944. There had just been a supply drop during the night from the British and this particular group had assembled to collect the packages. I had been in contact with them over several months, mostly through a neighbour of mine – who is not in that photo, I hasten to add.'

'So,' interrupted Rocco, 'you were not part of this group?'

'God, no! Nice of you to think so, young man, but I wasn't

courageous enough for that. I did provide certain…services for them and for other groups in the region, however.'

'Photographic services.'

'Yes. The Germans had closed down my shop but I was able to secrete enough supplies to carry on my work in a limited capacity. If anyone needed a photo for documentation, for example, I was able to help. It was a very small contribution, you understand, but… Anyway, the group in this photograph was a link in a somewhat fractured communist chain across central France. Most groups were part of the FTP – the *Francs-Tireurs et Partisans* – but this lot weren't affiliated to others in the region, so I was interested in making a record of them. They argued a lot, as I recall, mostly about politics.'

'And they didn't mind you taking this picture?'

'Far from it. They were delighted.' He took another sip of whisky. 'They said they intended sending a copy to Moscow, to demonstrate how they were carrying on the worldwide fight against Fascism. Can you imagine it, the reaction of those ghastly boot-faces in the Kremlin receiving a photo like that? As if they would care!' He laughed and shook his head. 'They probably thought they'd get the Order of Lenin or some such bauble for sucking up to the Party.'

'I take it you didn't share their political views?' Rocco said.

Poudric shook his head. 'We had our own problems – like a war being fought right in our front room – without trying to overthrow our own establishment for the sake of someone else. Bloody fools.' He stared off into space for a few seconds, before saying, 'So which one are you interested in, Inspector Rocco?'

Rocco had thought about his approach on the way down. If Poudric had known the people in the shot personally, he might be reticent about divulging any information about them. He didn't want to lean on the old man, especially given the background of the photograph. And who knew what sort of chain reaction it might set in motion, with old ghosts uncovered and memories disturbed that might be best left alone? But if this was the only lead he had, leaning might be his only option.

He reached across and placed a finger on Didier's face. 'This man.'

Poudric studied it carefully. 'I remember him vaguely, but I must confess I didn't take much notice of him as a subject. He wasn't the most interesting character, you understand; always mouthing off, though, about the proletariat and the revolution – the *glorious* revolution, mind; funny how it's never sordid or inglorious or ruinous. I thought he was a relentless little bore. As you can see from where his hand is resting, he seemed to think he had some degree of ownership over the woman, although I'm not sure the feeling was reciprocated.'

'Do you recall his name?'

'There were no names. It was the one stipulation: curiosity about backgrounds or origins wasn't tolerated. It was tough enough getting this close, without pushing my luck too far. Especially with him.' He tapped on Didier's face, then pointed to another, the one face turned away from the camera. 'And this one.'

'What was so special about them?'

'Well, your man just gave off an air, you know? Hot-tempered...like a mongoose on heat, ready for a fight with anyone. Unpleasant.'

226

'And the other?'

'Ah, him. The enigma.'

'Why do you say that?'

'He didn't want his photo taken, made that clear from the start. When I took this, in fact, I thought he was going to shoot me. It was only the intervention of the others that stopped him. Silly, really – it only made me more interested.' He smiled knowingly. 'We're tarts for new subjects, we photographers.'

'What did you do?'

'I waited and took a shot when he wasn't looking. Caught him full on, almost.'

'Why an enigma, though?'

Poudric hesitated, then said, 'You'll have heard of the SOE?'

'Of course.' The Special Operations Executive. Run out of London with a staff of British, French, Belgian and other volunteers, they fed, supplied and assisted the Resistance movement all over France and beyond. Dropping by parachute into occupied territory in the dead of night, creating havoc wherever they went, their exploits had reeked of romance, daring and excitement and had long passed into the stuff of legend.

'I think he was an agent. He was passing through, organising supplies and distributing funds to the Resistance groups, one of the men said. French – I could tell that much by his speech – but definitely not a member of this lot.'

'What makes you think that?'

'Frankly? He was too clean. Too…correct. Officer class, at a guess.'

Rocco glanced again at the man, but he couldn't see how

a glimpse of a half-face could tell him anything more about Didier Marthe. Even less if the man had been part of the shadowy world of the SOE. Their secrets remained buried deep. Still, you could never tell. 'Do you have that other photo?' Perhaps if he got a look at the full face, it might stir some memories among those who knew about such things. He was thinking about Massin; he'd been part of the officer corps once. Maybe he could ask around among old colleagues. It was a long shot, but it might help tell where Didier had gone after the war, and what he had become involved in.

Links in the chain.

Poudric looked regretful. 'Not yet. It's here somewhere, I know it. But not all the photos I took have remained where they should. Like I told the woman who called here not long ago on this very subject, these things have a life of their own.'

Rocco felt a jump in his chest. 'What woman?'

'She came by a few weeks ago. Late one night, when I was in my study. She said she was a History student researching the Resistance in the war, and had read about my work building a wartime photo archive for the library. She asked if I had any shots of the communist groups around Poitiers. As it happened, I did.' He opened the brown folder and took out a copy of the print Rocco had brought with him. 'I dug it out when I knew you were coming.'

Rocco stared in disbelief. 'It's the same shot.'

'Correct. She asked if she could have it, but this was the only one I had. She was very insistent and asked me to make a copy, so I printed one off while she waited and kept a copy. She paid me, too.' He turned over the photo and tapped the logo on the back. 'Hah. I even used my old shop stamp on the back without realising it. Habits, Inspector; very hard to break, some of them.'

'She paid? That was generous, for a student. What was her name?'

'Agnès Carre. No address, though. Actually, I thought she was a little old for a student – I have trouble telling, these days. But things are changing all over, aren't they? As to where she lived,' he shrugged expansively. 'No idea. She didn't say.'

'What did she look like?'

'Plain. Smartly dressed, yet instantly forgettable. That is all I can say. Even her accent was neutral. Sorry.'

'No matter. She never came back?'

'No. I thought she might, being a student: they're always after free stuff that nobody else has got. But she never did. I told her I had other photos somewhere, but she didn't seem interested, not once she spotted this one. She said she was travelling, so I didn't press her.'

Rocco stood up. He'd got everything he was likely to get. 'It might be helpful if you could locate that other photo.' He handed Poudric his card. 'Call me when you do, please.'

Poudric took the card and studied it carefully, then looked up at Rocco with a faint frown. 'You realise that none of the people in these photographs will be able to help, don't you?'

'Why do you say that?'

Poudric shrugged. 'Simple. They were betrayed to the Germans. Every last one of them. They were captured in a raid one night when they met up for a group strategy briefing called by the SOE man. It was about a week after I took this photo.'

'What happened to them?' Rocco could guess the answer, but had to ask.

'They were shipped directly into Le Struthof for questioning.' He shook his head in sadness. 'Like most who went to that place, they never came out again.'

Rocco drove back to Poissons, feeling as if he had stumbled into one of those moments when time seemed to collapse in on itself. In spite of knowing Poudric was wrong – couldn't possibly be right unless his own eyes had deceived him – hearing the blunt news about the fate of the faces in the photograph was like a body blow.

He'd heard of Le Struthof. Natzweiler-Struthof, as it was known, was a Nazi concentration camp in the Vosges mountains, specialising in taking captured Resistance fighters from across northern Europe. Such was Hitler's malevolence towards spies and saboteurs, many went into the camp and were never seen again, victims of its infamous gas oven, their brutal fate forever denied public knowledge by the camp's poor record-keeping.

He thought about what Poudric had told him. Many members of the Resistance fell into German hands, either by carelessness, chance or betrayal, and the stories and suspicions surrounding their fate were often open to rumour, some true, some entirely false, depending on perspective. The fact was, though, that whole groups had been broken up and killed, their numbers and organisations scattered to the winds.

Was Agnès Carre, the mystery woman who had called on

Poudric, a genuine student, anxious to redress some kind of balance, or was she someone with a far deeper agenda?

And what was the explanation for Didier Marthe's face appearing in this particular group photograph? Was it merely some luckless, now dead soul who happened to bear a passing resemblance – maybe even a family member? Or was it Marthe who, by an astounding twist of luck or circumstance, had escaped being scooped up by the Germans? There could be, Rocco reasoned, a darker explanation. If it was Didier in the photo, and not just a lookalike, then it could come down to one thing: someone had learnt of his escape and, for whatever reason they harboured, had finally caught up with him, seeking some kind of retribution. It would certainly explain the attempts on his life.

The only question was, who was after him?

It was gone five by the time Rocco arrived back in a deserted Poissons. The co-op was dark as he passed by, and when he got home, there was no sign of Mme Denis. He parked the car and climbed out, and was debating taking a long bath when the familiar rattle of a 2CV sounded in the lane. It was Claude, looking harassed.

'Lucas,' he called, clambering from his car and hurrying up the path. 'I think Didier's back.'

'You've seen him?'

'No. I went back to the Boutin house earlier to secure the shutter we broke, and heard a noise from Didier's place. I didn't think much of it at the time: put it down to birds or the wind. When I'd finished at Boutin's cottage, I went round to take a look. The cupboard by the back door was open. One of the guns is gone.'

CHAPTER THIRTY

Two days later, with no further sign of Didier and no closer to solving the mystery of Nathalie Berbier's murder, Rocco was growing twitchy with impatience. Stop-and-detain bulletins had gone out on Didier Marthe, with warnings that he was armed and dangerous, but he wasn't about to hold his breath. Such bulletins often relied on the stupidity of criminals doing something to bring them to the attention of the police, rather than a thinly spread police force spotting a face in a crowd.

He had twice driven down to the *marais* and sat staring at the lodge in impotent silence, aware that if he followed his instincts and broke in, he would probably have to suffer the consequences of discovering that Massin was no longer able to help him. Yet deep inside, he knew there was a connection somewhere that could propel the case forward, if only he could risk taking the plunge. Even so, he had driven away both times, aware that ending his career here through an act of impulse would solve nothing in the long run.

He had relied on Claude to trawl the village for any snippets of gossip about Didier, but that had also proved unhelpful. The man had hardly set out to make himself popular since his arrival a few years ago and cared nothing about public opinion.

In the end, out of a sense of frustration, he rang Michel Santer, seeking any information he could provide on Philippe Berbier. Santer had the nose of a true cop and picked up information almost by osmosis. If there was anything on the industrialist, he would surely know.

'You kidding?' Santer laughed. 'You think I move in those exalted circles? The man's a living legend…and a friend of the president. I bet if you asked them, the esteemed sewer workers of Paris will tell you even his shit's squeaky clean. What are you looking for, anyway?'

Rocco didn't entirely trust the phone system to talk too openly. It wouldn't be unheard of for the Interior Ministry to have someone listening in, and he didn't want to draw Santer into a mire by association.

'Just curious,' he said vaguely, hoping Santer would catch on.

Santer did. 'Um…you ever been to Clermont? It's on Route 16 out of Paris, about twenty kilometres east of Beauvais.'

'I know it.'

'Should take you about forty minutes to get there in that battle bus of yours,' Santer continued. 'I'm due some time off. Meet me outside the town hall at noon. You can buy lunch.'

* * *

Clermont was quiet when Rocco arrived and saw Michel Santer standing looking in the window of a fabric shop near the town hall. It was just on midday.

'Thinking of taking up knitting?' said Rocco as they shook hands.

Santer smiled lugubriously, his grip warm. 'I'm saving that pleasure for when I retire. It's about as far from police work as anything else I can think of.' He nodded to a restaurant across the street. 'It's your treat, don't forget. I should warn you, I'm hungry.'

Inside the restaurant, they sat and ordered lunch. While it was being prepared, they did the small-talk ritual over drinks, discussing who had moved where and when, who was up for promotion and who was on the way out. After the food was served and the waiter retreated, Santer raised the subject that had brought them there.

'So,' he said, chewing on a slice of bloody steak. 'How are you settling down out in the sticks? Got to meet any of the local vermin yet?'

'Only the fruit rats.'

Santer raised an eyebrow and Rocco explained about his housemates.

'Jesus, how do you sleep at nights? That's creepy.'

'Actually, I'm growing used to them. They're harmless.'

'Well, good for you.' Santer sat back and took a sip of wine. 'So. Philippe Bayer-Berbier, rich bastard. What's the deal with him?'

'For a start, how did he get to be rich?'

'You aren't the first to ask that. The truth is, nobody knows for sure. He wasn't born that way: his parents were medium-rank professionals by the name of Berbier;

the Bayer bit came later – and not his wife's, either. She's deceased. You met the mother?'

'Yes. Armour-plated and vicious.'

'Also thought to be behind his social climbing. Mummy-knows-best kind of thing, I reckon.'

'You saying he added the Bayer name?' It wasn't unknown for names to be hyphenated by wives seeking a specific identity in a marriage, but Rocco had never heard of a man adding a name of his own. Mother's influence, no doubt.

'Must have done. Maybe he thought it had a better ring to it for all his moving and shaking. Anyway, he started out dealing in reconditioned army trucks after the war, when the haulage industry was on its arse. Before long he was buying into other businesses. He has the Midas touch, apparently: can't help making money.' He shrugged. 'If I was his accountant or bank manager I'd know more, but I don't. Where's all this coming from?'

Rocco gave him a quick summary of everything he knew so far, including Berbier's attempt to gloss over the death of his daughter, his call for helpers from the Interior Ministry and the information from Sophie Richert.

Santer shrugged, playing devil's advocate. 'Fair enough. Maybe he's an overprotective father. Heavy-handed, even. You can understand him being miffed about her getting knocked up – any father would be. He has a reputation to protect.' He grinned. 'Something you or I will never have to worry about.'

Rocco grunted. 'True enough. Even so, there's something there that bothers me. He was taking a hell of a chance getting her body away from the Amiens morgue – and I still don't know how he found out she was there. It could have easily blown up in his face, interfering with procedure like that.'

Santer was sceptical. 'That I doubt. Believe me, Lucas, I've seen a lot of these people and the way they operate. They have friends everywhere...and where they don't, they call on contacts who do. People like Berbier also believe in their untouchable status – like the old aristos and royals. They don't get into trouble because they simply don't believe they can. And that belief breeds arrogance. It's as if they think they can walk through walls. I've seen people like Berbier walk away from charges that would have had you and me locked up in a second.' He shook his head. 'If you think he's hiding something in connection with his daughter's death, you won't find it out in the open.'

Rocco saw the sense in what Santer was saying, but he wasn't going to give up that easily. 'He's a rich businessman. Men like that have secrets.'

'True. They also know people: people who can make nasty things happen.'

'Meaning?'

'Meaning if you don't watch your back, you could end up seeing the dark end of a muddy ditch.'

Rocco stared at him, looking for a sign that he was teasing. 'You think?'

'No question.' Santer moved his plate away and leant closer. 'I checked with a mate who used to work in a division dealing with financial crime. A couple of years ago, one of Berbier's factories near Toulouse was hit by a strike. It was serious stuff, union men coming in from miles away and threats on both sides. Dangerous practices were being encouraged inside, according to the workers, and a couple of assembly line people had been killed. Anyway, the strike for better equipment and conditions began to spread to other factories and looked like going national. Then two of the ringleaders travelling along a clear, open road down near Bordeaux died in a crash.'

'It happens. So?'

'A military fuel tanker ran over their car in broad daylight. The tanker driver claimed the car swerved across the road in front of him, and a half-empty bottle of pastis was found in the front of the car. It was written down as a drunk in charge. Without its two main leaders, and with an under-the-table pay-off, the strike folded.'

'And the tanker driver?'

'He died ten days later in a shooting incident while on manoeuvres.' Santer shrugged eloquently. 'End of story.'

Rocco sat back, frustrated but hardly surprised. If it was true and Berbier had instigated the accident, it proved he was capable of using strong-arm tactics when it suited him. That made him no different from a handful of other business leaders who had cut corners and slipped into criminal territory to get what they wanted. It still didn't take him any closer to finding out why Berbier was so coy about his daughter's death. Reputation and scandal were polar opposites, and sufficient reason for anyone to want to hide unpalatable truths. But times were changing fast, in France as well as everywhere else. The Sixties were ushering in more than just a passion for long-haired youth and loud music, the Beatles and Johnny Hallyday. Moral outrage was no longer the potent force it had once been, and a man like Berbier would be able to weather the scandal of a pregnant, unmarried daughter easier than most.

There had to be something else. 'That's it?' he asked.

'It's all I have. If I get anything else, I'll let you know.'

'Inspector Rocco?' It was a man's voice, gruff with authority, cigarettes or too many late nights.

'Speaking.' Rocco hadn't been back from his meeting with Santer more than ten minutes and was fast becoming disenchanted with his phone, wondering why it was that it rang so often early in the mornings or when he was just getting in. It had never been like this in Clichy, with an office to work in. If he wanted to escape the calls, he simply went out to a crime scene for a while.

'Detective Bertrand, Rouen commissariat,' the man introduced himself. 'Forgive me for disturbing you, Inspector, but I think you might be able to help me.'

'I'll try,' he said cautiously, wondering if an old investigation had caught up with him. Some cases never let go, coming back to haunt you years after they had concluded, or were gathering dust in a pending tray.

'You made a visit recently to an Ishmael Poudric in the Saint-Martin retirement village near Rouen. Is that right?'

'Correct. Why?'

'Before I answer that, could you tell me the purpose of your visit?'

Rocco stifled a groan. Surely he wasn't about to have to apologise for stepping on someone else's turf. Then he remembered, hadn't Massin cleared this with the local office? 'I was investigating an attempted murder involving a former member of the Resistance near Poitiers. There was a group photograph Poudric took during the war which we found during our investigation. I thought it might give us a lead. My visit was run past your office in advance by *Commissaire* Massin in Amiens.'

'That's not the problem, Inspector, don't worry. I'm not that territorial.' The captain's voice contained an element of patience. 'But I think you might want to come down here. We have a situation.'

'Go on.' Rocco felt the air around him go still. This was going to be more bad news. He knew it.

'Poudric is dead. He was found in his study earlier today, stabbed through the heart.'

CHAPTER THIRTY-ONE

Rocco arrived near Poudric's house to find the expected posse of police vehicles and eager onlookers spread along the street. He negotiated the barriers and flipped his card to a uniform at the gate, and was nodded indoors. He found a tired-looking individual standing in the kitchen doorway, rubbing his eyes.

'Rocco?' The man stifled a yawn and put out a meaty hand. 'Louis Bertrand. Sorry – I was up all last night chasing a bastard of an arsonist halfway round the city. Now this.'

Rocco shook his hand. 'No problem. Did you get him?'

'Yes. His dad's a local councillor, would you believe? He had the cheek to deny it – and there was his little git of a son stinking of petrol and smoke right there in the living room.' He shook his head at the thought. 'I was tempted to flick a match near him: he'd have gone up like a Roman candle.'

'What's with the heat?' said Rocco. The air was heavy and musty, as if the heating had been jacked up to its maximum temperature.

'It was like this when we got here. We turned it down so we could work, but the place is well insulated.' Bertrand bent his head towards the study. 'We haven't moved the body yet. Thought it best to let you take a peek first.'

Inside the study, two men were checking through the papers on the desk, having to work over the reclining form of Ishmael Poudric lying in his chair. His head was thrown back and his arms hung by his sides, as if he had simply fallen asleep, too tired to find a more comfortable position. His mouth was open, Rocco noted, but there was no shock or surprise on his features, no frozen expression of pain.

He moved round for a better look. A patch of blood no bigger than a small child's hand showed on the front of Poudric's jumper.

'No sign of other wounds?' he asked.

Bertrand shook his head. 'None. He didn't answer his door to the postman this morning. There were a couple of parcels for him and a signature was needed. When the postman called back later and pushed the door, it opened. Poudric was right here, where you see him. The postman called us immediately.' He lifted his shoulders, suggesting a complete lack of ideas. 'No bad history, no rows with neighbours who, between you and me, are too old and infirm for this kind of nonsense, anyway – and no sign of a robbery.' He puffed his cheeks in frustration. 'If there's anything you can tell me, I'd be glad of the help. Our local medic reckons he's been dead over ten hours, but it's not easy to be certain because of the heating. I think the killer knew what he was doing.'

Rocco understood. Concealing or blurring the time of death usually had one purpose only: to allow the killer to

241

prepare a convincing alibi for being somewhere else at the time.

He bent closer. There were no cuts to Poudric's hands, no defensive wounds to suggest the photographer had seen the knife thrust coming. Whoever had stabbed the old man had taken him by surprise.

'We think he was standing when he was stabbed,' Bertrand continued, pointing to the floor beneath the desk, where one of Poudric's slippers had come off. 'He probably fell back and the killer eased him into his chair.' The detective pulled a face. 'At a guess, I'd say he knew his killer and was comfortable having him in here.'

Rocco couldn't argue with that. He played the scene in his head, picturing the sequence of events. An elderly photographer, welcoming someone he knew. No threat, no sign of danger, relaxed in his own home. It fitted.

'You found my card. Where was it?'

'Ah.' Bertrand nudged one of his colleagues, who handed him a buff folder from the corner of the desk. Rocco's card was stapled to the top right-hand corner. 'This was it, on his desk but under a pile of other stuff. He was building a library of war pictures, it seems, cataloguing photos from the period.'

'That's right.' Rocco opened the folder. Inside were two black and white photographs. One showed the diminutive figure of Didier Marthe standing next to a tall man with his back half-turned to the camera. They were close, as if deep in conversation. The second snap was the one Poudric had mentioned. It showed the tall man by himself this time, sitting at a rough table in a clearing. He was wearing a heavy coat, work boots and a soft cap pushed to the back of his head, and seemed unaware of being captured on camera. He was busy examining what Rocco recognised as a British Sten gun. On the table alongside him were a revolver and a box of ammunition.

But Rocco wasn't looking at the weapon. He was more interested in trying to control his reactions when he saw and recognised the face of the man who was holding the Sten with such easy familiarity. A man who, according to the late Ishmael Poudric, was long dead, a victim of German repression.

Philippe Bayer-Berbier.

CHAPTER THIRTY-TWO

After giving Detective Bertrand a potted version of his own investigation so that he could complete an outline report for his superiors, Rocco made his way back to Poissons, his mind in a whirl. So far, he had a puzzle of several disjointed parts, and no signs of being able to connect them with any degree of logic. He ticked them off in his mind. A young woman is murdered in a tiny rural village, her death quickly glossed over by her father, a rich industrialist and former Resistance hero. Living in the same village is a scrap man who appears to have covertly taken over the phone of a previous subscriber, for reasons not yet clear. According to a wartime photographer, the same man was part of a Resistance group, and was pictured alongside a French SOE agent. That agent is now the same highly placed industrialist and war hero…and father of the dead woman. Yet the agent and the rest of the Resistance group were allegedly wiped out by the Germans.

And now the photographer linking the two men had been murdered.

Rocco wondered if Poudric had realised the identity of the SOE man and talked to someone he should not have.

He was accustomed to having to shuffle leads like cards in a pack; it came with the job and required a degree of objectivity and creative thought which he mostly enjoyed. But so far in his career, gang murders apart, the majority of his cases had involved people known to one another and often in close proximity in their local community, which made connecting the links relatively simple. This one, however, not only stretched across distance and time, but social levels, too.

He pulled up along a straight stretch of deserted road. He felt a headache coming on. A run of fields looped off into the distance, bare and empty of movement. He turned off the engine and lowered the window, allowing a breeze and a few crows in a nearby spinney to keep him company.

He got out and walked away from the car, hands thrust into his pockets while trying to make sense of it all. Clearly Didier Marthe knew Philippe Berbier. And the phone number in the Félix Faure flat just as clearly linked Didier with Berbier's daughter, Nathalie. Yet logic said they could not have been further apart, by all the factors of birth, wealth and social backgrounds, as well as the generation gap and the kind of fashionable circles the young woman had moved in.

He stopped and took out his gun. The MAB felt warm and comfortable, nestling in his hand with solid familiarity. He spotted a make-do scarecrow standing in a sugar beet field fifty yards away. It was a simple cross of sticks wearing a threadbare waistcoat and a holed trilby, and served little useful purpose if the casual proximity of the crows was any indication.

Rocco took aim. It was too far for anything sophisticated, but he took a deep breath, released it slowly, then squeezed the trigger in a double tap followed by a single. The old hat snapped off at a wild angle and the sticks holding it exploded in pieces. The crows protested loudly, hauling themselves scrappily into the sky as the gunshots rolled away across the fields. Lucky, he decided pragmatically. Against regulations, too; Massin would have his balls if he knew. But it had served to release the tension and frustration he was feeling.

And in spite of the lack of clarity about who knew whom, he was a step closer than he had been earlier that day. He had another connection, another link in the chain.

He pocketed the gun and walked back to the car.

Rocco was dreaming, running through a cold, grim marshland, tendrils of mist hanging around his face, strangely immobile and vertical like the hanging fronds of exotic vegetation. He was trying to reach the other side, pushing desperately with his feet but going nowhere, the ground as sticky as glue. A bell was ringing, insistent and piercing. Did that mean his time was running out and the exercise was nearly over?

He snapped awake, mouth gummy and sour. That bloody phone again. He groped in the dark and found it, snatching it to his ear.

'Inspector Rocco?' It was a young woman's voice crackling down the line. Distant, but clear enough. 'It's Sophie Richert.'

'Jesus. One moment.' He struggled out of bed and switched on the light, shook his head to clear away the last fragments of sleep. He took a glass of water off the table and swallowed a mouthful. It tasted tepid and gritty, metallic. He sat down, composing his thoughts. He'd convinced himself that he would never hear from Sophie Richert again, not outside the fashion pages of some magazine, anyway. He said calmly, 'My apologies. Are you back in Paris?'

'No. New York. Sorry – were you asleep? I haven't got used to the time difference yet.'

'No matter. What can I do for you?'

'I have to talk to you...there are things I need to say.' She stopped as if suddenly unsure.

'That's good. But why now and not earlier?'

'Because it's safer. From here, I mean. I hope you understand.'

'I see. Go ahead.'

'I didn't want to say before, but Nathalie...she was thought of as a poor little rich girl; her father a war hero and a rich businessman, connected to diplomats, all that.' She hesitated, and for a moment Rocco thought he'd lost her, that her nerves had got the better of her. Then she continued. 'It wasn't like that.'

'How do you mean?'

'She wasn't rich. Her father was, but he never gave her anything. Her mother died several years ago, and that tore her apart. Her grandmother was still around, but all she really cared about was her son. Everything Nat had, she earned herself. She wanted to be independent...to be her own person, you know?'

'I understand.'

There was a choking sound. 'She should not be dismissed as just a…a spoilt girl who got into trouble. That's so unfair.'

'I agree, it is.' Rocco wondered where this was going. An attack of the guilts for running out after her friend's death, perhaps? Then he recalled Viviane saying that Nathalie's father paid her rent. 'She had the flat, of course.'

'That was just for show. He wanted to be seen as generous and caring…but it was to keep Nathalie under his thumb. Beholden to him. They didn't get on.'

'Why not?'

There was a long pause.

'Sophie?' Rocco prompted her.

'She knew things.'

The line pinged with static.

'What sort of things?'

'Stuff about how her father made his money…how he managed to become rich and powerful at a time when so many others had lost everything.'

'Did she give you any details?'

'No. She said it was too dangerous to talk about. She mentioned it once when she got drunk, after she found out she was pregnant. She was so unhappy… I think it very nearly all came out. But something stopped her.' Sophie cleared her throat as if she had found this difficult. 'The only thing Nathalie ever said was that for a man who started out as a simple army captain, her father managed to end up owning lots of land. He acquired it just after the war, when he began buying things.'

'Things?'

'I think she meant companies damaged by the war.

"Corporate rescue", she said he called it, like it was heroic or something.'

Or profiteering, as it's called in some parts, thought Rocco cynically. 'Go on.'

'She said that, in spite of him being rich, some of the land he had acquired in his business deals was useless. He was always moaning about how he'd been cheated because there was nothing he could do to profit from it.'

'Why useless?' Any land, Rocco thought, was worth something. Especially if you didn't have any to begin with. It gave most people a feeling that they belonged somewhere. No doubt to an industrialist like Berbier, however, different rules applied.

'She said some of it was mountainous and good only for a few sheep. The rest was all lakes and marshland.'

Marshland.

Rocco felt a cold chill go through him. 'Where was this marshland?'

'Somewhere in the north, I'm not sure. I think she was talking about where she...where it happened. North and boring, she reckoned. All beetroot and cabbages and people scratching a living in the fields. I don't think she meant that how it came out; she was actually a very nice person.'

Rocco had never met Nathalie Berbier, but in his experience, breeding came through at times of great stress. And sometimes that breeding was revealed as an ugly truth. Still, that was all over now; a pattern was beginning to emerge. The only question was, would it lead anywhere? A distant father-daughter relationship, parental meanness, a soured and suspicious atmosphere based on resentment.

Cue almost any family in the land. It didn't amount to a crime.

Then Sophie spoke again, her voice dull. 'I told you Nathalie hated the man Brouté.'

'Yes.'

'She hated her father more.'

CHAPTER THIRTY-THREE

Early next morning, eyes gritty through lack of sleep, Rocco dragged himself to the Amiens office in search of Desmoulins. He tracked him down to a side office, talking on the phone and making notes. Desmoulins spotted him and waved him in, then ended his call.

'Hi, boss,' he said cheerfully. 'I hear you've been busy.' He nodded at the phone. 'That was a call from Rouen, checking you out. A Detective Bertrand, talking you up after you met with him yesterday at a crime scene. His boss just got the report and wanted to hear more about the case. I hope you don't mind; *Commissaire* Massin was busy, so I filled him in on what little I knew, without giving any names, though.'

Rocco nodded and explained why he had gone to Rouen. 'Thanks for taking care of it. You'd better fill Massin in on that phone call, for the sake of procedure.'

'Will do. They've put out a bulletin on the student, Agnès

Carre, who visited him recently. He said you'd know all about that.'

'Yes. She was looking for a war photo. The same photo we found in Marthe's house. Can you do your own records search on her, too? Could be a waste of time, but another pair of eyes might turn up something useful.' He rubbed at his face and yawned. His whole body was beginning to shut down, overcome by tiredness.

'No problem. You look like you could use some of our special coffee.' The detective stood up and left the office, returning moments later with a large mug and some lumps of sugar. 'Sorry about lack of finesse, but the maid's off. This is strong enough to raise the dead.'

'Now that would be a miracle.' Rocco stirred in sugar and sank a large gulp of strong black that threatened to melt his teeth, then eyed Desmoulins carefully. The detective seemed unusually chipper and he wondered why. 'Did you win the lotto or something?' he asked.

Desmoulins grinned. 'Not quite. Massin told me about the photo coming from a shop in Poitiers. I used a bit of lateral thinking and reckoned that if this Didier Marthe came from that area, maybe Tomas Brouté did, too.'

'Christ, that was a leap. A good one, though. I should have thought of it myself.'

'I used Massin's name and got the mayor's office in Poitiers to run a priority check on the civil register of births for a Tomas Brouté in the area.' He shrugged. 'It was a long shot but you have to try these hunches occasionally, right?'

Rocco waited, then said calmly, 'Spit it out, for God's sake, I'm desperate here.'

Desmoulins looked pleased with himself. 'In December

1912, a Lisanne Brouté, spinster of the parish, gave birth to a son, named Tomas, Didier. No sign of a father, even a reluctant one.'

Rocco played devil's advocate. 'Coincidence. Both names are fairly common.'

Desmoulins didn't even blink. 'The registrar's name was Marthe.' He raised his hands. 'What can I say?'

Rocco closed his eyes. It fitted. Didier was about fifty, although he looked older, easily accounted for by a hard life and a lot of time working in the sun. It was a moment to savour, and he could well understand why Desmoulins was feeling so pleased with himself. 'Bloody good work,' he said. 'Brilliant. Can you get copies of the paperwork?'

'All on order. The mother's dead – I got them to check the death records as well. No way of checking what happened to the kid, unfortunately, but I think we know that, don't we?'

'We do. He plays with bombs for a living.' Rocco stood up, energised by the news. He was beginning to wonder why Didier had chosen to settle in Poissons-les-Marais. Doubtless it was for no better reason than chance and circumstance. The war had stirred up society's mix in more ways than one. Whereas people had tended to stay in their home regions all their lives before that, the ending of the conflict had encouraged some to move around a lot more, seeking jobs, new faces and places, often to start afresh and roll away from bad memories. Especially the latter. And for those in search of a new identity, France was a big place in which to get lost. Especially for a man trying to hide the fact that he was supposed to be dead.

That immediately led to thoughts about Berbier and his

253

place in the story. But his ruminations were interrupted by the phone jangling. Desmoulins answered. He listened for a moment, then looked at Rocco and held out the receiver.

'It's for you. Lamotte from Poissons? He sounds stressed.'

Rocco took the phone. 'Yes, Claude.'

'Sorry to chase you down, Lucas.' Claude sounded breathless, as if he'd run up a flight of stairs. 'I guessed you'd be there. Something's not right back here. You know Francine at the co-op?'

'I've met her. What about her?'

'She's gone missing.'

'When was she last seen?' Rocco met Claude outside the village café and told him to get in. He'd driven back as fast as the road would allow, elbowing aside those vehicles too slow to respond to his lights and horn, an echo of the urgency and worry in Claude's voice riding with him. He'd left Desmoulins ready to call in extra help if needed, and to explain to Massin what he was doing. He'd also left a note describing the photo of Berbier and asking Massin if there was any way he could check the industrialist's SOE credentials. He'd have preferred explaining the reasons himself, but Desmoulins now had the bit between his teeth and would carry a convincing argument for the request being met. It might come to nothing: even Massin might find his authority blocked at the level involving former intelligence service records. But the fact that questions were being asked would be felt like vibrations along a telegraph wire, and that might prove a useful catalyst.

'Yesterday afternoon. She served two people before

closing, but since then, nothing. She didn't open this morning, and two delivery trucks dropped stuff in the backyard without getting a signature. Someone thought they saw her driving out towards Amiens, but it was only a fleeting glance. She might have been going for special supplies.'

'Or making deliveries.' Rocco drove the short distance to the co-op and skidded to a stop outside.

'What?' Claude looked at him.

'She told me she was going to make a delivery to the lodge down on the *marais*. Another weekend party, apparently.'

'Christ.' Claude slapped the side of his knee. 'I never thought of that.'

Three women in traditional dark dresses, aprons and headscarves were standing near the front door, scowling furiously at the windows as if that alone would gain them admittance. *Like ravens at a funeral*, thought Rocco. He led Claude round to the rear of the shop, ignoring the women's shrill demands about when it would be open, and pushed through the gate. He found himself in the yard and threaded his way between two rubbish skips, pallets of new stock and several empty bottle crates to the back door. A garage stood empty to one side. The door was open, with an axe and a pile of chopped wood just inside, and the usual garage-type rubbish on a bench at the rear.

'What are we doing?' Claude demanded. 'Shouldn't we go straight to the *marais*?'

'Not yet. We'd look pretty stupid if she was here all the time, ill in bed.' Or worse, Rocco avoided saying. He tried the door, but it was locked fast. The windows were reinforced with wire mesh and steel bars, no doubt a condition of the insurance agreement. He went back to the garage and picked up the axe and walked back to the door. He jabbed the head of the axe through the thick glass panel, then reached through and found the key. Seconds later, they were inside.

It took moments to confirm that the building was empty. Rocco checked behind the counter, where he had seen Francine filling her delivery orders. There was no sign of the blue crate she'd been working on, he noted, nor any paperwork to go with it. And no sign of her car. It meant she had gone out on a delivery and was taking a long time to do it. Too long.

'We'd better secure that back door,' said Claude. He nodded at the women outside, who now had their faces pressed up against the window, watching silently. 'Once word about this gets round, it won't be long before someone pays the place a visit.'

'How about…Arnaud, is it?' Rocco remembered the handyman Mme Denis had mentioned. 'Could he do it for the time being?'

Claude nodded. 'That's his wife out front – I'll get her to organise it. She'll watch the place like a Rottweiler until it's done and enjoy the drama.' He went outside ahead of Rocco to make the arrangements, then joined him at the car.

Rocco drove fast for the *marais*. Alongside him, Claude was muttering and staring out at the passing scenery as if he might manage to summon up the missing woman by willpower alone.

Rocco felt for him. A small community like this bred closeness and a protective instinct among its members. And someone as harmless yet as fundamental to their needs as

Francine would arouse strong feelings of concern. He tried to quell his own fears by telling himself that she had merely taken off for a break, that she had got tired of being on duty in the shop all the time without relief and had gone shopping. If so, all she would have to worry about was the fall-out of small-community public opinion going against her for letting them down. But that would soon fade: people still needed supplies, and he had the feeling Francine was quite capable of dealing with sniping from dissatisfied housewives upset because they couldn't buy their cooking oil when they wanted to.

What bothered him more, however, was the thought that she might have walked into something down on the *marais* that she couldn't handle: something more than just a few dissatisfied crones in black dresses and aprons.

CHAPTER THIRTY-FOUR

Philippe Bayer-Berbier put down the telephone in his study and went to stand at the window, his brow creased in worry. He had just received a call from his contact in the Interior Ministry, informing him that Inspector Rocco had been signed in at a crime scene in Rouen the previous day. A retired war photographer had been murdered and Rocco's card had been found on his desk, left from an earlier visit. Word had only just filtered through from the Rouen criminal investigations office that Rocco had returned at the request of a local detective, and had provided some background information on the dead man. So far, there was no information about why Rocco was interested in anyone in the Rouen district.

Berbier chewed his lip. The bloody man was what the English so eloquently called a bad penny, he reflected sourly: always turning up when and where he was least required. He tried to relax; the muscles in his shoulders were bunching with tension, something he had experienced more often just recently than he was accustomed to. Following his daughter's untimely and messy death, which had been bad enough, and the investigation unrolled by Rocco, he had also learnt of the sudden disappearance to America of his daughter's neighbour and friend. While that by itself might have been an entirely innocent coincidence, he had since ordered Nathalie's flat to be cleared and cleansed as a precaution. He had no reason to think anything remained there which might be found by the police or – God forbid – the press, but it was a possible loose end. And loose ends were what had got him to this situation.

He breathed deeply, feeling his heartbeat gradually settle. Even if the young neighbour knew anything, had picked up some idle chatter from his daughter, it was unlikely she would be a problem all the way across the Atlantic. But he would still have rested easier being reassured that Rocco would not be able to get to her.

He wondered about the dead photographer. Ishmael Poudric, his contact had said. The name meant nothing to Berbier; names from that period were fading with the years, along with the faces. But the man's former address during the war – Poitiers – had touched something deep inside him, awakening unwelcome echoes of the past and bringing back memories of dark nights, cold, wet weather and the ever present danger of discovery or betrayal. The more he thought about it the more he recalled seeing a man with a camera with one particular group of Resistance fighters. He himself had always instinctively avoided having his picture taken. But the others had been arrogant and stupid, encouraging the man to follow them. In the end it had made no difference: they had paid for their carelessness with their lives.

All except one.

Berbier winced at that, wondering how he could have been so utterly foolish, so naive as to have trusted his future to one man. Better he should have taken out his knife and dealt with the little ditch rat there and then. Instead, he'd tied himself to the treacherous cretin for life, an unholy alliance forged by his own greed.

He turned to his desk and looked at a sheet of paper containing a list of the police personnel in the Amiens *préfecture*. He'd had it sent over by his man in the Interior Ministry. It was a chance request prompted by an instinctive desire to know more about what and who he was dealing with.

Right at the top was a familiar name.

François Massin, district *commissaire*.

He picked up the telephone on his desk and toyed with the wire, studying the name and wondering. He and Massin had met once at the military academy, when Berbier was a visiting lecturer on intelligence and guerrilla tactics. He barely remembered the man, only that he had been thin, ascetic and lacking any sense of brotherhood, to most members an essential part of the officer corps. To Berbier's mind, not having it wasn't necessarily a bad thing: too much military thinking was tied up in mindless tradition, anyway. But what he did recall about Massin was first, his observance of the rule book, and second, that he had since received a stain on his record from his time in Indochina. More than anything, for someone who doubtless wanted to reach the top of his profession before it was too late, that made Massin malleable. And taking advantage of a man's weaknesses was something Berbier understood only too well.

He read the *préfecture* telephone number off the sheet and was about to dial when there was a knock at the door. It was his driver.

'What is it?'

'An update from the Ministry, sir. The duty operator in Amiens says a woman has disappeared in Poissons-les-Marais. A local shopkeeper.'

'So?' Berbier's mind was still on Massin, deciding what approach to take. Senior policemen could be arrogant and unpredictable, especially those with something to prove. He had little regard for the man, but he would still have to be careful not to overplay his hand.

His driver shuffled his feet and continued, 'The investigator Rocco was present when the call came in and left the office the moment he heard. He seemed unusually concerned, they said.'

Berbier put down the phone, a ripple of tension fluttering through him. He would call Massin later. For now, this took precedence. He had arranged for an intercept of information passing through the Amiens office for this very possibility. If Rocco was on the move, he wanted to know about it. Why the inspector should be unduly concerned about a shopkeeper disappearing he couldn't fathom, and nor should it matter. But anything related to Poissons-les-Marais or his daughter's death had been flagged for his attention. And Rocco was undeniably part of that.

He made a quick decision. Things were coming to a head; he could feel it in his bones. 'Get some men over there and find out what's going on. You know who to look for.'

'Yes, sir.' The man nodded and left.

Berbier sat down behind his desk and steepled his hands in thought. There was still time, if he played it right, to derail Rocco's further interference. He set about mentally composing his phone call to Massin.

CHAPTER THIRTY-FIVE

Rocco skidded the Citroën into the *marais* at speed, the tyres throwing up dirt and gravel and sending up a mad scramble of birds from the trees as the engine blasted the silence apart. Alongside him, Claude closed his eyes and held on tight, muttering what might have been a prayer to the god of all travellers.

In spite of telling himself that Francine's absence might be purely innocent, a part of Rocco's brain was telling him that there was only one place where she might be – and not entirely of her own free will.

He felt the front wheels skating on soft earth as they approached the main lodge along the narrow track. With just a few centimetres of solid ground on either side, he had little room for error. But now was not the time for caution. If his fears were correct, everything depended on getting to the lodge as fast as possible. He felt the steering wheel twitch as the ground tried to suck in the front offside tyre, and a flurry of black mud sprayed into the air and plastered itself across the windscreen. He switched on the wipers but they merely smeared the mixture across the glass, rendering the ground ahead barely visible. Rocco thrust his head out of the window and watched the ground by the front wheel, conscious that at this speed, if he made a mistake and hit wet soil, they would plough right off the track and into the nearest stretch of unforgiving ooze.

Then they were into the turning circle in front of the lodge. Rocco stamped on the brakes, sending the heavy car into a sideways drift and spraying debris across the front of the building. They finally lurched to a stop within arm's reach of the veranda.

He turned off the engine and leapt from the car. He was carrying the axe from Francine's garage. The front door was locked and solid, as before, and he already knew by the feel that the axe would make little impression. He hurried round the side of the building, checking the shutters for weaknesses, signalling Claude to do the same the other way.

They met at the rear of the building.

A familiar blue crate of groceries lay spilt on the ground near the back door.

When Rocco last saw it in the co-op, it had been nearly full. But not now. A box of sugar lumps lay on the ground, with a line of ants helping themselves to the contents through a tear in the soft cardboard. Flies and wasps were feasting on a ripped bag of apples and a bunch of grapes, the fruit already turning soft and brown in the heat, and a carton of milk had ballooned and burst open. A furious army of smaller insects was taking full advantage of the bounty, a moving carpet of black dots in the spreading yellow film.

He prodded at the back door. It was shuttered, like the front, but seemed less solid. Taking a step back, he swung the axe, putting the full weight of his shoulders behind it, and felt the blade bite deep into the wood of the shutter. Glass burst and tinkled to the floor. He swung again immediately, aiming at where the lock should be, and felt the blade hit metal. Another swing and the shutter sagged in the middle. When he ripped the axe free again, one corner came away, bits of paint flaking off like confetti. A final blow and the shutter disintegrated, showering them both with wood splinters.

'Shit,' muttered Claude, impressed. 'Next time I need some wood chopping, I'll give you a call.'

Rocco kicked the door in and dropped the axe. He drew his pistol and cocked it.

'You ready?' he said. Claude nodded, eyes glittering with determination. He had produced his own automatic pistol and was holding it steady with both hands.

They stepped into a kitchen bright with daylight reflecting through the ruined door, off tiled walls above expensive work surfaces and a stainless steel sink. A large wood-burning cooker stood against one wall, with cupboards full of crockery, glasses and pans nearby. The floor was covered in heavy-duty matting of the kind Rocco had once seen in a private yacht club bar, and everything looked clean and untouched.

He stepped across the kitchen to a doorway leading to the main part of the lodge. A quick scan of the room and he went through, going down on one knee and sweeping the room with his pistol. Claude followed, moving to the other side of the doorway.

The room was a large single space, scattered with cane sofas and chairs, all liberally covered with soft cushions and throws. The polished hardwood floor was draped with expensive rugs, and a pair of large, elaborate oil lamps with fluted chimneys dominated the room. The walls below the windows were lined with cupboards.

'Jesus,' breathed Claude in admiration. 'How the hell did they get all this stuff in without anyone seeing it?'

'At night, probably,' said Rocco. He pointed to an open stairway across the room. There was no light, and it looked dark. Too dark. He motioned Claude to stay where he was and moved back into the kitchen, opening drawers and cupboards. Seconds later he found a supply of candles and two torches that worked. He went back into the main room and tossed one to Claude.

'I'll go first,' he said softly. 'You stay down here in case anything happens.'

Claude's eyes were huge in the reflected torchlight. 'Like what?'

'You'll know, believe me. If anything does, get outside and wait – but make sure it's not me before you start shooting.'

Claude nodded and moved across to the side of the stairway, where he merged into the gloom.

Rocco had done this before several times, moving into darkened rooms and up ill-lit stairways. The main threat was to the lead man. It never got any easier and nobody had ever been able to convince him that taking it slowly was any safer than going in at a mad rush with gritted teeth and a blood-curdling battle cry. He took a deep breath, checked that Claude was ready, then switched on the torch and charged ahead, legs propelling him up the open stairs.

He emerged into another large area like the one below, and swung the torch in an arc. There was absolute silence apart from his own breathing. His heart was thumping and he wondered what it would take to get him back to a peak of fitness. A short flight of stairs shouldn't be this stressful. He breathed deeply and called down to Claude, who came up to join him, adding his light to the room.

At first glance, it resembled an open-plan office divided by low screens. The difference was, each space contained a low, single bed and cabinet, and a small oil lamp. Small rugs covered the wooden floor, and the beds were spread with thick duvets and heavy, plumped pillows. The air was scented with pine. Across the room, above the kitchen area, were two open doorways with reed curtains. Rocco checked and found they were toilets with showers and small hand basins. Bottles of liquid soap and hair products stood in steel racks, and at floor level, small cabinets opened to reveal thick bath towels and pre-packed slippers, toothbrushes, combs and toothpaste.

'All mod cons,' he said. Whoever had furnished this place had decided that the guests should not go without the basics.

'You can say that again.' Claude had opened one of the bedside cabinets. Inside was a selection of porn magazines, tubes of jelly and a basket of sex toys. The last time Rocco had seen such a display was when he helped bust a brothel masquerading as a private gaming club in Clichy.

Clearly, guests here did not mind sharing even their closest and most intimate leisure time with their colleagues. Maybe it was part of the attraction.

Back downstairs, they checked the cupboards built into

the walls. One was a well-stocked drinks cabinet full of expensive spirits and liqueurs; another housed a top-of-the-range Danish Bang & Olufsen radio and sound system wired to speakers dotted strategically around the walls. Others held a large supply of books, records, board games and – to complete the collection – a film projector and an extensive library of pornographic movies.

Rocco tilted his head. 'You hear that?'

'Hear what?'

'Precisely. You could slaughter a pig in here and nobody would hear a thing. The place is soundproofed. Just right for noisy parties. Doesn't attract any attention if things get out of hand.' As Rocco's torch played across the cupboard, he caught a tiny glitter of colour at the base. An object was wedged in the gap between a rug on the floor and the framework. He bent down for a closer look.

It was a yellow-and-white earring in the shape of a marguerite.

CHAPTER THIRTY-SIX

'So she was here, then. The Berbier girl.' Claude followed Rocco out of the lodge and kicked the door shut behind him. It bounced open again, trailing the ruined lock and splinters of wood. He let it swing.

'I think we knew that.' Rocco felt oddly deflated by the discovery, the piece of jewellery merely underlining the fact that, apart from the crate of forgotten groceries, they had still found no trace of Francine Thorin. But why was the crate left out here to spoil? A few items had been taken, but he didn't think a random thief would have left anything behind: a prize of fresh supplies like that was simply too good to miss. No, if it was anyone, it would have been Didier, snatching whatever was easy to carry and wouldn't spoil too quickly. A man on the run has no time to plan his menu.

'They must have been put off,' he said half-aloud.

'Who?'

'The guests for the latest party…the one this stuff was intended for. They must have heard the news and cancelled… or received a call telling them it was off.' A murder in the area will do that, he thought sombrely. People aren't keen on partying with a killer on the rampage.

'I can't believe it.' Claude swept his arm around at the lodge with an expression of disgust. 'All that inside…and happening right under our noses. And nobody in Poissons knew a thing.'

'Someone did,' Rocco corrected him. He switched off the torch and stared out across the *marais*. 'Didier Marthe knew.'

'Just him?' Claude puffed out his lips in disbelief. 'Yeah – you're right. Something else I find baffling: that a worm like him had anything to do with this…this *extravagance*.'

'You mean a nonentity having access to wealth?' Rocco shook his head. 'Half the crims in the world are nonentities on the outside. It's what makes them so hard to spot.' He nudged the crate with his foot. 'Anyway, I doubt it was his money he was playing with. He was just the local fixer.'

'You think he had partners?'

'I'd bet my car on it.' He thought he knew who that partner might be, but proving it would be the interesting bit. But that was his job. He looked around, a thought tugging at his subconscious: something wasn't right about this scene. Then he realised.

The blue crate. A car.

'She couldn't have carried the crate all the way down here,' he said softly. 'And someone saw her driving. So where's her car?'

They scoured the immediate area around the lodge. The

ground was soft, which should have been ideal for finding traces of a car. But the surface had been laid with several layers of wood chippings and dried reeds, and other than a mess of indistinct footprints around the crate and the back door, there were no definite furrows to show the passage of a vehicle.

'Hang on.' Claude walked round to the front of the building, to where Rocco had left his car. He inspected the ground where the soil was harder, and looked up towards the nearest bed of reeds that led to the lake. He pointed and said dully, 'Over there. *The bastard drove her into the lake!*'

They ran across to the reed bed. Most of the stronger reeds on the bank were more or less upright. But beyond that, it was clear that something heavy had ploughed right through into the murky water, chopping down the thinner vegetation and carving a trough through the soft mud. A blueish glimmer of metal caught the light just below the surface, and Rocco felt the hairs move on the back of his neck as he realised what he was looking at. It was the roof of a car, just visible through the murk.

'What car did she drive?'

'A Panhard,' said Claude. 'Duck-egg blue, I think. It probably drove like one, too. Don't tell me—'

'It's here.' Rocco turned and headed for his car.

'Wait! Can't we do something?' Claude skidded down to the water's edge, staring at the area where the car was sitting.

'Like what?' Rocco called back. There were no bubbles to indicate trapped air slowly escaping, no signs of life. If Francine was down there, she was beyond any help they could give. 'There's no point.'

'How do you know that? You don't!' He made to step into the water.

Rocco stopped him. 'Actually, I do,' he said gently. 'I've seen enough cars go in the Seine to know. And it's been down there too long. No car is that waterproof, believe me.' He gave Claude a look full of sympathy. 'I'll go to a phone and get a recovery team out here…drag it out to make sure.'

It was mid-afternoon before a police recovery unit complete with a diver had arrived and were winching the Panhard with agonising slowness out of the lake onto the bank. By that time both Rocco and Claude had had to restrain each other from going in the lake to investigate the contents of the car themselves. As it ground out of the water and reeds, a stream of near-black water sluiced out of the battered doors and windows, bringing with it a choking stench of mud, stagnant water and rotted vegetation topped off by a cloud of heavy blue smoke from the motor winch on the recovery truck.

The roof and door pillars of the car had caved in under the pressure of being hauled out, but the shell was still intact. The driver's door had been left open, according to the diver, but he had found no trace of a body on the outside.

'Could she have fallen out?' said Rocco.

The diver shook his head and spat expertly into the water. 'There's no current down there; she wouldn't have drifted anywhere.'

Even before the last of the water had drained away, Rocco and Claude were bending close by the car, disregarding the filth pouring over their shoes and staring at the interior with a shared feeling of dread.

It was empty.

'Thank God,' Claude whispered, and made a rapid sign of the cross. One or two of the police team echoed the gesture, while the others looked almost disappointed. Claude glanced at Rocco. 'What now?'

'We find her, wherever she is,' Rocco said darkly. He stepped away from the vehicle, squelching through the muddy detritus and nodding his thanks to the team leader. 'And when we find her, Didier's going to wish he'd never set eyes on this place.'

It was a short walk through the trees to the Blue Pool, and Rocco led the way, his long stride soon leaving Claude behind. They were followed all the way by the stink of mud and the sound of the recovery team packing up their gear. It was probably a waste of time, Rocco decided, as they arrived at the edge of the sparkling clear water. But he had to be sure. He had seen too many examples of the blindingly obvious being ignored, only to find that it was obvious for a very good reason.

But the pool reflected silently back at them, cool and clear and empty.

CHAPTER THIRTY-SEVEN

'Why are we still here?' said Claude. The last of the recovery unit had left, along with the few onlookers from the village. It had plunged the *marais* back into a heavy silence, punctuated only by the occasional plop of fish jumping and the clatter of wings as a bird took flight through the trees. It would take some time for the wildlife to regain its normal composure after the crackling roar of the winch and the babble of voices. But it was just a matter of waiting, as Rocco knew only too well.

'She's still here, that's why. Francine.' Saying her name sounded odd, even intimate. Rocco had changed into his new boots, squeezing the muddy water from his socks and putting them back on. It was uncomfortable but bearable. Then he'd checked his pistol, slipping out the magazine and working the mechanism two or three times before replacing it with a satisfying click. He had also pocketed two spare clips from the boot of his car, instinct telling him that if

274

he had to use the weapon today, it would not be at close quarters, nor would it be convenient to pop back and seek replacement ammunition.

Claude watched with worried eyes, then checked his own weapon.

They sat in the car with the doors open, waiting and watching. Gradually, like an audience at a concert growing increasingly comfortable with their surroundings, the birds began to find their voices again. A pair of crows appeared, hovering for a few moments in harsh disagreement before touching down in the treetops; a flight of pigeons clattered to a rough landing lower down, ungainly and noisy; smaller birds appeared, too, their singing faint at first, until they grew confident that Rocco and Claude were not going to erupt from the car and ruin their newly regained tranquillity.

A flight of mosquitoes found Claude's side of the car and buzzed around his head, and he swiped at them in vague irritation.

'They don't bother you,' he said, glancing at Rocco. 'Why's that?'

Rocco shrugged. He'd lived with mosquitoes as big as seagulls once, but they'd always left him alone. Others had not been so lucky, and he'd assumed it was down to bodily chemistry. 'They know bad karma when they see it.'

'Karma? What's that?'

'For them, mostly a rolled-up newspaper.'

'I hope she's OK,' said Claude at one point, shifting in his seat. 'Francine, I mean. She's a nice woman.' He glanced at Rocco. 'But you know that.'

Rocco nodded. 'Nice enough.' He wondered where she was, and prayed that not giving way to irrational panic and running through the *marais* like a madman had been the right decision to adopt. Time would tell. 'She told me about her husband being killed in a factory accident.'

Claude raised his eyebrows. 'Really? I didn't know she'd been married.' He pursed his lower lips. 'How did I miss that?'

'About eighteen months ago, she said.'

Claude turned and stared at him. 'No way.'

'Why no way?'

'She's lived here for over two years, that's why – and alone. You must have misheard her.' He turned away with a meaningful chuckle. 'Not that I blame you. She's a fine-looking woman. I mean, enough to turn any man's head to mush.'

After sitting in silence for a few more minutes, Rocco got out of the car. Something about what Claude had said was disturbing him, but he couldn't work out what it was. It wasn't necessarily the conflict in the detail – that could be easily explained away: people got dates and times wrong for all manner of reasons, grief being a major one. But there was something else tugging at his subconscious, a related thought, and he couldn't pin it down. Maybe some action might dislodge it.

'I want to see inside the other lodge.'

'Why? You think she might be in there?' Claude joined him, easing cramped limbs.

'Maybe.' He hadn't forgotten that they had found the back door open the first time he had come down here. It didn't necessarily mean Francine would be there, but it was another obvious place to check. It was easier than sitting around doing nothing.

Claude nodded. 'I'll get the axe.'

'No.' Rocco stopped him. 'We'll check it out quietly first.' He locked the car, then led the way past the first lodge, skirting the lake and stopping every now and then to listen. The birds had ceased their activity only momentarily, then, reassured that neither man was about to start blasting holes in the trees, took it up again.

'You do a lot of that,' said Claude at one point, as Rocco stared upwards, ears cocked for any unusual sounds, sifting through the normal and looking for the out of place. 'For a city man.'

'Do what?'

'Sniffing the air, listening to the trees. I could hire you out in the shooting season – we'd make a fortune.'

Rocco continued walking. He was aware that his habit of tuning in to his surroundings, a hangover from his army days, seemed odd to other people. It had been the same among his colleagues in Paris. Entering buildings, walking silently along darkened alleyways or listening for the slightest indication of something out of place, he'd been more gun dog than human, alert for anything that did not fit. The habit had saved his life on two occasions and he wasn't about to give it up as a cranky idea just yet.

They arrived at the second lodge and found it locked tight, front and back. They did separate tours of the building, studying the ground carefully for footprints, but found nothing obvious. If anyone had been here recently, they had left no obvious trace. So who had locked the door again?

'Didier'. Claude read his mind. 'He's always around here; I bet he couldn't resist getting a key copied so he could nose around whenever he felt like it.'

Rocco nodded. It made sense. 'How do we get to Didier's house?'

'Follow me.' Claude set off through the trees. On the way, they passed the third building Claude had referred to earlier. It was like something out of a children's spooky comic, Rocco observed. Dark and dank, it had a drunken porch, broken shutters, and if there had once been any paint on the clapboard sides, it had long gone, leaving raw wood deep with cracks. The window glass had gone and the roof had the sad, sway-backed look of a neglected pony.

They continued until they reached the banks of a stream, and the tree-trunk bridge Rocco had seen before. Didier's house was just visible on the far side.

They crossed the bridge. Rocco remembered what Claude had told him, but figured that he wouldn't have crossed if he still thought the bridge was booby-trapped.

The front door stood half-open at a drunken angle. Rocco kicked it open all the way and drew his gun, then held up a hand to Claude and listened. Nothing. No sounds, nobody scurrying for cover, no furtive scuff of movement on the stairs.

He stepped across the threshold. The place hadn't been touched since he and Claude had last been inside. The cellar door, he noticed, was still locked and the shoe he'd kicked against it was still there exactly as he'd left it.

He went through the kitchen drawers, looking for keys. Most were full of rubbish, crumpled bills, receipts and cuttings from newspapers jammed in on top of odd tools, random items of cutlery and endless tangles of string and wire.

Claude joined in. Moments later, as he moved an old coffee

tin on a shelf to check behind it, they heard the dull rattle of metal. Claude upended the tin and a cluster of keys fell out.

Rocco grunted but said nothing. He was busy looking at some of the newspaper cuttings he'd found and very nearly ignored. They were dated over a number of years, culled from various papers or magazines. All were on the same subject.

Philippe Bayer-Berbier.

Most portrayed him in business mode, buying a company here, sealing a merger, appearing at a function with other business leaders and politicians, the urbane, charismatic and confident industrialist, comfortable among his kind. There seemed to be no specific reason for the cuttings and Rocco surmised that Didier, for reasons of his own, had been keeping a close eye on Berbier, watching his progress over the years. It was as much an unsettling light into Didier's world as it was to Berbier's, and he marvelled at the way two such different men had been joined over the years by their shared history right through to the present day.

Claude joined him and held up the keys from the coffee tin. They were shiny and well used. 'None of these fit the cellar. In fact, they don't look like they'd fit anything here.'

Rocco nodded and dropped the papers in the drawer. They told him only that Didier had an obsessive interest in Berbier. And that's how it would look to a magistrate. It wasn't a crime, nor did it prove that the men even knew each other. But to Rocco, it confirmed that there was still a connection, even after all this time. And that was enough to be going on with for the moment.

'Let's go.' He led the way outside, with Claude scrambling to catch up with him.

'What about the cellar? Francine—'

'She's not down there.' He put his gun away.

'How do you know? We haven't even tried.'

'I know, believe me.' He didn't bother explaining about the shoe. Right now, all he wanted to do was get back to searching for Francine before it was too late.

The second lodge was a smaller, rougher version of the big one, and looked to be more of a genuine weekend place than its neighbour. Claude went through the keys and eventually found one that worked. They slipped inside.

The search took even less time than the other lodge. No signs of expensive alcohol or dubious films, no toys or magazines, much less any kind of sound system. And no Francine. It seemed to be what it was built for, nothing more, nothing less.

Rocco stepped outside once they had searched the place thoroughly, and looked across the nearby lake with a feeling of increasing desperation, not helped by the apparent normality of the scenery around them. It was tranquil and motionless apart from a kingfisher flitting about on the far side, and one or two moorhens and coots stalking over the lily pads in search of bugs. Higher up in the branches, the smaller birds carried on their singing as usual, aware of, but more immune to, the events down at ground level.

Elsewhere, life carried on as usual. A droning noise sounded in the distance, probably a tractor, and a child's cry drifted through the trees from the direction of the village. A cow bellowed, a cockerel hawed faintly. Normal noises in a normal world.

Then the droning noise stopped.

Moments later, so did the birdsong.

CHAPTER THIRTY-EIGHT

Commissaire Massin was in his office reading a report from one of his detectives and feeling a gradual surge of apprehension building in his gut. He'd just spoken to a Detective Bertrand in Rouen, following a briefing from Desmoulins, and was trying to work out what Rocco was up to. Desmoulins was either unaware or not saying, and Rocco himself was conveniently out of touch somewhere in Poissons, looking for a missing woman. Her disappearance was apparently out of character, but possibly tied in with a missing patient from Amiens hospital being sought for assault on a cleaner. Desmoulins had told him that Rocco had been sufficiently concerned as to leave immediately, briefing him on his way out to his car.

Desmoulins had also advised that the murdered photographer near Rouen was the same man who had taken the photo of the Resistance people during the war – the former owner of APP – and that the entire group had subsequently died at the hands of the Nazis in the camp known as Natzweiler-Struthof. Included in their number was one Didier Marthe...the same man now being sought for the assault and theft at the hospital.

Even more intriguing – not to say worrying – was that Rocco had identified another person photographed among the group shortly prior to their demise: a French SOE officer. If he was correct, then that man was also very much alive, and now known throughout France as a pillar of the establishment.

Philippe Bayer-Berbier.

Massin sat back and fingered his chin. He was aware of the concentration camp and its grim history, and how few, if any, Resistance people had come out alive. He wasn't sure precisely how Berbier's survival was connected with the murder of his daughter, Nathalie, but no doubt that would become clear in due course. If Rocco was allowed to take his investigation that far.

What he was struggling with was the request Rocco had passed to him via Desmoulins: to find out the nature of Berbier's history with the SOE. Privately, he reckoned it would be a non-starter. Men like Berbier, even those who were known to have had a background in wartime subversion and sabotage, were rarely keen to allow those records to be made a matter of public detail. And a man like Berbier, who was acknowledged even by his supporters to have a somewhat shadowy history from the period immediately following the war, would be even less likely to allow it.

Rocco. The man was like a rough-trained bulldog: let him loose and he attacked anything and everything, secure in the knowledge that he was doing his job, no matter where it took him. It was useful at times, having a man like that, but it also generated enmity and bad feeling for those caught in any fallout. Like himself.

He turned and studied the one photograph he had decided to put up in his office. It showed him in police uniform, proud and determined following his award of a distinguished pass mark at the academy. It had not, over the years, led to the higher echelons of the service as he had envisaged, but he had not completely given up on progressing higher. There was still time.

He had another photograph, this one kept buried in his desk drawer. Also of him in uniform, this time in the distinctive Lizard pattern camouflage, and taken shortly after his arrival in Indochina aboard a French military flight. He'd been empowered with a single brief: to pursue action against the communist Viet Minh with all urgency and aggression. It had been his last photocall in military uniform and the memory of it still caused him moments of pain and humiliation. A humiliation renewed each and every time he saw or heard of Lucas Rocco.

It still surprised him that the former sergeant had given no indication of their shared history, either by expression or deed. Could he have forgotten that day on the front line? A day etched in Massin's own mind as though with acid? He doubted it: men like Rocco did not forget easily. He shook his head, angrily dislodging the thoughts that brought shame to him in the still night hours and plagued many of his daytime moments, too. He turned instead to the investigation Rocco was pursuing.

Maybe, just maybe, if he could keep Rocco on a tight

enough rein, a move higher up the ladder might be achieved riding on the back of a successful murder investigation. On the other hand, he recognised, it would be he who might end up with egg on his face if Rocco performed as usual, barging his way through people's lives without due thought to the consequences. People like Philippe Bayer-Berbier, for example, he thought wryly, suppressing a shudder. God forbid that he should let Rocco go anywhere near that man again: Berbier possessed too many friends in high places and, no doubt, too many favours he could call in if he really wanted to kill somebody's career stone dead, merely by lifting a telephone.

He swung back as his secretary poked her head round the door. He was going to allow Rocco a bit more rope. By all accounts the Rouen police were highly impressed by the unselfish help he had given them, and that could only reflect – had already reflected, via Bertrand's commanding officer – on himself. Maybe this could serve his own needs after all. Especially if the case involved bringing in someone of note, which would run through the halls of the Ministry like wildfire and enhance everyone associated with it.

'Sir?' his secretary prompted him urgently, waving a hand. 'Important call from Paris. Line one.'

Massin tried to remain calm. Most calls from Paris were important; they usually came from higher up the chain of command and required a sharp mind and sharper reactions to whatever news they brought. The only question was, would it be good news or bad?

'Who is it?' It had to be one of at least three senior staff members.

'A Philippe Bayer-Berbier, sir. Shall I put him through?'

CHAPTER THIRTY-NINE

'We've got company,' said Rocco. He stepped away from the lodge, instantly on the alert, glancing towards where he had left the car.

'How do you know that?'

Rocco pointed upwards. 'Hear that?' Everything was silent: the trees, the lakes, the undergrowth; even the breeze seemed to have shut down its whisper, leaving the air muggy and still.

Claude nodded. 'Damn. I hadn't noticed. I'm getting slow.' He followed Rocco's glance. 'What do we do?'

'We go and see who it is.' Rocco walked back along the path. It could be nothing, maybe a local come to fish. If so, no problem. If it was anyone else, he wanted to see them before they saw him.

As they neared the final bend in the path before reaching the main lodge, they heard a rumble of male voices filtering through the trees, followed by a short, sharp whistle. Then silence.

Rocco felt his scalp move. Whoever the new arrivals were, they had a communication system going. At a guess, they'd arrived at the front of the lodge and found his car. The whistle had been a warning to keep their eyes open.

That automatically left out anyone from the village or the police.

When the lodge came into view, Rocco knelt down behind some reeds and motioned for Claude to do the same. The voices had stopped, but the men must still be close by.

A man appeared at the rear corner of the building. He was heavily built, with cropped, black hair and wore a dark suit, white shirt and tie, and was carrying a gun. He moved cautiously, sticking close to the wall of the lodge as if listening for noises inside. He tried the rear door and found it open, then flattened himself against the wall. He gave a low whistle. Moments later he was joined by a second man from the other side of the lodge, similarly dressed and also armed. They communicated in a series of hand signals before slipping inside. A bark of laughter from the front of the building indicated at least two more men present.

Rocco recognised the tactic: the men at the front were a distraction while the other two checked the place out.

'Are they cops?' whispered Claude.

'Not the kind I'm used to,' said Rocco. 'Cops would go straight in.'

'So who, then?'

'City boys looking for Didier is my guess. Come on.' He eased away, leading Claude back down the path deeper into the *marais*.

* * *

Rocco didn't like the odds.

An unknown number of men, two of them armed and acting as if they had been trained in the military. If they were after Didier as he suspected and looking to settle a score, all well and good. He probably deserved everything he had coming. But there was still no sign of Francine, and if the men were up to no good and stumbled on them here in the *marais*, they might not be keen on having any witnesses to their activities.

He and Claude reached the second lodge and waited behind its cover. The minutes ticked by, the silence hanging like a blanket around them, stuffy and threatening. Then a stick cracked not far away, followed by a faint splash and a man swearing. Rocco eased back. It confirmed what he'd thought: clumsy feet in this environment meant city folk not used to walking on soft, unforgiving ground. One of the men had stepped on a branch, then off the path into water.

A white oval appeared above the undergrowth. A man's face. He was standing on the path thirty metres away, studying the smaller lodge. He had one hand held out, warning those behind him to hold back.

For Rocco it was enough. They couldn't stay here. The men were constrained by the single path, and evidently cautious about moving forward too quickly. They had probably been briefed about Didier's background and prickly nature, but would soon move forward.

He and Claude retreated further along the path to the ruined building. Once over the bridge leading to Didier's house and the village, they could get to a phone and summon reinforcements. Facing one armed man, maybe even two, might have been feasible for him and Claude, given that they were familiar with the area. Going up against four would be idiotic, and Rocco had no desire to go down in the annals of police history as a brave but dead fool.

As they slipped past the ruined lodge and headed for the bridge, Rocco heard a noise. He stopped, a hand on Claude's shoulder. A cat? Kids squealing? It sounded ghostly, a half-cry out of keeping with the surroundings.

Claude had heard it, too. 'Christ, what is that?' he whispered.

'It's coming from in there.' Rocco pointed towards the ruin. Did they have time to investigate or would the four men bypass the second lodge and come pounding along the path? He shook off his concerns. It didn't matter; they were here to find Francine, and this was the one place they hadn't yet looked.

'Come on.' He moved through the tangle of undergrowth and up to the front door, drawing his gun. The wood looked worm-eaten and rotten and smelt of mildew, and it didn't look as though anyone had been here in years. This was a waste of time…

He heard the noise again, this time close by.

He stepped through the doorway, feet crunching on wind-blown debris and rotten wood. It felt as if the whole building was trembling under his weight, and he wondered how safe the roof was. He looked around the room. It was a time capsule, rotting into the floorboards and decaying where it stood. An armchair had sunk like melting ice cream, its fabric tattered and faded to a uniform dull grey and trailing on the floor; a dining table had tilted drunkenly on one corner and a cupboard door hung off its hinges, revealing a bare interior covered with rodent droppings and layers of accumulated dirt.

Rocco moved across the room to a door at the back. It led to what had once been a small kitchen. More rotting wood and peeling walls, and the wreckage of a table and chairs, but with one difference: a pathway had been trodden through the clutter from the back door to a filthy square of colourless carpet near the side wall. Amid all the nature-inspired mess, it looked too out of place, too deliberate.

He signalled for Claude to keep an eye on the front of the building, then bent and flipped back the carpet.

Underneath was a trapdoor. A metal handle was recessed neatly into the wood.

Rocco pocketed his gun and heaved the trapdoor open, flooding the darkness below with light and revealing a nightmarish scene.

Francine Thorin lay staring up at him with bulging eyes, her hands lashed above her head to a thick wooden support post set in the earthen floor. A rough gag had been taped across her mouth, and she was making the high keening sound they had heard earlier, and rocking backwards and forwards, her entire body shaking with terror.

CHAPTER FORTY

'Thank God!' Francine gasped as Rocco tore away the gag and binding. She sagged against him, tears flooding down her face at the realisation that she was finally safe, her fingers digging into his arms in desperation. 'That man...he was going to kill me...!'

'Shush now,' Rocco whispered, gently touching a finger to her lips to stop her signalling their presence to the men out in the *marais*. Her face was bruised, with cuts on her skin where she must have been dragged into the hole, and her hair was a tangle of dirt and cobwebs. He didn't like to think of what she had suffered alone down here in the dark, not knowing whether the man who had taken her would ever come back or not. 'You're safe now. But we must get you away from here.'

She nodded, deep in shock, eyes locked on his as she gripped him even tighter. He smelt her perfume, soft and fragrant in contrast to the musky smell of the grim surroundings, and held her for a moment, dispensing with the normal advice of keeping a distance from crime victims. Above anything in the manuals, she needed contact and the reassurance of closeness, not official distance.

He turned and whistled softly to Claude, who appeared above them. His jaw dropped when he saw Francine, then he recovered quickly and grinned with relief.

'Christ on a pony! Here – reach up.' He bent and took Francine's hand, and hauled her out of the hole as if she weighed nothing. He turned to Rocco. 'We'd better move. They'll be here any second. I think they've picked up our tracks along the path.'

Rocco heaved himself out of the hole and made for the back door, pulling Francine after him. Once outside, he checked the path to the front and was shocked to hear voices close by. They'd left it too late; the men must have given the second lodge a miss. There was no time to get Francine to the bridge without being seen. She was only able to move slowly, her legs still cramped from her confinement.

He drew his gun and flicked off the safety. Time to set up some delaying tactics.

He caught a movement from the corner of his eye among the trees to the side of the lodge, and spun round. One of the men must have circled around to the side. He brought up his gun, finger tightening on the trigger, and was shocked to see Didier Marthe's face staring back at him. The scrap man was dressed in brown hunting clothes and carrying a shotgun. He looked pale and drawn, his face smeared with dirt.

For a brief second Didier wavered, staring at the three of them in desperation, especially, it seemed, at Rocco, then

Francine. Rocco got ready to open fire. Then a man's voice intruded, approaching along the path at the front of the ruined building.

In a flash, Didier turned and was gone.

Rocco turned to Claude. 'Get her across the bridge and don't look back. Call Massin or Detective Desmoulins in Amiens and get a squad out here on the double.'

'Why, what are you going to do?' protested Claude. 'There are too many—'

'Don't argue – there's no time.' Rocco turned and ran after Didier, heading away from the bridge and deeper into the *marais*, crashing noisily through a tangle of dry reeds. Behind him he heard a shout from the men on the path. He didn't stop to see if they were following.

He was counting on them doing just that.

There was no sign of Didier. The scrawny little man had moved like a greased pig, helped by his familiarity with the terrain and the colour of his clothing blending in with the vegetation.

Rocco drove on, pushing through the undergrowth and praying he wouldn't stumble into a bog or become entangled in the patches of brambles snaking everywhere. He heard a crashing sound behind him and men calling to each other. The pursuers had been caught off guard for a moment, but if they were fit and quick, they would lose no time in regaining the initiative.

He saw a clear patch through the trees ahead and veered towards it, calculating that he was now heading back in the general direction of the main lodge. Less bothered with catching up with Didier than he was drawing the men away from Claude and Francine, he put on a burst of speed.

Suddenly a stretch of water covered with a layer of scum appeared in front of him. He swerved to go round it, then moved back in the direction where Didier had gone. More sounds of pursuit came from behind him, and he realised that one of the men was getting close, the noise of his progress through the undergrowth coming uncomfortably near. He could even hear the other man's harsh breathing, but was comforted by the knowledge that while running, he couldn't shoot with any accuracy.

He felt one boot sink into soft earth. He staggered, dragging against the pull of muddy soil around his ankle, and saw a dull blackness reflecting back at him under a layer of coarse weed. *A bog!* He tore his foot free, nearly losing the boot, but managed to stumble away towards another clear patch to his right. It put him back on course for the main lodge. If he could reach his car…

A shot rang out, startling in its loudness and clipping a branch from a tree near his head. *Damn – they weren't messing.* He was tempted to ignore it. Stopping to fight would be stupid: he was outnumbered and too big a target, and he had the feeling these men had all seen action; they would not be put off by one policeman with a gun. Better to get away somewhere safe and hope Claude managed to call up reinforcements before it was too late. Even so, they had to learn that he wasn't going to run for ever or give up too easily.

He stopped and turned, dropping to one knee to reduce the target, and sighted on the gunman charging through the brush thirty metres behind him. He took a breath and fired twice, and saw the shoulder of the man's jacket jump as a shot struck home. The man was knocked sideways and there was a loud splash as he fell into the bog.

Rocco turned and continued running as two shots came in quick succession from further back in the trees, losing themselves harmlessly among the branches overhead. Undisciplined, he decided; they might have been trained once, but their discipline had gone. Indiscriminate shooting like that could only threaten their own men while giving away the shooter's position. A volley of shouts came as the others raced to cut him off, but found their progress impeded by the sheer perversity and tangle of nature in the raw.

Rocco was tiring fast and getting short of breath, the effort of pushing through this terrain far more wearing than trotting along a level road. He had few illusions about what might happen; there were three of them and one of him. Much more of this and the outcome would be short, sharp and fatal.

Moments later he burst through a hanging veil of thin branches and was relieved to see the lodge and his car right in front of him. Snatching his keys from his pocket, he ran to the driver's door, fumbling the key into the lock with a trembling hand and trying not to shoot himself in the process.

He threw himself behind the wheel and started the car, tramping on the accelerator. The heavy car responded instantly, leaping forward and fishtailing across the clearing…but heading straight for the lake as the steering wheel spun out of his hand.

He grappled with the wheel as a shot pinged off the bodywork. Then desperation enabled him to regain control of the wheel just in time. He slewed the car around at the last second and headed at full speed for the track back to the road. In the rear-view mirror, he saw three men emerge from the trees and run after him.

He smiled grimly, remembering the man he'd shot, and the splash.

One down, three to go.

CHAPTER FORTY-ONE

Rocco blasted out onto the main road and spun the wheel to the left, then trod with calm deliberation on the brakes and brought the Citroën to a stop. He didn't much care where he went right now, as long as the men followed him and not Claude and Francine. He glanced back down the track and saw a black DS parked in the bushes to one side. It could only belong to the gunmen. He waited, anxious for signs that they were coming. If they weren't, he'd have to head for the village and hope he could find the other two before the men caught up with them.

A figure burst into view from among the trees, running onto the track. A man in a suit. Rocco waited until he was sure the man had spotted him, then trod hard on the accelerator and took off for the station. He drove as fast as he dared on the narrow road, intent on keeping a lead while still drawing the men after him. There was a long straight stretch of narrow road from the station down to where it intersected with the road to Amiens, and he knew that they would be able to see him all the way. If he didn't turn on to the main road, they would know there was only one way for him to go: the cemetery.

He thought about Didier and where he might run. If the scrap man had any brains left, he must know that he was finished here. The police were after him for theft and assault; Rocco wanted him for kidnap; and now the four – or was it three? – men behind him wanted him for God knew what reason. But he had a good idea it was something to do with Berbier.

He saw the station crossing coming up fast. It wasn't much, simply a weighted wooden pole to stop traffic when a train was approaching. Only now the pole lay in splinters on the ground, and nearby, a section of a car's wing and a scattering of broken glass. Standing by the broken barrier and scratching his head was Paulais, the stationmaster.

The moment he recognised Rocco's car, Paulais ran to the side of the road and pointed towards the cemetery, waving him through and shouting incomprehensibly as Rocco roared by.

Now Rocco knew for sure where Didier had gone. It would be the one place where he felt safe; the one place he believed no sane person would dare follow.

A white Renault with the driver's door hanging open was skewed across the track twenty metres beyond the cemetery gate. Part of the right wing was missing and all the glass down that side had gone where Didier had collided with the crossing barrier.

Rocco stopped the car and climbed out, checking the

cemetery and surrounding fields. He was almost certain the fugitive would have gone straight for the wood, but he had no desire to be proven wrong by getting himself shot in the back. He also wanted to make sure that there were no visitors inside, and that they and the gardener, Cooke, were in no danger.

He drew his gun and jumped over the gate, checking the rows of headstones. The covered walkway was deserted and the tool shed in the corner looked locked tight. There was no sign of Cooke. One thing less to worry about.

He stopped by the central cross where Nathalie Berbier's body had been found, and turned to study the dense wood covering the hill at the far end of the cemetery. It looked dark and forbidding, and he was surprised at how quickly the daylight had slipped away. He checked his watch. Six o'clock. He'd been so busy with the hunt for Francine and the chase through the *marais*, he'd been unaware of time ticking by.

He breathed deeply and checked his gun. Took out a spare ammunition clip. Then he walked out of the cemetery and started up the track towards the wood. The ground here was deeply rutted and hard, and he stayed to one side, ready to throw himself down by the cemetery wall if Didier appeared. He realised that he was still wearing the rubber boots; hardly the best gear for a manhunt, but he doubted it would matter much, not once he was among the trees. He tried telling himself that coming here alone was stupid, that he should wait for help to arrive from Amiens. But deep inside he knew it would take too long. If Didier got away from here, they'd never find him again. He heard a car engine and turned. The black DS had passed the station and was barrelling along the road towards the cemetery, kicking up a furious cloud of dust in its wake. It showed no signs of stopping for the main road.

Rocco now had no choice. Going back to lead them away was no longer an option. They would be on him before he could get back to the road, and even if he got that far, their car was far more powerful and would soon overhaul him in a chase.

He turned and jogged up the track into the trees, and whatever was waiting for him.

CHAPTER FORTY-TWO

François Massin put down his phone with a trembling hand. He hadn't been expecting the call from Berbier, still less had he been quick enough to deal with the man in the way he would have liked. But as the voice had dripped like acid into his ear, part cajoling, part threatening, laying out in carefully camouflaged terms what his future might be – would be if he wasn't able to appreciate the 'delicacy' of the situation – he had begun to feel a deep anger building inside him.

He stood up and walked around his office, uncertain about what his immediate response should be. He had few friends in the senior ranks of the police service – mostly his fault, he acknowledged that, and there was little he could do about it now. But right now he could have done with some wise advice on how to handle internal politics. Being threatened by the likes of Philippe Bayer-Berbier, even in the subtle, 'friendly' tones the man had employed, was something he had never faced before. Yet he was all too aware of the enormous power the man wielded among the ranks of senior policemen and politicians – men who could decide Massin's fate at the snap of a finger. In a straight test of wills, he would be no match for that kind of influence.

He found himself standing before the photo of his younger self in uniform. So proud, he recalled his feelings at the time. So intense. And so determined to redeem himself and regain some of the self-respect he'd lost in the army.

And now this. He shook his head. He'd be an idiot to go up against Berbier, no matter what Rocco said the photo suggested. It would be professional suicide. He'd have no allies, no backing and would become a pariah with no fate but a lonely, humiliating resignation and a disappearance into obscurity.

It was not the ending he had envisaged for himself. And with that thought, he hated himself more than at any time in his life.

A knock sounded at his door. He straightened his shoulders and called, 'Come in.'

It was Desmoulins, looking flushed. Captain Canet hovered behind him, face tense.

'Urgent call from Poissons, sir,' said Desmoulins. 'Officer under threat. The missing woman has been found and there's been gunfire...several armed men are in pursuit of Inspector Rocco.'

'What?' Massin stepped towards the two officers. 'What men?'

'That's not clear, sir. One of them – the kidnapper – is Marthe, the man from the hospital. The caller said the others look like ex-military. Rocco's been forced to go to ground in the local *marais*.'

Massin turned away in a moment of indecision. Ex-military men who were prepared to go up against the police? Impossible, surely. What if Rocco had stumbled on some kind of official operation? Careers could be fatally damaged if the wrong response was made. Yet if it was true, and the men were not part of the state, then it boded ill if it was allowed to go unchallenged. He glanced at the photo on the wall. He hadn't done much to be proud of since those days. Now he was embroiled in a battle of wills with an enemy he could hardly see, let alone fight.

'Sir?' Canet prompted him. 'The lads are ready to go. Your orders?'

Massin turned. Desmoulins had his service weapon strapped on and a bunch of car keys in his hand. Canet, too, was armed and looked ready for action, his eyes bright. Behind them in the corridor, he sensed the presence of others.

He nodded. Maybe this would be a new start. If not, he could deal with his future later.

'You'd better get them moving, then, hadn't you?'

CHAPTER FORTY-THREE

Rocco felt chilled. Stepping into the trees had been like walking into one of the giant cold rooms used by meat wholesalers in Les Halles, in Paris. Thirty paces into the wood had taken him out of the light and into a world of shadows and shifting vegetation. He stood still and waited. As long as he stayed low on the slope and off the skyline, and wasn't silhouetted against the outside, he should be safe. He shivered, in spite of his coat, and sank to his knees, listening for the faintest sound of movement, of anything alien.

The quiet here was almost crypt-like. Barely a whisper penetrated from the outside, and if the men approaching up the track were still in their car, he couldn't hear the engine. He realised the advantage Didier would have in this landscape. The scrap man would be in his element: he knew the terrain like the back of his hand. To anyone else, it was a hostile environment.

Something hard and unyielding was digging into Rocco's left knee. He shifted his weight and looked down. A shape too uniform to be natural lay half-buried in the leaves and weeds. He shrank back, his gut going cold as he made out the familiar nose of a large artillery shell. He had no idea of the size, only that it had probably been designed to take out an enemy fortification or bury the occupants of a trench where they stood.

He lifted his knee and backed away, his thigh and back muscles protesting at having to move so slowly and carefully, stepping from one clear spot to another. It was all a gamble, he knew; God alone knew what he was treading on here. Most of the stuff had probably been buried deep, but over the years had risen gradually to the surface as the trees and vegetation grew and the elements flushed through, breaking up the surface soil and allowing the subsoil to yield up its deadly secrets.

The harsh whine of an engine penetrated the wood as it tore up the track at speed. The DS driver was making no attempt at subtlety, and Rocco heard a hollow crump as the Citroën's soft suspension bottomed in one of the many deep ruts.

He stayed where he was, breathing easily, confident that he couldn't be seen – at least, not by the gunmen. The thought made him want to spin round and search the immediate area for signs of Didier, but he resisted it. If the men came charging in here, they would be moving from light into shadow, fuelled by adrenalin and the desire to take him out as quickly as possible. Their vision would be slow to adjust and their control diminished, giving him ample time to identify the threat and move away.

As it would Didier.

As if on cue, a crackle came from deep in the wood to his rear. Rocco turned his head slowly, and was immediately rushed back to a time and place where every bush harboured an enemy, where sudden movement was to invite a rattle of automatic fire or a tripwire-linked explosion. He swallowed, his mouth dry, and felt a familiar tremble in his calves. For him, it had always been the legs, he remembered. For some men in the moments immediately before battle, it had been the hands shaking or the eyes flickering uncontrollably. For others it had been dark humour and dry laughter. Each had covered their own minor betrayals by gripping their weapons tighter, by thrusting their hands under their arms or simply by shutting their eyes and mouths and praying. In his case he had waited it out, because sooner or later it had always stopped.

A car door slammed and a voice drifted up from the track. The engine fell silent. Rocco watched the light, aware that somewhere behind him Didier would be doing the same.

Then he saw a flicker of movement and a dark shape appeared. A man with a handgun, head swinging from one side to the other, unaware or simply uncaring of the danger he was in. Another appeared nearby, further down the track. But this one was cooler, perhaps more experienced. One second he was there, the next he had melted to the ground.

Rocco didn't wait for the third man. If he stayed here, with Didier behind him and others coming at him from the track, he'd be trapped, especially having to take time to study the ground before every step.

He began moving in a monkey crawl, edging back down the slope towards the cemetery. He was counting on Didier having moved higher, where he would feel in control looking down on the newcomers. Rocco instinctively preferred being closer to the cemetery boundary where the going might be easier and where he could track movement against the skyline.

A shot rang out and he dropped to the ground. A sharp voice shouted a query, followed by a brief reply, then silence. Shooting at shadows, he decided. City rats nervous at finding themselves out of their own environment, in an alien world of shifting light.

He took advantage of their confusion to move, this time across the side of the slope. Then he waited, resting and watching the trees where he thought Didier might be hiding.

For the next twenty minutes he followed the progress of the three men from the car as they blundered their way through the trees. Occasionally they would call to each other, checking their positions with a hollow laugh or a brief acknowledgement, their locations pinpointed by the snap of a branch or the scrape of fabric on the thorny underbrush.

Another shot, followed by two more, this time higher up. Two voices were raised in query, one in alarm, and Rocco realised he'd lost track of the third man. He must have penetrated the trees further up the slope, trying to catch Didier unawares.

He crabbed sideways, knowing the two other men were not far away. Then a shape appeared barely ten metres from his own position. The figure was moving fast across the slope with little regard for danger, crashing noisily through the undergrowth. Not Didier, Rocco decided, but one of the gunmen, responding to the shots by circling across the lower slope to move up behind where he thought Didier's position might be. The man hurdled a tangle of briar, then stepped onto a fallen tree trunk and jumped down the other side.

CHAPTER FORTY-FOUR

The explosion came the moment the man landed. Rocco felt the shockwave brush his cheek, followed by a flash, then a billowing gust of debris burst upwards, shaking the leaves and branches high in the trees and raining down again with a rattle. It was like being caught in a monsoon, the vegetation trembling under the onslaught and drowning out nearly all other sounds.

Except for the man screaming.

It began as a long, high-pitched cry, cutting through the trees and sending shivers down Rocco's back. Amid the screaming was a gabble of words, distorted and meaningless, and he knew by the choking noises which followed that the man had taken the force of the blast in his belly and legs. He was again taken back to the jungles of South-East Asia and other explosions, other damaged men in similar circumstances.

Then came a single gunshot. The screaming stopped.

Didier. Two to go.

Rocco heard movement to the right of where the man had fallen, and a branch snapped. A sapling swayed, drawing an immediate shot from the left, followed by a shout of triumph. He knew what that signified, too: Didier was play-acting the inept fugitive, waiting for the men to come to him and drawing them across dangerous terrain.

The two remaining followers called out from their respective positions, and Rocco saw one of them move from behind a tree. After the fate of his colleague, the man stepped forward with a new awareness, checking the ground carefully in front of him. Every now and then, he whispered the fallen man's name. *'Marc! You OK? Marc!'*

For a second, as the man moved steadily closer towards the scene of the explosion, Rocco wanted to tell him not to bother. That his colleague was dead. But he knew it was futile. If Didier was waiting, then he already had the man in his sights and nothing Rocco could do would save him.

Then the last man appeared higher up the slope. He glanced down and located his colleague, signalling his presence with a faint whistle before turning to check the area around him.

Rocco froze, aware that he was out of cover. All the man had to do was look his way and he would certainly see him. Even as the thought occurred, the gunman's gaze swept across Rocco's position before moving on. He breathed a sigh of relief.

Then the man's head snapped back, processing the image he had seen. With startling speed, he turned and opened fire.

Rocco was already sliding sideways into cover, praying

he didn't trigger an explosion. He felt the first shot brush his cheek. Another clipped a branch close to his shoulder, showering him with splinters. He swore and landed in a briar, feeling the thorns slicing his face. Something sharp dug hard into his ribs and he continued rolling, knowing that the man lower down the slope would have seen the movement and would be tracking him.

He couldn't stay here. He forced himself upright and brought up his gun, counting on the element of surprise. He ignored the stinging in his face and the stabbing pain in his side, and saw the nearest man turning towards him. His colleague was a shadow in the background, also moving round to get his own sighting.

Rocco fired first, triggering shots as fast as he could, then threw himself towards a patch of clear ground behind a tree. As he did so, he heard a scream of pain, and looked up to see the man he'd fired at staring down at his leg. Instead of a bullet wound, however, a sharpened stake was protruding from his thigh and blood was pumping from the wound.

A Didier Marthe booby trap.

Two shots crashed out. The wounded man was punched sideways into the undergrowth, his jacket shredded. His colleague, realising his danger, turned and fired blindly into the trees before throwing himself into a patch of sweet nettles.

A split second after he landed, a huge explosion shook the ground, stripping the nearest trees and showering Rocco with debris. It set off another explosion, then a third and fourth, each one crawling across the slope like some malevolent being.

It was a deadly chain reaction. All Rocco could do was

cover his head and hug the ground, aware that the course of the explosions would have no pattern, no rhyme or reason. Whatever horrors lay mouldering beneath this part of the wood from the Great War over forty years before were evidently delicate enough to have been set off by the violent movement of the earth and the battering shockwaves of the first blast.

He heard a tree coming down, followed by another, the crash of their fall preceded by a tearing noise as their upper foliage ripped through the trees around them, the fractured roots unable to hold them upright. It was as if nature itself had decided to join in the fight. The ground shook with the concussion, then a heavy branch landed just a hand's reach from Rocco's head, and a shower of leaves and small branches carpeted his back.

Then utter silence fell. *Or had he gone deaf?*

Rocco shook his head and spat out leaves and dirt. He looked up cautiously and lifted his gun. A few leaves fluttered gently to the ground, a faint 'tick' marking each landing, and a distant drone of car engines being driven hard drifted across the landscape.

The cavalry. Lights, but no sirens. Someone, he thought vaguely, knew what he was doing. Sirens often spooked criminals into precipitate action, doing things they hadn't planned. A restrained but obvious approach in force, however, looked far more sinister and inevitable.

He breathed a sigh of relief and rested his head on his forearms. Then he heard the rustle of someone moving away through the trees.

Didier.

He slid out from his position and moved up the slope

towards the man he'd shot at, and found him covered by a fallen tree. His upper body was shredded and bloody, and it was impossible to tell if any of Rocco's shots had hit home first. The sharpened stake had pierced his inner thigh, although it hadn't killed him. What had done the damage was the enormous shotgun wound in his side, exposing ribs and belly, where Didier had caught him side-on. He moved past the body to check on the other man.

The last gunman was staring up at him from the edge of a crater in the bed of sweet nettles, eyes wide in shock. His lips moved soundlessly, the words unformed. Both legs were gone just below the knees and he was losing blood fast from the femoral arteries. Rocco knelt by his side, careful not to put too much weight on any one spot. He used the tip of his gun barrel to flick the man's jacket open and check for secondary weapons. There were none. As he dropped the jacket back, the man whispered something.

'Help...me!'

It was Berbier's driver.

Down the track, the approaching vehicles switched on their sirens to muddy the air and intimidate. The 'Ride of the Valkyries' moment, some cop drivers called it. They must have seen or heard the explosions and decided that the time for subtlety was past.

Rocco hadn't got much time. Even if this man didn't die of shock in the next few minutes, he would soon be beyond reach of anyone, sheltered by a screen of medical and judicial barriers. Either that or he would simply disappear, spirited away where he wouldn't be able to answer awkward questions.

CHAPTER FORTY-FIVE

A trolley clanked somewhere along the corridor of Amiens central hospital, and footsteps squeaked as a nurse hurried by in rubber-soled shoes. A telephone rang and a man's voice rose in query followed by laughter. Someone coughed noisily.

The usual noises. Unusual circumstances.

Rocco lay back on a bed and breathed deeply while a nurse applied a dressing to his ribs with cool hands. He wanted to sleep, but knew that was delayed shock. Sleep was a luxury for later.

'You were lucky,' the nurse commented cheerfully. 'It took off a chunk of flesh and nicked a couple of ribs. A bit to the side and we'd have been laying you out downstairs alongside the others.'

He grunted but said nothing. He hadn't realised he'd been shot, mistaking the pain in his side for having collided with something solid. His mother had been right after all: no pain, no sense.

Berbier's driver hadn't been so lucky; he had talked long enough, but died just as help arrived. With two of his friends also dead and the man Rocco had shot at missing in the *marais*, it had been a costly exercise for whoever had sent them.

Maybe the fourth man would surface one day, Rocco mused, a nasty surprise for some unlucky fisherman sitting quietly by the lakeside.

There was no sign of Didier, although one of the cops who was a hunter had found traces of blood on the far edge of the wood. It didn't prove Didier had been seriously wounded but it might be enough to slow him down and come to someone's attention. Rocco wasn't going to hold his breath on that one.

He had called out a warning when help had arrived, knowing he could easily end up the innocent casualty of a trigger-happy cop if he wasn't careful. He waited for them to come to him, feeling their way carefully over the ground, checking for more traps and lethal ordnance. It had taken twenty minutes, and he'd used the time to rest and lay still, studying the canopy overhead and thinking about what the driver, named André, had told him. He'd felt unaccountably tired, as if he'd run a marathon, and had closed his eyes for a moment.

Sensing movement after what seemed a long time later, he'd looked round to find Captain Canet staring down at him.

'You did all this?' Canet looked aghast at the carnage all around. 'It's a war zone!'

'Sweet Jesus.' It was René Desmoulins, peering over the officer's shoulder and holding his pistol in a meaty fist. He looked disappointed. 'You couldn't find it in you to wait for us, then?'

As soon as he was able to convince them to let him go, Rocco drove back to Poissons to find Claude, who told him that Francine was in Amiens hospital.

'She's in a mess – suffering from shock,' he said, eyeing Rocco's ruined clothing and bloodied face. 'When we got across the bridge into the village, I asked her what had happened but she became hysterical. I couldn't get a word out of her. Luckily Thierry's wife used to be a midwife, so she was able to calm her down with something. Thierry took her off to Amiens. You must have just missed her. You OK? You look like shit.' The words came out in a gabble, propelled by a mix of shock and relief.

Rocco nodded. 'Thanks for the encouragement.' He felt as if he'd been trampled by an elephant, but at least he was still on his feet.

'Sounds like you might have some questions to answer,' said Claude, when Rocco filled him in on what had happened. 'The big *képis* don't like unexplained massacres, especially when the press gets to hear about it. It makes them nervous, having to explain why some hotshot investigator from Paris blows up half the countryside. It's bad for the tourist industry.'

'I didn't know there was one.' Rocco was busy thinking about Francine and her incarceration. She must have surprised Didier at the lodge while delivering the groceries, and he'd panicked and locked her away where she wouldn't be found. At least he hadn't buried her in one of the marshes or dumped her inside her car in the lake.

Claude shook his head and sniffed. 'That's the problem

with newcomers – they always bring their shit with them.'

Rocco drove home, where he washed and changed into fresh clothes. News about the source of the explosions, which had been heard all over the village, had filtered through the community, and Mme Denis fussed around, scooping up Rocco's coat, shirt and trousers and pronouncing the first two salvageable, but the trousers beyond all help.

He waited for her to brush the coat into a semblance of something civilised, then asked Claude to take him back to Amiens.

Claude looked doubtful. 'Are you up to it? It's late. Where are we going?'

'I want to interview Francine.'

'Interview? After what she's been through?'

Rocco tossed him the keys. 'Don't ask.'

It was already dark by the time they arrived at the hospital. The press had received a briefing from Massin about the explosions in Poissons, and although it was deliberately short on detail, it contained enough salient facts for them to put out an early story the following day. Unfortunately, it hadn't kept them away for long, and they were already back clamouring at the entrance for late developments and the identities of the dead gunmen.

As the two policemen walked through the shadows across the car park, Rocco drew Claude to a stop before they reached the door. Something was niggling at his mind like a bad itch.

'You said earlier about newcomers bringing trouble with them.'

Claude looked abashed. 'Sure. It was just a crack. I didn't mean anything personal.'

'I know that. But who were you thinking of, apart from me?'

Claude puffed out his cheeks. 'Well, now you mention it, I suppose…Didier. Mostly.'

'He's been here – what, three years, you said?'

'About that.'

'Who else?'

'Let me see…there's Alain Dutronc down at the far end of the village, near my place…he arrived here about six months ago. He's a quiet drunk, about eighty-five years old and doesn't get out much. Then Mme Denis – she's been here a few years. A bit of a gossip, but she's OK.'

'She's not local?' He remembered her saying something about having lived in Poissons long enough to know there were always surprises. At the time, he'd taken it as a statement about a lifetime's knowledge of the village, or at least many years. With hindsight, it now took on a slightly different meaning.

'She turned up several years ago,' Claude confirmed, 'with her husband. Not sure where from. He died and she stayed on. Someone said she lost her family in the war. I don't know much about her, to be honest.' He shrugged. 'I don't push people to tell me their life histories.'

Rocco mulled it over, remembering how he'd felt sure someone had been inside the house and moved the photograph of Didier Marthe and the Resistance group. There was also the curtain caught in the window, which he was sure hadn't been like that when he'd left. Was Mme Denis more than a friendly neighbour? Had she used a spare key to see what he was doing here and how far he'd got with his investigation? But if so, she wouldn't have needed to open the window to get in, even if she were able to.

'And Francine, of course. But you know about her.'

Claude's voice interrupted his thoughts. Francine Thorin. Young, pretty, interesting. A widow. Friendly.

'Tell me again.'

'She arrived about two years ago.' Claude shrugged. 'That's all I know. She doesn't talk much but she's sociable enough, fits into the community. I mean…she's not exactly a good-time girl, you know what I mean?'

'No secret life, then.'

'If there is, that's what she's kept it – secret. But I don't believe that.'

'You didn't know she was a widow,' Rocco pointed out.

'No.' Claude frowned. 'I didn't.' His frown deepened. 'Look, where is this going? She's had a rough time, with the kidnapping thing.'

Rocco ignored him. Two years ago. He felt something about that time frame tugging at his memory. Was it significant?

'What else happened in Poissons two years ago?'

'How do you mean?'

'Apart from Francine arriving.'

'Ah. Let me see…there was Jean-Po Boutin dying. Nasty business, but it was an accident. I told you.' He lifted his eyebrows. 'That was it. Nothing else major, as far as I can recall.'

Rocco nodded, watching a flurry of activity under the lights by the entrance to the hospital as a crowd of press people gathered around a man in a white coat. They fell back as the man shook his head and waved what looked like a stack of papers, the laugh on them.

Rocco was having difficulty trying to marshal the facts of the various comings and goings around Poissons, and deciding whether they were relevant to his case and why the time frame had lodged in his mind the way it had. Mme Denis arrives several years ago with husband; husband dies. Didier Marthe arrives three years ago. Francine Thorin turns up a year later. Jean-Paul Boutin dies at about the same time.

Didier takes over Boutin's telephone shortly after.

Nathalie Berbier dies in the *marais*.

Ishmael Poudric dies near Rouen.

And years before that, at a time of huge upheaval and horror, a group of men and a woman vanish off the face of the earth.

Except that two of them came back.

Discount Mme Denis, he decided. He wasn't sure why, but instinct told him that anyone with her sense of humour couldn't be bad.

'That's a weird thing, now I come to think of it.' Claude had his hands thrust into his pockets and was staring up at the night sky with his face screwed up as if delving into the secrets of the universe.

'What?'

'Well, coincidence, that's all. For the first month or so after coming here, Francine lived in the house where you're staying.'

CHAPTER FORTY-SIX

Rocco stood just inside the cool side room and watched the slim figure lying in the bed. It occurred to him with a sense of irony that Francine was in the very room vacated not long ago by Didier Marthe. Maybe, he thought vaguely, wondering if he wasn't still feeling the effects of being shot, the hospital liked to save rooms for patients from the same postal area to give them a feeling of community.

There were no machines here: none of the tubes and wires associated with the wounded, injured or about-to-pass-on; none of the atmosphere normally pervading the space where the seriously ill seem to hover on the doorstep to the next world. It was merely a room where a woman was sleeping.

Bed rest, he'd heard it called.

The doctor he'd spoken to said she was in a fragile mental and physical state, nursing vivid memories and trying to come to grips with being safe after her imprisonment. It would take time, he'd added, a less than subtle warning for Rocco to go easy on her. Mental trauma, he'd added pointedly, was not like gunshot wounds, where the scars were mostly physical.

As Rocco moved towards the window he became aware of the patient's eyes tracking him across the room.

He stopped. 'How are you feeling?' He wondered how many times she had been in his house, either using the key from her own time living there or entering through the French window. It wouldn't have been difficult to do. She would have seen the photo and it would have triggered... what?

'OK.' Her voice was a rasp, echoing sleep and probably drugs. She looked around as if acquainting herself with her surroundings, eyes flickering as they settled on each new item in the room. Then she looked away from him, face turned to the wall. He thought she might have fallen asleep, but when he leant over, her eyes were open.

'You OK to talk?' he asked, and sat down before she could say no. His side ached and he felt the bandage tight across his ribs, but it was bearable.

'What about?' Her voice was clearer but lacked strength and vitality.

'What happened?' When Francine said nothing, he explained, 'That was a question, not a reply.'

Her face turned towards his, but she didn't look him in the eye. This close, he could see that the cuts on her skin were vivid red, but already starting to close and fade. The bruising he'd seen on her cheeks in the ruined lodge had diminished as if by magic, and he guessed that a kindly nurse had applied some discreet make-up.

321

'Are you interrogating me?' Her eyes were big, serious.

'I wouldn't call it that,' he said carefully. 'But I do need your help.'

She sighed and nodded. 'I went to make the delivery.' The words came out stronger this time. 'To leave the crate outside the main lodge as I'd been instructed.'

'Was it by phone?' He knew the answer but needed her to confirm it.

'What? Yes. Yes, by phone.' Francine looked confused for a moment, eyes almost closing. 'A man. Several days ago. He said to leave the stuff at the back door and he'd arrange for it to be taken inside. So I did.'

'Go on.'

'I'd just got there, and was putting the crate down, looking for a safe spot to leave it where the birds wouldn't get at it. Then the door opened and he came out.'

'Who? Did you recognise him?'

'No. I...no, I didn't see his face. It was too quick.' She shook her head, her hair falling across one side of her head. 'Just too quick.' A tear slid out of her eye and down her cheek. 'I never saw him.'

Rocco had to resist the temptation to brush the hair away. 'Not even when he tied you up? Not a glimpse...nothing?'

'I told you. No.' Her voice dropped to a murmur. 'He told me to look away or he'd drop me in the *marais*, where nobody would ever find me. He kept talking about the Blue Pool.' She shuddered and looked at him. 'Did you hear about it?'

Rocco nodded. 'I did. But it's not true – it's just a geological oddity.' He wasn't sure about that but he wanted Francine to feel safe. Secure.

'If you say so.'

'Did he at any time say what he was going to do? Why he was keeping you there?'

'No. He said he had…things to do. Things to finish. I was his *laissez-passer*, he said. I didn't know what that meant. I kept asking him why but he didn't seem to have any idea. I thought I was going…to die.' She gulped and a tremor went through her shoulders.

'Pity you didn't recognise his voice.' Rocco kept his tone matter-of-fact, yet probing. The art of suggestion often accomplished what direct questions could not.

'I suppose.' She still wouldn't look at him, but he could see her eyes were wet, red-rimmed. 'I heard a nurse say earlier that there had been explosions and several men killed. What happened?'

'Some men followed the man who kidnapped you into the woods. They trod on some abandoned ammunition from the wars. They're all dead.'

'What about the man? What happened to him?'

Rocco paused, stuck for an answer. If he told her Didier was dead, and no longer a threat, the truth would soon come out; he'd be a liar and for what reason? If he told her Didier was still out there, she might retreat into a shell and not come out again. Then something hit him like a cold shower.

She hadn't asked about the dead men. She was only interested in Didier. Who wouldn't show at least some curiosity about who the dead men were? Was that because she already knew?

He forced himself to push on and said, 'He got away but he's badly injured. Don't worry – we don't think he'll be back.'

323

She looked him in the eye for the first time, and he found the directness of her gaze oddly disturbing. It was almost as if she was trying to probe his mind. Then she sighed and turned her head away.

'So why me? Why do you think he attacked me? Kept me prisoner?'

He wasn't surprised by the questions, but found himself fastening on her tone of voice. He'd dealt with crime victims more times than he could recall: the targets of burglaries, assaults, even two kidnaps. They often asked the same question: 'Why me?', as if trying to understand if there was a personal element to what had happened. Nearly always they had been fearful, resentful, even angry, as if they'd been plucked out of the crowd with deliberate intent.

Yet Francine sounded almost detached. Analytical. Calm, even.

He was tempted to tell her that no, it had been purely random, the act of a desperate man. She'd simply been in the wrong place at the wrong time. But something stopped him. 'Why do you think he did it?'

She spun her head to look at him again, then frowned.

'What do you mean? I told you, I asked him but he never said. How would I know what it was?' Her skin flushed and he held her gaze, watching her eyes. She turned away again.

Rocco stood up, gently patted her arm. 'OK, I'll leave it for now. We'll talk again later, when you feel rested.' He paused, sensing she was waiting for him to leave. Then he said, 'One more question, though, for the press outside. They know you're in here; they're looking for background details. Is Thorin your family or married name?'

'My family name.' Her voice was a whisper, the response automatic.

He left her.

On the way outside he waved to Claude, who was busy chatting to a pretty nurse, then used the telephone on reception to call the office. He asked to speak to René Desmoulins and gave him another job to do. This one, he said, was urgent.

CHAPTER FORTY-SEVEN

Rocco got Claude to drop him at the office, then went in search of Massin.

Word had gone ahead and the senior officer was waiting for him in the corridor. He waved Rocco to a room just down from his office and spun the blinds to blank out passing foot traffic.

'You did good work,' Massin began, taking a tour of the room. It was an impersonal space with a long table and a few chairs. A police radio loudspeaker extension was located at the end of the room. Massin walked over and switched it on, and a flow of voices interspersed with static filled the air. He returned to face Rocco and sat down at the table. 'Nearly got yourself killed in the process, though. You enjoy living on the edge like that?'

'No. It was the way it worked out.'

'Pity you didn't bring back any live ones.' Massin tapped the table with a bony fingertip. 'It would have been useful finding out who employed those men.'

Rocco wondered if Massin was playing at being obtuse or merely cautious. 'Did you trace the car registration?'

'Of course. That was easy. It was one of several stolen in the Paris region over the past five or six months. All Citroën DS, all official in appearance. It was probably kept in a lock-up until it was needed.' He snapped his fingers, struggling for a phrase. 'What's the underworld description for such vehicles?'

'Use, abuse and lose.' It was also the term employed by crime squad members in Paris for cars used in armed robberies and bullion heists. The driver would be in a police uniform and the car plus the cap would be enough to fool the target long enough to gain access and carry out the job. After the job, the cars were dumped or torched, often both. He wasn't surprised by the revelation, merely disappointed. It would have been useful to have a line going back to the owner.

'Appropriate. You've spoken to the kidnap victim?'

Rocco nodded. 'She didn't see a face, though.' He went quickly through his chat with Francine, but he could see that Massin wasn't really listening. He wondered what was on the officer's mind. He soon found out.

'I tried to find out some of the information you requested,' Massin said, and waved a finger pointedly at the ceiling and walls. 'I got nowhere. In fact,' he straightened his tie, 'I was told in no uncertain terms to leave it alone. I may not care to be told that, as a professional policeman, but I have to recognise that there are certain...lines of questioning that it would be foolish for anyone to pursue without a clear and solid reason.'

'But what if those lines are connected to a murder investigation and another one of attempted murder?'

'You don't know that for sure. Thinking it does not prove it. Surmising something is not enough – you know that.'

Rocco reined himself in. He'd virtually resigned himself to thinking that Massin would not have tried too hard to find out about Berbier's past, not if it meant pushing his nose into official files. Yet by Massin's elaborate finger signals just now, was he actually suggesting the room might be bugged? If so, this put things on an entirely different level. He answered equally enigmatically. 'I understand. At the moment, I have lines of enquiry to follow, but nothing concrete.'

'Pity.' Massin looked disappointed, even pained. 'Exactly what information do you have on the…subject in question?'

The radio had fallen silent while they were talking, and was now emitting a faint hiss of static. Rocco walked over to it and moved the dial until a renewed welter of chatter came back. He turned up the volume, then returned to sit next to Massin. It was time to put what information he had down on the table.

He spoke quickly. 'I know Philippe Bayer-Berbier passed through the Poitiers area during the war sometime in 1944. He was on a re-supply trip, delivering essential funds and other material to Resistance groups in the region. He figures in the photo I mentioned – the one with the APP logo on the back.'

'But not recognisably.'

'Not in that one, no. But there is another, full face, taken at the same time. It's definitely him.'

'Go on.'

'According to the photographer, Poudric, shortly after the photos were taken, the entire group was caught while holding a meeting one night. The meeting had been called by the SOE agent.'

'The one you say was Berbier.'

'Yes. The entire group was shipped to Natzweiler-Struthof. They never came out.' He paused, then added, 'Except for Didier Marthe and Philippe Berbier.'

Massin looked at him with narrowed eyes. 'If I read you right, that's quite an allegation. You're saying…what, exactly?'

'Either Berbier and Marthe must have known what was going to happen and stayed away, or they managed to talk their way out. Since neither of them was ever seen in the area again, and I've never heard of the Germans doing deals, I'm leaning towards the former. They simply stayed away and moved on. It's the only explanation.'

'But why?' Massin looked perplexed. 'What would bring two men like this together? They had nothing in common except for the fight against the Germans. That alone might bring them into contact on the battlefield, but nothing more. Do you have an ounce of proof to back this up, such as a meeting or an exchange of correspondence?'

Rocco took a deep breath. The only proof he had was currently on the run, wounded, resentful and unlikely to give him the spit off his tongue, let alone information. He had a theory, but he was still working on it. Neither would be enough for Massin to take this any further forward.

Massin read his face. 'I see. So what do you have?'

'I'm waiting for a piece of information which I think will tie it all together.' A domino effect, he wanted to add, but wasn't sure Massin would believe him. He wasn't sure he believed it himself.

Massin opened his mouth to speak, but was interrupted by a knock at the door. He stood up and opened it to find Desmoulins standing there holding a piece of paper and trying to hold back a grin.

'Note for Inspector Rocco, sir.'

Massin took the paper, closed the door again and handed it to Rocco without looking at it.

'You must try not to use members of staff here as your own private detection unit,' he said dryly. 'Is that by any chance the information you've been waiting for?'

Rocco looked down at the piece of paper and saw two names. One dead, the other alive. He felt a kick of something low down in his stomach, but wasn't sure whether it was elation or something less welcome.

'It is. May I go?'

Massin nodded and waved a hand. 'Do. But if this falls flat, I suggest you enlist in the Foreign Legion. They're always looking for men with self-destructive tendencies.'

Back at the hospital, this time with Claude alongside him, Rocco stepped into Francine's room and waited for her to sense his presence, as he knew she would. She turned her head, and he watched with a feeling of disappointment as the uncertainty grew on her face.

He motioned Claude to sit by the window. He'd already warned him to listen and remember, but to show no surprise, make no comment.

'You again.' Francine rolled carefully to face him, her face pale.

'Me again.' He drew up a chair and sat facing her. He took out the group photo that Poudric had taken and showed it to her. Allowed her to take it from his hand. To study it.

She said nothing as her eyes slid across the faces. There was no reaction, no sign of recognition.

She shrugged. 'I don't understand.' She handed it back to him. Her voice was flat, unemotional, but a pulse was beating in her throat.

'Really?' Rocco crossed his legs and tapped the photo on his knee. 'I think maybe you do. That you understand very well.' She said nothing, so he continued. 'The woman in this photo was called Elise. She was born in Poitiers in 1910, and lived in the Rue Colonel Magnon, at number 25. Her parents were André, a baker's assistant, and Claudine, a laundry worker. Elise married once, but her husband was killed in an agricultural accident just before the outbreak of war. She reverted to using her maiden name.'

Still nothing.

'She was helped by the local union of farm workers – an unofficial group who cared for their own. It was almost unknown here at the time, this kind of little collective. They were probably more politically and socially aware than most, although certainly with no pretensions of moving higher, but happy to be doing what they could. They looked after her, gave her work whenever they could and helped her find a home. Some called them communists.' Rocco brushed some lint from his knee, keeping his voice level, almost casual. He wanted to see some reaction. 'Then, when the war came, a few locals joined the Resistance movement: those with certain skills or equipment, who knew how to disrupt, to destroy. Not all with military training, not experts, but passionate enough to feel they had to do something. The people who had helped Elise did the same. But true to form, they had different objectives and formed their own group... an offshoot of what became known as the FTP – the *Francs-Tireurs et Partisans*.'

Claude shifted in his chair but said nothing, leaning forward with interest.

'For Elise, it must have been like repaying a debt, to join their ranks. To even be asked, that was something. What she didn't know was that the group realised that a woman could, in many ways, be more useful in some situations than a man. A single woman was less suspect, could move more freely; they were less likely to be stopped by patrols, and if they were, could – especially a good-looking woman like Elise – talk their way through.'

Rocco stood up and walked across to the window. He felt her eyes on him all the way. Claude looked as if he was about to speak but Rocco gave a minute shake of his head. 'One of her colleagues in this fledgling underground group was a man named Tomas Brouté. Tomas took a shine to Elise...well, who can blame him? He wasn't much of a catch: he was born a bastard, had nothing to offer and was quick-tempered and aggressive. Dangerous, even. It didn't put him off, though. He used to hover around her all the time, hoping to catch her favours. He even began to treat her like his own...no doubt quick to warn others away, even placing a proprietary hand on her whenever the situation presented itself.' He turned and flicked the photo onto the bed, just like he had done with Didier.

'As he did there.'

She didn't look down. Stared right back at him, her expression blank.

'In summer 1944, the group was betrayed. The details are a little sketchy, but it seems they were picked up by the Germans one night during a meeting. They were sent to a place no sane person ever wanted to see: a concentration camp called Natzweiler-Struthof. The men, the woman – all of them.' The clank of a trolley sounded from out in the corridor, and a door thumped, followed by the squeak of soles on tiles. 'None was ever seen again. Until recently.'

Francine's eyes had closed. And suddenly Rocco felt sorry for her; for the memories he was releasing, for the realisation that more was known than she could possibly have imagined ever would be. But he forged on. He had to.

'The man named Tomas had a second name: Didier. His surname was Brouté, after his mother. He probably didn't care much for it – couldn't do, anyway, because people would have remembered it too easily. You're probably ahead of me here.'

No reaction.

'It doesn't matter. Unknown to anyone at the time – especially the other members of the group – Tomas had allowed his desire for Elise to get the better of him. Or maybe he'd just grown sick of the other members of the group because they wouldn't allow him to do whatever he wanted – I'm sure he had the skills if not the lust to want to go out killing Germans whenever he could, but uncontrolled, that would have had serious consequences for the local community. Whatever his reasons, he decided to betray the others to the Germans. Only, in his twisted mind, he hadn't quite allowed for the fact that the Germans would take everyone in the group, no matter who they were. The result was, Elise disappeared into the camp with everyone else. All except Tomas, who slipped away. And survived. He couldn't risk keeping his surname of Brouté, after his mother, because that would have been too easily recognised locally and someone might have put two and two together. He'd have been strung up as a collaborator. So he took his second name and the surname of the registrar on his birth certificate, and moved away from the Poitiers area and became someone else. He became Didier Marthe. And eventually, years later, he arrived in Poissons-les-Marais, where nobody knew him. Where he could start a new life.'

He leant forward and picked up the photo, tapping Francine on the shoulder with it until she opened her eyes and looked at him. He held it up for her to see, one finger on the thin man near the end of the group.

'That's Tomas Brouté, as he was known then. Now miraculously alive and calling himself Didier Marthe.' He moved his finger. 'And that's Elise, isn't it?'

Francine stared up at him, a glint of something in her eye. Was it resentment? Anger? Or something like a muted appeal for help? He couldn't tell.

'I don't know anyone called Elise,' she said finally, her words a whisper.

'Really?' Rocco felt a flutter of irritation. Maybe she was tougher than he'd thought. 'You should do. You shared the same surname.'

Her eyes flickered. 'What?'

'You've never forgiven the man who betrayed her, have you? Elise Thorin was your big sister.'

CHAPTER FORTY-EIGHT

Claude's chair creaked dangerously as the *garde champêtre* shot to his feet with surprise.

'Lucas, are you crazy?' He sounded shocked and angry, puffing out a blast of air in disbelief.

Rocco ignored him. He had his eyes firmly on Francine's face, watching for a sign – a hint – that she was about to fold. This couldn't go on for much longer.

'You don't know anything.' The response was sudden, so faint he almost missed it. She hadn't moved her head, but her shoulders had gone limp.

It was the beginning. Time to push it as far as he could. He held the photo alongside her face, then beckoned Claude over and made him look. Made him compare.

'Tell me what you see. Don't think about it – use your instincts.'

Claude resisted at first, his face red and his eyes hating Rocco for what he was suggesting. Then finally he looked. And started.

'*Jesus!*' He crossed himself, then looked again. Rocco knew Claude didn't need to look at Francine to check the similarities – they were there, now plain to see. They had missed the resemblance before because the very idea wouldn't have even entered their thinking. In terms of time, then was then and now was now – a whole world and too many years apart. Elise then was a similar age to Francine now. Seen side by side, the characteristics were too close to ignore.

'Elise and Francine Thorin,' said Rocco. He didn't need to look at the paper in his pocket, which Desmoulins had handed to Massin. 'Born to André and Claudine. There never was a marriage, was there? No husband killed in a factory accident. That was merely a fact you borrowed from your sister's life and adapted to suit your needs.'

He sat down again.

'Please tell me,' he said softly.

'Elise was sixteen years older than me,' she began, and reached out to take the photo from Rocco's hand. She smoothed her fingers across it, brushing away imaginary dust. 'I was twelve. She used to talk about the men in the group, but not the things they did against the Germans. It was too dangerous even between families...in case someone talked. She said Tomas was insanely jealous of the other men, who were all so confident and brave and...could talk to a woman like her. He was always trying to start an affair with her, but she wasn't interested. He was dangerous. She thought he was unstable. They used to argue, and she had to pretend to be friendly with him because he was always trying to start fights when one of the others so much as looked at her. Especially the newcomer.' She stopped and a tear dropped onto the photo. She didn't seem to notice.

'The SOE agent?'

She nodded. 'I didn't know what he was – just that a man had arrived from somewhere to help the group. I knew Elise meant England because I heard the plane go over the night he arrived. She was out with the others, so I knew something was happening. The planes only came from England; small square ones with enough room for a couple of people and the supplies they dropped. She came back smelling of kerosene, for the signal flares.' She cleared her throat. 'Anyway, the new man was tall and handsome and sophisticated – an officer, Elise said. Charismatic. Somebody who had seen places. I think she was attracted to him, but he hardly noticed.'

'You met him?'

'No. I saw him in Poitiers once. Elise pointed him out to me. Even being undercover, he had a way of holding himself.'

'Did she know his name?'

'No. Nobody did. He had a code name: Cormorant. A silly name for a man like that, don't you think?' She shrugged, not expecting an answer. 'He brought supplies for the group, and money to pay people.'

'Bribes?'

'Yes. Officials in the town hall and the railway, others who needed money to do things for the group. A lot of money, Elise said. He was also calling on other groups in the region.'

'What happened?'

'She overheard Tomas – Didier – talking with this new

man a few days after he landed. He was French, so she understood. They were arguing about the money. The agent was telling him that it had got lost in the drop; that it must have fallen into a lake and sank because the coordinates had brought them too close to water that night and the parachute had drifted too far on the wind. The argument got quite violent. Didier said the man was lying, that there was no wind that night. Elise told me the same thing. Too much wind would have blown the parachutes off course.'

Rocco found he was holding his breath. He didn't dare look at Claude for fear he might break the spell and Francine would shut down.

'What then?'

'Didier then told the agent he'd followed him out one night and seen him concealing a package in an abandoned cowshed. He threatened to tell the others if the man didn't give him a cut.'

'Which he did?'

'Yes. The agent told the group that the money was lost, then he and Didier split the package. But the rest of the group found out. I think Didier began to spend his share and someone noticed. Elise said that word would have got back to London and the two of them would have been hunted down and killed.'

Claude butted in. 'And your sister told you all this? You, a twelve-year-old girl?'

Francine nodded. 'Why not? She told me lots of things. She taught me lots, too.' Her eyes glittered with what could have only been secret pride, and Rocco felt a worm of disquiet as he wondered what else lay beneath that expression.

'Go on.' Rocco stared hard at Claude, a warning to stay quiet.

'Didier told her everything because he wanted to impress her. All it did was increase her contempt for him. In fact, she thought he was making it up, a braggart. She still thought that at the end.'

'What happened then?' said Rocco.

'A couple of nights later, the men in the group met in a deserted quarry where they had their equipment concealed in caves dug out of the rock. It was a strategy meeting called by the agent. But Elise said they were going to use the meeting to confront him and Didier about the theft. They warned Elise to stay away, that it might be dangerous. When they got to the quarry, the Germans were waiting.' She sighed with a deep shudder that seemed to embrace her whole body. 'That same night, the Germans raided our house and took my sister away. I never saw her again.'

'What about Didier and the other man?'

'They disappeared, too. Nobody saw them again. As far as anyone knew, they were taken at the same time. But now I realise that they weren't even there, otherwise they'd be dead.' Her face twisted with bitterness. 'How did the Germans know about the exact time and location of the meeting? It must have been because Didier and the other man betrayed the group – it's the only explanation.'

'But you didn't know that at the time.'

'No. Of course not.' She shrugged. 'It was just a horrible part of the war. Then, just over a couple of years ago, I saw a face in the newspaper. I thought I was going mad, delusional. It was the same face, the same smile...older, of course, but definitely the same man, now very important and rich. That's when it all hit me: when I realised that he must have got away...that Didier hadn't been bragging about the money after all.'

'So you reasoned that if the agent had got away, there was a chance Didier had, too?'

'Why not? They were in it together – traitors both.'

'So you came after Didier and tracked him to Poissons.'

'It wasn't like that. I followed the other man first, for two weeks, when he was visiting his factories. Him I knew where to find: he lived in the public eye, so rich, so important. I wanted to learn all I could about him. One of his factories is here in Amiens. It makes plastic buckets for export to Germany. Can you believe the irony of that?'

Neither man said anything.

'Anyway, after his visit, he drove out towards Poissons and turned off the road into the *marais*. I followed him on foot. He met up with another man at the big lodge.'

'How did you manage to follow him all that way?' muttered Claude. He hadn't said 'you being a mere woman', but the inference was clear.

'I worked for the tax authorities before coming here. I had to spend time with their investigators, watching people. It was easy. If he saw me on the road behind him, he probably looked right through me. Elise also taught me how to be invisible, how not to stand out.'

Rocco thought about the description Ishmael Poudric had given of the woman who'd called on him. *Plain... instantly forgettable.*

'And the man he met – that was Didier?'

'Yes. I recognised him immediately. He'd been to our house twice, chasing Elise, so I'd seen him up close. He had

340

a way of looking at women...and twelve-year-old girls. He was a vile little man. Repulsive. They were standing outside the lodge, arguing. Then they left. I knew where I could find one; now I wanted to find where the other lived.'

'Which you did.'

She nodded. 'It was simple. I followed him through the *marais* until I came to his house.'

'Was it you who pinned the photo to the board in his kitchen?'

She hesitated just for a second, then nodded. 'Yes. But that was much later.'

'To make him run?'

'No. To make him squirm.'

'Did he ever realise who you were?' He meant at any time; if Didier had taken her deliberately, it would point to motive, to planning. To recognition.

'No. I was a kid when he last saw me.'

'Did you ever enlighten him?'

'No.'

'Not even after he took you?'

'No.'

Rocco took a turn around the room to ease the sting in his ribs. The tablets the nurse had given him were wearing off and it was hurting like hell; he hadn't noticed it for a while, too absorbed in what he was doing. He returned to stand in front of her.

'You could have gone to the authorities.'

'And told them what?' Her eyes flashed. 'That I, as a twelve-year-old girl, remembered from all those years ago seeing a little weasel and the great industrialist and war hero stealing and cheating and betraying? Who would have believed me? Who would have cared? Would *you*?'

He had no answer to that. She was right: it was too old, too long ago. Best buried and forgotten, along with countless other crimes and misdemeanours. But not for him. There was one more detail he needed her to give voice to. Essential, in fact. 'The face you saw in the newspaper; the man you followed to Poissons. The SOE agent. He has a name?'

'You know it. Philippe Bayer-Berbier.' The words came out flat, lacking any feeling.

Seconds ticked by before anyone spoke. Then Rocco said, 'What were you thinking of doing when you found these two men?'

She shrugged again, this time looking him straight in the eye. There was nothing there, though: her eyes were empty. The very absence of emotion was utterly chilling.

'I was going to kill them.'

'How were you going to do that?' he said finally. Another tour of the room had not eased the discomfort in his ribs. He felt as if he had nothing else left to ask. Claude had sunk into his chair, incredulity on his face.

'Any way I could. I was going to bide my time. As to how, Elise told me. She blew up a train once, when it was in a siding. I was a good listener. I nearly did it, too.' She gave a half-smile, eyes drifting, and Rocco felt the last vestige of sympathy fall away.

'So Elise knew all about explosives?'

'Enough.'

'And guns?'

'Naturally.' She sounded proud of the fact, and he wondered how much of that was for her own skills, picked up at her big sister's knee.

He glanced at the photo again, at Elise holding a dagger as if she knew how to use it. 'And knives, too.'

This time she said nothing. Simply stared at him, a flicker of something crossing her face, then gone. *She was ahead of him; knew where that question was leading.* No matter. It was all he needed.

'Did you kill Nathalie Berbier?' He was pretty sure he knew the answer to that. He'd failed to judge Francine Thorin correctly until now. But Poudric apart, her approach to getting revenge was fairly basic: she focused on and went directly for those she held responsible for the death of her sister. Her response confirmed it.

'Is that who the dead woman was?'

'You didn't know?'

'No. Why would I?'

He believed her. There was something undeniable in her reply. Besides, he knew she'd had no prior contact with the lodge or anyone else in it until she had been taken by Didier. He nodded and stood up. As he reached the door, he turned and asked casually, 'Who was Agnès Carre?'

She turned on her side away from him and pulled the covers over her shoulder, shutting him out. 'Someone I once knew,' she said softly.

He glanced at Claude, who lifted an eyebrow. That she hadn't denied knowing the name might be enough. That and having admitted to pinning up a copy of the photo in Didier's house. Enough to prove that, after seeing the photo in Rocco's house in the Rue Danvillers, and realising only then that the photographer, Ishmael Poudric, was a loose end that needed clearing away, she had driven back to Rouen and murdered him.

Tidying up loose ends. No doubt something else Elise had taught her.

He walked out of the room and called the office. After a few false starts, he was told Massin was still there. He was put through. He gave the senior officer a summary of events, then asked him to arrange for someone to come to the hospital and serve Francine Thorin with an arrest warrant for the murder of Ishmael Poudric and the attempted murder of Didier Marthe.

CHAPTER FORTY-NINE

The *marais* at night was a ghostly environment. Musty smells, strange sounds and the furtive movement of wildlife echoed in the ever-changing and almost invisible landscape. With a weak moon flitting through thin cloud cover, it was a mass of shifting shadows, too, adding to the unreal quality of the place. Rocco had spent too many nights on surveillance in city streets and back alleys to be anything but easily bored by inner-city stillness and its lack of vibrancy; but this place had an undercurrent all of its own that was almost a relief to a bored cop.

He was lying beneath the overturned aluminium boat near the reeds, a few paces from the back door of the main lodge. Arriving on foot just after 02.30, he'd slid underneath the curve of its side, dragging in a square of canvas tarpaulin to form a groundsheet against the damp grass. The location gave him a clear view of the lodge and the approach along the path into the *marais*, but the road and the turning circle in front of the building were hidden from his sight. He had debated waiting in the reeds across the far side, giving him a view of both approaches, but a sneak look earlier had revealed soft, marshy ground underneath. He'd also dismissed the interior of the building: it was too restrictive and Didier would expect it of a city cop, anyway.

In the end, the boat had been the only solution.

He hadn't mentioned his intentions to anyone, mainly to prevent Claude from insisting on joining him. Two-man surveillances were easily spotted, and he'd seen so many fall apart through the presence of two breathing souls trying hard to remain still. In addition, he had no guarantees that the scrap man would come back here. For all he knew, he was a hundred miles away by now, nursing his wounds. Yet something told him otherwise. Too much had been happening in a very short space of time for Didier to have gained access to his home for long, and if he wanted to remain at large – and he was too much of a survivor not to – there were things he would need, like money. And that meant the locked cellar. Didier didn't seem the sort to have faith in bank accounts.

He shifted his weight to ease the pain in his side. The nurse at the hospital had said it would be uncomfortable for some days, and had given him a supply of painkillers if it got too much to bear. Unfortunately, he'd forgotten to bring them with him.

He tensed as something pale entered his field of vision. But it was too high off the ground to be human. He relaxed as an owl flashed briefly through a patch of moonlight. Soundless and white, it glided into the trees and was gone, swallowed by shadows. Then a fox appeared, trotting

346

nimbly along the path and nosing under a fallen branch before disappearing among a heavy growth of reeds. From his position, Rocco could feel the cooler air coming off the lake, and heard a variety of plops and soft swirls as the creatures of the water went about their business. At any other time, he would have enjoyed the opportunity to study the place. But now was not it.

Time had passed quickly. When he tilted his watch towards the moonlit gap near the ground, he saw it was 04.00. The time most cops on surveillance detail found the hardest to stay awake. Not criminals, though; they loved the hours leading to dawn, like feral cats on the prowl, going about their unseen business.

He yawned, mouth threatening lockjaw, and wished he'd brought coffee. A strong caffeine hit would have worked wonders right now, but he knew that a hunted man like Didier would pick up the smell from fifty paces away.

He checked his watch again. 04.10. Now time was hanging. Then he tensed as a crackle of grass came from his left, and he heard the familiar, faint whistle-brush of undergrowth against fabric.

A bird flitted up into the trees and a swirl of water in the lake behind him indicated something moving nearby. Whatever it was had come through the trees from his left, following the line of the track from the road. He cursed. The boat was tilted to the left, with the lower edge against the ground, and he wouldn't get a sight of the intruder until he or she moved across his front nearer the lodge.

Was it a moonlight hunter? Someone else from the village on a foray for fish or fowl?

Silence.

Something brushed against the hull of the boat and Rocco froze, half-expecting his cover to be lifted away. He was sure he could hear someone breathing. A man, it had to be. There was a sour smell, like that of disturbed water or mud mixed with body odour.

A faint cough, followed by a sigh. Rocco tensed, ready to follow the boat upright, gun at the ready. Instead, he heard a metallic click and a footfall. Whoever was out there was moving away.

He lay on his side, giving him an extra few centimetres of view under the curve of the boat. A shadowy figure crossed between him and the lodge, paused for a moment, then continued walking. Stopped again as the clouds shifted and pale moonlight flooded the clearing. The figure had moved in an odd, crablike fashion, as if normal walking was too hard, and was now standing slightly bent over, as if nursing a bad back. Or a gunshot wound.

It was Didier. He was standing in full view. He had a bag slung across his shoulder and was holding a shotgun, his battered bush hat a clear marker. He stood there for a few moments, head turning to scan the shadows like an animal at bay, and Rocco swore he could hear the man sniffing like an old bloodhound.

Then he was gone, moving soundlessly along the path towards the second lodge until he vanished into the shadows.

Rocco counted to fifty, then lifted one side of the boat and slid out. He followed the direction in which Didier had gone, keeping the tall reeds between him and the path. It was hard on his stomach and thigh muscles, but a relief to be out in the open where it gave him the chance to take out his gun and get the blood circulating in his veins. If Didier spotted him and swung that shotgun on him, he wanted to be able to defend himself.

He came in sight of the second lodge and hunkered down on the path. He was sweating, his heart going like a train, and he resolved to get back to some morning runs after this was over. Nothing too energetic, though. Just enough to make him feel better than he did right now, which was tired and flabby.

He counted to twenty, impatient to have it ended. There was no movement in the lodge, no signs of light. With a last look around and his chest pounding with tension, he crossed the clearing past the lodge and moved along the path towards the final lodge and the bridge to Didier's house.

He reached the last bend in the path and paused. No sounds or movement. He was about to step forward to view the ruined building, when something touched his leg.

He looked down.

His shin was resting against a thin sliver of silver strung across the path.

Tripwire.

CHAPTER FIFTY

Rocco pulled his leg back, balanced agonisingly on one foot. If the wire was released too quickly, it might still trigger whatever device was waiting for him. He put his foot down, then lowered himself to the ground. He began probing the immediate area with his fingertips, nudging aside stems of grass and dead reeds.

The ground was clear. That left the wire itself.

It was drawn tight across the path, held by two metal spikes driven into the ground. He couldn't see what the wire was connected to, but it ran off to his right after being curled around the spike, before disappearing into the reeds by the side of the path. He leant over and ran his fingertips along its length, stopping abruptly when he encountered something cold, round and metallic, held in place by three more spikes. He recognised the shape immediately.

Grenade.

Rocco felt a chill move across his shoulders and down

into his groin. If he had triggered the tripwire, it would have tugged the secondary wire, setting off the grenade just as he moved level with it. It was a mantrap, of the type he'd seen in Indochina and other places. One of the simplest forms of killing device with the minimum of hardware: a grenade pinned in place by pegs, sticks or in a bamboo cup, with the pin balanced and waiting for the lightest of tugs to set it off. Cheap, easy to place and deadly.

He waited for his breathing to settle and wondered what other little surprises Didier had waiting for him. This one had been simple to put in place: with practice – and if anyone was practised in the art of killing it was Didier – it would have taken seconds to ram the spikes home, string up the wire and drop the grenade in place. What he didn't know was whether Didier was carrying more such devices.

He stepped past the grenade and continued along the path to the bridge. No time to disarm it now...and trying to do so in this light would be a quick way to blow off his face. He could see the roof of Didier's house. No sounds came from it, no light. No movement.

He eyed the dark bulk of the bridge. The last time he'd crossed it, there had been no tripwires or booby traps. But that was then. Didier had changed the rules of engagement. If he'd once spiked the bridge to deter a few kids, he'd do it for a cop with even fewer regrets.

Rocco shook his head. Was he giving the man too much credit? Would it be another tripwire or a pressure plate and some *plastique*? Whatever, he didn't care to take the risk, and discomfort won out over death or dismemberment. He moved past the bridge and slid down the bank until he reached the water, which was cool and flowing smoothly.

He slid his feet into the depths, feeling the cold moving up his legs until he was standing knee-deep, with tendrils of weed holding his calves in a gentle embrace. If Didier put in an appearance now, he reflected, bringing up his gun, he wasn't going to waste any time on semantics: he'd shoot him where he stood.

The water gurgled noisily around his legs as he moved forward, and he reached the far side convinced that his approach had woken half the village. Clambering up the far bank, he looked across to the house and saw a dim light burning just inside the open door.

Before swinging over the top of the bank, he eased off his shoes and emptied them of water, then squeezed out his socks. Replacing them, he waited for the moon to slip behind a cloud, then stood up and walked across the open yard until he fetched up alongside one of the two large artillery shells either side of the door. From inside came the clinking sound of glass, followed by a heavy sigh. Didier drinking.

The clouds shifted again and suddenly moonlight flooded the yard. Rocco felt the hairs on his neck stirring. If Didier happened to poke his head out of the door, there was no way he could miss seeing him. He lifted the gun to head level and waited. There was nobody to see what went on here, no one to enforce the rules and regulations determining calls for surrender or the dropping of arms; one sign of the little man and his big gun and it would all be over. Then he heard a rattle of a key and the sound of a door being tugged open. The cellar.

Rocco waited until Didier's footsteps faded away down the steps, then stepped inside the house. The shotgun was lying on the kitchen table. He picked it up and placed it out of sight behind a chair, then slid off his shoes and followed Didier down into the dark.

He was at the bottom of the steps before he saw a dim light at one end of the cellar, through a narrow doorway. He stopped to allow his eyes to adjust and checked the floor for obstacles. The atmosphere down here was surprisingly dry, and smelt faintly of nothing more noxious than machine oil. He moved away from the steps and edged towards the light.

Didier had his back to him. He was kneeling in front of a large metal cabinet, with a leather bag by his side. He was dropping items into it in rapid succession, using his one good arm.

Rocco took in the room at a glance. The doorway where he was standing was a cheap plywood partition to section off this end of the cellar from the rest. Apart from the metal cabinet, there was a table, an armchair and a wardrobe. Along one wall was a wine rack filled with dust-covered bottles. A radio stood on a shelf on the opposite wall, with a line of thin paperback books below it. Cheap novels and ageing wine, Rocco noted. Didier's attempt at a higher form of life than the one he presented to the outside world.

Something must have changed in the atmosphere to alert the scrap man, because he uttered a shrill sound and spun round, dropping something on the floor.

It was a thick wad of money bound together with a rubber band. Alongside it lay a film reel.

Rocco leant against the wall and made sure Didier could see the gun in his hand.

'Come back for vital supplies?' he murmured. His voice sounded unnaturally loud in the confined space. He gestured for Didier to stand up.

Didier did as he was told, his eyes hot, black holes in a yellowed face. If he was alarmed by Rocco's sudden appearance, he wasn't showing it. The stump of his arm was sheathed in a filthy bandage and covered with a plastic bag, and dried blood the colour of a milky chocolate drink showed where it had seeped through the gauze. He hadn't shaved and looked even gaunter than Rocco remembered. And sick. He was amazed the man was still standing.

'What do you want?' Didier demanded. 'Money?' He nodded at the wad of notes on the floor. 'Take it, it's yours. If you let me go.'

'No chance.' Rocco stared at him with disgust. 'You think you can just buy yourself out of this?'

'Why not? It's what you people do, isn't it – take money to look the other way?'

Rocco stepped forward. He resisted the impulse to lash out, instead nudging Didier into the armchair. He bent and flicked open the bag. It contained a few items of clothing and more cash in rubber bands. And something wrapped in greaseproof paper.

'You taking a holiday?'

'What's it to you?'

'They came to kill you, didn't they? The men in the woods. What was that about – thieves falling out?'

Didier said nothing, simply sat hunched in the chair with a brooding menace.

'Of course, you know he'll get away with it.' Rocco hitched one hip onto the corner of the table, his gun resting

354

on his thigh. Didier stared fixedly at it, but said nothing. 'People like him always do. They're like greaseproof paper – nothing sticks to those ex-SOE types.'

At the mention of the SOE, Didier's eyes shifted. A bright light was shining there, and Rocco shrugged elaborately, feigning indifference. 'Still, what's new, eh? Shit always sinks, you know that. He must have had his life planned since that night in forty-four. Lose the money, come back for it later when nobody was about and sail off into the sunset. He was on his own out there, with nobody to watch him. So what could go wrong?' Rocco snapped his fingers. 'Ah, silly me. You were there, weren't you? Threw a bit of a spanner in the works I expect. But he was adaptable – the SOE had taught him that. He tipped some of the money your way and off you went like two honeymooners, set up for life.'

'*Bastard!*' Didier was breathing heavily, his jaw working. A dribble of saliva oozed down his chin and his good hand was shaking as if he'd been holding a road drill for too long.

'What was that?' Rocco leant forward. 'Didn't quite catch it.'

'I should have had more!' Didier spat out, pushing himself forward in the chair. 'He cheated me...kept me under his foot all these years and treated me like filth! If it wasn't for me, he'd have been under the guillotine a long time ago!' He kicked suddenly, catching the corner of the metal cabinet with his boot. 'But what I've got in there, he'll live to regret it.'

CHAPTER FIFTY-ONE

It began to ease out, like pus from a gangrenous wound, and Rocco listened, rhythmically swinging his leg. The regular movement seemed to calm Didier, keeping him talking as if hypnotised, a metronomic inducer of all his innermost secrets.

'I knew he was up to something. He spent too much time out on his own at night, walking in the fields near the drop zone. Why would he risk that unless he was looking for something? One night I followed him. I saw him with an oilskin package – like they used for wrapping stuff. He took it out of a ditch, in a drop canister.'

'Money?'

'Yes. I watched him counting it.'

'How much?'

'I forget.' Didier shrugged. 'It was a long time ago. Back then, anything was worth having.'

'Go on.'

'I said I wanted a cut. He refused at first, then agreed. Knew I'd tell, otherwise. He gave me a wad, said he was heading south to get the escape pipeline out. But the others found out what he'd done and threatened to tell London. He agreed to meet them, to give the money back. But he got in touch with the Nazis instead and told them where the meeting was taking place. He didn't turn up, of course.'

'How do you know it was him?'

'Because they were waiting, weren't they? The Germans. At the quarry.' His eyes glittered sharply. Sly. 'It could only have been him.'

'Or you.'

'Me?' Didier shifted his arm, and a spasm of pain crossed his face. 'Why the hell would I do that?'

'Because you argued with one of the men over Elise.'

'*Elise?*' Didier looked surprised by the mention of the name. Then a shadow of understanding crossed his face. 'Christ, is that what that daft bitch Francine told you? She's not right, that one. Follows me here and then tries to kill me, can you believe that?'

'You knew?' Rocco thought back to his talk with Francine. She had clearly thought otherwise.

'Of course I did – I knew as soon as I first saw her. She looks a lot like her sister. She's cracked, you know that? I stayed out of her way. Can't be doing with people like that.'

'You didn't feel threatened by her turning up here after all those years?'

'No. Why should I?'

'Because it's impossible to believe, that's why!' Rocco felt annoyed by the man's play-acting. 'The whole of France to choose from and you two pitch up in the same small village?'

Didier gave a sign of agreement. 'OK. It was spooky, I grant you. But stranger things have happened. As far as I could tell she didn't recognise me...never gave a hint. I thought it best to leave it that way.'

'But you can see how she might have seen things – about her sister and you. And you were the only other survivor.'

'Yeah, all right. I had a thing for Elise...but I wasn't that put out just because she wouldn't play. And it wasn't me who told the Germans. I turned up early but I smelt them before I got there. You think I wanted to be hunted down by every Resistance gunman in France for betraying the group? No way. The kid's got it in her twisted mind that it was my fault. Well, it wasn't – it was Berbier's.'

Rocco waited for more. It sounded plausible, unless you considered that Didier had probably erased from his mind his own involvement over the years, lumping all the responsibility on the rich, powerful, well-connected Berbier, despoiler of the working masses. He'd no doubt been in awe of the man at first, with his exotic SOE cloak-and-dagger appearance. Maybe he still was.

'So you had to disappear. But you didn't lose touch with Berbier, did you? You decided to milk him.'

'So what? He could afford it. It was only right.' He shrugged. 'It was fate. I saw his photo in the papers one day not long after the war...realised who he was, who he'd been. I watched him making himself richer over the years. Kept in touch, though: a phone call here, a note there – just so he knew I was out there. Then he approached me. Said he'd acquired a place in the country where he wanted to hold parties for business contacts. Fat, rich sickos who liked to live it up away from home. People he wanted to influence. He couldn't be involved, though: he needed me to run the place, be the fixer.'

The fall guy if anything went wrong, more likely, thought Rocco. Two birds with one stone. 'He paid you for this service?'

'Of course he did. Paid me well, too. Couldn't not, could he? He thought I'd got proof of what he'd done with the Resistance group. I let him believe it, that's all.' Didier chuckled proudly, then coughed wetly, clutching at his chest. 'All I had to do was manage the place, get it cleaned after each session and keep it stocked with stuff.' He glanced up at Rocco. 'You've seen inside?'

'Yes. Sleazy as a Montmartre bordello. Where did the girls come from?'

'His people arranged it. Young, fancy bitches from Paris, mostly, earning money on the side...or rather, on their backs. After a couple of sessions, I started taking notes. On the sly, of course. Big names, some of the people who came down here. Influential. Even a couple of – what do you call them? – civil servants. Grey drones in grey suits who probably couldn't get it up any other way. Then I realised Berbier was doing the same, only using his driver with one of those movie cameras.'

Rocco nodded. He glanced at the film reel on the floor. It chimed with what the driver had said before he died: Berbier was the controller, using the lodge for his schemes, and Didier was the factotum who knew too much. It was the reason the men had been sent after Didier: a reel was missing. The man had gone too far; become a liability. The danger of the reel getting into the wrong hands had been too great to ignore.

'He was going to use it for blackmail?'

'Not for the first time.' Didier took a deep breath, his chest rattling. 'You think he got all those business deals because he was good at adding up? He'd got it planned. Or his mother had.'

Rocco pictured the haughty old woman in the Bois de Boulogne, and saw nothing in the image to counter the idea. She was undoubtedly an old snob and social climber, and probably ruthless in steering her son to her idea of greatness. Manoeuvring business and official contacts for advancement would have been as natural to her as breathing, as would keeping him at arm's length from anything that might rebound on him. Hence the need for a middleman. Didier.

'She's a nasty cow,' Didier continued. 'I met her a couple of times. She treated me like something she'd picked up on her shoe. But she's no better: the idea for the lodge was all hers.'

Rocco was no longer surprised. It fitted. Set up a party venue out in the sticks, invite a few 'friends' for the weekend to have a good time, send a couple of girls out, lots of booze... and a man with a camera. Most business types relied on a day at the races, theatre tickets, that kind of inducement. But this was a whole lot better. Risky, though, no matter how carefully Berbier kept his distance from the nasty stuff. If it ever went public that he'd used blackmail and sex to further his businesses, it would blow the lid off his empire along with a lot of important names in high places. The repercussions would be enormous.

Massin would have a fit of indecision.

'Where did his daughter come in?'

Didier hawked and spat on the floor. The gobbet lay there, a sheen of bright red catching the light. He studied it for a moment, then said, 'I didn't know who she was at first. She was just a tart sent to join in the fun. One of them, anyway.' His head dropped and he groaned faintly.

'When did you find out?'

'After a couple of visits. She told me who she was…it seemed to please her, like she was rubbing his name in the dirt.'

'That must have gutted you, seeing her there: the daughter of a man you hated, who'd made it when you hadn't.' He said it with flat deliberation, twisting the knife that was already there.

Didier didn't react. He considered it for a moment, then shook his head. 'It meant nothing to me. She was just proof of how corrupt he was, him and his kind. In the end, I figured it was something else to bring him down.'

'When did he find out she was coming here?'

Didier looked up. 'He arranged it!'

'I don't believe you.'

Didier pulled a face. 'Believe what you like – makes no odds to me. I heard a couple of guests talking. One was a fat bastard from the Interior Ministry; he had a thing for her… always had, apparently. Wanted to get in her pants. They like young girls, him and his sort.'

Rocco thought that was a bit rich. If what Francine had said was true, Didier wasn't above showing an interest in young girls, either.

'Go on.' He needed to keep him talking, to draw out more facts. He didn't think he had much time left.

'Well, it's obvious. Berbier was using her – his own daughter. It wasn't the only time, either.' He shook his head. 'I thought I was rotten; not like him, though. He's worse. He thought she was weak.'

'What happened?'

'To Nathalie?' He shook his head. 'I don't know. She arrived that last time, and that was the last I saw of her... until I found her in the Blue Pool.'

The atmosphere in the small cellar was heavy, and Rocco tried to work out whether Didier was that good at lying, or whether he'd managed to convince himself of his innocence in this case, too, like the betrayal of the Resistance group. He waited, using the interrogation tactic of silence.

Eventually Didier continued. 'One moment she was inside, the next she was out and gone. It was a noisy business, lots of drinking and stuff, people yelling. I think it got out of hand in the end, especially with the fat bastard chasing the girl. Eventually the guests cleared out and left me to fix up the place. There was some blood on the sheets upstairs... could have been the fat man.'

'Does he have a name?' Rocco wanted to track him down. Dispense some justice. Might be better if Massin did it.

'No idea. His was one name I never got. Some were cagey like that; didn't trust anyone.'

'And the uniform?'

'They liked the girls to dress up. It was an excuse to treat them like sluts.'

Rocco waited. But Didier seemed to be sinking fast, as if tired out by all the talking. He wondered how long the man could last. He already looked as though death was hovering on his shoulder, grinning in expectation.

'So you didn't kill her, the daughter of a man you hated?'

Didier's head jerked. 'No way! That's not down to me. Him, yes – I'd gladly see him dead and buried. But you can't lay that one on me.'

Rocco let it go. 'But you placed her body in the cemetery.'

'Well I couldn't have the cops snooping around the *marais*, could I? This was my livelihood...my pot for the future. If the cops found the lodge and all that stuff, Berbier would have turned it all on me. I knew what he was capable of.'

'Did you tell him?'

'As soon as she ran off. He went berserk.'

'What happened?' Rocco had to force himself to remain calm. He was within a whisker of finding out what had happened to Nathalie, he knew it. All he had to do was keep Didier talking.

'I waited for him, didn't I?'

Rocco nearly slid off the table. 'Berbier came down here?'

'Like a snake down a rabbit hole. He was really pissed off at Nathalie. He'd had a phone call from one of his friends earlier, saying how she'd had a fight with the fat man. He said he was coming down to teach her a lesson.'

Rocco felt a drumming in his ears. So that was how Berbier had found out about his daughter: a phone call from Didier, and another from one of the guests. After that, strings were pulled. Friends in high places. He wondered if the magistrate who had signed the papers had ever been a

363

guest here. If so, there might be some film of him—

Wait. Something didn't match. 'You told him she was missing? Not that she was dead?'

Didier screwed up one eye and thrust his good hand down into the chair as if bracing himself against a stab of pain.

'Christ, you're slow, aren't you?' he sneered. 'She ran off and hid in the *marais*. It's a big place...no way was I going out looking for her in the middle of the night, so I rang him. I wanted to stay out of it. Nothing to do with me if his kid hates his guts. He arrived with that driver of his just before dawn, then went searching for her.'

'Him and the driver?' Rocco pictured André, last seen dying in the woods. Whatever sins he had committed had finally caught up with him.

'No. The flunky stayed here, watching me. I was cleaning up.'

'What then?'

'Berbier came back. Said he'd found her and was leaving. I assumed she was in his car. After they'd gone, I took a walk around, just to make sure nothing had been left lying around for the locals to get hold of.' He sat back, eyes blank. 'I ended up at the Blue Pool. She was lying there, just under the water. Nothing I could do but pull her out. She was dead.'

'What did you do?'

'Nothing. After a bit, I wrapped her in a plastic tarpaulin and left her under the boat while I figured out what to do. There were people about, so I had to be careful.'

'How long before you dumped her?' He didn't bother asking why the war cemetery: to Didier, it would have been ghoulishly appropriate.

Didier shrugged, no longer interested. 'Three days...
maybe four.'

Rizzotti had been right. Rocco stared at the floor,
picturing the nightmare scene, trying to imagine how any
father could murder his own daughter.

When he looked up again, Didier was smiling.

And holding a hand-grenade in his lap.

Rocco felt his gut lurch. Cursed himself for being so careless.
The grenade must have been secreted down the side of the
chair. In a room this small, if it went off they'd have to hose
the pair of them off the walls.

'What now?' he said.

'I get up and leave. You stay. First, though, put the gun
down.'

Rocco did as he was told, but stuffed the gun in his
pocket. It was no use to him now, not with what Didier was
holding. 'What are you going to do? Where will you go?'

'My business. You'll never find me.'

'Don't bet on it.'

Didier scowled, shook his head. 'How did you get
here?'

Rocco wondered why he wanted to know that. Surely
he'd noticed his wet trousers? Then he realised that Didier
wasn't taking in much at all. He was talking and listening,
but something in his brain was focused solely on getting out
of this room with his money. And the film. Anything else
not an immediate threat was a distraction to be ignored.

Instinct made him lie. 'I came along the main street.'

Didier nodded and stood up with difficulty, face pinched
with pain. He was nursing the grenade against his chest with

his good hand. He swayed drunkenly but righted himself with a shake of his head. The grenade pin was almost out, Rocco saw. Just a flick of a thumb away from spinning across the room and sending them both to hell.

He tensed, waiting for his moment, then stopped himself. If he rushed Didier, the pin would come out. No way to stop it. No way to put it back.

'What were you going to do with Francine?' He was trying to buy time, he knew that. It was pointless, but when it's all you have left, it becomes a currency, like anything else.

Didier frowned, the question throwing him. 'What?' He shook his head. 'I wasn't going to do anything with her. She's a sick bitch... I don't need to get my fun with women like that. But she was a useful bargaining tool.' He smirked. 'I figured you'd back off if you knew I had her tucked away. I'd have told you where she was eventually, once I was clear of this place.'

Rocco thought he recognised the truth when he heard it, and nodded. Maybe the man had at least one redeeming feature after all.

Didier coughed suddenly, and a pink bubble appeared at the corner of his mouth. He licked his lips and blinked very slowly, as if his eyelids had become sticky. He shook his head again, nodded towards the floor. 'Pick up the money and the film, put them in the bag.' He waited while Rocco complied, then put out his bad arm so that Rocco could hook the bag's strap over it. He moved aside and nodded at the chair. 'Your turn. Sit.'

Rocco sat.

'What's in the bottom of the bag?' He had a good idea

already, but confirmation might be useful. It was heavy and smelt faintly familiar. Like a brick of C4. Not that knowing would help him much. But any delay might give him the tiny edge he'd need to get out of this.

'What's it to you?'

Rocco shrugged. 'Just interested.'

For a moment Didier said nothing. He simply stared at Rocco in a detached manner. The silence lengthened, and Rocco wondered if he'd pushed it too far, or whether Didier was about to fall over and drop the grenade. But then he turned and walked away.

As Didier moved up the stairs, Rocco looked around the room, his gut churning. He knew what was about to happen; what the end would be. He wasn't meant to leave this room. Didier would get to the top, then flick out the pin and toss the grenade back down the stairs and slam the door. End of another problem. The thin partition across the room would offer no protection, merely adding to the deadly debris coming Rocco's way. Minced meat and the beginning of the long, dark night.

He listened to Didier's footsteps fading, crunching on grit. A split second before the door slammed, he heard a metallic *ping* and the rattle of the pin on the floor. Then a leaden thumping noise as the grenade bounced down the concrete steps and wallowed across the floor towards him.

CHAPTER FIFTY-TWO

Rocco found himself wondering how long Didier had set the fuse for. Six seconds? Ten? Three? A split second later he was throwing himself across the room, hurling the armchair towards the partition doorway and grabbing the metal cabinet. He ripped it away from the wall and threw it across the gap, too, then upended the wardrobe. It might not be enough, but it was all he had, a barrier against certain death. Trying to go for the grenade instead would merely be a quicker way to die.

At the last second, he dropped flat to the floor. Covered his ears. Opened his mouth.

The grenade went off.

The noise in the confined space was unbelievable. The concussion shook his whole body and he felt a hundred needle stabs of pain in his hands and across the back of his head. Something hot touched his leg, then was gone, and the air was sucked away from him, making him gag with the effort to breathe. The room filled with choking dust and he felt a shower of debris falling across his back.

The light went out, bringing total blackness.

Then Rocco was up and hurling himself towards the stairs by instinct, clawing past the cabinet and wardrobe and wondering how long he had before the ancient building caved in on top of him.

He reached the door at the top and kicked it open in a fury, slamming it back against the kitchen wall. The lights were on. He drew his gun and checked the empty room. Saw through the dirty window a pale shape on the other side of the stream, moving crablike along the path into the *marais*.

He lifted the gun, then heaved painfully, emptying his stomach on the floor and coughing, dropping to one knee. Eyes streaming and disorientated from the effects of the explosion, he looked around and saw the room tilt. For a second he thought it was the cellar ceiling giving way and dragging the house with it. Then he realised his sight and balance were playing tricks.

He was in no shape to follow Didier. Not yet. He needed his shoes, anyway. Running through the *marais* in his socks would be murder.

He got to his feet, swaying momentarily, then pushed himself off the wall and went to the kitchen sink. It was filthy, the God-awful smell enough to make him throw up if he hadn't already emptied his guts. No taps, but a jug of water stood on the side. He gulped at it, the liquid swamping down his chin and across his chest, cool and refreshing. He swilled out his mouth and spat a mixture of saliva, dust and blood into the sink. Not too much red, he noted vaguely;

must have bitten his lip when the grenade went off.

He'd been lucky.

Shoes, he reminded himself dully. He had to get his shoes. And something from the cellar. But what? He couldn't remember, only that it seemed important. His brain felt fried. He rubbed his face, trying to instil enough control to do the right thing. He listened to the creaking of the building around him. It seemed to be settling on its haunches like a mortally wounded animal with a series of cracks and groans.

The cellar. Now.

Rocco groaned and took a deep breath. He desperately didn't want to go back down there, but he had no choice.

No more than two minutes later, Rocco returned to the kitchen with a cardboard box tucked under one arm. He'd caught a quick glimpse of it, thrown on the floor when he'd upended the cabinet, and found it again by feel. The one glimpse had been enough. Inside one of the open flaps he'd seen the glossy sheen of black-and-white photographs. They were grainy and of poor quality, but good enough to make out clearly the faces of the men involved. And the girls they were with. There was also a notebook stuffed down one side, crammed with names and dates. The handwriting was untutored and shaky, but still legible.

Didier's proof.

He walked out of the house, gun held aloft. He doubted he'd get to use it: Didier would be long gone by now, scurrying away through the *marais* like the little weasel he was, on his way to freedom and obscurity.

He stepped on the bridge, trusting Didier not to have

endangered his own escape route. He wasn't sure why he was coming this way, or what he was going to do when he got across. He'd be better off taking the photos to his car and leaving Didier for someone else to worry about. He'd fall over if he didn't rest soon. That wouldn't be good. Humiliating, even. Christ, he felt tired, he just wanted to go home and sleep for a week.

But going home wasn't what he did. He chased criminals.

He was halfway across the stream when the explosion came. Flat and vicious, the sound echoed across the *marais* and ripped the night apart. It shook the trees, emptying the *marais* of birdlife in a surge of flapping, frantic wings and cries of protest. Rocco stopped, thinking he'd sprung one of Didier's traps.

Then he realised he could still feel his legs. Knew what it was.

Didier. He'd run into his own tripwire.

CHAPTER FIFTY-THREE

The street near the Bois de Boulogne still wore an air of tranquil exclusivity. The house martins were singing discreetly, the cars were parked nose to tail and the usual dog shit was scattered liberally across the pavement; all was well with the world in true Parisian fashion.

Soon change that, thought Rocco. He climbed stiffly out of the Citroën and sniffed the air, welcoming the familiar smell of city fumes topped with the hint of coffee.

'You sure you don't want me up there?' Claude was in uniform. He'd discarded his boots in favour of polished shoes. On the way into the city, he'd mentioned that the circumstances called for correctness: the official face of the law. He had also refused to wait at the end of the street.

Rocco wasn't sure about correctness. Not yet. But then, it had been a long time since he'd worn any kind of uniform. 'I'll be fine. If I'm not, you'll soon hear.' He paused and tapped the car roof. 'Thanks, though. Good to have you along.'

He had endured a bit of attitude from Claude on the way down. Part self-imposed guilt at not knowing about Francine's double life and how she had taken them all in, part his annoyance at Rocco taking on Didier by himself. Rocco still wasn't sure what had upset Claude most: being left out or not being able to put a bullet in Didier's head himself. He'd hardly even bothered playing with the car radio.

As if reading his mind, Claude took out his gun and laid it on the seat beside him. 'Just shout. I wouldn't mind using this on someone. Just the once.'

As Rocco crossed the pavement and reached up to press the entryphone button, a black car drew up behind his own. A man climbed out, leaving a uniformed driver behind the wheel. The newcomer wore a suit and carried a briefcase, and was holding up the ID of a senior officer of the Judiciary Police. He looked tough and businesslike and nodded cordially to Rocco.

'George Bleriot,' the man said. 'You ready to do this?'

Rocco returned the nod. Massin had told him someone would be needed to ensure that everything went to order: someone with sufficient powers to do whatever was required. He reached for the button but the gate was already open. He pushed it back, walked across the cobbled yard, past the green cherub in the dry fountain. No fancy car, he noted. Not that they had anyone to drive it, anyway.

He banged on the door, the sound echoing up the stairs. He tried the handle. It turned. The door opened. As he'd expected, the old woman met them halfway up the stairs. She looked aggressive and determined, one clawed hand gripping the banister like a bird of prey about to launch itself into the air.

He'd already decided that if she gave him any shit, he'd toe-punt her down the stairs, followed closely by her treacherous, murderous, double-dealing son. Bleriot would just have to pretend he hadn't seen it.

'Where is he?' he said, walking straight at her.

She moved aside at the last second, gesturing at the same doorway he had used before. As he brushed past he picked up the same sickly-sweet perfume.

It reminded him of death and decay.

'What do you want?' she hissed, glaring at them in turn. 'What are you here for? This is an affront – an insult. I will be calling the Ministry—!'

'You do that, you old witch,' Rocco said calmly, 'and I'll make sure you end up in a cell with half a dozen heroin addicts doing cold turkey.'

'Wha—?'

'If he doesn't,' Bleriot added, 'then I will.'

They found Berbier in his study, staring out of the window. He was dressed in an expensive grey suit, with a blue shirt and discreet burgundy tie, to outward appearances a composed and powerful figure, at ease with the world.

'What's the meaning of this?' He turned to face them, chin jutting forcefully from his collar. But Rocco sensed there was little conviction in the words or the pose. There was a shaving nick on one side of the man's chin, and a tiny spot of blood on his shirt collar.

A scuff came from behind and Rocco glanced over his shoulder. Berbier's mother had followed them into the room. Her chin was trembling, although whether out of fear, indignation or old age, he couldn't tell.

No phone call to the Ministry, then. She wouldn't have had time.

'End of the game,' said Rocco. He took a black-and-white photo from his pocket and flicked it onto the desk so both the Berbiers could see. It showed Nathalie, pupils heavily dilated, one breast falling out of a white blouse, being pawed by a fat man with a sweaty face and greedy eyes. In the background stood a pair of large oil lamps. He now knew who the man was, and Massin would, about now, be dropping a heavy dossier with other photos onto the desk of his superiors.

A very chill wind was about to blow along the corridors of power.

An intake of breath came from Berbier *mère*, but her son showed no reaction other than mild irritation.

'I don't understand,' he said.

'Don't you?' Rocco wanted to punch him. 'You don't recognise your own daughter being groped over by one of your official 'friends'? You don't recognise a room in one of your own properties – a place you use for your pals to meet up and treat as a convenient whorehouse?' He glanced at the old woman, who seemed to be trying to hoist herself into another dimension by sheer willpower.

Berbier said nothing.

'I have to inform you,' continued Rocco, 'that a dossier is currently being placed before the Interior Minister, with photos like these,' he nodded at the desk, 'and a reel of film, showing activities at this property involving men of substance and position – that's my description but I'm being sarcastic only because I actually feel like throwing up – who were there at your invitation and with your connivance.' He paused while that sank in. 'Actually, let's cut the bullshit: you used the place so your buddies could have fun while you filmed them for blackmail purposes to further your business dealings. You also had your own daughter there to entertain these men and play the whore.'

Berbier's mother flinched at that and closed her eyes. It seemed to be the first honest emotion he'd seen from either of them.

'I also have the testimony of one Didier Marthe, also known as Tomas Brouté, that while working as an SOE officer in 1944, you accompanied a supply drop near Poitiers and conspired to steal money from the Allies...money destined for use by the Resistance. Then, in collusion with Marthe, you informed the Germans of the whereabouts of the Resistance group, to prevent them informing London of your crime. The group was captured and taken to Natzweiler-Struthof concentration camp, where they were executed. That money set you up nicely after the war, didn't it? Nice going.'

'That's outrageous.' Berbier looked stricken, but his voice was surprisingly quiet and calm. 'I know nothing of these events.'

Bleriot, in the background, was frowning at Rocco as if uncertain of his ground.

'Really? So we won't find a record of your mission to Poitiers during nineteen forty-four, accompanying operating funds which were reported "lost"?'

'No. That's a complete fabrication. It must have been another officer.'

Rocco felt his disgust for the man reach new heights. Not content with a life of deceit and betrayal, he was clearly willing to pass off the blame onto someone else, no doubt counting on official secrecy to protect him.

'You could be right, of course.' He watched as Berbier's face registered a momentary relief, then added, 'Except that the officer accompanying those funds went under a unique code name...and we happen to know what that was from someone who was there at the time. Funny things, code names: they protect the identity of the user, which is good. But they tend not to be used more than once.'

Nobody spoke.

'The code name was Cormorant.'

'No...there's a mistake!'

The words burst in a whisper from the old woman's lips, too instinctively to be anything but recognition. She would have heard the name over the years, knew it instantly for what it was.

Rocco looked at her. 'Did you know about this?' A hint was all he needed for the structure Berbier had built to collapse. She could be the weak link.

But the old woman had recovered quickly and was staring at him with contempt, her jaw muscles working furiously as she tried not to look at her son.

'Never mind. After the war, Marthe remained in contact with your son who paid him to look after the property in this photograph, to fix it up for weekend parties. Co-conspirators all those years. Mostly it was to keep Marthe from going to the authorities and revealing what he knew.' He looked at Berbier. 'You didn't know what proof he had squirreled away, so you had to keep him sweet...and keep him where you could watch what he did. What you didn't know was that he was keeping a record of who came and went over the years. It seems he didn't trust you further than he could throw a bus.'

Berbier said nothing.

'Very well.' Rocco took out another photo. It was time for the big guns. Instead of dropping this one on the desk, he handed it directly to the old woman. If his instincts were right, she might turn out to be Berbier's undoing. All he had to do was shake her foundations to the point where she couldn't deny her knowledge any longer. The photo showed another man having sex with Nathalie. She looked unconscious, brutalised, mascara streaked across her cheek, her eyes swollen. She was wearing the uniform of a Gestapo officer. The same uniform she had been wearing when she died. The dark mark he had seen for himself on the body showed on the side of her neck, where she had been bitten.

The old woman uttered a noise midway between a whine and a cry of protest. Rocco stared at her.

'That's what your granddaughter was subjected to. You saying you didn't know?'

'*I didn't!*' She flung the photo away as if it was burning her fingers.

'You sure?' Rocco was relentless. 'You saying you didn't know she was doing this to earn money? That she had no option because she couldn't get any from her father for the operation?'

'Operation?' She looked at him, then Bleriot, then at her son in evident confusion. 'Why would she need money for an operation? What was wrong with her – was she ill?'

Berbier said nothing. But a vein in the side of his neck was pulsing heavily and his breathing had become laboured.

'What?' the woman repeated, grasping Rocco's arm, her nails digging into his skin through his coat. 'Tell me.'

'Your granddaughter was pregnant,' he said softly, this time without malice. 'Probably by one of the men your son was going to blackmail. She needed the money to go into a clinic and this was the only way she could get it. I have the testimony of a friend of hers to the effect. Your son, it seems, had a reputation to preserve.'

Berbier's mother seemed to sag, her face in torment. Then she turned on her son, lashing out with a spindly hand and scratching him deeply across one cheek. The score mark raised blood, a bead of which ran unchecked down his face. '*You filth!* You promised me...you said she was safe...that she was at a friend's party that night when the...the accident happened. *And you knew?*'

'This is all unsubstantiated rubbish,' Berbier said, his voice shaking. He stared at Rocco with glittering menace. 'I will be making a protest to the minister immediately and you, my friend, will end up in prison for this.'

'I wouldn't count on it.' Rocco reached into his pocket and looked at Berbier's mother. 'When I examined your granddaughter's body, she was wearing a single earring.' He pointed at the photo, where the earring in the shape of a marguerite was plainly visible. 'The other was missing.'

She stared at the photo, then nodded slowly, her voice a whisper. 'Yes. One was missing when she...when her body came home. I gave them to her when she graduated. She looked so pretty in them...such a pretty girl.' A sob broke loose from her chest and shook her thin frame, and she looked about to collapse.

Rocco opened his hand, capturing the moment. Nestling

in his palm was the other earring, the one he'd found in the lodge.

The old woman gave a small cry. Her hand flew to her mouth, eyes fastened on the jewel in recognition. She looked as if she was about to be sick.

'It was no accident, nor was it at a friend's house,' continued Rocco. 'Nathalie was running away from a man who was raping her. A man known to your son. She ran into the surrounding *marais* in panic, hid there for some hours. She was drowned in a pool of fresh water close to the lodge where these pictures were taken.'

'Drowned? By who?' Her eyes looked haunted. 'By Marthe? By that horrid little man?' She ignored her son as if he were no longer there. 'The man in the photo?'

'No. Not Didier Marthe.' He was on shaky ground here, but since neither Marthe nor the family driver were alive to dispute what he said, it made little difference. 'Nor the man in the photo.' He looked closely at her, judging how much he could say, how much she might believe. 'Your son's driver, though, he was there.' He waited, hoping she might connect the dots.

'André?' The woman looked at Berbier, but he failed to meet her eyes. 'But André...he *worshipped* Nathalie...he would have gone through *hell* for her...' She stopped and grasped her son's sleeve. 'But wait. That night...André went out at about four in the morning...with you.'

'André didn't kill her,' Rocco assured her. 'He couldn't have – he was with Didier Marthe all the time. He told me himself just before he died and Marthe confirmed it. There was only one other person present in the *marais* who could have.' He kept his eyes on Berbier just long enough to make the point, and felt the atmosphere harden to a brittle texture. 'Some people will do anything to preserve their reputation. Isn't that right?'

Rocco left Bleriot to arrange the arrest, and walked downstairs. He needed some fresh air, away from the rotten sickness harboured within the building. He felt tired and drained and his ribs were hurting like hell. He was also frustrated, not least because there were still many questions to which he doubted they would ever find complete answers.

But they had enough to begin proceedings, of that he was certain. And Massin had turned out in the end to have the bite of a bulldog. According to Canet, who had called in while Rocco was being treated in hospital, the senior officer had surprised everyone by going out on a limb to get the investigation going and to prevent it being stifled by interference from Berbier's powerful friends.

Massin. Rocco still wasn't sure about him or his intentions. No doubt his star would be in the ascendant after this, with elevation further up the greasy pole of seniority. It was the way of things.

Quite where his own star might be going was another question. He knew too much about Massin's past – and would any boss like to be in that position? Somehow he doubted it. Only time would tell.

Claude was waiting by the car, chatting to Bleriot's driver and smoking. Rocco walked up and bummed a cigarette. He didn't usually indulge, but he'd had enough fresh air; now he needed something to occupy his hands, even if it choked him.

'All done?' said Claude, holding a flame to his cigarette.

Rocco puffed tentatively, the smoke scorching his throat. Harsh but bearable. A bit like some forms of justice. He looked up into the sky, where pigeons were playing fighter planes over the expensive rooftops of Paris, and found himself wondering what the fruit rats were up to in his attic. Noisy little bastards.

'All done,' he confirmed, and flicked the cigarette into the gutter to join the dog shit.

'I suppose you'll be staying on here now, then.' Claude gestured towards the north-east of the city, towards Clichy. His expression was bleak at the prospect. 'Going back to fighting big-city gangsters.'

'No.' Rocco shook his head. After this lot hit the fan, he'd be about as welcome in the city as an attack of the plague. Not that he was bothered. 'Big-city gangsters are predictable. I like a real challenge. Come on, let's go solve some more crimes.'

ACKNOWLEDGEMENTS

With grateful thanks to David Headley, my agent; to my editors; and to all the folks at Allison & Busby who have made this more than just a manuscript with covers, but a real book.